WHITEWATER KILLER

KENT TREIBER

This is a work of fiction. Names, characters, places, and incidents either are the product of the author's imagination or are used fictitiously. Any resemblance to actual persons living or dead, events, or locales is entirely coincidental.

ISBN-10: 1475221908
ISBN-13: 978-1475221909

ACKNOWLEDGEMENTS

My wife Joette has given me unstinted support and encouragement throughout the development of this book. Her reviews and suggestions have been invaluable. Thank you love.

My friend Hank Schriefer, retired from the San Jose PD, has not only given me insights into police investigations and culture, but did the tough review of the book that I asked for. Golf friends Doug Clark, Grass Valley PD and Mike Dickinson, California Highway Patrol, have provided key information and more cultural understanding. My thanks to the following law enforcement professionals: Parris Bradley, retired from the Aurora, Colorado PD; Tom Stuart, Tucson PD; Jeff Markham, retired from the Lake County Sheriff's office; Randy Billingsley, Nevada County DA's office; Keith Smith, retired from the Waterloo Iowa Police Crime Lab. Thank you all for helping me make the book's police characters authentic and to depict the investigations realistically. All errors in procedure are mine as are the omission of some of the necessary, but less exciting, parts of police work. I realize that California DOJ agents rarely are involved in a case like this. They are organized and staffed for such a role and could provide valuable assistance in a multijurisdictional case involving small agencies.

Tech writer and editor Susie Holic, a friend for forty years, helped me deal with this arcane language of ours. Thanks to Bob Center for detailed discussion of the Tuolumne River's rapids and kayaking techniques. Thanks to Terrie Collins and Joann Kaleel for information on the real estate business. Don Hanson, Harvey and Mary Landsman provided helpful reviews. To other friends and family, thanks for your support and encouragement.

For links to maps, visit KentTreiber.com.

1. WALNUT CREEK, CALIFORNIA; FRIDAY

Sophia didn't know about her awful role in the mystery when she stepped out of the chilly department store. The fragrance of blossoms and new leaves drifted on a gentle breeze and she took a deep breath, her heart expanding with joy and gratitude. Sophia thought that it was a wonderful day, having no idea how terribly wrong she was.

It had been a long, cold and wet winter, and this spring day held the promise of renewal and the warm summer to come. Sophia tossed her long black hair and turned her beautiful face to the sun, letting its warmth thaw her as she walked through the parking lot. Her Italian heritage graced her with an olive complexion that was enhanced by a recent suntan into a healthy glow. Sophia's nose was chiseled, her eyes the color of dark chocolate, and her lips full and sensuous. "Pouty" her husband called them, and he found them irresistible.

So far, the day had been great. Her morning meeting with the Big Brothers, Big Sisters board had produced a promising fund raising idea. She had loved shopping at Niebaums for her daughter Jill's birthday present. Jill was going to love her new jeans outfit with the designer stitching on the pockets. Funny how some thread on the pockets multiplied the cost by 10. Maybe now Sophia would not need to rummage through her daughter's closet to retrieve her own favorite denim jacket. It gave Sophia some pride that she was still so fit and stylish that her 14 year old daughter loved to wear her mom's clothes. Sophia had not let herself go the way her younger sister had; she had worked hard at keeping her figure.

Sophia was looking forward to meeting her husband Pauli and friends tonight at a wine tasting dinner. What a good life. She could hear the sound of her Jimmy Chou heels clacking against the concrete floor of the parking structure as she approached her white Lexus RX350 SUV. Even though it was afternoon, she could feel the change in temperature as the thick concrete, shaded from the sun, gave up the cold it had absorbed during the chilly night. Putting Jill's package in the back, she pushed the button to close the rear hatch and moved toward the driver's door. "Excuse me miss," she heard from off to her right. "might you have a cell phone that I could use to call road service?" Sophia turned to see a good looking man with a bushy black mustache wearing a suit and a white straw cowboy hat walking toward her. "Certainly, just a minute," was the reply of a confident woman who liked to help people.

Sophia was digging around in her purse for her phone as the man approached. As she pulled the phone out and looked up she saw him on the other side of her car's hood, his hand reaching out holding a strange black object. She heard a pop and had a brief glimpse of colored confetti. Zzstap! Before the messages of pain could even travel to her brain, Sophia's body was reacting to the electrical charge. Every muscle was contracting as if her life depended on it and she went down, hard. Sophia was on the pavement, curled into a fetal position, conscious but struggling to comprehend what was happening. As she began to absorb the reality, the awareness of terrible pain was joined by an overwhelming and growing sense of terror. When she could assemble a thought she just kept repeating to herself, "This can't be happening to me. This just can't be happening."

The man in the suit walked up to Sophia, his finger squeezing the Taser's trigger again to give her more of a charge. Looking around to verify that there were no potential observers, he squatted down and put her phone, and the Taser into her purse. Throwing the strap of her purse over his shoulder, he picked up Sophia's 110 pounds as if she weighed nothing. In seconds he carried her two parking spaces to the right and put her in the back of a large SUV.

Closing the back of the SUV, the man checked the parking lot again. There was nobody in the vicinity. He opened the rear driver's side door and crawled into the back. Nothing was visible through the dark tinted windows. Soon he emerged and checked his surroundings again. Still seeing nothing, he pulled out a battery powered leaf blower, walked back to Sophia's car and ran the blower for a minute, blowing away the confetti-like ID tags from the Taser cartridge. Returning to his SUV, he climbed into the driver's seat and put the blower on the passenger side.

The SUV exited the parking structure, turning left onto Broadway. In three minutes the massive vehicle was traveling north on Interstate 680.

2. TUOLUMNE RIVER; TUESDAY

Jake Appleby took a minute to savor his environment. He turned around, taking in the canyon walls carpeted with green, the cloudless blue sky, the blue green color and rushing sound of the Tuolumne River. The complex smells in the foothill air made him wonder why he ever spent time in a city. A western scrub jay, quiet for the moment, was foraging for insects at rivers edge. A grey squirrel bounced along a limb of a nearby oak, chiding the interlopers. Jake absorbed all of this through his pores, it felt peaceful and right. To steal a term from Robert Heinlein, he was *grokking* the world around him.

At age 39, Jake was in good shape although he battled with a spare tire every time his solid six foot two frame accumulated more than 210 pounds. His gym work kept his body looking good, but he tended to keep it to himself by wearing loose fitting clothes. Even today, his river garb included a loose fitting long sleeved nylon shirt over his wet suit. A scar obtained on a teenage hunting trip started high on Jake's forehead then disappeared into thick, wavy, dirty blonde hair. His nose was a bit pointy. His blue eyes could twinkle to go with a wry smile or they could go ice cold. He refused to shave for river trips, so he sported blonde stubble this morning.

Every year Jake organized a whitewater rafting trip with a group of his buddies, rotating through the good rivers of California and the Rogue in Oregon. Jake was a skilled kayaker who could handle all of these rivers. Most of his friends were not kayakers, so rafts were the only choice on buddy trips. This year the trip was on the Tuolumne, queen of California whitewater. Seven friends were along on this trip: a couple of friends from his computer career, four Sacramento cops and his partner at the California Department of Justice (DOJ), Celia Moreno. They were using two paddle rafts, each with four of the group as paddlers plus a guide. The rafts could handle six paddlers, but ran fine with four. Since they were taking the one day trip, they didn't have a lot of gear to carry.

Twenty miles upriver from the rafters, the O'Shaughnessy Dam drowns the Hetch Hetchy valley, providing the water supply for San Francisco 140 miles to the west. This time of year the river was running full from snowmelt, though today the flow was low enough for rafts to make the run. Jake had given the group a few minutes to enjoy the unspoiled scenery of the 1800 foot deep Tuolumne Canyon. A few beaches were along the river, but rocks of all sizes and shapes dominated the shores. The canyon walls were covered in vegetation common to the lower foothills: many species of oak, occasional madrone, the ugly and sticky grey pine. The bushes include buck brush, California buckeye in its flowering stage, glossy green poison oak, thorny wild blackberry and red-trunked manzanita. Because wildfires had been suppressed through much of the twentieth century, the trees and brush on the northern exposure canyon wall were often so dense that the land was impassible. On the southern exposure canyon wall the greenery was somewhat sparse and the native grasses dominated because of the brutal sun during the dry summers.. Since it is a wild and scenic river, access to the Tuolumne was controlled by the Forest Service; they didn't expect to see many people. While many species of wildlife inhabited these hills, during a raft trip all you could expect to see were birds, squirrels and an occasional trout.

At Meral's pool, elevation 1400 feet, the group prepared to put into the river. The air and sun would be hot today, but the water was bone chilling snow melt, so everybody was wearing wet suits. They were shod in old athletic shoes or river sandals. Everybody wore flotation vests and helmets, survival gear if you had an unplanned departure from a raft.

Del Hodges and Harley "Porky" Hill, Sacramento PD patrolmen, needed the guide's instruction and paddling practice because it was their first raft trip. The others were a bit bored,

Large # characters w/o extraneous folks gratuitously added

but tolerated the refresher. They knew that you don't want to be learning in the middle of a class IV rapid, common on the Tuolumne. Del and Porky learned that commands from their guide like "all forward, left side back," and "take a break" told them who, when, and which direction to paddle.

Terry Rocker and Steve Devlin were partners working in the Sacramento PD Violent Crimes unit. The detectives watched the rafting lesson since it had been a couple of years since they had been on a river. Terry was "thin man": six foot three but only 170 pounds. A blonde crew cut topped a pale face with blue eyes. Terry was the smart ass of the group, popping off whenever he could. In contrast, Steve was a small hulk. At five foot eight he packed 190 pounds of muscle that he worked hard to maintain. He had a pale Irish complexion and black Irish hair. Steve was an excellent detective whose hobby was women.

Before they started, in the police tradition of practical jokes, Jake had a story for them. "There's a rumor that South American candiru fish have been released in the river. Just in case it's true, you should know about them. The fish are drawn to warmth, so a candiru sometimes follow a stream of urine to its source, swims up the urethra, and flares its barbed fins. It takes surgery to remove one. Just keep that in mind if you feel the need during the trip."

"No shit?" said Porky.

"That makes me cringe," said Steve Devlin.

"Yeah right," came from Celia.

It was nine thirty by the time they started downriver. Jake, Celia, Terry, and Steve were first with Chris Poulter as their guide, sitting on the back of the raft. The paddlers sat on the outside tube of the raft so that they could make powerful paddle strokes. Since the raft would tip and bounce down the rapids and their hands were busy with the paddle, they kept their feet wedged into footholds or under a thwart. Aside from paddling on command, their job was to avoid falling out of the raft and becoming "swimmers". The term "swimmer" was a bit of a joke because the power of the water in a rapid overwhelms the feeble efforts of even the strongest swimmer.

As the rafts started out, they could already hear the roar of the upcoming rapid even though they were floating on swift, but placid water. In the second raft Porky Hill was watching the scenery float by and the first raft floating a hundred yards in front of them. All of a sudden, the first raft and its occupants dropped out of sight. "Whoa, what happened to them?" exclaimed Porky.

"They dropped into the first rapid," said their guide Chick. "We're next."

Porky was nervous. Even though he was used to physical activity, he didn't know how he'd deal with what was coming. The unknown was daunting; on the one hand he'd like to postpone getting into it, on the other he wanted to get the initiation over with. He'd been told that the first rapids were big, a graduate course instead of an introduction.

Jake and Celia's raft was splashing and crashing down the Rock Garden rapid, a class IV introduction to the day's whitewater rafting. The rapid twisted through giant boulders that offered a maze of routes downstream. With the amount of water in the river today, Rock Garden had two routes that worked. Underwater rocks created a series of standing waves across their path. For each of these, the raft would go up on the wave and down into the trough. After cruising through the first three waves, the nose of the raft dropped into a trough and the top of the next wave broke over them, spraying everybody with foamy white water, generating some *whoops* from the paddlers and instant goose bumps. Two waves later they dropped into a trough and then were inundated with a solid sheet of chilly water from the next wave. At the bottom of the rapid, everybody was wet, though Jake and Celia were in front of the raft and bore the brunt of it. Celia was shivering; the cold water had sucked the heat right out of her. She yearned for some sun to warm her back up, but the river was shaded by the canyon wall that towered above them; no sun until they rounded the next bend.

After a second class IV rapid, they were above class IV+ Sunderland Chute. A class IV rapid is formally described as whitewater, large waves, long rapids, rocks, maybe a considerable drop, likely requiring sharp maneuvers. Risk of injury to swimmers is moderate to high. Class V rapids require expert skills and can be maim or kill you. Rafts normally portage around class VI rapids

As they drifted towards Sunderland Chute, orange and black dragon flies cruised and darted above the river, at times flying backward to get their fill of small fliers. Jake thought that the life of an adult dragonfly was cool, far better that the nymph stage where they breathe through their rectum like some politicians he knew.

Jake's attention came back to the raft when Chris said "do all you can to stay in the raft in this rapid, swimming is dangerous. There's a hole at the bottom that would be hard to swim out of and it's so full of foam that you might not float. When I yell out *down*, I want you all to drop to the bottom of the raft with your paddles sticking straight up."

The paddler's heart rates climbed in anticipation as Chris positioned Jake's raft at the correct entry point above the rapid. One instant they were in charge and the next instant the current took them like they were in the grip of a giant fist. The raft accelerated, then made a left turn and dropped into foaming whitewater. Within seconds they were again dripping wet but they were too busy and cranked up to notice. "All forward" shouted Chris over the incredible roar of the water as he pointed the raft away from a massive boulder tilted out of the river in front of them. "Faster," yelled Chris as he could see that they were losing the battle to avoid the boulder. They got some motion to the right, but not enough.

The river pushed the left side of the raft up onto the sloping side of the boulder while the right side stayed at water level. On the left, Jake muscles bunched as he grabbed a safety line and hung on. The current pushed his side of the raft higher and higher until he was looking almost straight down on Celia who was on the right side. Jake could see Celia's eyes widen as she realized that they were likely to flip, making them all swimmers with a chance of being trapped under the raft. There was no time for directions, but Celia and Steve who were now on the bottom-side leaned left into the center and delayed the flip. The raft started sliding across the boulder as the current dragged it downriver in addition to pushing the left side up. Jake's heart thundered as the they teetered on the edge of a flip. Mother luck was with them this time, they were pushed downriver off the rock and stayed upright.

Before anybody's hearts could slow, they accelerated into white chaos. "*Get Down*," shouted Chris and they scrambled to sit on the bottom of the raft. By the time that they got down, they were buried alive by foaming white water.

Celia hadn't taken a breath before the water enveloped them. She tried breathing through her mouth and got water instead of air. She felt panic rise like a skyrocket, then got it under control with the thought, I *will* be able to breathe. Time dilated for Celia. It seemed like she was immersed in the water for a full minute but it was only fifteen seconds before she emerged into the air, still hurtling down the rapid.

Everybody else was screaming something but the roar of the water drowned them all out. Celia just took in a lungful of sweet air, ecstatic to be able to breathe again. Damn, she thought, that was on the hairy side of fun.

Jake saw the big hole coming up on the right and had an image of the entire raft being sucked into its maw and never getting out.

Chris called, "everybody up," then "All forward double time" so they could pass by the hole and get a "take a break" command from Chris. A few more seconds and they were finished with the rapid and into an eddy for a needed break.

"Fantastic, what a rush," exclaimed Terry. "I thought we were screwed when we were on that boulder."

"Damn, that was unbelievable," called out Steve.

"We came so close to swimming," said Celia. "I thought we were done. Then I damn near drowned in that foam."

Jake replied, "It was close. We were lucky that we got off that rock on top of the raft instead of under it."

"Yee haw," they heard from the second raft as it finished the Chute with all its passengers on board.

Jake was thinking about what a blast it was to run rapids. Every time he ran one something was different. There's speed, chaos, the incredible power of the river, danger and the adrenaline rush. Significant skill is required to stay out of trouble. In rafting, most of the skill was the guide's. When kayaking, the skill had to be yours.

They were happy to have a peaceful section of water after the Chute, it allowed their hearts to slow and their bodies to relax. On this stretch, the entertainment was a pair of Merganser ducks that came racing up the river in high speed flight, their serrated bills pointing the way and their Mohawk hairdo blowing in the wind. After a minute, they came back, did their three point landings and began searching for frogs and fish.

As they finished Ram's Head rapid, Chris maneuvered them into an eddy to rest. Every rapid had an eddy or two below it, usually on the side of the river. The water in an eddy tends to be still or have a slight current upstream, thus giving the river runner a place to pause.

They were watching the second raft finish the rapid when Steve said, "What the hell is that?" and pointed across the river. All eyes turned to see what he was pointing at. Atop a large granite boulder at the edge of the river was something that looked bizarre. It was so out of place out here that it didn't make sense at first. "Oh shit," breathed Jake. "We'd better paddle over there." Chris turned the raft so that they'd end up at the boulder and commanded "all forward."

As they closed in on the boulder, Steve said "damn, I think that's a head propped up by rocks. I sure hope that it's a mannequin." After a few more paddle strokes, Celia said "I don't think it's a mannequin." As they reached their goal, they saw a milky white face with silky black hair reaching down to the boulder. The eyes were open and seemed to be looking at them, but they were dull. They'd all had experience in the morgue and in the field – it was a human female's head. There didn't appear to be any blood on either the head or the boulder. The head seemed to be clean and the hair seemed brushed, though a few strands waved in the light river breeze.

Celia spoke up, "we've got one sick bastard behind this one. I hope that she was dead before he did the big cut."

"She looks detached to me," piped up Terry.

"Man, you're on this one early," responded Jake to the cop humor. "I'd guess that this was a good looking woman." He noticed that the other raft was in the eddy across the river, the occupants looking over at them. "Stay over there," he yelled at them. The world no longer felt peaceful and right.

"I don't see any people or anything else that might be evidence," said Celia. "Me either," echoed Steve. "I think that the first thing to do is call it in," said Jake. "Does anybody have other ideas?" When nobody spoke up, Jake told Chris, "let's move back to the other side so we can talk."

As they paddled back across the river to where the other raft floated, Jake yelled out "Okay, we've got a crime scene here, so we need to be careful about destroying evidence. For the moment, just keep floating in the eddy. Since the DOJ may be involved in this case, I'm going to take the role of first officer on the scene. Everybody OK with that?"

The Sacramento cops murmured assent. Chris asked, "How long are we going to have to hang around here? We don't have camping gear and this single day run leaves us just a couple of hours of spare daylight. Running this river in the dark would be as smart as driving through a city blindfolded."

Jake responded, "Finishing the trip could be a problem, but we'll have to put that discussion off for a while. I need to get people heading this way. Can you pull out my bag?"

"Sure," said Chris, starting to open a waterproof gear bag in front of him.

Jake said, "Porky and Dell, why don't you guys cruise up and down the shore on this side, looking for anything that might be evidence."

Chris handed over Jake's small duffel bag and Jake pulled out his GPS and his sat phone. A lightweight handset that worked with the Iridium low earth orbit service, the phone was provided by the DOJ because Jake often worked in the Sierra Nevada Mountains where cell phone service was spotty. Jake started the power-up sequence on both devices. Once the GPS was up, he got their location: 37 50'21.52" N, 120 4'42.03"W. He pulled out a notebook and pen and wrote down the location, time and date, weather conditions and river flow rate.

The satellite phone finished booting and indicated a useable connection. They were lucky. Operation in steep canyons wasn't always possible because you couldn't view enough of the sky to pick up the required satellites.

Jake's first call was to the head of the Central Valley Forensic Unit of the DOJ. "Vern, this is Jake Appleby." Unlike the old satellite communications, Iridium doesn't have an annoying delay before you hear the response of the other person.

"Hi Jake, how ya doin?"

"Well, I was doing great until we stumbled on a crime scene up here on the Tuolumne River. I'm sure that the sheriff is going to want your help so I'm giving you a heads up. Can you get me the direct number for the Tuolumne County Sheriff?"

"It's 209-555-7901 Jake. So what kind of crime scene are you looking at?"

"We've got the head of an adult female on top of a rock in the river. We're staying on the water for the moment and haven't spotted any other evidence so far. You have any immediate suggestions?"

"You've got just a head, nothing else?"

"So far, only the head."

"OK, watch out for carrion eaters; buzzards and crows. Make sure that they don't get to your evidence. Look for circling buzzards that might indicate locations for other body parts. What's the access to the scene?"

"We came down the river but that's not a good route for your crew. You'll need to drive down Lumsden Rd, the local name for Forest Service road 1N10 that parallels the river on the south side. The road's no good for regular cars and you'll have to hike through brush to get to the river. You should check it out on the topos and Google Earth. Here's our location: 37 50'21.52" N, 120 4'42.03"W. The sheriff's people will know the road."

"Thanks Jake. It sounds like we should be treating that road as well as hiking routes to your location as crime scene. Evidence in the dirt gets compromised easily, so I'd request that the sheriff lets us go in first."

"Will do Vern. I need to call the sheriff and get them moving. You'll hear from us. Why don't you guys come up and do a television CSI thing here. We can just head on down the river and you can do the forensics, then solve the crime."

"Yeah right, that'll happen. Talk to you later," said Vern as he hung up.

Jake keyed in the sheriff's number and pressed send. "Sheriff-Coroner Raskin's office," squawked the phone.

"This is DOJ special agent Jake Appleby. I have a major incident that the sheriff needs to know about right now."

"Wait one," replied the handset.

Jake knew that calling the sheriff directly was the correct political move, but he was hoping that Raskin would get the right people involved, not come roaring out to the crime scene himself. Some "suits" screw up investigations by contaminating the crime scene while they attempt to show their power and gain press coverage. He knew that sheriffs, since they are elected, have extra pressure to show presence.

The phone returned to life: "Tyler Raskin. Who am I talking to?"

"This is Jake Appleby, California DOJ special agent, sheriff. In an improbable coincidence, I and some other law enforcement personnel were on a recreational raft trip down the Tuolumne when we encountered what appears to be the head of a human female, posed on top of a boulder in the river."

"So much for a calm spring day. Just a head, you say?"

"Yes sir. The head is the only evidence of human presence that we can see from the water. We've stayed on the water in order to preserve the crime scene for forensics. Before we continue, I should give you our location and sat phone number in case we lose connection."

"Go ahead."

"We're at 37 50'21.52" N, 120 4'42.03"W and you can get my sat phone with 011-8816-3314-1039."

"Got it. You have no suspect?"

"No sir. We haven't seen anybody since we started down the river. There's a small chance that the perp went on down the river but I think it's probable that he came in and out using the forest service road near here. There's no indication that this was the kill site. We don't know how much time has elapsed since the posing, though I'd say it was done today based on the lack of damage from birds and because there's no visible deterioration. It's your case sir, but I have some suggestions about how to get started."

"All right, you can quickly give them to me now, then again to my people when I get them assembled. Hold on a minute while I get the roundup started."

"Yes sir," said Jake.

A minute later, the sheriff was back: "go ahead with your suggestions, agent."

Jake listed them off: "roadblock the ends of Lumsden Road to keep people from entering and check anybody coming out as a possible witness or the perp. Because of the fragile environment for forensics, keep all personnel out until forensics gets here. If you have a plane or a copter, scout downstream from us in case the perp is on the river. Keep any helicopter away from here because we don't need any downwash that destroys evidence."

"That all sounds reasonable, we'll see what my people think. I'll get units headed toward roadblock locations now."

"Yes sir."

"We'll call you in about 10 minutes." The connection dropped.

Jake knew that the sheriff's office was in Sonora, about an hour away. Of course, DOJ forensics people, who were needed on something this complex, were even further away. He hoped that some patrol units were closer and they could close up the forest road soon.

Five minutes later, the sat phone rang. He answered, "Jake Appleby".

"Agent Appleby, this is Sheriff Raskin. I've got my team here on speakerphone. I'll have them introduce themselves."

A series of voices followed: "Lieutenant Evan Harris, Field Operations. Captain Manny Perez, Investigations. Sergeant Larry Murray, Investigations, Investigator Andy Katashi, Crimes Against People.

Raskin came back on: "Appleby, why don't you start from the beginning describing your situation there and any recommendations you have."

"Yes sir," answered Jake, and then proceeded to repeat the story and answer questions. At the end he said, "I've got one additional recommendation."

"Go ahead," said the sheriff.

"This scene is so clean that I think that gathering forensics is going to be tough. I suggest that you call in DOJ forensics right now and get them on a plane into Pine Mountain Lake's airstrip so they have time to work before dark."

There was silence. Jake figured that there was some nonverbal communication going on in Sonora.

"We'll do that," said Sheriff Raskin. "We're going to get off the phone now and get moving."

"I'll see you when you get here," answered Jake, then he hung up.

"So, what're they like?" asked Celia.

"So far, professional," replied Jake. "We'll see how it works out. It'd be nice to have a full team without anybody needing to feather their cap. It'd be good for us to bail out after they get here and interview us. They'll feel less threatened and might work better with us."

"I agree," said Celia. "What's the time frame?"

"It's going to be several hours before they get DOJ forensics looking at the forest road. I suspect they'll be quite slow getting down here so that they can pick up whatever's out there without destroying it by hiking around. Best case, they'll be down here by 6 or 7 o'clock, giving them a couple of hours before sunset. By the time they interview us I'm guessing that we'll be hiking out in the dark."

"I think that you should let the rest of the crew finish the trip," said Celia. "They can't help here and they might hurt. There's no reason to ruin their day any further. The two of us can handle the scene."

"You're right C," responded Jake. "I might catch some shit about it, but it's the right thing to do. What else?"

"Pictures."

"Oh crap. I can't believe that I forgot pictures." Jake spoke to the other raft crew: "Did you guys find anything at all on this shore?"

"No Jake," responded Porky, "not a damned thing other than bird shit on a rock."

"Did anybody bring a camera?" asked Jake.

"I did," spoke up Porky, "I bought this waterproof camera bag so I could record the trip but I've forgotten to use the damned thing."

"I need to use it for the crime scene, but I'll get it back to you," said Jake. "Has anybody observed anything at all unique here other than the head on the rock?"

The only sound was Porky retrieving his camera from his waist pack.

"All right then, here's what I propose. Celia and I will stay here in one raft to guard the scene and work with the crews that are on their way. The rest of you take the other raft and finish the trip. Any problems?"

"Yeah, that's a chickenshit way to get out of the poker game tonight," complained Terry. "I was going to take everything you had."

"Snowball's chance in hell, you dreamer," responded Jake. "I'm going to pass my notebook around, everybody needs to list their name and contact info for the sheriff's investigator. When you get back to the cabins don't get too drunk because the guy may decide to interview you tonight.

"We'll need to leave some of the gear with you to avoid being overloaded," said Chris.

"That's fine Chris. Hey everybody, have a ball on the trip, it's a great run and I hate to miss it. We'll see you at the cabins late tonight."

"Sure you hate to miss it," quipped Terry. "I think you'd prefer be alone with a beautiful chick."

"Yeah right," said Celia. "Get your ass downriver."

3. ALONE

Jake and Celia watched their friends float around the bend 800 feet downriver and disappear. There was nobody in sight and no prospect of seeing anybody for hours.

Jake looked at his partner. Celia, he observed to himself for the hundredth time, was not only a good looking woman but a good person and a good cop. Just a kid at 32, Celia was five foot eight and he guessed that she weighed under 140. Her raven black shoulder length hair complemented her light brown complexion and deep brown eyes. She had an attractive face though her nose that was a touch too broad. From what Jake had observed, she had a great body, on the lean side. Jake knew that Celia was in great condition because of her dedication to the martial art taekwondo. They'd first been partners as Sacramento PD patrol officers and he had practiced taekwondo with her for two years before dropping out. It had taken him quite a while to get to know her; she was a private person. After a year or so Jake had learned that inside Celia's tough shell there was a mellow and caring person. She could be a bit moody, so he needed to pay attention to what was going on with her and try to work with it. Jake maintained boundaries between them because they were partners, but there were temptations. He figured that with his track record, if he tried to start a relationship he'd just lose a friend and a great partner.

Jake had moved through the police department, getting promoted to detective and doing a short stint in homicide before passing the California Department of Justice's Special Agent exam. He had hired into the Investigations and Intelligence Bureau, one of eight bureaus including forensics, firearms, and narcotics. His Major Crimes Unit regularly got involved in cases that involved multiple law enforcement jurisdictions.

Celia had followed Jake's career path, moving a year or two behind Jake. Jake had helped her make the move to the DOJ and they had partnered up again a year ago. He thought they complemented each other well, making a good team.

"You daydreaming Jake? You need to take pictures of the boulder and the head. I'll keep an eye out for birds."

"Uh, yeah," responded Jake. He grabbed the camera and started taking pictures. He expected that the forensic guy's photos would be used, but you never know what might happen so you take pictures as soon as you can. The light through his viewfinder momentarily went dark. "what the hell was that," he exclaimed, lowering the camera.

"A damn turkey vulture that came out of nowhere," replied Celia. "He soared over us, clearing the rock by 10 feet."

"I'm sure that he's figured this thing for a snack now. I bet that he has some buddies around, wanting to make it a party. Vultures are big time cowards so I'm guessing that they won't come to eat as long as we're close by, but we'd better keep a close eye on them."

"A great way to spend an afternoon, looking at turkey vultures," answered Celia. "Ranks right up there with dumpster diving. I'll keep an eye on the birds, you'd better call the office and let them know what's happening. You know that the suits are going to want a piece of this. While you're at it, call the Missing Person's Unit and see if we have candidates in the database."

Jake understood the need for "politics" in order to work with other agencies and people with a wide range of personalities. He also understood that the public needed positive feelings toward law enforcement, otherwise the public would be less cooperative and law enforcement would end up with lower budgets. Beyond that, he hated ass kissers and publicity seekers. Since the DOJ was led by the Attorney General, an elected official, there were plenty of political animals and publicity hounds. Christ, if you looked at the Attorney General's web site you'd find it studded with "AG did this, AG did that" PR pieces.

They portrayed the AG as three supermen doing all the DOJs work himself.

In the Bureau of Investigations and Intelligence where Jake and Celia worked, the vast majority of workers and bosses were about getting the job done until you reached the Bureau Chief, Charles Browning. "Chucky the hound," as many people called him, constantly focused on publicity and worked to have himself as the highlight. Since he was now campaigning for the Attorney General job, he was worse than usual. The hound was going to slobber over this crime.

Jake pulled out his sat phone and verified that it still had a good satellite connection. He decided to see what he could get out of Missing Persons before he called their boss. "C, I'd call this a white female, shoulder length black hair, age 34 plus or minus 8, no identifying marks on the face. The eyes are too clouded to call a color. Whadya think?"

"Add in two piercings on left ear, can't see the right one. I'd call the eyes brown."

Jake called the DOJs Missing and Unidentified Persons Unit, described the situation and description. "I'm just looking for possibles, women that have gone missing in the last month. I'll hold while you look." He leaned back against the raft, closed his eyes and thought about the kind of people that kept him in the murder investigation business. So many of them were just stupid, greedy, and brutal, but this one looked to be different. A killer who would stage like this is a fiend in several senses of the word: evil, an enthusiast, proficient. Given the mutilation, the perp was going for shock value. He'd succeeded. Most killings of females had a sexual aspect that was not yet visible here. Jake guessed that this was going to be a difficult, if not impossible case and the DOJ needed to be a part of it.

A voice emerged from the phone. Jake listened and wrote in his notebook. "Okay John, thanks for the work. I'll pass this on to the primary investigator."

"Whad you get," asked Celia.

"We've got two possibles," responded Jake. "One from Pasadena missing sixteen days, one from Walnut Creek missing five days. They've got dental for the Pasadena woman. Too bad we don't have an internet connection so we can see the faces."

"That's a start," said Celia. "Okay now, quit dragging your feet and call the boss."

She reads me so well thought Jake. Even though he got along well with their boss Sam Nakamura, the suits above Sam were going to be on this case like flies on shit. It wouldn't be fun. "You got me," he said. He lifted the phone once again and called.

"Sam, this is Jake. I wanted to give you a heads up on the situation Celia and I have here."

Celia muttered, "Oh man, you're bad."

"You remember that we were taking a raft trip down the Tuolumne?"

"Yeah. You, Moreno and some other people, right?"

Jake described the events of the day and suggested that they should be involved in the case.

"It does sound like we should be involved. Sheriff Raskin's a good guy but he's got a political job and I don't know his investigators. Play it sensitive at the start, don't go pissing in anybody's boots."

"I'll hold my bladder for a while boss."

"If the vic isn't a lowlife or prostitute, the press is going to eat this up big time. I'm going to have to let Browning know."

"I figured as much," said Jake with a notable lack of enthusiasm.

"What do you need from me Jake?"

"Nothing right now except for keeping your eye on the politics,"

Sam knew how much Jake hated having management intrude on his cases. While he sympathized, Sam played his role in management by not knocking his superiors, at least to his employees. "I'll be watching, Jake. You keep me up to date."

"Yes sir. I'll call you when there's news or when we get out of here." Jake disconnected the call.

"It's done, C. Ten bucks that we hear from Browning before forensics arrives."

"No bet. I've got plenty of other ways to throw away money. Let's talk about the coincidence. The chance of this head being placed here just when we're on the river is infinitesimally small. That gives us a connection to look for."

"You're right C, though the connection could be to somebody else in the rafting party," answered Jake."

"We should look for connections to everybody," acknowledged Celia, "but I have a strong feeling that the connection is to you and I. What the connection is, I haven't a clue. It could be one of our old cases or because we work for the DOJ. This doesn't smell like one of our old cases, but I need to look through them. If the connection is to us, who knew that we would be here? We should have a small list of people outside of law enforcement and family members."

"Good points C, you should run with it."

They sat there for several minutes, each of their minds chewing at the situation as the river gurgled by. Bit by bit, they relaxed into waiting for forensics and the sheriff's people to arrive.

Celia broke the silence: "Well, you screwed up again Jakey. You got me alone in a beautiful place, but you royally buggered up the ambiance with this one piece of your décor."

4. CELIA

Sitting in the raft through the late afternoon, Celia was enjoying the peace and calm of the river canyon. They'd had nothing to do for the last couple of hours and had more hours before somebody would show up.

She spent minutes just watching the sun glinting off of ripples in the water as they danced an ever changing pattern on their way to the sea.

Celia began daydreaming about life and how it led her to this place and situation. She'd grown up in Vacaville as a normal daughter of high school teachers. Even though she was second generation American from Spanish and Chilean heritage she'd had to deal with some "Mexican" prejudice from school mates. It was painful, but she'd learned that kids could be vicious, picking on anything that they saw as a weakness. As an adult, the only time she'd seen that behavior was when a lowlife was trying to get to her. She didn't think of herself as "ethnic" or a minority and that worked well in most of today's California.

The normal life was shattered one night during her freshman year at Chico State. She was raped while on a date with a huge football player named Ed. Between her intoxication and his size, strength and aggressiveness she didn't' have a chance. Celia was depressed for weeks. For a long time she couldn't share the horrible experience with anybody but the confessional. The response she received there made her back away from the church that had always been part of her life, though she kept thinking about God.

Celia developed a resolve: She wouldn't be a victim again and she would do her best to protect others from having their lives damaged and destroyed. She began taking classes in taekwondo martial arts and developed a dedication that many students didn't share. She got serious about college and switched her major from Psychology to Criminal Justice with a minor in Psychology.

Two years later at a party Celia walked into a room and there was Ed, climbing all over a young redhead who wasn't looking too happy. He recognized her and called out, "hey baby, you were good, I bet you want some more Big Ed – we'll do a threesome."

The girl whined, "Ed, please."

"Don't get your muff in an uproar, baby," answered Ed. "I'll be fillin' it up right soon." He gave her a light slap on the right cheek.

Without a word Celia walked up to Ed, spun, and drove her heel into his solar plexus. As he began to gasp, she finished her spin and struck an upward blow to his nose with the heel of her right hand. Four seconds after it started, Ed was on his knees trying to breathe while tears and blood dripped from his face.

Celia said to the redhead, "come on, we're getting out of here." She grabbed the girl by the arm and walked her out of the house.

Reflecting on the memory as she floated on the river, she still felt good about it. It wasn't enough, but it was good.

Celia landed her first job with the Sacramento Police Department right out of college. She was proud of her accomplishments in law enforcement. She had learned a tremendous amount working on patrol and as an investigator. The current job in the DOJ was bigger, with more scope and the opportunity to travel around the state. In addition to putting bad people away, she gave guest lectures at Chico State and Sacramento State.

One downside of the changes was the impact on her family. Her parents disapproved of her career choice and were upset and angry about her separation from the church. The problem was aggravated because she wouldn't explain why she changed. Family visits that used to be so warm and cozy now tended to be tense, even when the disapproval didn't boil to the surface.

Another downside was the impact on relationships. Her values, many acquired from her religious upbringing, made casual sex unappealing. Despite that upbringing, she'd had an affair in her mid twenties that made her a major fan of sex combined with love. That relationship had ended and nothing had come along since. Being a female cop was difficult and her career goals required her to walk a thin line so she'd be viewed as a cop first, woman second. She could *never* get involved with somebody at work because it would get out, guys wouldn't think of her as a competent cop, instead they'd sexualize her.

Celia was stirred out of her reverie by a tickling feeling on her right knee. She had learned years ago from a bee that brushing at an insect before you looked was a bad idea. Peering down, she was surprised to see a beautiful yellow and black Tiger Swallowtail butterfly resting on her knee. It appeared to be looking at her, slowly opening and closing its wings. They contemplated each other for several minutes. When the butterfly launched itself toward its next destination she sent a goodbye after it.

Celia came back to the present, realizing that she was stiff from sitting in one position so long. The sun had descended beyond the western wall of the canyon, they were in shadow.

5. TROOPS APPROACH

Sheriff's Investigator Andy Katashi was excited, but nobody would have had a clue. His expressionless face and stoic behavior hid his feelings. At a slender five foot ten he was not intimidating but if you paid attention you could see that what bulk he had was muscular. His straight black hair, black eyes and slightly slanted eyes identified his Asian heritage. Katashi was third generation Japanese-American, not a common racial background in the Sierra Nevada Foothills.

Katashi was excited because he was lead on a dramatic murder case, something that was quite rare in Tuolumne County. Murders didn't happen often and they were usually mundane events involving drugs or escalation of domestic violence. So far, this one looked like it was in a different league. Katashi's intelligence and work ethic had led to his investigator's position, but he wanted more. He hadn't worked with DOJ forensics before, but had heard that they were the best in the state, so he'd be learning.

Katashi was waiting at the Pine Mountain Lake Airport for the DOJ forensic team to show up. He was standing just outside of Gold Country Aviation's building where he expected the DOJ plane to stop. The small public airport was adjacent to the private community that was built around a diminutive, but beautiful lake. In addition to water sports, it had golf, tennis, and a stable among its amenities.

Hearing the distinctive sound of turboprop engines, Katashi spotted a twin engine plane on a downwind approach leg just north of the airport.

Five minutes later the beautiful Piper Cheyenne III twin taxied up and stopped. The whine of the turboprop engines wound down and peace returned to the airport. Two men and a woman climbed out, two began unloading cases and one walked to meet Katashi.

"Hi, I'm Vern Lund. Are you Andy Katashi?"

"I am. Welcome to Tuolumne County," said Katashi as they shook hands. "I'll pull my vehicle over to the plane and you can load up."

Ten minutes later the group pulled out of the airport in Katashi's SUV. Ten minutes after that they reached the roadblock at the intersection of Ferretti and Lumsden. The deputies who had set up there reported that nothing had happened. No vehicles had come out and none wanting to come in. One of them climbed into Katashi's vehicle and they drove down the dusty forest road. Vern monitored their location using a GPS that displayed a topo map or the area.

After two and a half miles, Vern said, "stop here, we need to start looking at tire tracks." They all got out and took a look at the road. The dusty surface captured tread patterns well in some spots. Unfortunately, it was difficult to make sense out of the jumble of different tracks. After a minute, Vern pointed to a track and said, "This appears to be the most recent track here, though we don't know if it has anything to do with our crime. Nancy, shoot a series on this track. Andy, I suggest that you set up your command post just behind us. We're close enough to the location that Jake reported; we'll make this the beginning of our crime scene."

Katashi pulled a small table and chair out of the SUV and set them up at the edge of the road. He stationed the deputy there with a crime scene log and instructions that nobody else was to enter the scene until he was advised otherwise. He radioed the sheriff's units at the roadblock they just passed and instructed them to leave one unit there and bring one unit up to the command post.

By the time the sheriff's unit arrived, Nancy had finished recording the tire tracks and crime scene tape had been strung across the road. Vern and his technicians started to walk down the road paying close attention to the surface and the sides of the road. Katashi and a deputy stayed 50 feet behind them, walking in their tracks.

After about a quarter mile Katashi noticed that the forensics people had stopped and were pointing at various spots on the road. Katashi walked up to them.

Vern said, "A vehicle with the same tire tread has turned around in the road here. We also have footprints, so it looks like the car was parked, somebody exited and walked towards the river then returned. Given where we are on the map, this could well be our guy."

"It's good to have that. We should get on down to the river while we've got a couple of hours of light," responded Katashi.

"I'll have my crew tape this off and record it while you and I try to find a clean path down that won't contaminate evidence," said Vern.

After instructing his people to record all the tire tracks and boot prints, Vern backtracked ten yards on the road then turned downhill toward the river. Katashi and a deputy followed. The going was slow because of the steep terrain, the brush, and the need to make sure no signs of human activity were on their route. They left flags of crime scene tape to mark the path that would be used by all but the forensics people until evidence had been collected from the area.

6. TROOPS ARRIVE

Celia was startled when the satellite phone rang. Jake got to it after three rings with a "Jake Appleby… yessir." On the phone, Chuck Browning, Chief of the Bureau of Investigations and Intelligence, said, "I received a briefing on your situation from Sam Nakamura. Illuminate me with the knowledge acquired since you talked to him."

"There's nothing new. We've been guarding the site while waiting for forensics and the sheriff's people to arrive. I heard a bit of noise just before you called so they may be up on the road."

"They should be at your location by now, I sent my airplane for them in order to expedite their arrival. The DOJ is going to be involved in this investigation and you will be our primary representative along with the Deputy Attorney General we assign to the case. I want immediate updates from you about any significant developments in this case and I want a status summary at eight PM every night, beginning tonight.

"Yes sir," said Jake.

The connection was broken.

"Chucky the hound," muttered Jake. "Another pleasant conversation."

"Wha'd he have to say," asked Celia.

"We're going to be on the case with a DOJ lawyer, call him with any significant developments and update him every night at eight."

"That'll be a pain in the ass. Why is he so into this case?"

"I don't know," responded Jake. "Given who he is and that he's running for Attorney General, I'd guess that it's about publicity. He figures to get lots of press using the head in the river for sensationalism."

"Great," said Celia.

They began to hear more noise: indistinct voices. It became clear that people were headed down the canyon slope towards them.

It took Vern and company forty minutes to reach the river even though the straight line distance was a fifth of a mile. When they reached the shore they spotted a raft thirty yards upstream. Vern yelled "Hey Jake, we've arrived." It was 6:34 and they would only have an hour and a half before the light would be too poor for crime scene work. In an outdoor crime scene, you stopped work at night if you could because it was impossible to find minute traces of evidence under nighttime conditions.

The group worked their way up the shore toward the boulder while looking for evidence in the path. There was nothing to be seen, but there were enough rocks on the bank that it wasn't too surprising. As they reached the boulder they stopped and examined its gruesome decoration.

"Welcome to the Tuolumne Vern," said Jake. "It's been a long wait. And I bet that you're Andy Katashi. I'm Jake Appleby and this is my partner Celia Moreno."

"Agent Appleby, you are correct. I am assuming command of the crime scene now. Would you please move your raft downstream to where we emerged from the brush, then tie it to shore?" was the cool response from Katashi.

Jake shared a look with Celia as they began maneuvering downstream as asked.

Vern already had his camera out and was recording the boulder and head.

As Jake and Celia stepped ashore and then tied up the raft, Katashi reached them. "Where is the rest of the rafting party?" questioned Katashi.

"We decided that there was no value to keeping them here, so we sent them on down the river," said Jake. "We have names and contact information for you."

"That wasn't your decision to make, agent Appleby. They should be here so I can interview them."

"None of them have useful information Andy." You can interview them tonight at our Mountain Meadows cabins if you really want to do that. We can debrief you on the group's experience and save you the time," replied Jake with a touch of annoyance.

"As first officer on the scene, you should have preserved the scene. That includes all potential witnesses. What other non standard decisions have you made?" asked Katashi.

"None," replied Jake.

"We'll see," said Katashi. "I'll interview you two separately and then you can return to your friends."

"Look," spoke up Celia, "we understand that this is your jurisdiction and your case. As DOJ agents we can provide you with some help as well as resources that the sheriff doesn't have."

"That won't be necessary at this time," responded Katashi. "I have the DOJ forensics people and that's all I need or want."

"Have it your way," said Jake. "Let's do the interview and we're out of here."

Katashi interviewed each of them, finishing by handing them his card and saying, "call me if you remember more."

By the time that Katashi was done with them, Jake saw that Vern was done with the boulder and was working his way upriver looking for traces. He called out, "Vern, we'll talk to you later."

"Sure Jake," responded Vern. "Talk to you later."

Jake and Celia began following the yellow tape flags up the hill. Their athletic shoes didn't give them good traction on the precipitous slope. They slipped and slid for most of the climb. When they reached the road they spotted the crime scene techs. After introductions, Jake asked what they'd found.

Nancy responded, "We've got tire tracks and footprints showing that the most recent vehicle on this section of road came in from the west and parked on the south side of the road over there. One person got out, headed into the brush towards the river and returned. The vehicle then turned around and headed back west. We've found nothing else along the road for a quarter mile in either direction. The shoe print indicates a men's size ten or a woman's size eleven. It's a standard Vibram sole so we're not going to ID a brand or model for you."

"What about the tires?" Jake asked.

"We should be able to give you make and model along with one or two sizes. They don't have any unique damage that would allow you to match a specific set of tires."

"Too bad the perp didn't leave his business card, but what you've got is a start, thanks," said Celia. "I'm sure you'll have to find a local bed somewhere tonight – our rafting group has cabins at Mountain Meadows if you don't find something else."

"Thanks, we'll see what Vern wants to do," said Nancy.

Jake and Celia walked west to the command post. The fine tan dust on the road puffed into the air with every footstep, coating their bare calves like it coated the brush on the side of the road. They introduced themselves to the deputy and asked, "Do you have somebody that can give us a ride to the Mountain Meadows cabins?"

The deputy responded, "In about a half hour. Got another car on its way."

"We'll wait," said Jake. "It'd take twice that long to get one of our friends out here."

The deputy asked, "You found this head? Was she a looker?"

Jake answered, "Well, she wasn't made up for the prom, but there appeared to be lots of potential."

"Not your everyday action up here," observed the deputy.

"Not normal anywhere," responded Jake.

Jake and Celia wandered off, waiting for their ride. "Time to call Browning," said Celia after checking her watch and seeing that it was eight.

"Yeah, the hound needs to be fed," said Jake. Jake keyed in Browning's number and pressed send. When Browning answered, he said: "Appleby here. We're up at the command post on the forest road that parallel's the river." He summarized the news and then said, "Our sheriff's investigator made it clear that he isn't interested in DOJ help other than forensics."

"His opinion is of no import," was Browning's response. "We are in this case and I expect you to overcome trifling obstacles such as this. If you encounter opposition that you cannot overcome, contact Nakamura or myself and we will deal with the sheriff."

"Yes sir."

"Continue to contact me as I instructed."

"Yes sir."

The call dropped.

"Well?" Celia said.

"He said to ignore Katashi, stay on the case, call for help if we have to."

"Okay, we can do that. We can't always make friends.

"Katashi is acting old school even though he's a kid. I haven't had a guy play turf control in quite a while.

"I hope that it's not a department thing."

Jake said, "This case buggers up my visit with Kaitlin. I need to call Fiona."

"I'm sure that will be a delightful conversation. I'll give you some privacy," said Celia as she walked back to the command post.

Jake took a deep breath, let it out, and called his ex wife Fiona. After she answered he said, "It's me. I'm very sorry but this case fell out of the sky into my lap today and I won't be able to get up there tomorrow morning."

The phone blared: "God damn you Jake Appleby. Once again you disappoint your daughter and me. Every time we depend on you, you turn around and crap on us."

"Fiona, Fiona," Jake breathed. "You're right to be angry, I'm angry that I have to cancel but there was no way to foresee this case and there's no way I can get out of it in the morning. I'll find a way to make it up to both of you."

"Yeah, I'll be holding my breath for that," growled Fiona. "It's this damn career of yours once again; it steps all over your family. Get out of it and back into computers where you can spend at least some time with your daughter."

"I know how you feel about the job Fiona. You know what led me here and that hasn't changed."

"Diane has been gone thirteen years Jake. Grief is supposed to be a process and by now you should be at the end of that road. You don't have to let that terrible tragedy control your life."

Jake's baby sister Diane had been raped and murdered at the age of 17. Jake had been driving to his parent's house in San Jose when he spotted her white Mustang with the red racing stripe parked two blocks from the family home. He stopped to look at the car and discovered her body wedged into the floor behind the front seats. Jake had never experienced death before; the shock and then grief was crushing. Jake's father Nick was a homicide detective with the San Jose PD, ensuring that triple the normal energy was applied to the case. A year went by and the killer or killers were not found.

Despite a lifetime of direction from his parents to steer clear of a criminal justice career, Jake made a decision to fight back against the creatures who wipe out other people's lives. Jake had been an early employee of Google, completely immersed in the offbeat creative culture of the company. With stock from his first startup and options from Google he was a wealthy man. He exercised his Google stock options and began his new career with twenty three weeks at the Sacramento Police Academy.

"Fiona, we're not going to get anywhere hashing over this for the hundredth time," sighed Jake. "As soon as I can break free, I'll get up there to see Kaitlin. Can you put her on the phone?"

"You're right about getting nowhere Jake. I'll get Kaitlin. Call me."

"Bye Fiona."

After a minute the phone spoke. "Hi daddy."

Jake's heart tripped at the sweet sound of his daughter's voice. "Hi honey, how are you doing today?"

"Okay I guess, but mom says that you're not coming tomorrow?"

"I'm sorry, but something's happened that's going to keep me down here tomorrow. I'd prefer to be with you kiddo, but I don't always get to do what I want."

"This happens all the time daddy. You said you were coming," said Kaitlin with a trace of whine.

Jake's guilt caught in his throat. "I'm sorry. As soon as I can get away I'll be up there."

"I guess I'll see you when I see you."

"You'll see me soon honey. Good night."

"Bye daddy."

Jake took a deep breath, let it out, then walked over to join Celia.

"Tough?" she said.

"Yeah, it is. It hurts to disappoint an innocent kid. It doesn't help my relationship with Fiona either."

They stood in silence for a couple of minutes, then saw a sheriff's vehicle heading toward them, trailing a cloud of dust into the darkening sky.

When they reached the cabins, they found their friends far ahead of them on the drinking and well into a poker game. There was some cold chicken and plenty of beer. Jake and Celia each grabbed a bottle of Sierra Nevada: Pale Ale for Jake and Summerfest for Celia.

"So what happened after we left?" asked Steve Devlin.

"Not a whole lot," replied Celia as she drained her first beer. We had a buzzard fly by then sat around until forensics and the sheriff's guy got there at 6:30. The sheriff's investigator was a bit of a prick – he wanted us out of there and was pissed that we let you guys finish the trip.

"Fuck him," said Terry. "We had nothing for him and it would have sucked to have missed the rest of the river trip. You were right Celia, Clavey falls was incredible. That first drop felt like you were dropping off the roof of a house and every bit of water you can see is crazy."

Jake piped up,"What she didn't tell you is that a couple of people have died in Clavey. They were kayakers though, rafting is safer. I'm glad you guys enjoyed it and I wish we had been with you. It was damned inconvenient of that lady to leave her head out there." Jake grabbed a drumstick and another beer.

"Any forensics turn up?" asked Porky.

"They didn't have a lot of time before they lost the light. As far as we know, they've just got vehicle and boot tracks on the road.

"Her old man did it," said Porky.

"That's a good bet, though posing the head in the river seems strange for a partner murder," responded Jake. "We have a couple of possible missing person's matches so maybe we'll find out who she is soon. Then we'll see about the old man."

"This could turn into a real whodunit," said Steve.

"You could be right," said Celia. "Speaking of whodunits, Jake and I were discussing what a coincidence it is that the head was posed in the river just in time for a group of law enforcement people to find it. Can any of you think of a personal or job situation that might have led to this? An old case maybe?"

There was silence for a minute.

"We had a case a couple of years ago," said Steve. "A woman was murdered and dismembered – parts of her showed up all over the place. We liked the husband for it but never put together enough evidence. I guess this could be the guy flipping us off."

"Can you check out his situation when you get back to work?" asked Jake. "See if somebody around him has gone missing. Let us know either way, would you?"

"Sure, we'll do that."

Celia asked, "Anybody else?" After a few seconds of silence she said, "We'd appreciate it if you'd keep thinking about it. Let us know if anything at all comes to mind."

"Enough of this crap," said Jake. "Who's dealing?"

7. SONORA

Andy Katashi arrived back in Sonora about eleven thirty. After setting up overnight crime scene protection, he had driven the DOJ forensics team into Groveland where he found them rooms for the night. He had called Paul at the Felippo Funeral Home and arranged to meet him and drop off the head for overnight storage. Captain Perez had scheduled an autopsy in the morning using a forensic pathologist who would drive up from the valley.

After seeing the head stored, Katashi drove to the sheriff's office to begin his paperwork. As he reached the office door, he ran into a deputy starting his graveyard shift who said "Hey Andy, did you catch the case with the head?"

"Yeah," said Katashi. "Is something up?"

"All I know is that some suit from DOJ was on the eleven o'clock news making a big deal about the head and the DOJ. He gave our department honorable mention at the end of his spiel."

"Bastards," said Katashi. "Thanks for the heads up."

Fuming, Katashi walked to his desk and slammed down his attaché case. Mumbling under his breath, he started on his paperwork, hoping to make enough progress that he could be in bed by three.

8. GROVELAND; WEDNESDAY

Jake was up at seven, moving slow after the evening of beer drinking. He couldn't bounce back quite as quickly as he had in his twenties. He dressed in a pair of Levis and a silk Hawaiian shirt. Jake wasn't much into clothes except for his collection of Hawaiian shirts.

After starting a pot of coffee using the ground Sumatra he had brought along, Jake walked over to the office and bought a copy of the Modesto Bee. As soon as he saw the paper, he exclaimed, "The son of a bitch did it again." On the front page, above the fold, was a two column headline *DOJ FINDS WOMAN'S HEAD ON THE TUOLUMNE*. This had to be Browning's work. Browning had held a news conference the previous night just in time to catch the eleven o'clock news and the morning papers. He had made sure that his name and the DOJ was emphasized as well as making the story as lurid as possible.

Celia was on the porch of the cabin drinking coffee with Steve and Terry. Jake dropped the paper in her lap and said, "look at your favorite suit's work," then he walked on into the cabin and poured his own cup of coffee. By the time he sat down on the porch, Celia had finished reading.

"I'm not too surprised Jake. This is why he's called Chucky the Hound. It's annoying as hell but there's nothing we can do about it. I bet that the sheriff and your buddy Katashi are more pissed than we are."

"Katashi's a lost cause already, but yeah, the sheriff won't be happy," said Jake. I hate it when Chucky does this. Not only is it embarrassing and pisses off people we need to work with, but it puts too much public light on the investigation. Giving the perp free information just makes it harder for us.

Terry finished reading and passing the paper to Steve, he said "our chief gets some PR, but this turkey's over the top. Nobody knows anything, nobody's had time to do anything and he's going for the big splash. Glad I don't have to deal with him."

Jake pulled out his laptop and used it to access the DOJ missing person's database. The first MP that satisfied his search was the woman from Pasadena. She had a ski jump nose that did not resemble their victim's. The next match was of an attractive woman with a light olive complexion. Jake pulled the card out of Porky's camera and loaded the pictures into the laptop. He then started looking through yesterday's pictures in a window alongside the Missing Persons picture. Selecting a picture taken from the same angle as the picture of the missing woman he said, "guys, come look at this."

Terry, Steve and Celia looked over his shoulders at the laptop's screen. "That's got to be her," said Celia.

Steve said "bingo."

"Fast work, buddy," said Terry. "She was sweet. Had some nice sweater puppies too."

"Showing your class again Terry," said Celia. "She's dead for Christ's sake."

Jake dug Katashi's card out of his pocket and called. After one ring and a boring voicemail message he responded to the beep with "Katashi, this is Jake Appleby. I've got a tentative ID on your victim. Call me at 916-555-7942."

Next Jake called the Walnut Creek Police Department, the contact for the missing woman. After telling the officer handling missing persons that the picture matched well with a homicide victim, Jake was switched over to Roger Minter, the lieutenant running the Crimes Against Persons unit. "I'm Jake Appleby, agent with the California DOJs Sacramento office. Yesterday on the Tuolumne River we chanced on some remains that look a lot like your missing person Sophia Mancuso.

"Shit, I didn't even know that she was missing," said Roger. "I know her from our local mentoring organization. Sophia is a nice person. How good is your ID?"

"All we have here is a head, but comparing it to the missing person's picture, it looks like her to us," said Jake. Give me your email address and I can send you the picture that looks like a match."

After sending off the email, Jake said, "The missing persons entry in our database doesn't indicate that dental records are available, but that'd be the quickest way to firm up the ID."

"You're right," replied Roger. "Maybe we can get the records without upsetting her husband too much. I don't want to jump the gun and tell the poor bastard that we have a head that looks like his wife. While I'm waiting for the picture, let me write down your contact information."

Jake gave him the information and told them that the Tuolumne County Sheriff had the remains at this point, giving him Katashi's contact information.

"I've got your email," said Roger. "Let me get that picture up. Shit, it sure looks like her. Damnit. Alright, I'm going to assign detective Torrey Bonner to this, first order will be to come up with dental records. I'll have him call you when he's got them."

"OK Roger, I'll be trying to connect with the autopsy," said Jake, then hung up.

"Why didn't you say Roger and out?" said Terry.

"I'm sure he'd never heard that before," responded Jake.

Jake called the Tuolumne Sheriff's Department, asking for Captain Manny Perez. He figured that he'd eliminate the Katashi problem by stepping over him. "Captain, this is Jake Appleby from the DOJ. We talked yesterday when you had your meeting with the sheriff."

"Yeah Appleby, I remember. What can I do for you."

"First of all I'd like to apologize for the press coverage. I wish I had control over that but I don't. I have some news about the case and then I'd like to be in on the autopsy if you have it scheduled. I've tried to call Andy Katashi but he doesn't seem to be available."

"Go ahead."

"There's a good chance that we have a match of the victim with a missing Walnut Creek woman. The Walnut Creek PD is going after her dental records."

"Having an ID would be good," said Perez. "The autopsy is scheduled for 11 at the Fellipo Funeral Home. You're welcome to attend. I'm assuming that you can arrange the forensic odontology work?"

"Yeah, our Missing and Unidentified Persons Unit does forensic odontology. I can make that happen. I'll be there for the autopsy and we'll see where we go from there."

"Why don't you plan on meeting with us here before the autopsy?"

"That sounds like a good plan. See you about ten."

"All right rafters, what say we pack up and go have a good breakfast in Groveland?" said Jake.

He got nods, murmurs and statements of agreement. The group disbursed to pack and load.

"Celia, why don't we stick to our original transportation plan. I'll drop my bike out of the truck and you take the truck back to Sacramento. You can check our old cases for the coincidence angle and I'll run up to Sonora and deal with things there." Celia and Jake had driven up in Jake's truck, loaded with food and beer and Jake's favorite toy, a 2009 Honda CBR100RR Fireblade superbike. The original plan had been for Jake to ride it up the winding foothill Highway 49 to see his daughter in Grass Valley.

"Sure," said Celia as she walked off to pack.

9. SONORA

After a tasty breakfast at the Foothills Café in Groveland, the group said their goodbyes and headed out. As Jake put on his protective jumpsuit he was getting excited about the ride to Sonora. While not a long ride, it was on country roads through rolling oak studded foothills. Traffic was light and most of the curves on the road could be taken at high speed. Jake knew that motorcycle riding was dangerous, but at this point in his life the adrenaline rush and the sheer excitement of riding a machine like his Fireblade was worth the risk. Its 174 horsepower gave it a 3.5 pounds/hp ratio with Jake in the saddle, far better than Ferrari's fastest road car, the 599 GTO, at 5.8. His Blade would leave the Ferrari in the dust, doing zero to sixty in under two seconds while the Ferrari took over three seconds, still better than twice as fast as most cars. The biggest challenge with the Blade was to moderate the use of its awesome power. The machine would get Jake to 135 in ten seconds, but if he hit much of anything at that speed he'd be toast.

When Jake upgraded to the Blade, he took three classes at a superbike school to improve his riding skills and understand his limits. He figured that skill was a way to moderate the risks of riding.

Jake left Groveland after all of his friends but by the time he reached the top of Priest Grade he had blown by all of them. Jake had to rein in the Blade as he descended seventeen hundred feet down Priest Grade like a corkscrew. Reaching Highway 49 he opened up but stayed under ninety most of the time. He slowed a touch as he blew through the old gold town of Chinese Camp, once full of Chinese and the site of tong wars, now closing in on ghost town status, the Chinese long gone.

Accelerating out of the town, he relished the sweet sound of a powerful high revving engine, so different from the low pitched rumbling roar of a Harley. Reaching the populated area of Jamestown, Jake slowed to the speed limit, worked his way into Sonora and pulled up in front of the sheriff's office, finishing the ride in less than half an hour.

Jake removed his helmet, took a deep breath and relaxed his shoulders. He walked into the office, identified himself and asked to see Captain Perez. Jake figured that he might have to work with Tuolumne County again, so he'd spend time cultivating a relationship if possible. In any event, he had time to kill before the autopsy.

"Captain Perez, it's good to meet you," said Jake as they shook hands.

"Good to meet you, agent," said Perez. "Andy's gone back out to the crime scene, but will be at the funeral home for the autopsy."

"That's fine, I wanted to meet you and give you what I have," said Jake.

"You know, Appleby, we have a long term good relationship with DOJ forensics and have worked with narcotics task forces, but have no experience with your Major Crimes operation. The eleven o'clock news and today's paper don't leave a good taste in our mouth."

"Yes sir, I understand that. I'm afraid that all I can do about the press interaction is apologize. Chuck Browning is three layers above me in the organization. On the other hand, I believe that Major Crimes can provide jurisdictions like yours with added value in the right situation. We tend to get involved with multi jurisdictional crimes, when we have more resources or expertise, or when an agency has a conflict of interest. Of course, our initial involvement in this crime is a curious coincidence, but it now appears that we have at least two jurisdictions involved."

"Tell me more about this Walnut Creek connection."

"Let me show you two pictures," Jake said as he pulled his laptop out of his backpack. Bringing it out of hibernation he turned it around so Perez could see the screen. "The picture on the left is one I took of the remains at the scene yesterday. The picture on the right is from our Missing Persons database."

Perez studied the pictures. "That's a match as best I can tell. Certainly worth pursuing."

"I emailed my picture to Roger Minter who runs Crimes Against Persons for Walnut Creek. It turns out that he knows the missing woman, they're both involved in some volunteer work. When he saw the picture of our vic he thought it was her."

"It looks like you've got an excellent lead," said Perez. "So far we have no hints that she is somebody local, but it's still early. Come back over here after the autopsy and we'll meet with Andy and his Sergeant."

"Yessir," said Jake as he packed up his laptop and headed out the door.

Shortly before eleven, Jake walked into the funeral home and found the lab that was used for embalming. The room had white cabinets and counters on two sides and a large stainless sink. Two wheeled stainless tables rested on a painted concrete floor that sloped towards a drain. The smell of embalming fluid was different than the smells of a morgue, but about as unpleasant. A cold place to pass through at the end of life. Jake met a still unfriendly Andy Katashi and the forensic pathologist, Jack Carver, who had driven up from Stockton.

"You guys haven't given me a lot to work with, but we'll find what we can," said Carver as he removed the head from a refrigerator and set it on the stainless steel table. Though no significant signs of putrefaction were visible, the odor of death was in the air. Jake disliked autopsies, but they were part of the job and often provided key information.

As he did the external examination, Carver said "we're not going to have a clue about time of death and cause of death may not be here either. I can tell you that the skin on the neck was precisely cut by a razor sharp knife or a scalpel. The cut appears to be postmortem. The x-rays that you had the hospital take show nothing unusual. Was there blood where you found it?"

Katashi replied, "None."

"Then the head appears to have been drained of blood before it was placed at the crime scene. We'll double check that observation once we get inside."

Carver continued the external exam in silence, then "There appears to be a trace of adhesive at the lower right corner of her lip. We can check its composition later."

"Duct taped her mouth shut," said Jake. "I'm sure you see that on a regular basis."

As he examined the right ear canal, Carver said "ho, we have some action. It appears we have a puncture of the right eardrum." The remainder of the external produced no more comments.

Carver then began the internal exam by cutting and peeling back her scalp. This whole part of the exam was a turn off for Jake. He could deal with dead bodies in the field but the slicing and dicing was unpleasant. Jake had great admiration for the ability of doctors to deal with blood and guts. He would have turned away if it hadn't been for Katashi's presence.

Jake's least favorite part was next. Carver started up the bone saw and it began its high pitched scream. As the saw bit into the skull, the pitch dropped and the smell of burned bone filled the air. Once the top of the skull was removed, even Jake could see hemorrhaging on the right side of the brain. After photographing the brain in situ, Carver removed the brain and said, "We have some significant damage here opposite the ear. The eardrum puncture and brain damage is consistent with the insertion of a thin pointed object through the ear then the manipulation of it to increase the damage."

The remainder of the autopsy produced no new information. It was one o'clock when Jake and Katashi walked out of the building to warm sunlight and delicious fresh air. Jake thought about lunch for about a millisecond and put the thought away. He said to Katashi, "See you at the office," then walked to his Blade.

In a conference room at the sheriff's office, Jake, Katashi, Perez and Sergeant Larry Murray got together. The room was the classic government conference room for worker types: bare and plastic.

"Andy, why don't you tell us what we learned from the autopsy," said Perez.

"The head appears to have been severed after death, using a sharp cutting tool and some care. We won't have any time of death information. One possible cause of death was the insertion of a thin pointed object through the right ear into the brain, followed by a stirring action to do more damage. He could have used an ice pick. No foreign material was found that might point to the killer. Other than that, nothing."

"That's not a lot of help," said Perez. "What do we have from the crime scene?"

"A good set of tire tracks. We should get make, model and size today. Boot tracks, size ten with a Vibram Tucson sole. Those soles are used by three boot manufacturers. One blue thread caught on a buckbrush. That appears to be all, though they were widening the search when I left."

"Whoever did this is looking damned careful," said Larry Murray. "This is as bad as the cases where we find a few old bones in the woods."

"You're right about that," said Perez. "The best we've got right now is Appleby's possible victim ID. Show them the pictures Jake."

Jake caught a dirty look from Katashi as he started up his notebook. Murray also noticed the look and frowned. Jake ignored it. When the machine was up, he moved it to where Murray and Katashi could see the screen. "The picture on the left is one I took at the crime scene. The one on the right is from the DOJs missing persons database."

After a minute, Murray said "Good matchup."

"Just because two women have dark hair and dark eyes doesn't make them a match," growled Katashi.

"The missing person is from Walnut Creek," Jake said. "I sent the victim picture to the Crimes Against Persons lieutenant there. He knows the missing person and thinks that the victim is her. We need to do a dental match."

After a few seconds of silence, Perez said, "This identification is the best lead we have at the moment. Andy, get the remains down to the Missing Persons Unit and let them do a comparison. Even if our victim is from Walnut Creek the case is still ours.

"Yes sir," said Katashi.

"I think that it would be a good idea to hold back the ice pick information," suggested Jake.

"I agree, we don't want copy cats and it would be good to have that in our bag," replied Murray.

Why don't we call Walnut Creek, give them an update," said Jake.

"Go ahead," said Perez, pushing the phone over to Jake.

Jake pulled out his notebook, found Torrey Bonner's number and punched it into the speakerphone. After a few rings, Bonner answered.

"This is Jake Appleby with the DOJ. I talked with Roger this morning about your missing person Sophia Mancuso. Roger said he was going to give you the case."

"Right you are," said Bonner. "I'm headed to her dentist's office as we speak."

"I'm in Sonora with the three Tuolumne County Sheriff's people involved in the case, Captain Manny Perez, Sergeant Larry Murray and investigator Andy Katashi. The autopsy was this morning and they're going to deliver the remains to the DOJ Missing Persons Unit this afternoon."

"Hold on, let me pull over and get out my notebook," said Bonner.

After a minute, Bonner came back. "Give me those names again."

They gave him the names, a summary of the autopsy and described the crime scene evidence that they knew about.

"That's a start," said Bonner. "Can you put me on the distribution list for the autopsy results and tell me whose running the forensics?"

"We'll do that," said Murray, giving him Vern Lund's name and number. "We've decided to hold back the ice pick information. Anything else?"

"Not at this point, I just need to get the ID done," said Bonner. "Thanks, I'll talk to you later."

Outside, Jake looked at his watch and thought for a minute. He pulled out his phone and called his ex wife. "Hi," he said. "I can get up there by about six and take you and Kaitlin out to dinner and maybe a movie if it's OK with you."

Silence for a second. "The off again, on again Jake Appleby I presume."

"I do the best I can Fiona," said Jake.

"All right, come on up. See you at six." She hung up.

Jake saddled up and started driving north out of Sonora. Lots of great twisties were between Sonora and Grass Valley. He was going to have to get on it and stay on it to make what was a four hour trip by car in less than three hours. It would be a fun ride but he was going to be wiped by the time he got to bed tonight.

10. GRASS VALLEY

Jake wasn't able to crank up much speed until he passed the turnoff for Columbia. The Columbia State Historic Park was a good ride from Sacramento and might be the best preserved of the California Gold Rush towns. The entire length of 49 was littered with old towns established during the Gold Rush when most of the population of California was in the foothills looking for gold or selling to the prospectors.

The initial wave of about a hundred thousand miners went after placer gold, the gold that had washed out of the mountains into the streams and rivers. While tough work, placer mining could be done by anybody with an able body since the foothills were all public land at the time. Millions of ounces of gold were retrieved in the first few years, but much of it went to the people that "mined the miners" by selling them supplies, whiskey and women. Few miners left the foothills with their fortune.

As Jake left the populated area, he cranked up his speed, enjoying the sweeping curves and his machine. The country was studded with magnificent oak trees and the wild grasses were lush green, just beginning their summer ripening in areas with shallow soils. It was a typical late spring day; temperatures in the low 80s and a clear blue sky. The scenery and the weather were lost on Jake, his focus was on the road and riding. He knew that he faced some danger on this ride, primarily from vehicles crossing the center line on curves or from people pulling onto the highway from side roads. If he stayed alert, the power and braking of his motorcycle could avoid these hazards. Slower vehicles in front of him weren't a problem since he could pass a car in about one second.

Cornering was the true joy of pushing a motorcycle and doing it well was a complex choreographed process. On a track, you learn each corner and develop the optimum way to ride it. On the road, you can't always see the full corner and often have just a split second to decide on speed and the line you want to ride. As you come to the corner you brake to your chosen entry speed, just like you would in a car. At the same time you're choosing the line you'll take, positioning the bike at the extreme outside edge of your lane for entry to the corner. Through the corner you're leaning to the inside, taking up a good portion of the lane, your inside knee inches from the pavement, the centerline or road edge markings flashing by in your peripheral vision. The exhilaration peaks as you begin to finish the corner and roll on the power, staying connected to the pavement while screaming down the road, headed for the next corner.

Jake was just getting into the rhythm when he finished the 12 miles to Angel's Camp, Calaveras County, in about eight minutes. As he drove through the small town at normal speeds, he reflected on the town's good luck. Mark Twain's first important work, *The Celebrated Jumping Frog of Calaveras County*, was published in 1865. The Jumping Frog Jubilee is a yearly event held in May, it had just finished a week ago.

Ripping off another seven miles, Jake slowed to get through the tiny town of San Andreas; established as a mining camp in 1848 San Andreas was a bit smaller than Angel's Camp and claimed less than 3,000 residents.

Fifty more miles and several small towns later, Jake reached Placerville at the junction of 49 and US 50, the main route to the south end of Lake Tahoe. For a few years during the Gold Rush, the town was named Hangtown because of the regular hangings that occurred there. Jake stopped at a gas station for fuel, a much needed bathroom break and an energy bar.

The 26 twisty miles to Auburn passed by Coloma, the original site of John Sutter's sawmill where gold was first discovered in California. The discovery was in January 1848, not long after the United States took California from Mexico. The territory that had been a sleepy, obscure backwater when gold was discovered became the 31st state of the union less than two years later.

Jake's high speed riding was finished for the day because 49 between Auburn and Grass Valley was a heavily travelled road. As 49 worked its way uphill from the lower foothills, the vegetation changed. Grasslands studded with massive oaks gave way to forests of smaller oaks, which then began giving way to a pine forest.

At ten minutes to six he pulled up to The Magic Inn, said hello to Paul and dropped off his backpack. As Jake was walking to Fiona's, he reflected that his hosts Paul and Betty were salt of the earth people who he enjoyed visiting. Betty worked in a physician's office and loved being a grandmother. Paul worked on their restored Victorian like the state worked on the Golden Gate Bridge: work from one end to the other then start over again. Paul was also a magician and really enjoyed people.

Five minutes after leaving the inn, Jake had reached Fiona's own restored Victorian house and was hugging his daughter.

Jake and Fiona were married when Jake was twenty four and working long hours at a computer software startup in Silicon Valley. Fiona was working on her internship hours toward a Marriage and Family Therapist license. They were deeply in love and, when they found time to be alone together, were all over each other. The list of situations where they had made love was fun to review. They had been married less than two years when Jake's sister Diana was murdered. While they both grieved Diana's loss, it drove Jake into police work. Though she tried to be supportive, Fiona didn't like his new career and was concerned about its effect on their family. Kaitlin's birth changed the equation, but he spent more and more time on police work, shortchanging his family. They tried therapy for six months but couldn't make enough changes, so after six years of marriage, Fiona divorced Jake and moved to Grass Valley with Kaitlin. He had made a large amount of money in the computer business, so the divorce settlement left Fiona financially comfortable. Jake still loved her and wanted them to get back together. Though frustrated by his behavior, Fiona still had strong feelings for him.

Jake gave Fiona a hug and said, "You know that I'm sorry about today. I would have much preferred to spend it with you two. This case dropped in my lap while I was on the river yesterday."

"I know you wanted to be here," said Fiona. "I know that your work's unpredictable, but that can be hard on us. No point in rehashing it. Let's have dinner together and then you can have some personal time with Kaitlin."

"Good plan. How about Mexican? We could walk over to the Sleeping Burro."

"Good, I love their quesadillas," responded Kaitlin.

"Works for me," said Fiona. "Let's go, I'm hungry."

They walked the five blocks to Main Street, then three more blocks down Main Street to the restaurant. Like many of the eateries in the area it had good food and nice ambiance but it wasn't something you'd brag about to a friend from San Francisco. Jake had a Negra Modello and a chili verde burrito. Fiona had a glass of chardonnay and enchilada suiza. Kaitlin had a mango soda and a chicken quesadilla.

"Any good news with your practice?" asked Jake.

"I've gotten one good new patient," said Fiona. "It looks like I've lost another, but she wasn't working on her issues, just wanted a magic incantation from me. We've got another psychologist who immigrated from the Bay Area trying to start a practice. He hasn't gotten his rude awakening yet about how tough it is to start a practice up here."

"I hope he has other income," Jake said. He knew that the area was overrun with counselors and psychologists; there weren't enough patients to go around.

The three of them talked through dinner, Jake encouraging Kaitlin to keep up her hobby of mountain biking since she lived in good mountain biking country and road biking was hazardous on the area's narrow winding roads. Jake knew that Nevada Union High School had a successful mountain bike team that would be a great experience for her when she was older.

When they had eaten all that they wanted, Jake paid the bill and they left the restaurant.

"That was great, I enjoy our time as a family," said Jake. "Fiona, are you sure you won't come to the movie?"

"No thanks, I'm going to head home. I'll see you when it's over."

"Come with me, chickadee," Jake said to Kaitlin. "Tell me more about what's been going on in your wonderful life."

Kaitlin began talking about her friends and school while Jake made appropriate noises of agreement, encouragement, and consolation. He was grateful that Kaitlin shared what was going on in her life with him and tried his best to encourage her. He and Fiona both felt that communication was a critical factor in relationships – if you can't communicate and try to understand each other, you're going to have a difficult time with the inevitable problems that pop up in life.

Kaitlin was just finishing her first year in middle school and was enjoying it. Jake encouraged her and was excited – he loved watching her evolve. To him she was becoming more and more a human being, though he realized that progress might be delayed by adolescence.

They walked up Main Street to the old movie theater at the corner of Church. As old as the building was, it was kept in good shape and had been modified to show three concurrent shows. They found a movie that appealed to Kaitlin. It started in forty minutes so they walked back down the street and bought some frozen yogurt. Walking down the hill (there were few level areas in the Grass Valley area), Jake was reminded that all you had to do was look up a bit and you'd see pine forest from almost any place in town. It was a nice, compact and historical downtown to stroll through. The downtown area of Main and Mill streets totaled about six blocks so you could walk it all in a few minutes. Some small shops were of interest to Kaitlin. On other visits, Jake had enjoyed the three tasting rooms associated with local wineries.

Jake's cell gave off its Celia music, so Jake picked it up. "What's up C?"

"Where are you?"

"I'm in downtown Grass Valley with Kaitlin. We'll be going to a movie in a few minutes."

"Well that's a good thing. I'm glad that you made time for her. Say hello for me. I'd like an update on the head case and it's about time for you to call Browning."

"OK mother, I'll call him. Why don't I call you with an update after I drop Kaitlin at home?"

"That'll work. Talk to you then."

Jake asked Kaitlin to stay inside the yogurt shop, then stepped outside and called Browning. "This is Jake, calling with your update."

"Go ahead Appleby."

"About all the autopsy found was that the neck was cut with a sharp instrument postmortem."

"That is all they found? No cause of death or time of death?"

"That's it," Jake said. He was withholding the ice pick information because he didn't want Browning leaking it to the press.

"What other case status do you have?" asked Browning.

"Wait one," said Jake as he waited for two attractive women shoppers to walk by. "We have a tentative ID for the victim, a Sophia Mancuso, missing from Walnut Creek last week. Missing Persons will do a dental match for us first thing tomorrow. We have a Walnut Creek detective wired in on the case. That's it for now."

"That is good progress Appleby. I'll expect such progress to continue. Call me if there are any major breakthroughs. I'll continue to require eight PM briefings nightly."

"Yes sir." The call dropped and Jake gave his phone a dirty look before putting it away. Browning was so stiff he must have a broomstick up his ass, he thought.

Shrugging it off, Jake collected Kaitlin and they walked back to the theater.

Their movie was in the main theater of the old art deco building. The ceilings and walls held designs painted in gold leaf and teal, a remnant of the 1940s, giving it the feeling of an old movie palace. It was a pleasant contrast to modern movie theaters where you felt like you were sitting inside a bland container. Both Jake and Kaitlin enjoyed the funny animated movie. On the walk home, Jake felt proud as he listened to Kaitlin's observations on the movie and life. His daughter was growing up and that was great. Jake thought about how nice the evening had been, a world away from murder and butchery.

Back at Fiona's house, Jake said good night to his daughter. After Kaitlin had moved off to her bathroom, Jake and Fiona held hands and looked at each other for a minute. Without a word, they moved to a full body hug and a deep kiss. Stroking her face with his hand, Jake started to move to the couch, but Fiona resisted. "No Jake, it's time for you to go."

Jake was disappointed, but he'd learned not to push her in these situations. "OK, but give Willie time to calm down before you throw me out."

Fiona giggled and held his hand for a minute, then walked him to the door.

On the walk back to the B&B from Fiona's house, Jake thought about the relationship he wanted and the one they had. He knew that Fiona loved him, but it had been years now and they weren't back together. They still made love and it was great, even though it didn't happen often. Suppressing the pain, he called Celia and gave her all the information he had, including the ice pick and that they were holding it back, even from Browning.

"I know you don't want the pick getting out, Jake, but cutting Browning out when he's demanding regular and thorough updates is liable to backfire on you."

"You could be right, C, you often are," replied Jake. "It just felt like the right move at the time. You know the hound is just running to the press with all this stuff and I just don't trust him to hold this back."

"Your call, your ass," said Celia.

"Indeed it is. Are you up for a trip to Walnut Creek tomorrow if the dental is a match?"

"Not a problem. Call me when you know."

"Night C."

"Good night Jake." The call ended.

Jake walked another block to the B&B, enjoying the peaceful evening. Getting into his own bed was his preference, but he had a personal rule about not riding his Blade in the foothills at night. The Sierra Foothills were full of deer. They were most active and difficult to see in twilight and nighttime. Hitting one in a car was bad enough, but hitting one on a bike at high speed would kill you. Because of that, he was a regular at The Magic Inn.

11. SACRAMENTO; THURSDAY

Jake woke up at six, brushed his teeth and went downstairs to the kitchen. Paul wasn't downstairs yet, so Jake left him a note and his key. It would have been nice to stay for one of Paul's great breakfasts and the accompanying magic tricks, but Jake needed to get down the hill.

Jake rode his Blade four blocks to Bob's Café, one of the few places that was open this early. The owner, not Bob but Sally, got him a big mug of coffee and then a stack of their great sourdough pancakes. Sally, attractive and hard working, had a penchant for hiring attractive waitresses. The food was good and the place was clean. Jake was a regular customer when he was in town.

When Jake reached Auburn he had a good view of part of California's Central Valley. An amazing geographic entity, the valley is 42,000 square miles, about the size of Tennessee. Flatter than Iowa, the valley drains from a three hundred foot elevation in the north and south to a thirty foot elevation in downtown Sacramento at the confluence of the Sacramento and American rivers, 75 miles from the ocean.

The Sacramento metropolitan area stretched out in front of him had a population of over two million, greater than Alaska and Hawaii combined. These people were spread out – except for the downtown area, few buildings were over two stories tall.

Jake made it to his condo just before nine. He had used some of his stock option money to buy his condominium; it was upscale from the units most cops owned. He chose a condo because he didn't want the maintenance hassles that came with a regular house. Jake relished the oversized garage that had room for his truck, Fireblade, Porsche Boxter and a small workbench.

As he entered the kitchen, he was greeted by an throaty, guttural *mrrrrrh* from Tank, his black and white cat. "OK, I missed you too," said Jake. Tank, short for cantankerous, was an independent cat. Tank usually gave Jake extra grief after a multi-day absence. Jake did a quick check of all the cat gadgets to support Tank: automatic feeder, automatic filtering watering bowl and a self cleaning litter box that connected to the spare bathroom's toilet. Everything looked OK, so Tank was just being crabby, not a surprise.

Jake took a quick shower and shaved, then put on his office clothes. Climbing into his red Porsche Boxter S, he headed for the office. Once he reached town, he was greeted by tree lined streets that added character and much needed summer shade to Sacramento proper.

Next to the DOJ office, Jake parked the Boxter in his rented space, then picked up coffee for himself and Celia. Black coffee for Jake, a decaf nonfat latte for Celia.

For a government office, the DOJ facilities weren't too bad. Agents like Jake were in a large bullpen, separated into partner clusters by shoulder high partitions that deadened sound a bit and gave some privacy. Jake had enjoyed a much better working environment in the computer business, but this was tolerable. He and Celia shared a cluster containing two desks, two filing cabinets and two guest chairs.

"Thanks for the coffee Jake," said Celia. How was the trip?

"The trip from Sonora to Grass Valley was fun. It was great to see Fiona and Kaitlin. The trip down the hill was just commuting. You know that what you have is not coffee C, it's had the caffeine removed and been polluted with a bunch of steamed milk."

"You're such a purist. Coffee blended with other flavors adds zest that you never experience," rebutted Celia.

"Coffee in its many sources, roasts and blends has plenty of nuance and variety for those with discriminating taste," was Jake's comeback.

"Yeah, yeah, yeah," said Celia. Let's get Vern on the phone and find out what he knows about the Tuolumne crime scene." She dialed Vern's Central Valley Lab number and put him on speakerphone.

"Morning Vern, this is Celia Moreno."

"Hi Celia, how are you this fine day?"

"I'm great Vern. Jake's on the line too. What do you have for us on the Tuolumne head case?"

"We don't have a lot," replied Vern. Nothing that will lead you to the perp, but some things that might help confirm a suspect. The vehicle was a large SUV or a half ton pickup with Bridgestone Dueler A/T RH-S P265/70R17 tires. Lots of those tires are out there and there was no unique tread damage on this set. The boots were a men's size 10 or women's size 11, plus or minus a half size. The boot tread is a Vibram Tucson design, but it's used by three boot manufacturers. I'll email you an image of the tread. We have soil samples in case you find boots or a car with soil, but the road soil was so powdery that I doubt you'll find it on anything other than a wheel well. Our least interesting find is a navy blue cotton fiber that was pulled out of a garment by contact with a buckbrush. The fiber is consistent with those used in sweatshirts."

"You're right Vern, that's not going to lead us to anybody and, by itself, isn't going to convict anybody," said Celia. "It's better than nothing though. Is there any wear or damage to the boot prints that might match a specific pair of boots?"

"The tread looks brand new, nothing unique about them."

"Thanks for the update Vern," said Jake. "This perp is either cautious or lucky to have left this tiny amount of generic evidence. How many people in California don't have a navy blue sweatshirt?"

"Not many Jake," said Vern. "You're right, evidence was scarce out there and what we found was nonspecific. We would have liked to have found more, but it just wasn't there. This case is going to take serious detective work or some luck."

"We appreciate the work Vern," said Celia. "If it's not there, you can't find it. We'll talk to you later." She hung up.

"Crap," said Jake. "I was afraid that we didn't have much."

"It's better than nothing though Jake, it'll make suspects either more or less likely. I'll go back to looking at our old cases to explain the "coincidence"."

"I guess I'll have to set up a new JARS case for this so we can get our reports into it," said Jake. "The dental comparison should come through soon."

The DOJs Justice Active Records System (JARS) was light years ahead of the old typewriter on paper method, but it still took a lot of time to produce clear and complete documentation in a form suitable for use in court. Most people had no clue as to how much time cops spent writing reports or how necessary they were.

There were lots of side benefits to the electronic system – everything that they tagged as a name, geographic location, business, vehicle, license plate, phone number, or specific item of interest was automatically indexed along with those from all reports on a case. The "active" part of the system was even more exciting. When any input to the system indexed an item that was already in an index of any case in the system, the "hit" was pointed out to the report writer, the lead investigator of the associated case, and the writer's of reports indexing the same item. The users could tailor this behavior and decide what type of notification they'd like. Each user could chose email, text message, or phone call. There was an effort underway to get all California police agencies to adopt this system, but the pace of adoption was slow. Jake's computer experience and interest made him better than most in using the system and in suggesting enhancements. He had been part of the task force that chose JARS for adoption by the DOJ.

After setting up a new case in the system with himself as the lead DOJ agent, Jake gave appropriate authorization to Celia, Sam and Vern as well as their investigative assistant, Suzie Eckerling. Suzie would be a key player, getting documents from other sources into the system and properly indexed. Jake asked Suzie to start with Katashi, Jack Carver the pathologist and Vern, then he started with his own reports.

Just before noon, they got a call from the Missing Person's Unit's forensic odontologist with the news that the

Tuolumne head's teeth matched the dental x-rays of Sophia Mancuso.

"Why don't you call Walnut Creek, tell them the news and that we're coming," said Jake to Celia. "I'll call our buddy Katashi and let him know that he's only part of the game."

"Sure," replied Celia as she looked up the number of the Walnut Creek detective. Finding Torrey Bonner's name and number, she dialed his office number.

"Bonner," he answered.

"Torrey, this is Celia Moreno at DOJ. We have a dental match between our Tuolumne head and your missing Sophia Mancuso. We'd like to come down and be part of your notification"

"I could have gone all day without that news," responded Bonner. "The match, I mean, not your wanting to be involved. When can you get down here?"

"Grabbing some lunch on the way, we should be there around one thirty."

"I'll see you then," said Bonner before he hung up.

Jake had already finished his call to Katashi, who had been as friendly as always. His loss of exclusivity on the case wasn't good news for him, but didn't seem to change his attitude. Jake and Celia grabbed keys for a DOJ SUV and started the drive to Walnut Creek.

12. NOTIFICATION

Celia and Jake walked into the Walnut Creek Police Department and asked to see Torrey Bonner. After a couple of minutes, a middle aged man of about five eleven with a hint of a belly and thinning brown hair emerged. He was wearing wrinkled brown slacks, a pale yellow dress shirt and a tie the color of meatloaf.

"Moreno and Appleby?" he said.

"I'm Celia and this is Jake," spoke up Celia.

"Good to meet ya, I'm Torrey Bonner, sometimes known as no boner Bonner. Why don't you come back to my office."

"That nickname could mean a couple of things," said Jake. "Should I ask?"

"It's boner as in mistake," replied Bonner. "After a few drinks, some guys get on to other meanings."

"I can see that opening," said Celia, showing that she was one of the guys.

As they walked down the hall, Bonner offered them bottled water with a caveat. "You know that researchers have found that bottled water can contain up to ten times the bacteria of tap water. I'm a drinking fountain kind of guy."

"I'm good," said Celia.

"Me too," said Jake.

As they reached Bonner's desk he said "Did you hear about the idiot who walked in here last month with a bag of coke, complained it was cut too thin and demanded that we arrest his dealer?"

"Sounds like a serious candidate for this year's *brain dead inmate* award," chuckled Jake. "I'm afraid that our perp is not related to him."

"So tell me what you know about what happened to Sophia Mancuso," said a serious Bonner.

Celia related the discovery of the head on the river, Jake described the autopsy and the forensic evidence, handing Bonner printed images of the boot prints and photographs of the head.

"So we don't have much," said Bonner. "My partner Julie Fortuna is gathering everything relative to the missing person's investigation. Do you have suggestions on how to handle this?"

"I think that we treat is like any other homicide; notify and look hard at the husband as well as anybody with motivation," was Jake's reply. "Celia has a great sense of whether somebody is experiencing real grief or not, so she's good to have at notifications."

"Sounds reasonable," said Bonner. "Let's see if we can find out where the husband is right now."

Bonner called Pauli Mancuso's Lexus dealership and found that he wasn't there. The second time was the charm, Mancuso was at home.

Driving to Mancuso's house, Bonner said "I hate notifications. I never know what to say and you never know how the survivors are going to react."

"Celia does it as good as I've seen it done," said Jake. "Do you want her to do it here?"

"I'd like to get out of it, but it's my responsibility," responded Bonner.

They drove up to what appeared to be a McMansion. Any three bedroom house in this area was worth at least five hundred thousand, this thing might be worth more like a million five even in the current real estate market. There was a lush green lawn on both sides of a circular driveway with colorful flower beds almost certainly tended by a service. The circular driveway connected to another driveway that went back to a three car garage. As they stepped out of the Walnut Creek unmarked car, they were engulfed in the sweet smell of newly mown grass. They had parked in the circular driveway just behind a spotless black Ford Expedition XLT with chromed aluminum wheels. Even though the big SUV shouted out "city dude's ride," it was capable of handling rugged dirt roads. Jake took a quick look and learned that the tires matched the tracks found near the Tuolumne site.

"Heads up, the tires make this vehicle a possible for the Tuolumne pose site," said Jake in a low voice. "A second good reason to look hard at this guy if it's his car."

The house had a ten thousand dollar front door set. The eight foot doors were flanked by two sidelights with beveled glass. After Bonner rang the doorbell they heard standard suburban background noise – a couple of leaf blowers and a lawn mower.

The door was opened by a middle aged man who looked like he could play a mafia guy in a TV show. He stood about six feet tall, had slicked back black hair, a good looking but heavy face with an olive complexion. He was wearing expensive looking black slacks and the top button of his deep blue silk shirt was unbuttoned. The only thing missing was the gold chain. He didn't look happy.

"I'm Walnut Creek detective Torrey Bonner; this is Celia Moreno and Jake Appleby from the state Department of Justice. "Are you Pauli Mancuso?"

'Yeah," responded Mancuso. "Have you found my wife? Is she all right?"

"Can we come in and sit down sir?" asked Bonner.

"Uh, yeah, come on in."

They walked through the doors into an entryway big enough for a kid's bedroom. There was a greenish marble floor, several pieces of quality wood furniture and a massive chandelier hanging from the twelve foot ceiling. They followed Mancuso into a living area that was furnished with expensive looking pieces, though there were far too many flowery items for Jake's taste.

Bonner asked, "Is your daughter at home, Sir?"

Sitting down, Mancuso said, "No, she's out with some friends. What's the deal here? Don't keep me hanging."

"Mr. Mancuso, I'm sorry to tell you that your wife is deceased," Bonner told him. "Please accept our condolences on what must be a shocking tragedy for you and your daughter."

Mancuso's face sagged as if he'd lost all muscle tone in an instant. He looked at the floor for a few seconds, and then his Adam's apple bobbed as he swallowed. "No," he whispered.

There was silence for seconds, and then Mancuso verbalized his denial. "This can't be true. Sophia isn't dead."

"I wish that were true," replied Bonner. "I'm afraid that we have definitive identification based on your wife's dental records."

"There must be some mistake," exclaimed Mancuso. "Show her to me."

"Sir, it's not necessary that you identify her and I suggest that you don't. It's far better that you remember Sophia as she was the last time you saw her."

"Show her to me. I insist on seeing who you think is my wife."

"Sir, if you want to do this, we can show you a picture," said Bonner in a calm tone.

"Let's see it. This can't be Sophia."

Bonner pulled a large picture of the victim's head out of his briefcase. He had prearranged this picture as the least gruesome of the bunch since it didn't show the severed neck and it was taken before the autopsy mutilated her. He placed the picture on the coffee table, saying "This is our victim, whom we have identified as your wife, Sophia Mancuso."

Mancuso stared at the picture, his eyes widening. His hands rose to cover his face and he choked out, "Oh God, take that thing away." He shuddered and then took several deep breaths.

Bonner asked, "Sir, can you confirm that the person in the picture is your wife, Sophia Mancuso?"

"Yeah," sighed Mancuso, his face still in his hands, his elbows resting on his knees.

"We'll send her remains to the mortuary of your choice, just let us know," said Bonner.

"Remains?" said Mancuso. "Oh God, this isn't that thing that was in the news? The head found in some river?"

"I'm afraid that you're right," responded Bonner. "Her head was found posed on a rock in the Tuolumne River. It may be of some comfort to know that her head was not severed until after she died. I'm sorry, but we have yet to find any additional remains."

"This is hideous. What kind of monster could do this to a sweet person like Sophia? How did she die? What did the bastard do to her?"

"We don't know what kind of person did this sir, but we'll be doing our best to find out," responded Bonner. "There are some nasty people out there. We don't have a confirmed cause of death and we don't know what went on between her abduction and her death. We have a lot of work to do so we'd like to ask you some questions now."

"That's great, you don't know shit. Go ahead."

"It's important for us to develop accurate and complete information on what your wife was doing prior to her disappearance and determine, as best we can, when and where she was abducted. My partner, Julie Fortuna, is reviewing the missing person's report and talking to the investigating officer as we speak. She will be contacting you soon to obtain as much additional information as you can provide. In the meantime, can you give us names of anybody who was angry with your wife, disliked her or harbored a grievance against her?"

"People liked Sophia, she was such a warm and caring person," replied Mancuso. "If somebody was upset with us, most of the time it was because of something I did or said."

"Why don't you include any people that are upset with you and conceivably would attack you through Sophia," said Bonner.

"The only name that comes to mind is Georgia Teller," said Mancuso. She hates Sophia for some reason, I'd guess jealousy. They were teenage friends, but Georgia's life went south while Sophia's has been great. I just can't think of anybody who would hurt Sophia just because they're mad at me."

"Thank you," said Bonner. "Please tell us about your wife. What did she do, what kind of person she was."

"Well, she grew up lower middle class. Her parents didn't have much education or money. She went to college though, and then got a teaching credential. When I met her she was teaching fifth grade. God was she beautiful. She loved the kids and they loved her. When we got married, I retired her from that job. No wife of mine is going to do union work. She's been raising Jill and running the house. She's on the board of two non profits that help kids.

"Thanks," said Bonner. "That will help us. As a formality, we need to ask some questions so that we can rule you out as a suspect."

"Me? I would butcher my wife? You've got to be nuts to think that I would do such a thing. Jesus."

"I understand that this is uncomfortable, but my boss would have my ass if I didn't ask, so humor me a bit."

"This is crap. Go on, get it over with."

"Please describe your activities on Friday the twentieth when your wife disappeared."

"It was a work day. I was at the office except for a Rotary luncheon. I had a meeting with my accountant and spent time with my sales manager. I left around five to come home and change for a wine tasting dinner that Sophia had signed us up for. When she didn't get home in time for the dinner and I couldn't reach her on her cell, I got worried. I called her sister and her best friend, but they couldn't help. I called the police who had no record of her and suggested that I call the hospital first, and then call back. The hospital had no information so I called back the police and made a missing person's report. I remember being surprised that I didn't have to wait on the report like you always see on TV."

"Thank you," said Bonner. "How about your activities on the day and night of Monday the twenty third?"

"By then you guys had found her car and car keys. I was totally freaked out and not functioning well. I'd kept it from our daughter, who was away on a trip with the school band, but she knew something was wrong because she hadn't talked to her mother for four days. I went to work but couldn't focus on anything, couldn't carry on a reasonable conversation. I went to lunch at Harrison's, had several drinks and decided to go home. When I got home I kept drinking until I fell asleep. About eight in the evening I woke up feeling like shit, drank some water and went to bed."

"Did you have any contact with people after you left Harrison's?" asked Bonner.

"Nope. I didn't want to talk to anybody except my wife."

"Jake, Celia, do you have any questions?" said Bonner.

"Is that your Expedition out front?" asked Jake.

"It belongs to my business, but I use it," said Mancuso. "A guy virtually gave it to us as a trade-in on a GX460."

"I know that your wife was driving a Lexus SUV, do you have other cars?"

"I've got a GS460 demo in the garage."

"Have you told your daughter that her mother is missing?" asked Celia.

"I had to tell her when she came home on Tuesday. That was awful and made me feel even more helpless. Husbands and dads are supposed to fix things and I couldn't fix this. Jill took it hard, she's scared. Telling her that her mom is dead is going to be a bitch. Man, how is she going to deal with a real nightmare like this?"

"Mr. Mancuso, I can connect you with a crisis counselor who can help you with notifying your daughter as well as some of the other activities connected to an event such as this," said Bonner. "Would you like me to call and have one come over?"

"Please, I can use that kind of help," said Mancuso. "I'm going to have to tell Sophia's friends and family as well. What a mess. Are they going to put Sophia's name in the paper as the victim? It would be horrible for everybody to visualize her being treated this way."

Jake spoke up. "We'll treat this as a sex crime even though we don't have specific evidence to back up that theory. That will let us withhold your wife's name from the media. This is such a sensational crime, however, that I suspect the media will be putting serious energy into digging up details, particularly if any of the national media pick up the story. There's a good chance that they'll find out that the victim was your wife. I'd suggest that you, your family and Sophia's friends all commit to a no comment policy for the media. You'll all be better off. Some media people are good and competent, but their interest is in selling, not in protecting your family."

"I wouldn't have believed that this could get worse, but it sounds like it will," said Mancuso.

"There's a good chance that you're correct," said Bonner as he stood up. "We'll need to talk to your daughter, when do you expect her home?"

"She's just a kid. Losing her mother is going to eat her up. This mutilation business, God knows what that will do to her. You really need to talk to her?"

"Yes sir, we do. Kids see things that adults don't and their viewpoint is different. Sometimes that can be a big help in an investigation."

"All right, she's supposed to be back here around four. I'll be here and if she can't handle it, you'll be done."

"Yes sir. Our crisis counselor should be able to help you deal with the impact on your daughter. We'll leave you for now and should be back around four. You'll be hearing from my partner and a crisis counselor soon."

"Yeah," said Mancuso, looking dazed. "You can let yourselves out."

"One more thing, sir," said Bonner. "Will you give us permission to search your house for information related to your wife's death?"

"Go pawing through my house? There's not going to be anything here of use to you. No, I don't give you permission."

"Very well sir," said Bonner as he walked toward the front door.

13. WALNUT CREEK

Moreno, Appleby, and Bonner found a private table in front of a local coffee brewing shop. They sat down to discuss what had transpired at Mancuso's house. As usual, the outdoor chairs were uncomfortable metal that was better at withstanding weather than at being pleasant seating. Traffic was light, the tree leaves were fluttering in a light breeze, it was clear and sunny, and the temperature was perfect. They didn't notice any of it.

"Damn, I'm glad that's over," said Bonner. "It was easier than notifying a wife, but not a lot. I think that I'd rather sift garbage than do a notification."

"I know what you mean," answered Jake. "It's one thing to be among blood and guts at a crime scene, a whole 'nother story to be in somebody's nice house telling them that their wife has been butchered."

"So what do you think of Mancuso and his story?" asked Bonner.

"I didn't smell anything wrong, but he could be a good actor," said Jake. "I'd still say that he might be good for it, since he's the spouse and his tires match the crime scene. How about you, C?"

"It felt like real grief to me," said Celia. "The denial and pain he expressed looked spontaneous and natural. I didn't get any sense that he was playing us. A psychopath might be able to fake the emotions, but I didn't see any other psychopathic traits. I'd say that he isn't our perp."

"Celia's good at reading people," said Jake. "Maybe we should take a poke at this Georgia Teller person before we get back on Mancuso."

"Sounds like a plan," said Bonner. Pulling out his cell, he called a clerk at the station to get a location on Georgia Teller.

It was a five mile drive to Teller's home. She lived in a decent looking trailer park, nice enough to be described as a "Manufactured Home Community". Her unit was a midsized beige double wide with a carport in front. Bonner rang the doorbell. After a minute, the door opened to reveal a woman who looked like she'd been ridden hard and put away wet. Her stringy blonde hair had been fried by a bad bleach job. Her face looked haggard and had more lines than it should have for a contemporary of Sophia Mancuso. She was slender except for extra wide hips covered with generic jeans. A logo t-shirt covered her torso. From the clear view of her nipples, she wasn't wearing a bra.

"Hi, I'm detective Torrey Bonner from the Walnut Creek Police Department. Are you Georgia Teller?"

"That's me," Teller responded. "What's happenin'?"

"We'd like to discuss a matter with you," said Bonner. "Can we come in and sit down?"

"Uh, yeah," said Teller. She stepped back from the doorway and they entered.

The interior looked clean, but piles of things were everywhere. There was a pile of newspapers, sorted piles of magazines, piles of catalogs, piles of folded clothes. They followed a path through the piles to a couch and chair.

"We're sorry to inform you that Sophia Mancuso is deceased," said Bonner. "We're investigating her murder and understand that the two of you were friends."

"Deceased? Murdered? Soph is dead?" Teller muttered.

"Yes ma'am," Bonner replied.

"How did it happen? How did she die?"

"We can't get into that now," said Bonner. "How long have you known her?"

"We were good buddies from middle school through high school," said Teller. "We saw each other after that, but we weren't buddies."

"Why was that?" asked Bonner.

"Well, she went off to college and I went to work. Then she married that asshole Pauli and got all rich and high society on me."

"So there's some ill feeling between the two of you?"

"I wouldn't call it that. It was just hard for us to, you know, relate. I gave her some shit about Pauli and she didn't like it."

"What was the problem with Pauli?"

"He's a fucking GQ. He's always dressed up fancy and thinks that he's better than everybody else because he's got money. He can't keep his salami in his pants even though he had a beautiful wife like Soph.

"Can you give us specific examples of his infidelity?"

"Well, I never watched him doing anybody, if that's what you're asking. Back when they invited me to parties I'd always see him rubbing up against some chick. He came on to me once, had his hand on my ass and whispered *why don't we go upstairs* in my ear.

"And what happened?"

"I grabbed his nuts, gave them a big squeeze, and walked away. Maybe that's why they quit inviting me to their parties. He probably told Soph some lie about what happened because she was cold toward me after that."

"Can you tell us where you were on Friday the 20th?" asked Bonner.

"You're kidding, right?"

"No, we'd like to know so that we can rule you out of the investigation."

"I caught the 10 o'clock flight to LA to help out my mom. She's in a bad way and I stayed down there until Sunday night."

"Thanks. We'll confirm that and it should rule you out," said Bonner. "What time was your return flight?"

"About five in the afternoon."

Bonner asked, "Jake, Celia, do you have any questions?"

"Ms. Teller, can you give us any names of the women you saw Pauli Mancuso flirting with or names of women he might be involved with?" asked Celia.

"Nah. I didn't know the women at their parties, all upper crust and all. He went after the young ones at the parties I went to."

As they got into their car, Jake said, "This woman and Sophia Mancuso sure got on divergent roads after being buddies in high school."

"Night and day," responded Celia. "It's hard to believe that they were ever good friends."

"If Mancuso's as big a skirt chaser as she says, we may have another motive," said Bonner. "Guys that think with their gonads do some stupid things. Maybe we'll ask him after we talk to the daughter."

"I'd hold off asking him until we do some checking," said Jake. "If he knows we're looking he could do some covering up."

As Bonner headed back to Mancuso's house, he said, "Yeah, you're right. Celia, why don't you lead the interview with the daughter? I'd guess that you'd do a better job than I can."

"Sure," responded Celia.

Jill Mancuso bore a striking resemblance to her mother. She had the silky black hair, the light olive complexion and the same beautiful face. This afternoon, tears streaked that face. At fourteen, she already had a nice figure. It wasn't hard to visualize hoards of horny teenage boys chasing her. Visually she appeared to be a woman, but as soon as she began talking you knew that she was fourteen.

"Jill, we're terribly sorry for your loss," said Celia after the introductions. "This has to be such a big shock that it's hard to believe. Can you tell us a bit about your mom?"

"We loved each other so much," responded Jill. A new tear emerged from her right eye and trickled down her cheek. "She and I did so many fun things together. Sometimes she could be, like, a mom, but I guess she needed to do that. She was working on my birthday party; it was going to be great. Now I guess I won't have one."

"Do you know what your mom was doing on the day she disappeared?"

"Not really. She dropped me off at school – I left that morning with the school band on our trip to Disneyland. I think maybe she was going to shop for my birthday present. She was so nice, why would anybody hurt her?" Jill said in a child's voice.

"I don't know, Jill, but we're working hard to find out," said Celia. "Can you think of anything your mom said or did recently that was out of the ordinary?"

"Umm, I don't know. Well, she said something about talking to somebody named Kim at dad's work. She sounded mad."

Celia glanced at Pauli. He looked surprised, then a bit worried. "Did your mom say anything more about this?"

"I don't remember anything," said Jill. "I just remembered that because mom almost never got mad."

"Thanks for talking to us, Jill. Your mom sounds like an exceptional person. Hold on to your good memories."

Jill sobbed as reality struck her another blow. As they left, Pauli wrapped his arms around her, trying to be of comfort.

In Bonner's car, heading back to the station, Bonner said, "Mad at somebody named Kim eh? You think she might be Mancuso's trouser rouser?"

"Quite possible," said Jake. "We need to check it out. I think maybe higher priority should be searching his place, checking his phone and credit card records. We've got three reasons now: husband, tires, and skirt chasing. If his wife was going to confront his girlfriend, that would be icing on the cake.

Bonner said, "you're right, Jake. Mancuso didn't give us any real suspects to look at and he's not passing the sniff test. "We might have enough probable cause for a search if we have his girlfriend admitting a relationship, but we don't have enough now."

"We could get the warrant to search the victim's premises," said Celia. "The kill site is unknown and could have been in or around the house. We should be able to include her phone and credit records. That may give us everything we need other than Pauli's cell records."

"Good idea Celia," said Bonner. I'll get working on a warrant, maybe the two of you could start checking out his business."

Jake and Celia left Bonner at his office and drove over to Mancuso's Lexus dealership. On the way they called Sam Nakamura using the car's Bluetooth system to make it a conference call. They gave Sam an update on what was happening.

"Sounds like you're doing what you need to do," said Sam. I have to tell you that Browning has assigned Don Foreman to be the Deputy Attorney General for your case.

"The man with no tan?" said Jake, referring to the year round white complexion of the freckled redhead.

"That's him," responded Sam.

"We don't have much use for a lawyer right now, he'll just be another person we have to update," said Jake. "I'm already spending enough time updating Browning."

"I understand, Jake, but you're going to have to call him anyway. You know how it works around here."

"OK, OK," replied Jake. "Give me his cell number and I'll call him tonight when I get some time."

When the call was over, Jake said to Celia, "You don't know Don Foreman. He's a competent lawyer but kind of a boring wimp. The worst part is that he kisses ass. Browning will know everything that's going on, not just what I tell him."

"You'd better get straight with Browning then. No reason to get wrong with him for no benefit."

"You're right, though I haven't lied to him. I just didn't tell him everything."

"Jake," said Celia, drawing out the word to indicate displeasure.

"Yeah, yeah. So, at the dealership shall we start with this Kim person?"

"Why don't we start with the manager and get a list of all the employees. Then we can get to Kim."

They reached the dealership, a classic luxury car facility. A two story glass showroom was surrounded by landscaping, a departure from the classic pavement and metal facility. Two rows of cars flanked the showroom and the entrance to the service facility was visible. Approaching the showroom door they could see four shiny new vehicles displayed around the floor. As they entered the building they were greeted by a smiling man in a grey suit, blue shirt and striped tie.

"Good afternoon folks, may I help you?" was the greeting.

"You can," said Celia. "We need to speak with your manager."

"May I ask what this is about?"

"Police business," replied Celia, displaying her badge.

"Oh," said the salesman, for once at a loss for words. "I'll take you to his office."

Entering a hallway at the back of the showroom, they passed by several small offices and came to an area carpeted in a rich blue, populated by a thirty-something woman behind a large desk. The woman had short blonde hair, a narrow nose, and her ample breasts were displayed artfully. As they approached, she looked up from her computer monitor.

"Cheryl, these are police officers. They want to see Otto," said the salesman, turning to go.

The smile that had started on the woman's face disappeared and her eyes widened. She picked up her phone, punched a button, and said, "Otto, two police officers are here to see you." A pause and then, "yes sir. He'll be right with you," she said to Jake and Celia.

A door opened and a well fed man appeared. Looking to be just under six feet and weighing about two thirty, he was wearing a black pin striped suit with a white shirt and a red paisley tie. "I'm Otto Stenson, the sales manager. Can I help you?"

"You can. I'm Jake Appleby and this is Celia Moreno. We're both agents of the California Department of Justice. We're assisting the Walnut Creek Police in the investigation of Sophia Mancuso's death."

"She's dead? Oh my God. How did it happen?"

"All that we can tell you is that it is being investigated as a homicide. In the meantime we need to gather some information from you and the other people associated with this business. First of all, when was the last time you saw Sophia?"

"Let me see, it was … It was about two weeks ago, she came by to talk to Pauli. She was always so sweet to me."

"Thank you. Now tell us about when Mr. Mancuso has been in the office from last Friday through Tuesday of this week."

"That's going to be hard. I'm not here all the time. We're open seventy six hours a week and I take Mondays off. Even when I'm here, I don't always know whether Pauli's here. We can ask Cheryl."

Between the two of them, it turned out that Mancuso had been in the office in the morning on Friday, Monday and again after lunch on Tuesday. None of this cleared Mancuso for the abduction time frame or the head placement time frame.

"Thank you," said Jake. "We'll be talking to everybody, but we'd like to start with Kim."

"Kim Stockman?" said Cheryl. "She should be here. She was our top salesperson last year, so she has the office looking out on the floor."

"Good," said Jake, happy that she had filled in the last name for Kim. "Here's a card for each of you, please call if you think of anything that you might think is relevant."

"I will, but I can't think of what it might be," said Otto, retreating to his office.

"Sure," said Cheryl.

As they walked to Kim Stockman's office, Jake said to Celia, "Why don't you lead on this one."

"That's fine," said Celia as she knocked on the office door.

The woman who opened the door was a tall drink of water. She was at least six feet tall in her bare feet. She had a large bust, shown to advantage by a nice silk blouse with three buttons undone. The rest of her, including her hips, was too slender but not anorexic. A tight black skirt ending five inches above her knees left just enough to imagination. An attractive face with blue eyes and cherry red lipstick was topped with what might be naturally blonde hair. A pair of expensive looking shoes stood at the rear corner of a nice oak desk covered with paperwork. She smiled and said, "What can I do for you?"

Celia introduced them and their mission. Stockman's reaction upon learning of Sophia Mancuso's death was different from that of the manager. At first she seemed surprised and shocked but then her face changed and she looked like she was calculating the possible effects of Sophia's death.

"When was the last time you saw or talked to Mrs. Mancuso?" asked Celia.

"I'm not sure," replied Stockman. "I think that she was in the office a couple of weeks ago. It's been a long time since I talked to her."

"Please tell us all the times you've seen Mr. Mancuso from last Friday through this past Tuesday."

"Really? You're looking at Pauli as a suspect?" The friendliness was gone now.

"Everyone is a person of interest at the beginning of an investigation," replied Celia. "So when did you see him in that time period?"

"Let me think. He was in part of Friday, I think the morning. I saw him Saturday and then again Tuesday afternoon."

"What about Monday?"

"I wasn't in the office on Monday, I didn't see him."

"Have you had a personal relationship with Mr. Mancuso?"

Stockman reacted with indignation. "Certainly not. I must tell you that I resent the suggestion. If you have no more questions, I have work to do." Now she was cold and angry.

"I do have another question," said Jake. "Where were you on that Friday, Monday and Tuesday?"

"You've got to be kidding."

"No, this is a homicide investigation, not a comedy. Please answer the question."

"On Friday I came in about ten and left around seven because we had no action. I sold an LX470. I joined friends for drinks and dinner. We danced a bit and I was home by midnight. On Monday I went into the City with a girlfriend. We shopped, had dinner, and went to see Beach Blanket Babylon. Tuesday I had floor duty here all day and sold an ES. Can I get back to work now?"

"Just as soon as you give us the contact information for your friends from Friday and Monday," said Jake.

They collected the information they needed and walked out of Stockman's office. The door closed forcefully behind them. Looking around, they saw two salesmen talking to customers. "Enough of this for now?" asked Jake.

"Enough," answered Celia. Let's talk to Bonner, pound out reports and get some dinner.

"Good plan," said Jake as they reached their SUV. "What'd you think of Stockman, C?"

"I think that she's on the phone to Mancuso as we speak. I can see Mancuso going for her, but I'm not sure how she'd deal with it. She's a player – you could tell that right after we told her about the homicide. I know she was thinking about how she could use this to her benefit. You could also see her decide that being nice to us wasn't going to buy her anything, which makes me believe that her alibis will hold up. If she was worried about them, she'd be playing us."

"As usual, a probing and succinct analysis," said Jake. I'd guess that there's a good chance that she'd been doing Mancuso and maybe now she sees a future bigger than being his fling."

"Yeah, a good chance. Maybe we can get some leverage on her through Mancuso's phone and credit card records.

"Speaking of that, let's talk to Bonner," said Jake, handing Celia his cell phone.

She punched in Bonner's number and put the call on the Bluetooth system.

"Bonner."

"Torrey, this is Celia and Jake," said Celia. "We just finished talking to Mancuso's sales manager and the woman named Kim, whose last name turns out to be Stockman. They don't give Mancuso a useful alibi. They don't conflict with his story either. The Stockman woman denies personal involvement with Mancuso, but we think that she's lying. She has alibis for the pertinent times that we expect to hold up. We're betting that she's already told Mancuso about the conversation. We'd like to see if Mancuso's phone and card records can put them together."

"I think that we'll have the warrant tonight so we can get the records for his wife tomorrow," said Bonner. "I've got an Assistant District Attorney heading for a judge right now."

"When are you planning to run the search?"

"I'll get it started at seven tomorrow morning and then head for the office. Mancuso's already had time to conceal and destroy evidence. Another night shouldn't make much difference."

"That works for us. We're going to hammer out our reports and send you a copy, then get some dinner. Any recommendations?"

"I like CJ's Steak House on North Main. They've got good meat and fish. I'd join you, but the wife already had something planned."

"No problem. We'll head for your office in the morning about eight."

Celia and Jake got rooms at a local Holiday Inn and collaborated on writing their reports using a JARS laptop package. They then used secure network software to put the reports into the DOJ system, maintaining security even though they were using a public network. Now that Bonner was identified in the system as part of the case, the system itself would automatically notify Bonner that reports were available for his online access. Since his department didn't use JARS, they'd have to set up his computer for secure access to it.

They found CJ's Steak House and headed for the bar. It was a standard midrange operation with a twelve foot polished wood bar and about ten tables. They settled into a dark brown vinyl booth that had a bit of privacy and a faint odor of stale beer. As usual, their choice of booth was in the corner with a view of the entry and bar. Cops like to know who's around. Jake had the twenty ounce margarita on the rocks, Celia had Kendall Jackson chardonnay. They talked shop. Jake said, "So backing up to get an overall view, how do you think that this case is shaping up?"

"Gee Jake, I think we've got a mystery. I think that Mancuso is weak as a suspect. Even if you ignore my feelings about his grief, he doesn't seem like a guy that would cut his wife's head off and display it in a remote river where it's sure to be found. I guess that the search will show if he's an outdoorsman, but I'm betting that he isn't. So far, the other potential suspects seem to alibi out, so if it's not Mancuso, we're nowhere.

"I agree that we have nothing but Mancuso, though we've only looked for a day. I can counter all of your arguments about him. Mancuso could either be good at faking grief or could just be realizing what he's done and actually grieving. The head in the river thing could have been creativity to throw us off – he could have found out a lot about the scene using the internet.

"You could be right Jake, it would make the case simple if Mancuso's our boy. I just hope that Sophia wasn't picked at random."

"You and me both. We have nothing to work with if she was random."

"Let's postpone thinking about that and have dinner as soon as you've called Browning."

"Damn, it is that time again. You know if I tell him everything that happened today that he'll release Sophia's name and claim that we're pursuing a suspect."

"If you don't tell him everything Jake, he'll get it from Don Foreman who will read the reports. No matter what you do, the press will get this and splash it on the front page. The head thing is too lurid, it's juicy because it involves a wealthy and attractive woman. I'd like to protect Jill from the public exposure too, but it just can't be done."

"I guess you're right." Jake pulled out his phone and made the call. He gave Browning the facts, but not opinions or hypothesis. When asked for his opinion, he said that it was too early; they didn't have enough information to have an opinion. As usual, Browning clicked off without a goodbye.

"He's one haughty son of a bitch," Jake said. "I'm sure that he believes that his shit doesn't stink."

"Lucky for you, you're done with him for twenty four hours. Let's get some food."

14. WALNUT CREEK; FRIDAY

At seven AM, Torrey Bonner, two squad cars and a crime scene crew arrived at Mancuso's house. Bonner rang the doorbell and a minute later a barefoot Pauli Mancuso opened it. A shadow passed over his face as he saw who was at his door.

"Mr. Mancuso, we have a warrant to search Sophia Mancuso's house and grounds plus vehicles that she used. I know that this will be inconvenient for you, but it's necessary for our investigation."

"You've got to be shitting me. Instead of looking for the killer you screw up our life even more? My daughter's not even dressed – you can't come in."

"I'm sorry sir, but the investigation requires that we find more information about Sophia," said Torrey Bonner. Unfortunately, we'll have to inconvenience you. We'll give your daughter a chance to dress before we enter her room, but she needs to be quick. Before you let her talk to any kids you may want to talk to her about this." He held out Mancuso's San Francisco newspaper. A two column, top of the fold story was headlined *Head Found in River Identified as Walnut Creek Woman.*

Mancuso looked at the headline. His mouth opened and closed twice without a sound. "Jesus," he croaked. "How is she going to deal with this? She'll have to go back to school and every kid will be giving her the look."

Have you talked to the grief counselor? They can help with this and the school thing. Before she goes back to school you'll want to talk to the school administrators about how they handle the situation."

They were interrupted by a flatbed car transporter backing into the driveway.

"What the hell is this?" exclaimed Mancuso.

"Sophia also used your SUV, didn't she?"

"Yeah."

"We'll have to transport it to our yard for the search. Once the search is completed, it will either be returned or impounded."

"Impounded? What the hell do you mean, impounded?"

"If your vehicle contains evidence of a crime, it will be impounded."

"You're going to convince my neighbors that we're criminals."

Bonner turned his head and saw a collection of people on the sidewalk, all watching the action at the Mancuso house.

"What a mess. You bastards," said Pauli Mancuso with venom. "My wife is brutally murdered, my daughter is traumatized and you arrive out of the blue to violate everything we own. You can bet the Mayor will hear about this."

"Yes sir. Now I need you to stay out of the way of my team. We'll do our best to leave your home in good condition."

Bonner gave instructions to the patrol officers and a copy of the Tuolumne boot print picture to the techs, who then launched into the search. Bonner did a slow walkthrough of the house, garage and yards to get a sense of the place in case evidence was discovered. He then headed for his office.

Bonner collected Jake and Celia from their loaner desks at the Walnut Creek PD and took them into a drab, windowless conference room. Bonner said with irritation, "Some asshole from the DOJ is in the paper claiming that he's hot on the trail and doing everything that is possible, blah blah blah."

"Oh crap, that's Chucky," said Jake. "I forgot to check the paper this morning. Can I see it?"

After reading the short article, Jake apologized. "I'm sorry, man. I should have told you to expect this. Chuck Browning runs the Bureau of Investigations and is nicknamed Chucky the Hound because of his publicity seeking. He's worse now that he's running for Attorney General. He often produces yet another example of our fine critical press printing inaccurate information. There's nothing I can do to shut him up, Torrey."

"I've seen assholes doing this kind of thing before, but this guy's bad. Kind of makes me want to go play softball instead of working on the case."

"We know what you mean," spoke up Celia. "It's hard to put up with guys claiming credit when they don't do shit. In the end though, we need to run the case and the people that matter will know that we did it. Let's get back to it."

"Yeah, I know, said Bonner. "It just pisses me off. I'd like your Browning to meet a couple of punks I know in a dark alley. Where were we?"

They talked about the search while waiting for Bonner's sometimes partner Julie Fortuna.

Jake looked up to see a spherical woman walk through the door. She didn't scrape against the door frame, but it was close. She had brown hair cut short on top of a spherical head and her face was set in a tight, no nonsense expression.

After Bonner did introductions, Fortuna reviewed the known information on Sophia Mancuso's abduction.

"At 9:40 AM, there was a charge of $21.00 from Shining Bright Car Wash on her card. She had a board meeting with a youth mentoring organization that ran between 10 and 11:30. The next thing we have is a charge of $22.42 at an upscale Chinese restaurant on North Main at 12:50 PM. They dug up the bill for us and it was for a single meal, so she was alone. The restaurant staff does not remember her. The next trace is a charge for $446.45 at Niebaums. She bought clothes in the junior's department at 2:18 PM. That was the last charge."

"At 11:10 on Saturday morning, we got a call from mall security about an abandoned car. The plate matched the number in the BOLO for Sophia Mancuso. A patrol checked it out. For all they knew, she could have run off with some guy she met and left her car there. When they checked it out, they found the car unlocked and a set of keys on the ground, right next to the inside edge of the left front tire. They called for an investigator and crime scene. Other than the keys, they found nothing on site, so they had the car taken to the yard and processed. The keys were hers. All they found in the car were the gift wrapped boxes of clothing from Niebaums, a fleece vest that her husband says she was wearing in the morning, and normal car junk. There was no purse and no blood. Only her prints were found, the car wash did a great job inside and out, saving us a lot of work chasing old prints."

"The investigator chased down the information I just gave you, interviewed the board members, husband, sister and several friends. All he found indicated a stable, upper middle class mother and wife. Given that, the primary theory was that she had been abducted at the parking lot. The investigator had his time off Sunday and Monday, he conducted more interviews of her friends on Tuesday and Wednesday. Nothing of substance turned up. The reports are all here," said Fortuna, holding up a file folder.

"It's too bad that your department doesn't use JARS, we could have just linked our overall investigation to yours and we'd have your reports and indexes automatically included," said Jake. "If you can get copies for us, we have somebody who can put them into the system."

"Sure, we can get copies made," said Fortuna.

The group talked about the next steps. Fortuna was to get an updated set of Sophia's phone, credit card and bank records; Jake was going to talk to more of Mancuso's employees. Celia and Bonner would put the crime information into the Western States Information Network operated by the DOJ to see if similar crimes were out there. WSIN was one of six regional systems that were part of the Federal DOJs thirty year old Regional Information Sharing System. California's newer JARS would automatically feed the older system, but in this case they needed to perform some manual work to get Walnut Creek's information included. The same situation existed for the Federal DOJs ViCAP system.

Jake walked to Mancuso's dealership because he needed some exercise. One of the problems with his current job was that he was out of town a lot, making it difficult to use a regular gym exercise routine. He always packed a set of exercise bands so that he could do resistance work in his hotel room before his morning shower. When he was at home, he made good use of his gym membership.

Jake had decided that he could use a room at the dealership for initial interviews of the employees. While bringing people to the police department had the advantage of more isolation and control, he could get isolation in a conference room and start interviews in a firm but friendly manner. As he left the morning meeting he had called Otto Stenson and had him line up people in a string of twenty minute sessions.

When doing interviews, Jake used a high tech smartpen that he had purchased at a big box electronics store. The amazing device was an audio recorder and a pen with a computer that linked what you wrote to the audio at the time that you wrote it. You could go back to a written note, tap the pen, and hear what was being said at the time the note was written. Not only did this give him a complete record with fast access to pertinent audio, but he could spend most of his attention on the actual interview as opposed to writing notes. The smartpen was so unobtrusive that most subjects forgot that the interview was being recorded. Best of all, you could download data from the pen to JARS. The system would store the audio data and support links from points in the formal report to the associated audio. JARS would also pass the audio through a voice recognition package and produce a rough transcript of the interview. The rough transcript also linked back to the audio so you could check what was said when you found something that looked squirrely. The smartpen was too fat to be stylish, but Jake didn't care at all, the thing was a godsend to somebody who'd had to search through a long recording of an interview just to find a simple statement.

Jake interviewed five of the sales people without getting much useful information. It appeared that Sophia Mancuso wasn't involved in the business and almost never came to the office. It also appeared that Pauli Mancuso was quite interested in women. He spent a lot of time looking and flirting, though none of the employees admitted to knowledge of anything deeper.

The sixth sales person had some good information. He said that he had been walking through the bar at the Beefeaters Grill in nearby Pleasanton and seen Mancuso kissing Kim Stockman in a corner booth. "It was dark, but I'd swear that he also had his hand up her skirt," he said. By checking the calendar in his phone, the salesman came up with January twentieth as the date. He had paid more attention to the two of them in the office since then and thought that they had something going, but were trying hard to keep it from people. According to the salesman, Mancuso had quit flirting with Stockman, but he often saw them with their heads together.

The last two employees didn't produce anything new or interesting. Jake then interviewed the office's accountant, who wouldn't talk about specifics without a warrant. Jake ended the interview, turned off his pen, and said, "Off the record, just give me an overview of the business financial situation."

The accountant relaxed a bit and considered his answer, then said, "I'll be honest, the great recession has hammered the bottom line. During the bubble, profits were immense. Last year, profits were down fifty percent from their peak, this year they're back up to maybe seventy percent. I don't do Pauli's personal finances, so I don't know how he managed his money. If he put away a reasonable percentage in the good times, he should be fine now. Towards the end of the bubble I sensed that Pauli knew the economy couldn't continue as it was. We're lucky that we sell luxury cars; the market for basic cars has been worse."

When Jake got back to Bonner's office, he told the team what he'd found. "It looks like Mancuso's out there dipping his wick, at least with Stockman and maybe others. Let's check credit cards for that date.

Fortuna leafed through a pile of paper and said, "Here we go, a hundred seventy two dollar charge at Beefeaters Grill on January twentieth. On the twenty first, there's a hundred and sixty two at the Pleasanton Palms Hotel."

"That would be the charge for the night of the twentieth," said Jake. "I'd say we had smoke in the grill then fire at the hotel. Why don't you check for more of this and look at the phone records for Stockman calls."

Fortuna went back to her desk with her papers and Jake asked Celia and Bonner for news.

"We got enough data into JARS to generate a Western States Information Network entry," said Celia. WSIN didn't come up with any similar crimes for us, so we went ahead and did the manual work needed to get JARS to put the case into the New ViCAP system. We did some ViCAP queries, but didn't come up with anything. We can try different queries later. So far, this case just doesn't match up with anything in the country."

"The preliminary results from the search of Mancuso's house are in, said Bonner. "We know that his tires matched the tracks found near the river, but they didn't come up with boots to match the prints you found. They did find an ice pick in the kitchen and a big old Bowie knife. Both of them looked clean, but the lab will check them. In the laundry they found a blood stained hand towel, it's at the lab. They also found a two hundred thousand dollar life insurance policy on Ms. Mancuso and a five hundred thousand dollar policy on Pauli. Nothing on the car yet. If he butchered her, he did it someplace else.

Julie Fortuna came back with her pile of paper, now sporting a bunch of paper clips. "We've got a good pattern," she said in her monotone voice. "Starting in January, we have eleven Thursdays with a restaurant and hotel charge on them, three times every month. They're not all at the same place, but they're all within an hour's drive."

"So we know he was out on Thursdays, but we have no direct evidence about her unless we get it from witnesses," said Jake. "Before we go to the trouble of finding witnesses, let's run a game on her, see if she'll cop to doin' the deed with Mancuso on a regular basis. If she doesn't, then we find witnesses."

Bonner agreed and called Kim Stockman's cell phone. Hearing one end of the conversation you could tell that she resisted the invitation to come right down to the station. She changed her mind when Bonner offered to send a patrol car to pick her up.

Twenty minutes later Bonner and Celia were in the interview room with Stockman. Jake and Fortuna watched the TV monitor.

"You have no justification for dragging me down here in the middle of my busy work day," exclaimed an irritated Stockman. "This is harassment and I'm going to file a complaint."

"Be our guest, Miss Stockman, but lying to a peace officer is far more justification than we needed," responded Bonner. "It behooves you to back off the attitude and start telling the complete truth regarding your relationship with Pauli Mancuso."

"What do you mean? I told this woman and her partner the truth yesterday."

"You gave us bullshit," said Celia. We have you in a bar with Mancuso's hand up your skirt, then at a hotel with him that night. There were quite a few other nights as well. Give it up, all of it, or you're looking at a minimum of obstructing justice."

Stockman started to reply, then slumped back down in her chair and seemed to deflate. After a few seconds of silence, she said, "Well, yeah, we did it a few times. Pauli's a good looking man who liked me a lot. He's got some talent in the sack that I took advantage of. That's all it was though, some laughs and some sex. I don't get emotionally involved with married men, that's a fool's errand."

"Give us the specific dates when you got together," said Bonner.

"Maybe I can do that," Stockman responded as she pulled out her calendar. "It was about three Thursdays a month. Pauli told his wife he was out for a poker game, but most of the time he and I were playing our game." From her calendar, she read off the dates that they had identified from the credit card records.

"We have evidence that Mrs. Mancuso confronted you," said Celia, expanding on what Jill Mancuso had told them.

"No, that didn't happen," said Stockman with some vigor. "And if it did, I would have dropped him like a hot rock. He was just a boy toy, not worth some kind of nasty confrontation."

"You didn't get preferences from his dealership?"

"Nothing that I couldn't have gotten elsewhere. I'm a high performer, better at this business than the vast majority of these people who think that they're car salespeople. I didn't need to do Pauli for business reasons."

"Let's go back to when you saw Pauli between last Friday and Tuesday," said Celia.

"I told you the truth. I saw him Friday morning, Saturday and Tuesday afternoon. Saturday was a last minute thing. He wasn't much fun to be with because he was worried about his wife being missing. I know that it was real because I got my hand under the tablecloth and into his pants but he just couldn't get it up. He went home after dinner and I did some clubbing."

"So now that he doesn't have a wife, what happens to your relationship?" asked Bonner.

"I don't know. He's not much fun right now, but he'll get past it. I don't see him as good for much other than laughs and sex. He doesn't have the money that he used to and I sure don't want to deal with a teenager."

"Is there anything else that you can tell us about Mr. Mancuso and his wife?"

"No. He didn't talk about her to me. As best I could tell, she was fulfilling her part as a piece of his life image, just like the house and cars did."

"OK, that's enough for now," said Bonner. "Keep this interview to yourself."

"Believe me, I don't need to tell people that I spent time in a police station," replied Stockman as she stood up and headed for the door.

Bonner, Fortuna, Moreno and Appleby gathered at Bonner's desk. "What did you think, Jake?" asked Bonner.

"That she's pretty and sophisticated on the outside, a bit ugly on the inside," responded Jake. "She gave us all the hotel dates we had. That suggests that she wasn't hiding parts of the affair. It also tells us that Mancuso wasn't playing this game with anybody else because we didn't find hotel bills for other dates."

"If you believe her, she had no motivation to get rid of the wife in order to have Mancuso to herself," said Celia. "On the other hand, I don't trust her at all. She'd lie if she saw any benefit to it."

"We don't have the staff to follow either Mancuso or Stockman, though we can make passes on their houses and the office to see what cars are there," said Bonner. "I think that I'll give Mancuso a couple of days until we get the lab results. Now that we have evidence of infidelity, we have enough probable cause to get his records. We'll pull his records and see if he and Stockman are calling each other or spending money. Then I'll bring him in and hit him with the affair and whatever else we've got by then. In the meantime, Julie will verify Stockman's alibis for Friday and Monday nights, then check on Mancuso's Friday afternoon and evening alibis."

"Sounds like a plan," said Jake. "Why don't we call Sonora and do a quick update?"

Bonner called Katashi at his Sonora sheriff's office desk. They exchanged updates and found that there were no positive developments in Sonora. Katashi had focused on finding somebody who had seen activity on Lumsden Road Monday night or Tuesday morning, but had no success so far.

Jake and Celia joined the thousands of people heading east from the Bay Area for the weekend. Traffic was slow all the way to Sacramento. They met Terry and Steve at the Blue Ball Inn for drinks, dinner and cop talk.

It was eleven thirty when Jake and Celia dropped off the DOJs SUV to pick up their own cars. Jake said, "C, I'll see you in the morning. Unless something good turns up, I'm going to take Sunday and Memorial Day off, I suggest that you do the same."

"Another good plan, Jakey. Mañana."

15. REFLECTIONS

The killer sat in his easy chair with a drink in his hand. He was feeling his power and gloating about his control. The police were clueless, just like he'd planned.

His thoughts turned to the unexpected selection of a victim who looked like his mother. That had never been part of the plan; the opportunity had arisen and he had grabbed it. Now that it had happened he felt great about it. He could remember being aroused by the terror in her eyes.

Mother had much to atone for. Until he was 14 and big enough to stop her, mother would make him take his clothes off, then whip his butt with a belt. The terrifying part was that he never knew when it was going to happen because it wasn't just when he displeased her. Starting out with intense anger, she was relaxed and happy when she finished abusing him. He finished those sessions feeling powerless and full of hatred. As far as he knew, his father had never known about the beatings. It was solely mother's recreation.

When he was 15, he'd witnessed her ultimate betrayal. He'd come home early from school and heard noises from his father's office. Thinking that he'd surprise dad, he opened the office door, then froze in shock. On top of the desk, on her back, lay his naked mother. Her legs were pointed up in the air and her calves were resting on the shoulders of their naked tennis pro. The pro kept slamming his cock into mother, who grunted with every thrust.

Regaining control of his body, he'd backed out of the doorway and closed the door without a sound. He'd gone to his room, laid on the bed and cried. How could she do this to them?

From that day on, he'd despised women. Much of the time it was to his advantage to keep his views to himself so he did that. He would date a woman for sex or if he needed one for a social event, but it took a great effort to rein in his feelings when he did so.

This bitch that he'd just dispatched gave him great release, he'd pick another one like mom and savor it even more.

16. SACRAMENTO; SATURDAY

Jake drove to work in the rain, the solid grey sky removing the color from everything, his windshield wipers slapping time. Jake was a spoiled Californian and knew it. Not fond of dreary weather, he was hoping that this was the last flatland rain for the season. Though the mountains had their summer thunderstorms, rain in Sacramento from June through September was rare.

Jake and Celia had an eight thirty meeting with Don Foreman, the Deputy Attorney General assigned to their case. They met him at their partner cluster in the DOJ building. It was common practice for an attorney to be assigned to a case, though not always right at the beginning. Lawyers were necessary for warrants and to plot a case's legal strategy. Jake wasn't happy with this selection, because Foreman was a sycophant of Chuck Browning, so Browning would have access to more details of the case. DOJ security policy limited Browning's access to case details in JARS, but the attorney on a case had full access.

Foreman was five minutes late. Even though it was Saturday, he was wearing a grey suit and a starched white shirt with a striped blue tie. At 155 pounds, he didn't fill out a six foot one inch frame. He had freckles and pale red hair; the man with no tan.

"Please give me a summary of the case and your current plans," said Forman after the greetings.

Jake and Celia gave him the short version of events, and then told him that they were going to leave Walnut Creek to the locals for a few days while they looked at the "coincidence" angle. Jake gave Foreman authorization to the case records in JARS. Security in JARS was layered, so none of the case information was available to the general DOJ population even though they had access to the system. When case index comparisons connected multiple cases, access was arranged by the lead investigators or, in trial phase, the lead attorney. The other major security feature, protecting both the DOJ personnel and the public, was that records put into the system were permanent; they could not be altered or deleted, they could only be annotated.

"I'll get back to you once I review the case records," Foreman said. "Call me if you need warrants or we get a major event."

"We'll do that," said Celia as Foreman turned to depart.

Next, they walked over to Sam Nakamura's office to give him an update. As their boss, it was important for him to have a handle on what they were doing. Once in a while Sam gave them direction. Most of the time he left them alone and watched their backs while he dealt with budgets and politics.

Celia gave Sam the case update. His response was "You don't have squat yet, do you?"

"It's thin, I'm afraid," said Celia. "The best we have is the husband and his fling at this point."

"Whoever did this is looking skillful or lucky," said Jake. "We've still got the coincidence angle to look at. Sam, can you find a way to get Browning off of this or at least to stop talking to the press? He's giving out too much detail and almost seems to be trying to pump up fear in the general public."

"I hear ya Jake, but you need to remember that I work for him, not the other way around. I've got no leverage at all to move him off the press thing. I'm sure that he's stroking the press to help his campaign."

"Shit," said Jake. "That means it will get worse, not better."

"Quite likely. Just stay as clear of him as you can, both of you. The upside will go to him and you'll catch all the downside."

Back at their cluster, Celia began checking into a coincidence lead, Steve Devlin's old dismemberment case. Jake started his reports on Friday's action.

After fifty minutes, Celia spun around in her chair and said, "The guy that Steve liked for his dismemberment case seems like a waste of time to me."

"How so?"

"Steve says that the guy's a complete slob. The body parts in his case were hacked up and tossed into waterways. Whoever did our victim is anything but a slob. That started me thinking about this coincidence thing. The category of people hassled or convicted by one of us doesn't make much sense. How would people like that know that the person they were angry with was going on a raft trip?"

"Hmm," was Jakes response. Thinking about it, he said, "It's possible that they could find out, but you're right, it's not likely. Yeah, we should make that angle low priority."

"I agree. I don't have anything promising to work on so I'm going to head for Vacaville and what's left of my family weekend."

"Another good idea. I think I'll get my daily call to Browning over with and head home."

"Are you doing anything special?" asked Celia.

"I'm going up to see Fiona and Kaitlin tomorrow. Maybe I'll do some kayaking on Memorial Day."

"Sounds good Jake. I'm gone," said Celia as she walked out.

"See you Tuesday," Jake called after her.

Jake called Chuck Browning to report and tell him they were done for the weekend.

"Browning."

"This is Jake Appleby with an update," said Jake. "I'm calling early because we're done for the weekend. The coincidence angle we were working didn't pan out."

"Once again, you are left with nothing?"

"That's close, sir. We've still got the husband of the victim who is being worked on by Walnut Creek."

"I expect some results, Appleby. The press is frantic about a beautiful woman disappearing and only a severed head being found. I need some information to fuel the media beast."

"Yes sir. The case is tough but we're working it hard."

"Appleby, I understand that you have experience in river kayaking?"

"Yes sir, I do a fair amount of it."

"This case has reminded me of my college kayaking days. I remember what a thrill it was to conquer a rapid-filled river. I'm reviving old kayaking skills of my own with some classes. I may need you to show me the way down some rivers."

"Yes sir, that could be done," said Jake, hoping that it would never happen.

"Good afternoon, Appleby. Remember, I need results."

"Good afternoon sir," Jake said as the phone clicked off.

What a pain in the ass, thought Jake. I hate having to deal with the stuffed shirt at all, but I like my job and I don't have to deal with him much. Kayaking doesn't seem like the sport for Chucky, he'd be more into polo or golf I'd think.

The hell with him, I'm going to have a good time with the rest of my weekend. There's a nice bottle of Dos Lunas reposado tequila waiting at home and I'm going to keep it company tonight.

17. ROSEVILLE; TUESDAY

He'd been sitting in his SUV, in the shade of the Roseville Mall parking structure for an hour now. Like a law enforcement officer, he'd been observing everything in sight. Now he had something: A dark haired woman had emerged from a Mercedes and was headed out of the parking lot towards the Niebaums department store. He picked up his compact binoculars and gave her a closer look. Bingo. She fit his needs. He sat back watching for a parking space near her car to open up and contemplated the coming action.

Twenty minutes later he noticed an elderly woman with a cane looking around in confusion. He got out of his SUV and walked over to her. "Can I help you ma'am?"

"I don't know," she said in a tremulous voice. "My car seems to have gotten lost."

"Well let's find the silly thing. Do you have a remote control key?"

"I do. Here it is," she said as she pulled a wad of keys from her purse.

"Just push the lock button and your car's horn should go off."

The old lady pushed the button and they heard a car horn. "I heard it."

"I think it came from further out in the lot," he said. "Let's head that way and try again."

An hour later, Gina Roberts walked out of Niebaums with two packages, excited about the spoils of her shopping expedition. She paused to pull out sunglasses to dampen the intense glare of yet another clear sunny day. Beautiful day, she thought. Thank God it wasn't one of those makeup-melting triple digit days. Too bad that she had to get back to work, but she had client meetings scheduled this afternoon.

Gina was five six, a beautiful woman of Italian heritage in her thirties. Her figure was good, though her hips were wider than she'd like. She had a lovely face and men loved to drown in her dark eyes. She always dressed well and today was no exception.

Gina had just put her packages in the trunk when she heard, "Excuse me miss, might you have a cell phone that I could use to call road service?" She located the source and saw a clean-cut man wearing a suit and a white straw cowboy hat walking toward her. The man's bushy black mustache reminded her of her uncle, though he wouldn't be caught dead wearing a cowboy hat and he didn't have enough hair to grow a pony tail. She didn't notice that he was wearing surgical gloves. "Sure, I've got a phone" she said, reaching into her purse.

BOOM! The world exploded into PAIN! Every muscle in Gina's body locked up and she found herself on the pavement.

"You're mine, slut," spat the man in the suit as he put the Taser back in his pocket then bent over and put a bouffant hair cap on her. He looked around to see if anybody was in a position to observe them. Seeing no threats, he picked up Gina, her purse and the parts blown out of the Taser cartridge, carrying them three parking spaces to the left and putting her in the back of a large white SUV.

After checking his surroundings again, he opened the rear driver's side door and crawled in the back. He zip-tied her ankles and wrists together, then positioned her face-up on a paramedic's backboard and strapped her down. Next he pulled out a syringe and injected her upper arm, not bothering with the traditional alcohol swab. A strip of duct tape that had been prepositioned on the side pillar went over her mouth. He duct taped her hands together, rendering her fingers and fingernails unusable. Done for now, he covered her with a large mover's pad.

Emerging from the back, he noticed a woman walking towards him. Instead of using the blower, he moved to the driver's seat and drove out of the parking lot at a normal speed. In two minutes he was on highway 65, two minutes later he was on Interstate 80. Daydreaming a bit as he drove, he thought about the unexpected pleasure the women were giving him, a free bonus that didn't compromise the plan. If he'd remembered the teenage erections he'd gotten just from pulling the legs off a grasshopper, he might have anticipated this additional benefit of the game. Fucking women, they were good for something.

After twenty minutes he exited the freeway and drove the SUV around the area in a narrowing spiral, looking for signs of police. Finding none, he pulled into the driveway of a decrepit ranch house surrounded by a large, dry, and weedy lot. The garage door opened, the SUV drove in, and the door closed.

The man got out of the car and paused to look around. A large chest freezer hummed and the air had a faint odor of chlorine. Seeing nothing out of the ordinary, he reset the alarm system. He then opened a cabinet in the garage and began taking off his suit, putting it in a plastic garment bag. He knew that the body shed DNA evidence all the time. For example the average person lost thirteen pubic hairs per day. To keep this under control, he donned a Tyvek crime scene jumpsuit with hood, shoe covers, and blue nitrile gloves. Opening the rear of the SUV, he unstrapped Gina, put her over his shoulder and carried her into the house.

Walking into a bathroom filled with turquoise tile, he put her on the floor, removed her clothes, and placed them in a black plastic garbage bag. Placing the bag in the hallway, he picked up a short, wide stool and placed it inside of the bathtub, then he slid another black plastic bag over the stool.

He picked up Gina's limp body and draped her body face down over the stool, her head at the end of the tub with the shower head. He then strapped her to the stool using two lengths of rope. Closing the bathroom door, he sat on the toilet seat and surveyed the room. Sterile and empty, the ugly old room had no shower curtain, towels, rugs or toilet paper. The only thing that wasn't built in was an 8x10 photograph taped to the mirror of the medicine cabinet over the free standing turquoise sink. At first glance, it looked like a head shot of Gina, but when you looked closely you could see several subtle differences. Gina's face was more round, her hair was shorter, and she didn't have the slight wrinkles radiating from the corners of her eyes.

The man leaned back, gazed at the photograph, and thought about how he had the control now. He waited for Gina to wake up because she had a role.

After half an hour had passed, Gina's head began to move and muted sounds came from behind the duct tape. The man stood up and uttered his first words since the parking lot. "Welcome back, my pretty. I have been anticipating your return since your participation is a necessary component of my production." He grasped her head in both hands and turned it to face him. Her eyes widened and the terror in them increased as she saw him wrapped in white. His feeling of power intensified.

He released her head, took a step back, and picked up a black leather belt. He lashed her bare buttocks with the belt; she jerked and a scream filled the bathroom, muffled because of the duct tape over her mouth. He lashed her again and called out, "How do you like it bitch?" He hit her twice more, then switched the belt to his left hand, grabbing a handful of Tyvek and erection with his right. Again and again he hit her, breaking the skin in places so that speckles of crimson blood flew onto turquoise tile. After fifteen strikes, he arched his back, called out "Aahhhh" and stopped.

For a few moments the only activity in the room was the feeble moans coming from Gina. Then he said, "Moan all you want. This is my show now."

He enjoyed it for a while, then tossed the belt into the bathtub, reached into the medicine cabinet and withdrew an ice pick. "Now for the finale," he said as he moved to Gina.

When she was gone, he removed the ropes, putting one of them tight around her ankles and the second looped through the first. He stepped into the tub and, struggling with the weight, put the looped strap into a large hook hanging from the ceiling. Pausing to catch his breath, he stepped out of the tub and retrieved a scalpel from the medicine chest. With all the emotion of a butcher he cut a precise, deep line across her throat, severing both carotid arteries which began gushing blood into the bathtub. He collected a sample in a small stainless steel water bottle that had been labeled with the number two. Next a baggie received some pubic and head hair. The baggie was labeled with a two.

Sitting down on the toilet, he waited for the blood flow to fade to a dribble. He thought about how much better this was than he had expected. The power was immense and the release was euphoric. What great bonus benefits.

The draining was finished. He finished severing her head and set it upright to drain.

After washing his gloved hands in the sink, he changed booties. Slipping an extra large plastic bag over the body, he unhooked it from the ceiling, carried it to the garage, and put it into the freezer. He came back for the head, removed the duct tape and cleaned it up. The head went into a bowl and the bowl into the refrigerator. He said with a smile, "Tom, you've been a baaad boy."

He took a respirator, a large bucket, a bottle of bleach and a two gallon garden spray container filled with 10% bleach solution to the bathroom. After cracking several windows he turned on a whole house exhaust fan. He cleaned and dried his tools, putting them back in the medicine cabinet.

An hour later he had finished cleaning up to his satisfaction. He wasn't so concerned about evidence relating to the victim, he just liked things neat and wanted to ensure that there was no evidence of his presence. The process had included a thorough cleaning of the SUV's interior.

Her clothes had gone through a wash cycle with lots of bleach and were in a new bag with the cleaning rags. In a separate bag went his Tyvek suit and respirator after they had been rinsed in bleach water. The bags went into the trunk of a five year old green Toyota Camry for later disposal. The suit was already in the Camry, in its own plastic bag destined for the cleaners. The alarm system was activated. Dressing in yet another set of clothes, he sprayed the garage floor with bleach solution, got in the Camry and left.

18. SACRAMENTO

Jake arrived at the office about eight thirty carrying a coffee and a latte. "Good morning C," he said in a cheerful tone. "Didya have a great and refreshing visit with the family?"

"It was good and bad Jake. It's great to see everybody and I have fun with my nieces and nephews. Then there's dad. I'm always feeling that disapproval of my work and that I'm single. Even though he knows that I won't go to church, he's always taking the family to Mass when I'm there and makes a big angry issue about it."

"Sorry to hear that, but I guess that's normal when you go down there."

"Yeah, it is. It's uncomfortable enough that I don't visit often, even if they're only 45 minutes away."

"Bummer. It's not good to have a family situation go bad."

"Thanks Jake. I do miss the close family we were when I grew up."

"I know what you mean. I can only handle a couple of visits a year to my parents. Even though dad and mom are in our business, they always insisted that we find other lines of work. I've gotten a lot of grief from them since I moved into law enforcement. It helps to take Kaitlin along because they get into the grandparent mode and off my back."

"Can I borrow her next time? I guess that wouldn't work."

"I doubt it."

"So did you have a good time with Kaitlin?"

"I did. We went out to the Empire Mine State Park, I hadn't been there in years. They have this room sized model of almost 400 miles of shafts and drifts. The longest goes down a mile. It's too bad you can't get into the mine, it's full of water. We also did some serious work looking online at her school assignments and grades. Can't have her thinking that dads are just for play. The three of us had a nice afternoon hike and barbequed salmon for dinner. On Monday I got out with some guys and kayaked the north fork of the American River."

"Good boy. Time to get back to work. I'm going to call everybody on our raft trip and find out who knew they were going."

"Sounds like a plan. You know that old Freud quote about "sometimes a cigar is just a cigar"? I still think that we have more than a cigar here, it's just too big a coincidence. While you're calling I'm going to review what we've got in JARS, talk to Walnut Creek and Sonora, then do some thinking."

Partway through his review of the case documentation, Jake encountered the description of the tires believed to have been on the perpetrator's vehicle. He sent Suzie an email, asking her to find out how many of those tires had been sold in California. Without unique marks that would identify a specific tire, knowing the tire model and size might be about as useful as knowing that the suspect had brown hair.

After several hours, they sat back to brainstorm or, as others might put it, to theorize and speculate.

"So why was Sophia Mancuso kidnapped?" asked Jake.

"The standard answer would be that somebody she knew wanted to do her harm," replied Celia. "With her social status and the upscale shopping location, you'd figure that the chance of it being somebody she knows goes up. We just haven't found the person."

"But we've looked at the most obvious people and they don't look good for it. We haven't turned up anybody else to even look at."

"We just haven't scrubbed her life hard enough to find the right suspect."

"Maybe," said Jake. "Bonner and Fortuna are doing some scrubbing."

"You know that the other answer is that she was just a victim of opportunity, that the kidnapper thought that the parking structure was a good place to get one. Or, he was driving by and spotted her, took her on a whim."

"If either of those variations is true, we're only going to solve this with luck or a mistake by our perp."

"Yeah. Any other ideas?"

"I guess it could be somebody trying to harm the store or Mancuso's dealership," said Jake. "That's hard to buy. Let's talk about why we only have a head and why the river."

"It has shock value. Like the damned jihadists cutting people's heads off. Historically it was a good way to off people and have a display for deterrence – the head on a pike kind of thing."

"But what's being deterred here? And an isolated river is not going to get a broad audience. We've even managed to keep the pictures away from the media"

Celia said, "I guess that could tie back to the department store or dealership; deter people from dealing with them? That still seems kind of thin though."

"The thing about this head is how nice it was. You know, surgically removed, cleaned up, with no visible damage. Even the hair looked good. That's not like somebody murdering with rage, it's … precise or respectful. Organized."

"I hope nobody respects me like that," was Celia's response. "You're right though, that is strange. Why would somebody kill her, then be respectful? Then there's the whole question of why would the killer take her head all the way to the Sierras to pose?"

"It could be that the kidnapper has a place up there, he took her there for the surgery. We should get Bonner and Katashi to check on Tuolumne places owned by people that knew Mancuso."

"Possible; worth a look," granted Celia. "I still think the head placement was because of somebody in our rafting group, I just can't find the damn connection."

"So on one extreme, we've got the theory that somebody connected to Sophia and having a place near Tuolumne did it. On the other extreme, she was a victim of opportunity by a weird dude who put the head on the Tuolumne to mess with somebody in the rafting group. We've got no real evidence of either theory, we're nowhere. Shit."

"Hang in there Jakey," said Celia. "You know the drill: think, dig, keep on truckin'." She knew from experience that Jake's impatience sometimes boiled over, taking his attention off the case. She thought that it was OK, that his impatience sometimes caused him to make waves that resulted in good things happening.

"Yeah, yeah. I think my truck's about out of fuel. I'm out of here, see you tomorrow." Jake walked out, leaving the case behind. He knew that parts of his brain would keep working on it, but he was going to let his conscious mind take a break.

Celia decided to call her friend Kaya Lane, who worked in the DOJs Violent Crime Profiling Unit. As a PhD psychologist she was smart and professional, as a Hopi descendent she came from an interesting culture, and as a girl friend, she could be great fun.

"Kaya, how're you doing?" opened Celia.

"I'm doing great, but I'm working on an ugly child molestation case and it's hard to avoid an emotional response," replied Kaya.

"I always try to focus on how satisfying it is to nail those slime balls, helps me to stay focused."

"Good approach. Doing anything fun these days?"

"I was on a cool raft trip a week ago, but it got spoiled when we floated into a crime scene."

"That was you? The Tuolumne River head thing?"

"That was me and Jake and a few other guys. I'd like you to take a look at the case and tell us what you think."

"You want? Not Jake?"

"Jake will want your analysis, Kaya. I think maybe you intimidate him a bit so he leaves the asking to me."

"Little old me? Intimidate?"

"You may be slim Kaya, but you're not little." Kaya was almost six feet tall and her great body tended to be in constant motion. "We'll both use what you come up with."

"OK, I'll take a look for you. Give me JARS access for the case. You want to meet for dinner and give me your take?"

"That'd be fun. How about the fish place on the river, off Garden Highway?"

"The Grotto? Sure. I'll see you about six?"

"I'll be there. Bye."

After a hard workout at the gym and a good Thai meal, Jake went home to an empty house. Tank was there and that was good, but Tank was just like most of his guy friends, you enjoyed time together, but didn't get close and personal. As Jake sat down in his Stressless recliner with his bottle of sipping tequila, he felt a melancholy evening coming on.

Jake started up Laurie Lewis' recording of *Who Will Watch The Home Place*. The beautiful music fed his feelings of loss. Somehow the music could get past his defenses; open his heart in a way that few things could. As he sipped, he reflected again how he had never cried as a teenager or adult until he sat at his sister's funeral. That experience seemed to have opened a gate in him that wouldn't close. In times where he reflected on loss, his eyes produced tears faster than his tear ducts could drain them. This didn't happen much in public, but when it did, he was embarrassed. Intellectually he knew it didn't make him a weakling but he'd been brought up in the "men don't cry" tradition. He'd decided that feeling emotions in certain situations was a good thing as long as they didn't control you.

It had been years since Diane's death and the ragged edges of the wound in his heart had healed, but there was still a hole there. It didn't come up often, just when he had one of these evenings. He and Diane had always been buddies, there was enough of an age difference that there wasn't much sibling rivalry. Their relationship was such a contrast to the poor relationship between him and his older brother, the family's star. Diane loved life and laughed at it often with Jake. Jake had enjoyed being a good big brother, letting her talk about the travails of adolescence, giving her some subtle hints about life. She'd loved riding on the back of his old Yamaha motorcycle, even more of a pleasure because it was forbidden by their parents. Jake tossed back the remainder of his glass then leaned back and let the memories and feelings engulf him for a minute.

Jake sat up, refilled his glass, and put on Alison Krause's haunting version of *Ghost In This House.* The lyrics and Alison's sweet voice mixing perfectly with the unique sounds of the Dobro took Jake to a place that was sad and beautiful at the same time. The lyric *two hearts on fire that once burned out of control* always brought up Fiona, their loss of a fantastic partnership and family. In many ways he thought that their marriage was another casualty of Diane's murder, but that they could have made things work if they'd been smarter and he'd prioritized things better. He kept trying to get his family back but right now it was a pale shadow of what they'd had. Somehow he just couldn't pull back from full immersion in law enforcement.

Another drink and Jake's mind wandered back to good memories of Diane and Fiona. He stared at the wall, seeing nothing as he walked that good road.

19. SACRAMENTO; WEDNESDAY

Jake felt something on his back. As he struggled to wake, he decided that it was Tank having a morning walk across his body. Jake's eyes didn't want to open, but he managed to slowly roll over and grab the cat who said *mrrrph?* Taking stock of his situation, Jake decided that he may have grown fur on his teeth and that he was running in compound low gear. He remembered the evening and guessed that he'd made it to the bedroom with just enough energy to crash on the bed.

When he managed to get into second gear he got up and walked to the bathroom. As he began the process of cleaning up, he made two decisions: Put the sad memories back into their compartment and get out with some friends tonight.

Downtown by nine, Jake took the stairs down to the computer development lab. He wondered why it had been put in the basement. Did the suits think that computer guys were moles, disgusting looking critters that lived underground?

Jake found the lab being used for one of his pet projects, integrating JARS with the California Automatic License Plate Reader (ALPR) system. Evolved from photo radar systems that tried to penalize speeding at a low enforcement cost, ALPR has a much higher potential as a law enforcement tool. ALPR takes a digital image of a vehicle and pulls the license plate number out of the data. The mobile version of the system was installed in a few highway patrol vehicles and some large city police department vehicles. Comparing the license plate number to a "hot list" of numbers, a hit would trigger an immediate message to the vehicle's driver and their dispatch system. A secure database of scanned images was kept in one of the DOJ computers and could be analyzed when information about a plate was desired.

The JARS project automatically moved plate numbers in and out of the state's hot list when a plate was put in a JARS case or when the case was closed. When a plate was added to a case, the database of scanned images was automatically searched and historical plate location information included in JARS.

The current weakness of the ALPR project was that too few plate reader systems were in operation. Attempting to learn from the United Kingdom, which has an extensive and effective system, the state project was beginning to deploy fixed systems on roadways.

Jake was a member of the design board for California's ALPR project. He'd organized workshops with DOJ attorneys looking at privacy issues that might be raised by the ACLU and others. Good security and concern about privacy issues had been woven into the project from the beginning. Jake knew that plate readers would turn out to be a law enforcement gold mine for locating stolen cars and plates, suspects, missing and suicidal people. In addition, it would provide traffic flow information and speed limit enforcement.

After working the morning with the team and a quick lunch, Jake went back to his desk.

"Did you get your fuel tank filled up?" was Celia's welcome.

"No, but last night I may have burned out the brain cells that were bothering me," replied Jake. "I'm going to get some more fuel tonight, Steve and Terry are coming over for steaks. Will you join us?"

"Sure, you need to have some brains amid all that beef," answered Celia with a tiny grin.

"Out of compassion for your ego, I'm going to let that go," responded Jake. "My morning with the JARS team was a good break, but I should get back to our case. I may not be raring but I'm ready to go."

"I just heard from Torrey Bonner in Walnut Creek. Their lab reports came in from the Mancuso search. The towel had blood on it alright, but it was menstrual blood, so Sophia or Jill just cleaned up an accident. The knife and ice pick were clean and they got nothing out of the SUV."

"So Pauli Mancuso is either skillful or he's clean," said Jake. "If he used another house for the deed and was careful with the SUV, he could still have done it. On the other hand, we could have a killer who has no connection to the victim. Have they found anything by scrubbing Sophia's life?"

"Nothing so far. No dirt and no enemies. Maybe she was an actual model citizen."

"Some are out there C, it's just that we don't come across them in this job."

"True. We do get a better class of criminal in this job than we did working for Sacramento, but not model citizens."

Their musings were interrupted by the arrival of Sam Nakamura, looking for an update. They told him that the case had turned into a grind; lots of work, few results, nothing that looked promising.

"You know that real cops have to grind sometimes," reminded Sam. "The perps aren't always stupid enough to fall in your lap. You guys are good, hang in there." His morale boosting done, Sam headed back to his office.

Celia said, "Jake, I asked Kaya Lane to look at our case and give us her reading. Let's go over and see her."

"Reading? As in crystal ball reading?"

"Cut the crap Appleby, you know that she almost always gives us some good stuff."

"Yeah, I know. Intellectually I know profiling can be a useful tool, I'm just not too fond of the soft sciences." Jake got up for the walk over to the profiling unit.

As they walked, Jake asked, "So, does Kaya have any witch doctors in her family tree?"

"Don't be a jerk, Jake. The Hopis have a large set of cultural/religious beliefs, but Kaya's work is based on psychology and the lessons from forty years of profilers." Celia looked up to see a grin on Jake's face. He'd been jerking her chain. She walked faster.

When they reached her office, Kaya got up and shook hands with Jake. Her raven black hair fell straight to her shoulder blades, contrasting with her white blouse. Her dark eyes were penetrating but she had a slight smile on her face as she said, "How've you been Jake? It's been what, six months?"

"I think it was around Thanksgiving. I'm fine and you're looking good as usual."

"Thanks," said Kaya. "Let's get to it. As you well know, you don't have much on this case yet, but what you do have tells us some things about your perp. I'm sure that you see you've got an organized killer here. Here are attributes that I'm comfortable with at this point: He's a white male, age from 25 to 45, above average intelligence, at least middle class. He's a self-centered person who manipulates people, feels no guilt or remorse for his actions. He'll pay lots of attention to the media. The head display was planned out and done for shock value. The goal of a person like this is often power."

"That makes sense to me," said Celia. "Are you not comfortable applying other known attributes of organized killers?"

"Not yet, we just don't have much to go on."

Jake spoke up, "So you're saying that a Hispanic or Asian person with average intelligence couldn't have done this?"

"You know better than that," replied Kaya. "These attributes are probable, but people are complex and varied; nothing is certain."

"Soft science," said Jake as he stood up to go. "We'll keep your ideas in mind."

Celia flashed Jake an annoyed look then looked at Kaya and shrugged. "Thanks Kaya."

On the walk back to their offices, Celia broke the silence, "Pauli Mancuso might fit."

"You said Mancuso's grief seemed genuine," responded Jake.

"I also said that a psychopath might be able to fake the emotions. His grief and concern for his child would all have to be acting, a major performance. Not impossible, but difficult."

"Why don't you pass Kaya's opinions on to Bonner. He can use them while investigating Walnut Creek suspects."

"I will."

Jake was thinking about his next steps when the phone rang.

"Jake, this is Julio in Missing Persons. I've just put a new one in the system and she looks like a sister to the one you found last week. Everything we have about her is in the system. Look for the name Gina Roberts."

"Thanks for the heads up, I'll take a look," said Jake.

Jake turned to his computer and got into the Missing Persons system, searching for Gina Roberts. The picture that came up on the screen made him sit back and say, "Wow."

Celia turned from her desk and said "what?"

Jake said, "Take a look at this. We may have number two happening. We've got a missing woman that looks just like Sophia."

Celia looked over his shoulder. "You're right, she's close. Another Italian or Hispanic beauty."

Jake clicked over to the textual information. "Lives in Roseville, didn't come home yesterday. She's some kind of account executive with a brokerage firm. I'd expect her to be well off like Sophia. I'm going to call Roseville."

Calling the number listed in the system, Jake reached the woman who handled Roseville PD's missing person cases.

A husky woman's voice: "Roseville Police, Sharon Klein."

"My name is Jake Appleby, I'm an agent with California's DOJ and I'm calling about your missing person's report on Gina Roberts."

"What can I do for you?"

"I think it's more like what I can do for you at this point," said Jake. "Have you read about the woman's head that we found on the Tuolumne River?"

"Yeah, but our woman just went missing yesterday, it couldn't be from her."

Jake rolled his eyes, then said, "I realize that your person is not our victim. What I wanted to tell you was that our victim looks just like yours, ours went missing when she was out running "errands" like yours, and I'm guessing that they were in the same socioeconomic class. I think that there's a good possibility that our perp's back at it and has your woman."

"Whoa, that's heavy. Most of ours come back after a long visit with some guy."

"I think that it might pay off if you looked harder at this case. The car of our victim was found in the parking lot of a Niebaums store in Walnut Creek. I know that there's a Niebaums in the Roseville mall so I'd suggest that you look there. I hope she's out with some guy, but I've got a bad feeling that she's not."

"Well that's a reasonable suggestion, Mr. Apples," said Klein, sounding indifferent. "We may have a unit check it out. Can I have your full name and a phone number for our records please?"

"It's Appleby, Jake Appleby. Use my mobile number, 916-555-7942." Jake hung up.

Celia gave Jake a questioning look.

"I think I interrupted her nap," he said. "Maybe they'll check out the parking lot. If they find Robert's car I'm sure we'll hear from them."

"Why don't I link our case to the missing person's report as a possible victim. Roseville uses JARS, so they'll have access our case's summary data without even talking to us."

"Good idea. Why don't you do that while I go get some good steaks. See you about six?"

"Sure."

At 5:45, Jake had just emerged from his shower when he heard the doorbell. He wrapped a towel around his waist and walked to the door. Since he was in law enforcement, he checked the peep hole first, then he opened the door.

Celia started with "I finished my errands early so I just thought …" She had never seen Jake without a shirt and he surpassed her fantasy. Not good. She averted her eyes a bit and tried to recover with, "I don't see any tattoos, Jake."

Always quick, Jake responded with "They're not where you're going to see them." His eyes twinkled and he had that wry grin. "Come on in, I'll be with you in a minute."

Celia walked in thinking, Girl, you didn't need to see that. Now you're going to have to get that picture out of your mind.

An hour later Steve and Terry had joined them, everybody had consumed at least two drinks, the steaks were on the grill. Everybody was getting refueled.

20. MIDDLE FORK, AMERICAN RIVER; FRIDAY

He left his kill house in the SUV, heading towards the morning light that had just appeared on the horizon. As he left the valley and began climbing, the sun rose, showing orange through the haze. Twenty five minutes later he had turned onto Driver's Flat Road and reached the fee station, just twenty minutes after "quiet time" for the Ruck a Chucky recreation area ended.

After his planning run, he had decided that paying the day use fee worked with his plan. Paying would protect him just in case timing was bad and a ranger decided to check vehicles while he was there. He handled the envelope with gloved hands and placed the clean ten dollar bill inside. The envelope asked for a vehicle make, model, and license plate number. He wrote in the make and the plate number, but transposed three digits. He figured that a ranger would pass this error as a simple mistake.

Driving downhill on two miles of a steep dirt road roughened by emerging boulders, he reached the river and the six basic campsites. After driving a half mile upstream on the worsening road, a pullout area provided room for the SUV. He emerged from the car, a dirty baseball cap low over his eyes, a beer logoed t-shirt and jeans covering the rest of him. A casual but careful look around verified that nobody was within sight. The only sounds were birds and the gurgling of the river.

He donned fishing waders and wader boots after assembling a fly rod. He moved a bowling ball sized object from a cooler into a large wicker creel, then the creel's strap was hung diagonally over his shoulder, transforming him into a fisherman.

Locking the vehicle, the fisherman headed towards the river on a narrow path worn in the dirt, surrounded by star thistle, the most successful invasive pest plant in California. The path ended at a small sand beach. He avoided the sand, sticking to the greenish serpentine rock veined with white quartz. Just below the beach the fisherman waded into the water and began fly casting. Working his way downstream he kept an eye out for people, but saw none. This area was screened from the camp sites by a bend in the river and shoreline vegetation. Being seen and remembered would, at worst, complicate the plan.

His pre-chosen boulder was flat topped and began protruding out of the river about four feet offshore. Gloving up, he picked up three rocks the size of cantaloupes and placed them on the boulder to support his arrangement. After one last casual look around, he pulled Gina's head from the creel and placed it on the boulder, facing upstream and propped up by his rocks. Using a small hairbrush, he touched up her hair.

Moving upstream and fly casting, he kept his eyes out for signs of people, but saw none. Careful to never appear in a hurry, he wasted no time getting back to the car, loading up the fishing gear and heading back up the hill. Turning off of Driver's Flat at the top of the hill, he breathed a sigh of relief. The planning hadn't prepared him for the level of tension he'd encountered. While the operation had been low risk because of all the preparation, about two minutes were critical. If somebody had popped up then, seen the head and him, he would have had to shut them up. Another body would have diluted the shock value of his display.

All had gone according to plan as he had expected. Law enforcement could catch many of your ordinary, stupid criminals. They didn't have a chance against him. After cleaning up, he could sit back and await the turmoil.

21. RUCK A CHUCKY

Paula Seldon was looking down on the Ruck a Chucky falls from the shore, standing on a giant boulder about 50 feet above the river. She was still dripping from Chunder rapid and vividly remembered her amazing ride down the Tunnel Chute rapid. She'd been scared in Tunnel Chute and she would have been terrified if she was in the raft going down Ruck a Chucky. All the passengers were portaging while the guide took their raft through a class VI dangerous rapid that dropped thirty feet. She'd walk, thank you.

A mile below Ruck a Chucky they finished their last rapid of the day and Paula breathed a sigh of relief. Rafting had been her boyfriend's idea and the Middle fork of the American River had been wilder than she'd experienced before; her stomach was still churning. She was taking in the scenery when she saw something on top of one of the boulders in the river. Hoping that it was one of the river otters the guides had talked about, she kept a sharp eye on it as the riffled water carried them closer. Her fellow paddlers were busy comparing their views of the trip.

"Oh my God!" she shrieked, startling everybody in the raft. "It's somebody's head! Oh God, oh God," she said as she began hyperventilating.

Their guide turned the raft so he had a better view, seeing a woman's head with bluebottle flies walking around it. "Son of a bitch. That's sick." As they floated past the rock, he dug into his dry pack to get the satellite phone they carried for emergencies. He heard a retching sound, turned and saw Paula losing her lunch into the river. I could do without that smell, he thought. When the phone powered up, he called the sheriff and reported what they'd found. Directed to stay there and protect the crime scene, he replied "Yes ma'am."

22. SACRAMENTO

It was another slow day for Jake. Yesterday the Roseville PD had found Gina Robert's car in the mall parking lot, just as Jake had suggested. The crime scene crew had found AFID tags from a Taser on the pavement near the car. The small confetti like AFIDs contained the serial number of the Taser cartridge that had been discharged. The car was being checked out, but Jake figured that they'd find that same thing they found on Sophia's car, nothing. He had talked to Roseville's Crimes Against Persons lieutenant and convinced him to treat the case as a potential kidnap/homicide. The lieutenant had assigned a detective named Rich Luton, who had talked to Jake for about an hour. Jake had given Luton "detective" authorization to the case information in JARS.

Luton had already filed two reports. The first was on his interview of Gina's husband who had reported her as missing. Not much there except that the husband had mentioned that there was an angry ex-husband. Luton was getting the missing woman's phone and credit card records. The second report was on the Taser AFIDs. Taser International maintained a database of cartridge serial numbers correlated with the cartridge purchaser and they ran background checks on their purchasers. All that wasn't of much use since the cartridge was one of several that had been stolen along with a Taser X26 device.

Jake and Celia talked about the weekend plan. Given the status of the case, they decided to remain in contact but take the weekend off if nothing developed.

As Jake stood up to leave, his phone rang. "Jake Appleby."

Listening.

"What's she look like?"

Listening.

"We'll be up, give me directions."

Writing.

"About forty minutes."

Jake hung up and turned to Celia. "We've got another posed head. Dark haired female posed in the Middle fork of the American River."

As they started out in Jake's Boxter, Celia called Kaya Lane, told her about the development and gave her directions.

They headed for the foothills using I80, getting past some of the rush hour traffic by using the siren and lights Jake had installed on the Boxter.

23. RUCK A CHUCKY

As they left the town of Auburn on Foresthill Road, Jake turned off the siren, leaving the lights on. Now they could talk and Jake was telling Celia about the road. "You can't see much from the car, but we cross the North Fork canyon on the tallest bridge in California, some seven hundred feet above the river. Bikers love the road – not much traffic and lots of sweeping turns. The downside for the bikers is that the Highway Patrol knows they ride hard here."

Turning right on Drivers Flat, they showed ID to a deputy and continued on to the fee collection area where they got a ride down into the canyon in a sheriff's SUV. Jake carried a gear bag with his satellite phone, a good camera, binoculars and other gadgets. When they reached the campground area, now crowded with people and vehicles, they introduced themselves to Sheriff's Detective Randy Moore who had the lead on the case.

Moore was about fifty with a thinning head of blonde hair and pale blue eyes. He had the look of a well muscled man who has let it go – everything was rounded. His work boots clashed with his slacks and open collared blue dress shirt, but were quite appropriate for the scene.

Jake explained the Tuolumne / Walnut Creek crime and mentioned that there was a woman missing from Roseville who was a candidate for his victim.

"We've just gotten this chaos under control," said Moore. "There must have been thirty raft loads come down through here. We had to get those people out of the way and canvas everyone that might have been here when the head was dumped. We've taped off the area around the head and stayed away.

"I've got some binoculars," responded Jake. "Let's get as close as we can and use them."

They got to the taped crime scene boundary, about one hundred feet upstream from the head. Jake pulled out his binoculars and a photo of Gina Roberts. After a long look, he handed the glasses to Celia and said, "What do you think?"

Celia looked back and forth at the photo, then the head. "Twenty bucks says that's her."

Moore took a look and said, "I won't take your bet. Knowing who it is will give us a big leg up. So many of the remains we find in these hills are tough to ID because they're not as fresh as this one."

Jake had pulled out his camera and attached the long telephoto lens. He took several pictures.

A short, hyperactive man, as thin as a stick, came up to Moore and began talking about the canvas of potential witnesses. Moore introduced him as Nathan Taylor, his partner on the case. Jake said hello, then left Celia with them and stepped away. Taylor's problem was that they hadn't been able to interview all of the raft company shuttle drivers who might have seen something. Some of them had left before any deputies arrived, some had to leave to get rafters out of the crowded area.

"You've got names and numbers of most of them?" asked Moore.

"Yeah, we got six of them," replied Taylor. "We just don't know who we missed."

"State Parks and Rec writes permits for all the commercial outfits," said Moore. "Find out who has permits, call the outfits you don't already have a name for and find their drivers."

"Uh … OK," said Taylor, turning to walk away.

"Nathan, before you chase the permits," said Moore, "get a ranger to open the fee envelope deposit box and collect the contents for us."

"Sure, I'll get it done Randy," responded Taylor as he walked away.

Moore looked at Celia and rolled his eyes. "Sometimes he's a little slow. He's just a kid, so there's hope that he'll get better."

Jake had walked off about thirty feet and was on his satellite phone talking to Sam Nakamura. "The head down here looks like it belongs to the Roseville woman. So now we've got two victims and at least four jurisdictions. I'm defining our guy as a serial killer. As much as I hate it Sam, it's time to start a task force."

"It looks like you're right, Jake. We need to make sure that everybody is communicating well or things will drop through the cracks. I can get Suzie Eckerling to set up JARS. I'll call the four departments and get them on board. You'll run the task force. Do you have a name for it?

"You can call it "whitewater", Sam. I need you to run it instead of me though. Your rank will give you more clout and I think I'm going to need all the time I can find. This case is looking like a nasty bitch."

"You're just avoiding administration Jake. I guess I can run it for you. I'd enjoy dipping my hands close to some real work for a change."

"Thanks. All the worker names are in JARS except for the Placer County people. Lead up here is Randy Moore, he's partnered with Nathan Taylor. Given that our perp's a repeater, we should have our first meeting on Sunday if you can pull this off."

"We'll see. It's late on Friday, it'll be hard to get hold of all the right people."

"OK Sam, let's both get to it."

"Later," Sam said before he hung up.

Jake looked around and saw that the crime scene crew still hadn't arrived. He couldn't see Moore or Celia, they must have walked off. He rolled his shoulders to get rid of some tension, then looked around to absorb some of the outdoors that he loved so much. The river was about seventy feet wide here, flowing quietly with just small riffles on the surface. You could see much of the bottom, the water not obscuring it, just adding a greenish tint. Lots of white flowered toyon bush grew near the river. Across the river, the steep north facing canyon wall was solid green; lots of oak with a few grey pine and old snags. Just downstream was a small beach, fool's gold glittering in the sand at the shoreline. A nice place, too bad it had become a crime scene.

Celia walked up and said, "Crime scene just passed the fee collection area, should be down here in a couple."

"Good. Do you know why they named this area Ruck a Chucky?"

"I haven't a clue."

"The gold miners named everything in these hills and sometimes their ingenuity was stretched a bit. The mining companies operating in this canyon got a reputation for bad food: rotten chuck. Somehow the tag stuck to the area and evolved into Ruck a Chucky."

"Once again, Jake Appleby, you've burdened my brain with an important fact."

"It's important for you young people to understand your heritage. Why don't you go tell Moore that you've got a profiler coming."

A minute later, Jake spotted a DOJ forensics van pulling in. He headed that way, figuring it contained his favorite forensics guy, Willy "Chocolate" Jackson. Out of the truck bounced a short, wiry black man with short hair and one of those chiseled jaws. One of the smartest men Jake knew, Willy had gotten his nickname from Willy Wonka's factory well before he got his PhD in forensic science.

"Welcome to Ruck a Chucky, Chocolate. Great place for Friday night fun."

"If it isn't the biker boy," came the response. "It looks like you've still got all your arms and legs. Did you get smart and sell that mutilation machine?"

"Can't sell her, Chocolate, she's the only woman I can hang onto and she takes me for quite a ride."

"That's quite a sad story. Where's your capable and much more attractive partner?"

"She's over next to the river with the Placer County detective."

"I always look forward to working with her; professional and beautiful too. Enough chit chat, what's going on here Jake?"

"A guy we've been looking for just got promoted to serial killer. The head of his second victim is on a rock over there in the river. Vern handled the first head, we found it on a rock in the Tuolumne River."

"That's the one that Browning keeps yammering about in the newspapers?"

"You've got it. He'll be on this new one like slime on a snail. So far this perp's been slick. Vern got almost nothing from the Tuolumne crime scene. I'm hoping that your superior skill and intellect will find something we can use."

"Compliments help, Jake. Bribery goes even further."

"Let's see… A BBQ in your honor if you nail him."

"That sounds attractive, we'll get on it."

"Hi Chocolate, good to see you here," said Celia as she walked up.

"Ah, the bright one of the pair. You'd better not leave this other one alone too long, he'll get himself into trouble," chuckled Chocolate.

"Trouble's his middle name," said Celia. "I sure hope that our perp left something for you to find here; our clue and evidence buckets have plenty of space for more."

"I need to get moving or it'll get dark and your buckets will stay empty," said Chocolate as he moved off to direct his crew.

Ten minutes later a red Toyota 4Runner drove up and Kaya Lane stepped out. Her black pants suit and low heels stood out from the crowd and would be covered with dust within minutes. She reached into the back seat and pulled out tennis shoes.

"Hi Kaya," said Celia with a smile. "Nice outfit."

"I know," said Kaya. "I should keep a set of field clothing in the office. The cleaners will take care of the mess. What's the story here?"

"We've got a female head posed on a rock in the river. From a distance it looks like a woman who went missing from Roseville on Tuesday. We're waiting for crime scene to give us close access."

"I usually takes three killings for a perp to get labeled a serial killer, but if this is the same guy I'd use that label now."

"We agree. Maybe he left us a present this time."

"We can hope."

"Let's go take a close up look at her," said Celia, noticing that crime scene had opened up a path for detectives.

Jake joined them on the path, greeting Kaya.

They approached the posed head from upstream and could see her face. Seeing it was tougher this time, they knew her name.

"Same dude," said Jake. "Down to the rocks used to prop her up and the brushed out hair."

"I agree," said Celia. "The rock's close to shore so it could have been a wader or a boater. The big difference is that this is a much more public area than the Tuolumne."

"Yeah, there's enough action here that he wouldn't stand out like he would have at the Tuolumne. I doubt that he was a boater. There's no need for a boat to get to the rock. Here comes Moore; why don't you shoo some flies away and I'll take pictures while he looks."

Randy Moore walked up to take a close look. They let him stare and think in silence. "Nasty crime," he said. "Vicious act to cut off a head, but then he cleans it all up into a sterile display. What do you think?"

"Same dude that did the Tuolumne posing," said Jake. "No way a copycat did this."

"How long's it been since the Tuolumne?" asked Moore.

"Eleven days. Not a lot of time."

"You're telling me."

"Our boss is organizing a multi-jurisdictional task force as we speak," Jake told them. We've got four jurisdictions and we don't even know where the victims were killed. I think that the first meeting will be Sunday."

"So much for my weekend trip to the beach," sighed Moore.

"I know what you mean, but if he's on an eleven day cycle we have no time to screw around," responded Celia.

"You guys will be busy for a while, but in the Tuolumne case, nothing has turned up in the hills except the posed head," said Jake. "I'd like to find the rest of her though; he may have dumped it up here someplace."

"There's a lot of empty woods in the area," replied Moore. "If he's as careful as he looks, the chance of us finding it anytime soon is slim."

"I know," said Jake. "I'm going to call Roseville on my sat phone and get them going. If I get the guy who's assigned, you want to talk to him?"

"Yeah," said Moore. "We should connect."

Jake called Rich Luton in Roseville. "Rich, it looks like we have Gina Robert's head here on the Middle fork of the American River."

"Shit. You sure?"

"Three of us have compared the head to a picture of Gina and think it's her. When I get back to cell coverage I can email you a picture of the head. Dental's the best way to make it positive, you don't want her husband to ID what we have."

"Yeah, that'd be a brutal thing to do to the guy. I know who the dentist is, but I'd guess that he's closed for the weekend."

"If you can dig up the records I can get a match done this weekend. Otherwise we'll just go on the assumption that it's Gina and her husband will have to wait for confirmation."

"OK, I'll try to find the dentist. What else?"

"We've got a serial killer here, so time's important. I'm going to push Placer to do the autopsy tomorrow. In the meantime, my boss is setting up a task force, calling your bosses as we speak. I think that the first meeting will be Sunday morning. In the meantime you could start investigating this as a homicide."

"We'll see if they'll authorize the overtime."

"Let me know if they don't, I can probably get it done. In the meantime I'll give the phone to the Placer detective who caught the case."

"Yeah Jake, talk to you later."

Jake handed the phone to Randy Moore, then turned to look at the head. Now that he'd done the professional things that needed immediate action, he felt his muscles tensing and the anger beginning to pulse in his head. Vicious animals destroying the lives of good people. It made him want to obliterate them, to squash them like the poisonous vermin they were. Jake let the anger wash over him for a minute, then began the conscious process of relaxing and going back to professional mode. The anger had to go back into its compartment.

"Jake, I met the deputy coroner," said Celia. "He said that they knew there'd be lots of pressure on this case, so they've scheduled an autopsy for eight thirty tomorrow morning."

"This is government, how can it move so fast?"

"Because we have some skilled and competent people in addition to bureaucrats."

"That would be shocking news to a lot of people, let's keep it quiet," said Jake. "I don't see any reasons to hang out here, let's get a ride back to my car."

Back in the Boxter, Jake emailed pictures of the latest victim to Roseville's Rich Luton, then called him. "I just emailed you the pictures. Any news on your end?"

"I lucked out. I got hold of the dentist and he was cooperative. I'm on my way to pick up Gina Robert's dental x-rays. Let me check and see if your pictures arrived. Yeah, here's the message." After half a minute, Luton was back, "I agree with you Jake, that's got to be her. Shit."

"We've got some urgency on the case now. We need to expect that our perp's going to keep on killing until we get him. Placer County's going to do the autopsy tomorrow morning, you may want to attend. We'll try to get the teeth matched tomorrow as well. Why don't you bring the x-rays to the autopsy in the morning"

"Sure. I'll see you then."

Jake started driving down the hill towards Sacramento. On the way, Celia updated their boss, left a message for Don Foreman, and lined up a forensic odontologist for the afternoon.

"You want to take the autopsy?" Jake asked.

"You had the first one, why don't you take this one. You might pick up on similarities that I wouldn't. Besides, I've got a long morning scheduled at the Taekwondo Club that I don't want to cancel."

"Life outside the DOJ? I suppose it keeps up the skills you need to be my bodyguard. OK, I'll do the autopsy."

Jake dropped Celia at her car. He then walked up to his office to call Browning. He summarized the events of the day for Browning, who had some questions.

"Two victims, two rivers, two weeks, zero leads isn't it?"

"Yes sir, that's one way to summarize it. We have plenty to look at though."

"Tell me what was different about this staging than the previous staging."

"So far, the major difference is the environment. Today's site has much more public access and presence. People camp, hike, and fish down there on a regular basis. The head could have been found by somebody other than a rafter. It also wasn't as safe a place to do a pose. More people around means a bigger chance of discovery during posing."

"Did somebody see him?"

"We haven't found anybody so far. If somebody had seen him with the head I think we'd have heard from them."

"Find this person, Appleby. This state doesn't need a serial killer preying on middle class women. If you need more resources, ask for them."

Jake said "yes sir," but realized that the connection was gone.

24. AUBURN; SATURDAY

Jake had a light breakfast in Auburn. After his first sip of coffee, he grabbed the front section of the Sacramento Bee. The headlines screamed, *Whitewater Killer Strikes Again.* The subtitle read *Serial Killer Roams Northern California.* Reading the article, Jake wasn't surprised to find it low on facts but high on emotion, opinion, and fear. Then there was Browning's posturing again, making himself seem the sole guardian of the legions of women who might fall into the grasp of this vicious killer. Well, he got the vicious killer part right. This kind of publicity would create pressure on them for a solution. Some of that was good, because they'd get resources when they asked. The bad part was that politicians would want lots of their time for updates instead of letting them work the crime. Sam Nakamura was good at keeping people off their back, but this would test him.

When his breakfast arrived, Jake switched to the sports section.

Jake drove the few blocks over to the county morgue and found a bit of a crowd. Rich Luton and Randy Moore were already there and the pathologist was garbing up.

The external exam turned up something on Gina's neck that had been obscured by her hair; a one inch smear of dark material. To everybody in attendance it looked like grease, but tests would be required to scientifically identify the material.

The remainder of the autopsy produced neither surprises nor new evidence. The head had been severed postmortem with a surgically sharp instrument. The right ear had been punctured with a thin instrument that had then penetrated the brain and caused major brain tissue destruction, intracranial and cerebral hemorrhage.

As the three detectives walked out into sunlight and delicious fresh air, Jake said, "With the exception of the grease, this is a carbon copy of the victim we found on the Tuolumne River. Blood drained, postmortem removal, ice pick in right ear. We can hope that the grease gives us something, but I won't be holding my breath. We held back the whole ice pick thing, I'd like to continue holding it back."

"Seems like the guy likes northern California, rivers, and sharp things," said Luton. "He appears to have a woodie for good looking Italian women."

"Right now he's looking more like a classic serial killer that may have no direct connection to these women," said Jake. "On the other hand, he could be masquerading as a serial to throw us off a more classic murder motive. We still need to look at connections to the women and connections between the women. In both of these cases we don't know where the actual murder took place, so jurisdictions are not only scattered, they're unclear. I hope that we can all work on complementary pieces of the investigation and share information through the task force and JARS."

"What's JARS?" asked Moore.

Jake explained that the Justice Active Records System (JARS) was an electronic repository for all information related to a case except for physical evidence. In addition to text, it stored all types of data including videos, photographs, and audio recordings. It was the case file, the murder book and much more. In addition to secure accessibility for all involved parties, the system automatically indexed things like names, geographic location, businesses, vehicle, license plate, phone number, or any other specific item of interest. Whenever any input to the system indexed an item, the "active" part of the system looked for a matching reference. Any "hit" was pointed out to the report writer, the lead investigator of the associated case, and the writer's of reports indexing the same item. The users could tailor this behavior to get email, text message, or phone call.

"You're making my head spin," said Moore. "I mean, I know how to use a computer, but this sounds kind of crazy."

"The basic system is easy to use," said Jake. "Taking advantage of some of the bells and whistles takes some education. Contact Suzie Eckerling in our office to get special case access since your department doesn't use JARS. She'll also take care of getting your material into the system."

"JARS works well for us," said Luton. "You still have to write the reports, but it's great at correlating information. Jake, I'm going to start my investigation with the victim's family."

"Good plan," agreed Jake. "I'd like Celia or I to go with you on the notifications and early interviews if you're OK with that."

"No problem as long as we do it on my schedule," responded Luton.

"We'll make that work," said Jake. "Do you want to wait for the teeth to do the notify?"

"As long as it gets done today, yes. Notifying the wrong people is something I'd like to avoid."

"We're going to finish up the canvas interviews of people who were at Ruck a Chucky yesterday," said Moore. "Where we can, we'll check out buzzard activity in that area in case the rest of the body got dumped."

"That all sounds good too. If you can work with Suzie, we can get the information you come up with into JARS and everybody can use it. Good plans, guys, I'll talk to you during the task force meeting tomorrow if not sooner."

"Tomorrow," said Moore.

"Call me when you match the teeth," said Luton.

Jake sent off a quick email to Suzie about adding Moore to the system. He then walked back inside to pick up the head for transport to the forensic odontologist in Sacramento.

25. SACRAMENTO

Jake dropped off the head and x-rays for the odontologist then went to grab lunch. As he finished eating, he got the call: The teeth and the x-rays were a match. Gina Roberts was their second victim.

Jake called Celia, told her about the ID, and asked if she'd go out with Luton for the notification and initial interviews.

"Sure Jake," Celia said. "I've had a good morning of ass kicking, I'm ready for some intellectual work. Give me Luton's number."

Jake found Sam Nakamura in his office and touched bases. Sam had just gotten the last commitment to the task force so they were up and running. With Suzie's help, they had all the players set up in JARS. Sam was about to enter Sunday's meeting into the system. The system would then notify all the participants. For participants who used smart calendars, the meeting would be added automatically in their calendar.

Jake found Suzie and they talked about the JARS setup for the case. "Did you get a call from Moore?"

"I did and he's set up with detective access to the case. I talked him through downloading our browser extension so he can get at it."

"Moore and his people will come up with a number of contact reports and other data. I'm afraid that you're going to have to scan them in and tag the appropriate items," said Jake.

"No problemo, that's my job. Besides, I just got a summer intern and I need some scutwork for him."

"Thanks Suzie," said Jake as he headed out to run some of those stupid errands you need to do to keep life functioning.

26. ROSEVILLE

Celia parked in front of the Roseville Police Department just before two o'clock. She'd called Luton, given him the news about the dental match and arranged to meet him so that she could participate in the notification and interviews.

Luton met her and took her back to his desk. Celia pegged Luton at six foot one, 190 with black hair combed back and eyes so dark that they looked black. She also noticed that he exuded fitness and would have been good looking if it weren't for his three-step nose. When she got to his desk she noticed a plaque indicating that he was part of Tri-City SWAT, a cooperative venture of three small towns to have an effective SWAT team. This guy was a stud, she just hoped that he had brains as well.

Luton showed her what he had on Gina Roberts and her husband; not much. He also had the name of Robert's ex-husband, a guy named Mason Resto. Resto had a restraining order requiring him to keep away from Roberts. He looks like fertile ground, Celia thought.

They took Luton's unmarked unit to the Robert's home. Jack Roberts answered the door, looking dejected. He was about five ten with one of those bellies that hung over the belt. Brown hair, hazel eyes and a somewhat doughy face topped off an ordinary looking guy. The home was large, new, and on a golf course.

"Mr. Roberts, I'd like to introduce Celia Moreno from the California Department of Justice," said Luton.

"Pleased to meet you," was Robert's automatic response. Soon he wouldn't be pleased at all.

"Can we sit down and talk?" asked Celia.

"Ah … sure," responded Roberts. They sat in the great room on facing black leather couches. Boldly colored art stared at them from stark white walls.

"Mr. Roberts, I'm sorry to tell you, but your wife has been murdered," said Luton, getting the monkey off his back.

For several heartbeats, there was no response. The doughy face then seemed to melt without a sound. Tears streamed from Robert's eyes as he said, "I knew it, I knew it. She was so beautiful and vibrant, I knew my life was too good to be true."

"We're sorry for your loss, Mr. Roberts," said Celia. "I can only imagine how terrible this news must be to you."

"She, she was so good, how could this happen," Roberts sobbed to himself. He began gasping for air.

Celia and Luton gave him a couple of minutes to compose himself.

Luton asked, "Mr. Roberts, can you think of anybody who might want to hurt your wife?"

Roberts furrowed his brow. "The only person I've ever known who was angry with Gina was her ex-husband, a fellow named Mason Resto. Before Gina got a restraining order, he used to harass her, but I can't believe that even he would murder her. She was just so nice to people; she didn't gossip, she didn't do mean things. This is just so awful, so crazy."

"How about Gina's work, were there potential conflicts with co workers or customers?"

"Gina never talked about anything like that. I guess you should talk to her boss."

"Mr. Roberts, we have to ask a few questions that will be unpleasant for you. Can you tell us what you were doing Tuesday afternoon and evening?"

"What was I doing? Well, I work every day, never leaving before five thirty. I'm an accountant for DeVille & Lombardy. Tuesday evening? Tuesday is bridge night, so I picked up a hamburger after work and drove to Blake Parson's house for bridge. We were done just after nine and I came home. That's when I realized that Gina wasn't home. She's *always* home when I get here. There was a voicemail from her secretary, frantically trying to reach her because a client was waiting for a three o'clock appointment. When I couldn't reach Gina's cell phone I called the police."

"Thank you sir. Were there any conflicts between you and your wife?"

"No no no. Gina and I loved each other. Our lives were ordered and wonderful."

"What can you tell us about your wife's activities on Tuesday?"

"I went through that with your Missing Persons officer. I don't know. We had our breakfast together, then we each went to work. I don't know about her work day."

"Mr. Roberts, did Gina have any good friends?" asked Celia.

"Well, she had friends. We don't, I mean didn't, socialize a lot and I can't think of anybody that Gina spent much time with. Most of our spare time was just the two of us and oriented towards performing arts. We subscribe to the Sacramento Philharmonic, the Music Circus, the Theater Company and San Francisco Opera. "

Luton collected names and numbers for the people and businesses that had come up in conversation. As he stood up to go, he asked Roberts "will you give us permission to search your house for evidence related to your wife's murder?"

"On TV, I see searches tearing places apart. I don't think that I want that."

"Sir, this is not TV. We do everything we can to leave your home in the condition we found it. A search might provide information that would lead us to Gina's killer."

"Well, I guess it's the right thing to do then."

"I have a Consent to Search form I need you to sign and then we can work out the logistics on the phone."

Back in the car, Luton said, "Guy seems kind of a dweeb, but I guess there have been some dorky serial killers, so why not him?"

"I think that the feelings Roberts showed were genuine, this is an absolute disaster for him," said Celia. "He didn't give us a lot to look at other than the ex-husband."

"Let's see if we can find the ex at home," said Luton as he accelerated away from the curb.

They approached Mason Resto's house in the Stoneridge West Village area of East Roseville. The streets were lined with large two story houses and young trees planted in tiny front yards. The neighborhood was a product of this century's first housing boom, worlds apart from the postwar boom housing built in the 1940s. Back then, Roseville was a tiny town of seven thousand revolving around a railway yard. Now over one hundred thousand people live there.

Resto wasn't into maintenance. The house looked a bit ratty, at minimum needing a paint job. The lawn was green, but shaggy and unkempt. The tree in the front yard needed pruning. A red Ford Expedition sat in the driveway.

As they walked to the front door, Celia took a look at the tires on the SUV. Sure enough, it had the Bridgestones. "Rich, lots of these tires are out there, but these are the same brand and size as the tread we found near the Tuolumne."

"That's useful, thanks," replied Luton as he knocked on the door.

After a minute the door was opened by a man dressed in black slacks and a dark purple dress shirt. He had slicked back blonde hair. Celia guessed that the platinum shade came from a bottle. A thin face with grey eyes and a pointy chin covered in stubble. Maybe four inches shorter than Luton, the man seemed to have an average build with a nascent belly.

"Yes?"

"Are you Mason Resto?" asked Luton,

"I am. What can I do for you?"

"I'm Detective Luton of the Roseville Police Department and this is agent Celia Moreno from the California Department of Justice. We're here to talk to you about your ex wife, Gina Roberts."

"Did Gina get herself in trouble?" Resto asked, a touch of hope in his voice.

"Can we come in and sit down?" asked Luton.

"Sure, come on in."

They walked through the door into an entry way that opened to a great room furnished much like the Roberts' house. The exception was a large leather recliner positioned in front of a television that displayed a baseball game. Gina must have furnished this place before the divorce, thought Celia. Unlike the Roberts' house, the room was dusty and the windows were dirty, though everything seemed in order.

"So why would you think that your ex wife would be in trouble?" asked Celia.

"Her holier than thou act couldn't last forever. She wanted to be rich so I figured that she'd cross the line sometime."

"She wanted to be rich?"

"Sure. She left me because I wasn't making enough money then she turned around and married a nebbish who had money."

"But you're not aware of any specifics?" asked Celia.

"No, I don't have anything to do with her, how would I know?"

"When was the last time you saw her?"

"I don't know. Probably about six months ago at the mall."

"And what was your interaction?"

"Interaction? She said hi and I ignored her."

"So you're angry with her?"

"I just don't care for people who use me. That woman ate it up when I was a football player and class president in high school, but when she got her college degree and started making real money she dumped me, leaving me with a big mortgage and hooking up with that geek."

"So what position did you play?" asked Luton.

"I played safety for my junior and senior year."

"So you like to hit people?"

"Well, it's part of the job description," said Resto with a smile. "I modeled myself after the Assassin."

"Jack Tatum, the guy that paralyzed Darryl Stingley back before you were born?" asked Celia.

"That's the guy," responded Resto. "Hell of a hitter. Coach had some films I watched many times."

"Did you play college ball?" asked Luton.

"I did, but not much. That coach played favorites. He played a guy that kissed his ass even though I was better."

"What do you do for a living, Mr. Resto?" asked Celia.

"I sell real estate. I'm good, I've sold a ton of houses."

"Things must be tough now after the real estate collapse."

"It's more of a challenge all right. The damn banks have done us all in because they won't make any loans and are foreclosing everybody. I'm dealing with it though."

"What office do you work out of?"

"I'm with Ellerson Properties. I used to be with White/Marsten but the bastards were cheating me."

"We know that Gina liked music and theater, do you have any hobbies?" asked Celia.

"That stuff that Gina liked is duller than a chain saw run in dirt. I went once or twice, that's all. I like pheasant hunting and fly fishing."

"Lakes or streams?"

"Mostly rivers. It was more fun when I could afford a guide. Damn banks have screwed up my fishing."

Celia looked at Luton.

"I have to tell you that Gina Roberts has been murdered," said Luton.

"Murdered? Really. So how'd she get it?"

"We don't have a cause of death yet," said Luton. "You don't seem bothered much by the news."

"Well it's a surprise. I guess it happens all the time. Too bad for her."

"Mr. Resto, where were you this last Tuesday afternoon?" asked Luton.

"Selling real estate. That's what I do, you know."

"We need you to be more specific about where you were and who you were with."

"Like an alibi, eh? Let me get my calendar." He walked back to the kitchen and returned with his iPad. "I showed some houses starting at five. "

"How about earlier?"

"I was at the office preparing for the showing."

"Who else was in the office?"

"I don't know, I don't remember useless details like that."

"What about Thursday night and Friday morning?"

Resto looked at his calendar again. "Thursday night I was showing houses to the same people I worked with on Tuesday. Friday morning I was out screening houses for a client."

"We'd like a list of those houses you screened."

"I suppose you do. That'd be more work than I'm interested in doing at the moment." Resto was smiling with his mouth, but those grey eyes just looked cold.

Luton looked at Celia. She rolled her head backward an inch towards the door. He stood up and said, "Thanks for your cooperation Mr. Resto. We'll have a few more questions later."

"Nice meeting you fine specimens of government in action," said Resto.

Celia and Luton walked out, got in Luton's car, and headed for the Roseville PD.

"That guy's a slick, nasty piece of work," said Celia. "He sure didn't care that his ex wife has been murdered."

"You got that right," agreed Luton. "I doubt that he's the only guy that wouldn't care if his ex wife is dead. He's one cold sucker though. You notice how he blames somebody else for his problems?"

"I did. He's all, I'm perfect, but everybody's screwing me."

"His story about college football is bullshit," said Luton. "He's too small for a college safety unless he had some unbelievable skill. I like him for the murder. He seems to have motive and opportunity. I'd like to search his house and truck but I don't think that we have enough probable cause."

"I'm afraid that you're right," responded Celia. "We should talk to him again."

"Yeah, maybe tomorrow," said Luton.

"What about phone and credit card records for Gina and Jack Roberts?"

"I'm hoping to get the Roberts records today."

They pulled up to the station. As they got out, Celia said, "Don't forget that task force meeting tomorrow."

"Yeah. You've done these before? Are they useful or just hot air movement?"

"The task force meetings I've done seemed productive. You get a much broader picture of what's going on; the communications and contacts can pay off."

"We'll see," said Luton without much enthusiasm.

On the way home, Celia called Jake to give him an update. "I doubt that the husband did it. He's got alibis that should be easy to check and I thought his grief was genuine. We'll need to check out Gina's place of employment on Monday. We may have a live one in the ex-husband. To quote Luton, he's one cold sucker. He didn't blink an eye when we told him that his ex is dead. On the other hand he showed no signs of knowing she was dead until we told him. We need to look at him harder."

"Sounds like a productive day," said Jake. "How's Luton?"

"He seems to know his shit. He's a SWAT guy so he's gung-ho though he's not excited about task force meetings. He doesn't seem to have a problem working with me. I haven't seen any Sherlock Holmes qualities yet."

"Sounds OK, that's good. Doing anything good tonight?"

"No, I'm just going to put in some report time then relax. I may be joining Luton's interrogation early tomorrow."

"Well get your beauty sleep."

"What the hell does that mean, Jake? I need some beauty?"

"No, no. I uh just uh spouted an old bromide. You, uh, don't need more beauty, you already have some," said Jake, pushing the foot in his mouth a bit deeper.

"Jesus Jake. Celia hung up.

Clicking his headset off, Jake felt bruised. Once in a while, Celia jumped down his throat for what he thought were thin reasons. That's just part of the package, he thought.

Jake called Browning and gave him a full report of the day's activities. Remembering Celia's admonition, he told Browning that Gina may have been killed with an ice pick but that they were holding it back

Home, tequila, bed.

27. ROSEVILLE; SUNDAY

At nine AM, Celia met Luton at the Roseville Police Department. They continued from there in Luton's car to the house of Mason Resto. The SUV was in the driveway again. Luton pounded on the front door and waited. There was no response that they could hear. Luton pounded on the door again, louder and longer. They heard a muffled sound from inside the house. As Luton was about to pound again, the door opened. Resto was standing there barefoot, wearing a silk robe.

"What are you doing here at this ungodly hour?" asked Resto.

"We'd like to talk to you again, Mr. Resto," said Luton. "Will you get dressed and come with us?"

Resto took in the scene for a few seconds, then a slight smile appeared on his face. "I may choose to go with you. It would be interesting to see how a real interrogation room compares to the television versions. I'll go get dressed." He closed the door in their face.

"What an asshole," said Luton. "I'd like to go through his place."

"I would too, but we'll have to find another approach unless we can get more probable cause."

Ten minutes later they had Resto in the back of the car and were heading for the station. Ten more minutes and they had him in an interrogation room.

"Mason, I'm curious as to why your house is neatly arranged but could use some cleaning," said Celia, trying to ease into the interrogation.

"It's simple," said Resto. "Cleaning is not my thing. Cash is tight right now so I haven't hired a cleaning woman in a while. Are you looking for some money on the side, officer?"

"So why did Gina have a restraining order against you?" asked Luton in a conversational tone.

"Oh that," responded Resto. "Right after the divorce I was pissed at her and needed some money. She got kind of upset about me being around, kind of a woman thing, you know?"

"So she gave you money?" asked Celia.

"A few bucks. She left me with the house but there was a big mortgage payment for only one person. She only helped for a while though. I managed to refinance so it's not quite so bad now."

"If she was so helpful, why does it seem like you hate her?"

"She wasn't helpful, she owed me that money for leaving me in a bind. She screwed me over, that's why I despise her. Good riddance."

"Why do you think she was killed?" said Celia.

"Maybe the new husband got tired of her greed or she stiffed one of her clients."

"Did you remember what houses you were looking at on Friday morning?" asked Luton.

"Haven't given it a thought. Well, this has been an experience but I've had enough." Resto got up and walked toward the door.

Luton said, "Whoa there."

Resto responded, "You can't detain me here, you know I'm free to leave." He opened the door and left.

Celia looked at Luton. "Well, we intimidated the hell out of him."

"Not your usual suspect," responded Luton. "We had to give it a shot, but it looks like this is going to have to be evidence based."

Celia and Luton walked over to Roseville Java. After ordering, Celia saw the newspaper headlines. *Browning Warns Women* headed a two column front page piece in the Sacramento Bee. She said to Luton, "Damn. Jake's going to shit a brick when he sees that. He just can't stand headline grabbing."

"Well I'd have to agree with him on that," said Luton. "I let the bosses get upset though, I just do my job. I should check out Ellerson Properties, see if Resto's boss or coworkers know anything. I've already got records for Gina and Jack Roberts, I can finish going through them today."

"Then there's Gina's work to check out," said Celia. "I think that we could get Jake to do that unless you want it for yourself."

"Help is good, I don't need to be the Lone Ranger. We'd better walk back so we can do your task force meeting."

They'd reached a conference room with a speakerphone with five minutes to spare before the eleven o'clock meeting.

28. SACRAMENTO

At twenty minutes past sunrise, Jake's morning coffee was dripping as he stepped out front to get his paper. He filled a large mug with *We Don't Shoot To Kill, We Shoot To Stay Alive* written on it and sat down in his Stressless recliner. He took a sip of hot, black coffee and unfolded the paper. The headline made him forget to swallow and he burned his tongue. After he gulped down the mouthful he said, "Son of a bitch. More Browning press."

Tank looked at Jake for a second, then went back to drinking water, thinking, *why is he bothering me?*

Jake read the article. *Chuck Browning, head of the California Department of Justice's Bureau of Investigation & Intelligence held a press conference Saturday evening to warn northern California women of the dangers they face from the Whitewater Killer. Browning said that the killer's pattern is to kidnap affluent women from the parking lots of upscale clothing stores. He warned women to be ultra vigilant in parking lots and suggested that they consider shopping with a friend to minimize the danger.*

Browning, a candidate for California Attorney General, went on to say that the women had apparently been killed with an ice pick and had been mutilated, (only the heads of victims had been found). Browning said that his bureau is now running a task force involving five law enforcement agencies focused entirely on apprehending the monster responsible for these killings. While he couldn't divulge details, his people are pursuing a number of promising leads in the case.

Arrogant, publicity hound asshole was Jake's first thought. This guy is doing more to scare women than protect them. The jerk publicized ice picks after I told him that we were holding that back. Then he makes sure that the killer knows that we know his kidnap pattern. All this to get his name on the front page. God, I can't stand the man.

Jake picked up the phone and called Sam Nakamura at home. After five rings he got a weak "hello?".

"Sam, this is Jake. Have you seen the Sunday paper?"

"Jake? Jesus, I haven't even seen my bathroom, you woke me up."

"Look, that bastard Browning is screwing up our case to get himself publicity. In addition to releasing information that he shouldn't, I'm sure he's pissed off every department we're working with. I'm not going to talk to him anymore, he can kiss my ass." If it was possible, steam would have been coming out of Jake's ears.

"I'm walking out to get the paper now, Jake. Cool down and let's see what can be done. OK, I've got the paper, give me a minute to look at it."

Jake got up and refilled his mug while he was waiting. He couldn't sit back down, instead he paced the kitchen floor.

"So Jake, wasn't the ice pick thing a holdback?" said Sam.

"Yeah, and I told him that just yesterday."

"That sucks. I could go over his head on this, but since the Attorney General endorsed Browning as his successor, it would backfire. I see the parking lot stuff as something the perp knows we know anyway. Browning's attempt to scare women doesn't hurt the case. Acting like the commander of California law enforcement will piss people off, but that's a done deal."

"Damn it Sam, I shouldn't have to deal with this. This guy should be supporting us, not screwing us up."

"I agree Jake, but we'll just have to live with it. There's no way to keep the case information from him, his boy Foreman has access to it all. If you refuse to talk to him, he's liable to pull you off the case. That should be my call, but if I chose not to follow his directive and went to the Attorney General about it, I'd lose."

"I may have a hard time remembering to call him."

"Early onset Alzheimer's? Illegitimi non carborundum, Jake."

"Yeah. See you at the task force meeting." Jake hung up.

Jake arrived at the DOJ building about ten thirty, having driven downtown with the top down in his Boxter, trying to enjoy the late spring morning. The DOJ had a slick room setup for remote conferencing. Most of its features wouldn't be used today because the remote participants weren't set up with the computer software yet. The justification for the room was that a quality setup would encourage people to participate. Meetings would take less time and be more efficient (if, of course, the leaders and participants could run an efficient meeting).

Sam Nakamura arrived with Suzie Eckerling. One of Suzie's several hats was to be the expert on the conference gear and software. Don Foreman walked in, dressed in a grey suit, the only suit in the room. At five minutes to nine, Willy Chocolate Jackson walked in with a "you sure know how to booger up a Sunday morning." The other participants began calling in.

Sam, as task force leader, kicked off the meeting. "Good morning everybody, I'm Sam Nakamura the task force commander." He read off names and organizations of the participants. "Between now and the next meeting I'd like you all to have our videoconference application installed on your laptops; talk to Suzie if you need help. For this meeting, please say your name when you speak up. We're going to make these meetings as short and effective as possible. The main purpose is to share knowledge and ideas in pursuance to capturing our perp. Historical information on the case is available to all of you in the JARS system, so we'll just be talking about recent developments, theories and plans. This time only, give us a brief historical summary. We'll start with Tuolumne Sheriff's Investigator Andy Katashi."

"Good morning," said Katashi. "The first victim's severed head was found thirteen days ago on top of a rock in the Tuolumne River. It was found by a group of whitewater rafters who were mostly law enforcement, including Appleby and Moreno from the DOJ. Forensics results were meager, they're in the system. We had agreed to hold back the probable cause of death as an ice pick, but some DOJ guy made it public this morning. Our recent activity has been in looking for property in our county that is owned by the victim's husband or one of the people connected to her. We've also checked with rental agents. Negative results. At this point we have no active investigation, though our department's people know we'd like to find a kill site and remains.

"Thanks Andy," said Sam. "Next is Walnut Creek PD detective Torrey Bonner."

"We believe that the first victim, Sophia Mancuso, was abducted from the parking lot of a Walnut Creek Niebaums store four days before her remains were discovered. There's evidence suggesting that she got back to her car in the lot before the abduction. Sophia was an affluent resident of Walnut Creek, a wife and mother. We've looked hard at the husband, but don't have much on him. He remains a person of interest and we'll be looking at what he was doing when this second victim was taken and discarded. We've now been through most of the victim's close connections but nobody stands out. Recently we've widened the circle of people we're talking to. So far, the victim is looking like a squeaky clean citizen. We've discovered nobody with any connection to Tuolumne County."

"Thanks Torrey. Now Placer County Sheriff's Detective Randy Moore."

"Remains were discovered last Friday in the Ruck a Chucky recreation area, on the Middle fork of the American River. The severed head was posed on a boulder just off of the shore and was discovered by a rafter. I guess that Willy Jackson will discuss forensics. The autopsy showed results identical to what I read about the first victim: head severed postmortem with a sharp tool, something similar to an ice pick into brain through the right ear. Given the state of the remains, she'd either been killed no earlier than Thursday or her remains had been isolated and refrigerated. Material that looked like grease was found on her neck hidden under her hair. Like Tuolumne, we were holding back the ice pick and frankly, I'm disgusted by the leak. We've now interviewed all but two people we know were down there during the relevant time frame, nothing we got stands out other than the head had to be placed between Thursday dusk and Friday afternoon. We had a nearby site with a lot of buzzard activity, but it turned out to be a dead cow. The department will continue keeping an eye out for the rest of her remains or a kill site. We're going to finish our interviews and revisit a couple of them."

"Jake Appleby here Randy. Have you gone through the permit envelopes deposited at the Ruck a Chucky entrance?"

"You know, I asked my partner to pull them, but I haven't heard anything else. Thanks for bringing it up."

"Next is Roseville PD detective Rich Luton," said Sam.

"The remains found in Ruck a Chucky were confirmed as Roseville missing person Gina Roberts on Saturday by the DOJ odontologist. Gina went missing Tuesday afternoon, we found her car in the Niebaums parking lot on Thursday. The trunk of her car contained two shopping bags, the receipt indicating a purchase in Niebaums at 12:50 PM Tuesday. The crime scene crew found AFID tags from a Taser near her car. The tags traced to a Taser that was stolen along with four cartridges. I'll be checking the victim's credit card records today. We've interviewed the husband, who claims good alibis, though we haven't confirmed them yet. The husband has consented to a search and we'll do it tomorrow. We talked to the ex-husband who wasn't bothered by hearing that she was murdered. He doesn't have an alibi for the kidnap time frame, but may have one for the dump time. The guy's slick and not cooperative. He didn't give us anything in an interrogation, then he just got up and walked out. He owns a red Ford Expedition that has the same type of tires identified on the Tuolumne case. We've got more interviewing and alibi checking to do tomorrow."

Jake spoke up, "Thanks Rich. Torrey, it looks like our guy's using a Taser. Was there any sign of that in or around your victim's car?"

"I've heard nothing about that, Jake. Her car was in the lot overnight before we found it, so the confetti could have blown away or been picked up by one of those vacuum trucks that cleans parking lots. We'll go back to the lot and look."

Sam said, "From the DOJs Central Valley Forensics unit, Vern Lund."

"Good morning. We did the forensics for the Tuolumne River pose site. As many of you know, we didn't find anything to lead you to a killer. We have tire tracks identified to a make, model and size, but about a quarter million of those tires have been sold in California, enough for over 60,000 vehicles. We have a boot tread, but again, there will be lots of boots using that tread. Neither had unique damage we could use for a specific ID. Last and least, we have a cotton thread, probably from a navy sweatshirt."

"Willy Jackson, DOJ Sacramento forensics."

"Much of the site in Ruck a Chucky had too much activity for us to pick up tracks, but we do have a track from a Korker wader boot. Just like Vern found, the posing boulder produced no evidence. The most intriguing evidence is the grease found on the remains. It's automotive quality grease with considerable foreign matter mixed in. The one component we've identified so far is ponderosa pine pollen. Ponderosa's will sometimes grow at a twelve hundred foot elevation in this area, but generally they're happy at two thousand feet or above. South of Auburn this gives you an area uphill from Highway 49. If you find a source for the grease, we can do a high probability match on it, but it won't exclude other possibilities. Based on the disposal site, your perp seems meticulous."

"Kaya Lane, DOJ profiling."

"Hi everyone. I've reviewed the records on both killings and I visited the second killing crime scene. I can give you, with a high probability, some characteristics and traits of our killer. We've got an organized killer, meaning that he plans what he does and is careful to avoid being caught. He's a white male, age 25 to 45, above average intelligence, at least middle class. There's a good chance that he was abused by a female parent and the victims may be chosen because they resemble that parent. I would expect that he tortured the victims even though we haven't seen evidence yet. It's possible that he'll take trophies from the victims: jewelry, personal items or body parts. He's a self-centered person who manipulates people, feels no guilt or remorse for his actions, and blames his problems on others. He'll pay lots of attention to the media. This head display was carefully planned out and done for shock value. The goal of a person like this is often power. There's a good chance that there is no connection between our killer and his victims. They could just be victims of opportunity."

Sam nodded at Jake to take his turn.

"Jake Appleby again. First of all I'm going to apologize for public comments made by a certain high level DOJ employee. They don't come from the people you're dealing with and we have no control over them. I know that you people are doing the real work and that you're critical to this investigation."

"With all due respect to my colleague Kaya, we know that profiling has hits and misses, so it's a tool that often works, but sometimes doesn't. In particular, we cannot be boxed in by the notion that the victims are chosen only by opportunity, we must do the hard work of looking for connections."

"I'm going to do some summarizing, ask some questions and make some suggestions. First, the connections and similarities. Two affluent and attractive thirty-something married Italian women. Both abducted from a parking structure after shopping at Niebaums on an afternoon. No witnesses to the abductions. Four and then three days after abduction, their severed heads were posed on a boulder in a river often used for whitewater rafting, kayaking and fishing. Postmortem head severing and a thin instrument through the ear are identical. Virtually no forensic evidence. Initial investigations of people of interest have not turned up hard evidence, though we've just started with this Resto character. We have not found the remainder of either body, we don't know where the murders took place."

"Now differences. The two abduction locations are 92 miles apart. The dump sites are 142 miles apart. We've got four different law enforcement jurisdictions. The first location has tough access, rarely sees anybody other than rafters, kayakers and occasional fisherman. The second location is much more public. The first victim had a daughter, no kids for the second. The first victim did volunteer work, the second was a financial planner. The discovery on the first victim was by law enforcement personnel on vacation, including Celia and I, a dubious coincidence. So far, nobody connected with the first victim does whitewater rafting, kayaking, or whitewater river fishing. The second victim has an ex-husband who fishes on rivers."

"You people are professionals and will have good ideas as you think about this case. Please share them via JARS or task force meetings. Some questions for the back of your mind: why heads? why rivers?"

"Now some guesses and opinion. This smelled like a serial case in the beginning and needs to be treated as one now. If you have *Practical Homicide Investigation*, review the section on serials. The people that do serials are either smarter or more cunning than our usual mopes, often know our procedures well and may have worked in law enforcement. They like to see themselves as victors over the police and may manipulate evidence to win their game. They tend to increase the rate of their killings over time. This guy may have been smart enough on his own to stop using Niebaums parking lots, but you know that he'll stop now that his pattern was pointed out in today's paper."

"Right now I think that it's important that we look hard for connections between the two victims. Torrey and Rich, if you disagree or need help, let me know. That's all I have; Celia?"

"This is Celia Moreno. I've been working on the coincidence angle. How could we be the ones to discover the first victim? We've decided that somebody we've busted isn't going to know when and where we were rafting. It would have to be somebody at least close to our normal lives. The other angle that we should all keep in mind is that this guy may be staging a series of murders to cover up a specific murder. That's all I have."

"This is Sam Nakamura. Does anybody have something to add?"

Silence.

"Fine," said Sam. "I'd like to remind all of you to ensure that all information goes into JARS. The system is, among other things, a murder book that you can all access. For those of you who don't use JARS and must produce paper for your local systems, please get your paper to Suzie ASAP and she'll get it into JARS. If you have a significant development occur between task force meetings, please use the broadcast function of JARS, it will notify everybody and add your development to the record. Our next task force meeting will be Tuesday at four PM. Please ensure that you've got our videoconference package operational by then. We're adjourned."

"Not bad Sam," said Jake after all phones were disconnected. "It went fast, we don't seem to have blowhards or slackers."

"Yeah, it should have given a bigger picture to the Roseville and Placer County people," responded Sam. "Let's see if we can't have significant input to Tuesday's meeting. Since I'm such a good guy, I'm going to give all of you the rest of the day off."

"You're such a benevolent dictator, Sam," said Celia. "I'm grateful to get half of Sunday for myself."

Celia walked out with Kaya and said, "Jake was hard on you in there, he just can't get past his bad experience with a profiler."

"Yeah, I could have done without his speech, but there's some validity to what he said. Profiling is an imperfect tool. His attitude and tone of voice implied that it was a poor tool, and he's wrong about that. What was his bad experience?"

Celia replied, "As a green homicide detective he bought a profile hook line and sinker and couldn't get a solve. The perp killed a second person while Jake was working the case. A year later the guy was picked up for another case and they found evidence for Jake's case. The perp didn't match the profile at all."

"I can see that making Jake sour on profiling, but he had his own part in the screw up. He should never have treated the profile as pure gospel."

"I'm sure that he knows that at some level. He'll get over it someday. If your profile works, that'll help. How about lunch?"

"Thanks, but I have a lot of shopping to do so I'm going to have to eat on the run. Let's do it another day."

"Take care, Kaya."

"Bye Celia."

29. ROSEVILLE; MONDAY

Jake drove from home to the Roseville Police Department, stopping along the way for a breakfast burrito at one of his favorite breakfast places, Pauline's. Jake enjoyed Pauline's because he was on a first name basis with the owner and the staff. Everybody chatted together about surface events in their life, making it a comfortable place.

Celia and Luton were already there when Jake walked in. Luton said "I thought that Celia and I would go over the Robert's phone and credit card records. Maybe you could check out Jack Robert's work alibi, then check out Gina Robert's workplace?"

"I can do that," said Jake. This was basic detective drudge work, but he was willing to show Luton that he could be a team player. "I'll plan to come back here when I'm done." He got up and headed to the parking lot, chuckling to himself about Luton's hanging on to Celia. Who but a male chauvinist wouldn't want to work with the pretty one?

Luton and Celia walked to his desk in a classic bullpen that smelled of too many guys and not enough fresh air. Celia got her laptop going and connected to Roseville's network. Luton gave Celia the phone records and started on the credit card data.

Celia began with a file from the telephone company containing the phone calls from Robert's home phone as well as a file from their cellular company. She fed them into a program that took the numbers, looked them up on the internet, and identified the owner of the number. Multiple entries of the same phone number were highlighted with their own color. Celia stepped through the list. None of the names rang a bell or looked interesting. Neither of the cell phones were used during the day of the kidnapping. multiple calls were listed from the home phone to Gina's cell starting at 9:28 PM. That made sense, the husband got home and was looking for his wife. Celia added the call list to the JARS case file. The system would index each number and look for matches.

Looking up, Celia saw that Luton was on the last page of the credit card information.

"I'm not seeing anything of interest in the Robert's credit card records," said Luton. We already knew that she'd made purchases at Niebaums before she was abducted. No further charges were made on her card. None of the charges that I looked at seem interesting."

Celia told him about the phone records. "Why don't we swap information to see if a fresh look brings up anything?"

"Sure," said Luton.

It was noon when they both decided there was no more information to find in the data and headed for lunch.

Jake had verified that Jack Roberts had been at work on the afternoon that his wife had been kidnapped. According to Robert's boss, the man was always at work and always working; a stereotypical accountant.

Gina's office was more interesting. She worked as a financial planner with a large brokerage firm, giving "free" planning to account holders. Jake and some of her clients understood that it wasn't free, the client paid for it via account charges and commissions on products that Gina recommended. Despite disclosures given on paper to clients, there was room for misunderstandings. Clients could become irate if they were steered into investments that performed poorly and they then realized that the firm took its cut off the top.

Gina's boss professed to love Gina's work, claiming that "she was a wonderful employee, her clients liked her and she did a great job for them."

"She didn't have an angry client or two?" questioned Jake.

"That does happen in this business of course. People ignore our talk about risk then want somebody else to be at fault when the risk becomes real and they lose money. Once in a while one of these clients will get aggressive and abusive. Gina hadn't had any of these."

"Could she have had angry clients that didn't confront the firm?"

"That's possible."

"I'd like a copy of Gina's client list."

"I'm sorry, but that information is confidential. You'll need a warrant to get it."

"That's unfortunate. We'll see what the DA thinks. Can you describe Gina's work habits and interactions with her coworkers?"

"Gina was a hard worker and pleasant to everybody. She wasn't a social person, at least at work. She brought lunch and ate at her desk. She didn't participate in the organized social activities we have. As far as I know, she didn't connect with any of our staff outside of work."

"Is there any other information about Gina that comes to mind?"

"I can't think of anything. I'm sad to lose her."

"Did Gina have a secretary or a teammate?"

"She had an administrative assistant. I'll take you to him."

They walked to the assistant's desk and Jake was introduced. Jake handed the manager his card and said, "Thanks for your time. If you think of anything, please give me a call."

Jake asked Gina's assistant, "Did anything unusual occur on the day that Gina disappeared?"

"It seemed like a normal day. She did get a call from her ex-husband, that doesn't happen often."

"Did she tell you this or did you answer the phone?"

"I answer most of Gina's calls and I answered this one. I'd guess that he was looking for money again, though he didn't say so."

"Did Gina call him back or talk to you about what he said?"

"I believe that she called him back, but I don't know what they talked about. Gina kept her private life to herself."

"On earlier calls from the ex-husband did you get any information from him?"

"Well, at least once he used the phrasing, "I need another loan". That implied to me that she'd been giving him some."

"Anything else?"

"No. The guy was self-assured and demanding but I didn't get a lot of information from him."

"On a different topic, did Gina have angry clients?"

"Angry? We had a few that I'd call concerned or maybe upset, but nobody that I'd label angry."

"OK, we may want to revisit that if we get a warrant for client names. Thanks for your help."

"Sure. Good to meet you. I wish you great luck finding the sonofabitch that killed her. She was a nice person, she didn't deserve that."

Back at the Roseville PD, the group exchanged information. As Luton summarized it, the phone and credit card information wasn't worth squat.

Jake described his interviews, mentioning the phone call from Resto. Then he said, "Probably some of Gina's clients have lost meaningful money in the last couple of years. These people could have motive, though how they'd connect to our first victim I don't know. The problem is that the office manager won't release the information and we don't have probable cause for a warrant."

"That line of investigation seems like a stretch, but we could keep it in mind if all else fails," remarked Celia.

"This case is strange enough that the answer might be anywhere," said Luton. "I'm betting that the answer is Resto, but I'll add Gina's clients to the bottom of my to-do list. Based on your interview, Resto lied to us about his last contact with Gina. I sure wish that we could get at Resto's house, car, and his records."

"We wouldn't want this to be easy," said Jake.

"Speak for yourself," said Luton. "I'm going home for an early dinner, then over to Jack Roberts' house to collect information that could help find a connection between Gina and your first victim. I'll be digging at the same information on Resto tomorrow."

"Jake and I will go check out the brokerage where Resto works," said Celia. "Talk to you tomorrow."

Jake and Celia left the Roseville PD, driving their cars ten minutes to the Ellerson Properties office. They found Pete Ellerson and introduced themselves..

"We need some information about Mason Resto," said Jake.

"Why?" responded a cautious Ellerson

"We're doing routine information gathering for an investigation into the murder of his ex wife," said Celia.

"Whoa. You think he murdered his wife?"

"He's one of many persons of interest, we're just doing routine checking. We have no opinion on Resto's involvement at this time," Celia said. This guy had no need to know what was going on with the investigation.

"Resto talks a good game, but he's sold only a couple of inexpensive homes in the last nine months. I'm thinking that he's kind of lazy."

"That won't produce much income," said Celia.

"No it doesn't. Not for him or for me. I've been keeping my eyes out for somebody to replace him. He made good money during the boom, but so did most everybody."

"Does he have friends at work?"

"Not that I know about. I mean, he talks to people on occasion, but I've never seen him buddy up with anybody. To tell you the truth, he's not a likeable guy. Like I said, he talks a good game, but his behavior can be sleazy."

"How about his ability to plan and organize things?" asked Jake.

"When he decides to work, his planning and organizing is great. I've seen him create great plans for marketing homes and manage negotiations well."

"We need to know whether he was here around midday last Tuesday and early morning Friday," said Jake.

"Tuesday. I wasn't in on Tuesday and wasn't here until after lunch on Friday. You're welcome to ask our receptionist and the other realtors. "

"Thanks for your time, Mr. Ellerson," said Celia as they headed for the receptionist.

Fifteen minutes later Jake and Celia were out in the parking lot next to Celia's car, a yellow Ford Mustang GT with a polished set of custom aluminum wheels.

"Nobody remembers Resto being here, so they won't give him an alibi for the snatch or the dump," said Celia."He still looks good for it."

"I agree, we just need some real evidence. Where are we going to find it?"

"This guy's smart, right? He should know that killing and cutting up two women would leave forensic tracks. He'd be smart enough not to do that at home. The guy's a realtor. In this market, houses get listed, don't sell, and come off the market. He has to know about empty houses all over the area and he could have duplicated any key that's ever been in a lock box. He could have chopped her in lots of places we'll never know to look at."

"That's an excellent, if depressing, point C." said Jake. "The resources it would take to check out every empty house that's been on the Multiple Listing Service are beyond what we could come up with."

"We could check for burglary reports where the owners found blood."

"That's reasonable. Why don't you pass that on to Luton. It's his department's territory."

"Will do," said Celia. She opened her car door and got in. Jake caught a flash of a long, good looking leg before she pulled her skirt down.

Jake said, "Steve and Terry are meeting me at the Blue Ball. Want to Join us?"

"Sure. See you there."

30. SACRAMENTO; TUESDAY

Rich Luton finished the half hour drive from Roseville to the East Sacramento home of Lia Iaconnelli, the mother of Gina Roberts. Her home was in a nicely kept neighborhood of small houses built in the housing boom that followed World War II. As with most of Sacramento, the street was shaded by large trees and the houses were fronted with lawns. The woman that opened the door looked like a slightly older version of her attractive daughter. The dark hair, olive complexion and deep, dark eyes told him that this was Gina's mother. The red in her eyes revealed that she had been crying. Luton's gaze followed the gold chain around her neck to the gold cross that fell gently between her breasts. He noticed her cleavage then quickly brought his eyes back to her face and introduced himself.

"Pleased to meet you, detective," Lia responded in what sounded like an Italian accent. Of course she wasn't pleased at all; dealing with her daughter's death was a terrible ordeal for her.

"I've never heard the name Lia before, it's a nice name." said Luton, trying to be sociable.

"It's Italian. I don't know how common it is in Italy but it's not common here. My parents moved to Sacramento from Italy when I was eight."

"Mrs. Iaconnelli, I'm terribly sorry for your loss. I'm working full time on your daughter's case and will do my best to bring the perpetrator to justice."

"I appreciate that, detective. I had always heard how difficult it was to lose a child. It's just crushing me and I can't get it out of my mind for more than a minute."

"I'm sure that it's more difficult than I can understand," responded Luton. "Can you think of anyone who might have wanted to harm your daughter?"

"Gina was such a nice person, everybody liked her. I never would have thought that somebody who knew Gina could harm her."

"What about her ex-husband, Mason Resto?"

"Mason is a sad boy. He was such a good looking and popular kid in high school, even a football star. That seems to have been the high point of his life. Imagine seeing that your life has gone downhill since you were eighteen. Gina, on the other hand, kept growing and blossoming. She had outgrown Mason by the time she was twenty five. Gina said that he's even gone downhill and gotten more bitter since their divorce. Despite all that, I just can't picture Mason doing such a horrible thing to my daughter."

"Might your husband have a different view, mam?"

"Oh detective, I thought you knew. My husband passed away four years ago. Now it's just me."

"Sorry ma'am, I didn't know."

"That's OK detective, I'm used to it now."

"Mrs. Iaconnelli, one of the areas we work on is identifying connections between a victim and possible perpetrators. In this case, we're also trying to find connections between Gina and another victim who was killed in a similar manner. Can you talk me through the highlights of Gina's life – where she went to school, where she's lived, organizations she's belonged to, friends and special interests she's had?"

"I can do that, detective."

Back in his Roseville office, Luton called Torrey Bonner in Walnut Creek.

"Bonner."

"Torrey, this is Rich Luton, Roseville PD. I've got life highlights for our vic, thought we could see if there are connections to yours."

"Sure Rich, let me get my file opened. You want to run through your list and I'll look for matches?"

"Sure. Tell me when you're ready."

"Go."

"Kit Carson middle school, Sacramento High School, Sacramento City College, Mills College."

"Hey, we have a hit. Sophia went to Mills College. Let's see, she graduated in … 1995."

"Gina graduated in 1996, so there's a year overlap. Do you know anything about the college?"

"Yeah, a bit," responded Bonner. "It's a small women's college over the hill from us in Oakland. Quite a while ago they tried to convert it to coed but there was a big uproar and it's still a women's college. You think there're any men's colleges left?"

"No. Men's colleges can't be politically correct."

"But women's colleges are?"

"You know how that goes. Not my problem this week," said Luton. Can you check out their connection at the school?"

"I'll give it a shot. Why don't you finish your highlight list."

"Yeah. Gina married in 1996 right out of college to a Mason Resto who went to Sacramento High, one year at Sacramento City College. She got a job with a company named Star & Hollings, a brokerage company. She's a financial planner and was still with them when she died. She didn't have any interests or hobbies that would generate non-local connections."

"None of that cross checks," said Bonner. "How about a list of friends and acquaintances for her?"

"Her mother and husband have promised me lists. I'll put them into JARS when I get them."

"Give me a ring when you do that. We don't use that system here, but Moreno hooked me up and I guess I can figure it out."

"I will. Talk to you later."

"Later," said Bonner as he hung up.

Just before four, Jake, Celia and Sam Nakamura arrived at the DOJs videoconference suite. Designed to make meetings between geographically disbursed people effective and as personal as possible, it was constantly being upgraded as technology evolved. Remote participants could be on a telephone, connected via a web browser, or by a conference application supplied by the DOJ. For this meeting, everybody should be using the application.

The people physically present sat on one side of a long table. Each place at the table had a microphone, video camera, power and a secure Ethernet connection for the occupant's laptop, which ran the conference application. On the other side of the room, mounted on the wall, were seven large flat screen monitors.

Suzie Eckerling was already in the room and had things ready for the second task force meeting. Over the next ten minutes, the local and remote participants showed up and at two minutes after four Sam started the meeting.

"This is Sam Nakamura. Those of you who are using the remote conference application should be seeing my image, name and organization in the upper left portion of your screen. The equivalent of this in our conference room shows the speaker currently having the floor on our central screen. On the bottom of your screen should be a scrolling window listing the participants who are signed on. When another participant is commenting, his or her picture will show up on the upper right of your screen. When the speaker is showing any form of visual, the visual will fill most of your screen. You'll catch on. I did and I'm not good with tech."

"I select the person having the floor based on your requests. If you have a topic to discuss, click the checkbox labeled 'ready to talk' on the lower left of your screen. If you want to comment on what's being said by whoever has the floor, just start talking. The system will pick the first to talk, display him or her on the right side of screens, and route the audio."

"Now to the business at hand. First Jake."

"I'd like to show you one of the features of JARS and how it relates to this case," said Jake. "JARS holds location information in a form acceptable to Google Earth, so you can see the geographical information relative to our case." Jake made a few mouse clicks and people's computer screens and one of the wall mounted screens filled with a Google Earth window showing a satellite view of North America. They could also see a mouse cursor replicating the one on Jake's computer.

"You'll see on the left a list of placemarks that have been identified for this case. I'll double click on "head one". The North America display zoomed in on a portion of a river viewed from an altitude of five thousand feet. "You can zoom in and out as well as move locations. I'll zoom out to show all of our current case locations and you'll see a pin on the Walnut Creek and Roseville shopping centers as well as the location where Gina Robert's head was found. It's obvious from this view that Lodi or Sacramento could be the geographic center of the action so far. This is a great tool; let it stimulate some geographic understanding and maybe ideas. That's it from me."

"Randy Moore," said Sam.

As Moore's image flashed up with the subtitle, "Randy Moore, Placer Sheriff's Detective," he said, "We've gone through all the permit envelopes to the Ruck a Chucky area. Most of them were people we interviewed on site. Two we haven't interviewed yet. One listed a license plate that isn't valid: 5XCS783 is listed by the DMV as junked. That particular envelope didn't have prints on the envelope or the $10 bill, so it smells bogus. This could be our guy, wanting a permit just in case the rangers were checking while he was down there. The make and model just lists "chev" so you'd expect the vehicle to be a Chevrolet."

"That leaves out Mason Resto's SUV," said Rich Luton.

"And Pauli Mancuso's," said Torrey Bonner.

"We've gotten a few useful bits from interviews," resumed Moore. "A red SUV of undetermined make and a white Chevy Suburban were seen and we haven't identified an owner for either. Witnesses remember a couple of fisherman. One had a creel, pretty unusual these days."

"Resto's SUV is red," commented Luton.

Nobody else spoke up. "That's it for me," said Moore.

"Rich Luton."

"I've focused on Mason Resto, the ex-husband of our Roseville victim. Our victim apparently has been giving Resto money, we have requested check images from the bank. He's got motive, he hates his ex wife. He's got opportunity since he has no confirmation of his alibi for the kidnap or dump days. He seems clever enough to run an operation like this and he fits much of the profile laid out Sunday."

Kaya's face popped up on displays. "I concur. I've read the reports on Resto and he seems to fit the organized offender profile. His clear lack of empathy for the victim is telling. The first victim may have been a trial run, intended to make us think that the second victim was also chosen at random."

"Pictures of Resto are in JARS," said Jake. "Could Placer show them in a six pack to campers?"

"We can give that a shot," said Moore.

"The search of Gina Robert's house yesterday turned up nothing," said Luton. "That's all I have."

"Torrey Bonner."

"Rich Luton and I got together looking for correlations between the two victims. The one thing we found in common is Mills College. I'll be heading over there tomorrow. We searched the Niebaums parking lot and found two AFIDs that came from the stolen group of Taser cartridges. Our perp must have used a Taser on Sophia. "

"Anybody else?" asked Sam.

Jake's image flashed up. "I picked up something using the JARS calendar/timeline tool. If you look at the calendar view of our case now, it stands out that the abductions and head poses are happening on Tuesdays and Fridays."

"Anybody else?"

Silence.

"OK then. Thanks everybody. We'll meet again Thursday at four."

31. SACRAMENTO; WEDNESDAY

Jake and Celia sat in their office and contemplated the case. "So what isn't being actively looked at by somebody on our four jurisdiction team?" asked Celia.

"That permit envelope from Ruck a Chucky is interesting to me," said Jake. "I didn't get the sense that Moore was going to pursue it, did you?"

"No, it seemed like he figured it had been processed and dropped into the case documentation."

"The envelope tells us some things about our perp. First, he probably thought through whether to fill one out or not and decided that it was better to do it. That suggests to me that he thinks through situations, analyzes risks, and is cautious. The small risk that he might be stopped without a permit and be identified down on the river was significant enough for him to take the risk of doing the envelope."

"I'd buy that thought, as long as I didn't have to pay much for it," said Celia. "If you follow that logic, then what he wrote on the envelope can't be far from correct. He wouldn't want the permit checker to encounter completely bogus information on the envelope."

"Indeed. So following the logic train a step further, he was driving a Chevrolet. Selling a ranger that you put down the wrong manufacturer would be tough. Based on the Tuolumne tracks, it's a pickup or SUV. He'd have to have the license plate number on the envelope be close to that on the vehicle so it would look like he made a simple error. The license plate format on the envelope isn't correct for a truck, so it's an SUV.

"Makes sense," responded Celia. "Because no prints were on the envelope or the money we can conclude that he recognized the danger in leaving an envelope and took measures to minimize the risk. Of course, by wiping the money he told us that this envelope was his."

"Yeah, used money always has prints on it. Of course a permit checker wouldn't have known that there were no prints, so that fact didn't increase his short term risk. If the perp had thought about the print issue early enough he could have picked up a ten someplace and not gotten his prints on it. The existing prints on the money would have led us on a useless chase, something he'd enjoy. He's not perfect."

"Perfect enough so far," commented Celia.

"He'll make his mistake. We just need to be sharp enough to see it. Let's play with the license number and see what we find. If you were checking permits, what kind of mistake on 5XCS783 would you find credible?"

"The first one that comes up is just a number transposition. Given that there are the right number of characters and the letters are in the right spot, I'd look at transposing the digits 783."

"So there'd be only six permutations of those numbers and one of those, 783, has already been checked. Let's see what the DMV database has for the other five," said Celia as she rolled up to her computer.

"We have five active plates, but only one is a Chevrolet with body type UT," said Celia with a tinge of excitement. "Plate 5XCS387 is registered to a Tom Ditkam at a Nevada City address. How can Nevada City be in a California DMV database?"

"You don't know about Nevada City?" chuckled Jake. "It's an old mining town only 3 miles from Grass Valley, maybe 30 miles from Ruck a Chucky. The town was named Nevada, Spanish for snow. When the desert to the east became a state and stole the name Nevada, the town changed its name to Nevada City.

"Thanks for the geography and history lesson, wise one. What do you think about our hit?"

"I think it's promising. I wonder if it's too easy."

"It could be. If instead of transposing the three numbers our perp changed just one of the letters, we'd have, uh, another

75 plates to look up. What's the highest number the state has used for the first digit?"

"I think it's six. Let's google that. "

A quick check determined that plates issued after 1993 would begin with 3,4,5, or 6.

"So if he only changed the first digit, we have another 3 plates. If he changed the first digit and transposed the last three, we've got 18. Of course if he changed a letter and transposed the last three we have…, uh, 75 times 6 gives us 450. Yuck."

"OK, command decision. We'll look up the 75 letter combinations and 18 number variations. If we split them up between you, me, and Suzie Eckerling we can knock it out quickly."

"You're in command? I'm surprised," said Celia with a hint of a smile.

"Well … I'm older," was Jake's comeback.

"You are old. Is it depressing?"

"I'm going to call Suzie."

An hour later they had come up with another six Chevrolet "UT" vehicles. They called Randy Moore in Auburn and described what they'd done.

"That's smart work," said Moore. "How about if my partner and I call these people with a real soft approach, like we're looking for additional witnesses?"

"I like that approach," said Jake. "This just gives us some place to look; it has no real evidence value. We don't want to spook our perp if he's one of these seven."

"We'll act like dumb country cops," responded Moore.

"Great. We'll email you the information and then we'll put it in JARS, linked from your report on the envelopes."

"Talk to you later," said Moore as he hung up.

"Suzie, can you package up the information for Moore and JARS?"

"Sure Jake, I'll handle it," responded Suzie as she got up to leave.

Jake called after her, "While you're at it, tag their addresses in our Google Earth location file."

"I'm ready for a seafood lunch Jake," said Celia. "Want to head for Old Sac with me?"

"Another fine idea C," said Jake. "Let's go."

After lunch, Jake pulled up Google Earth and looked at the registered locations for the license plates they'd found in the morning. Only three of them were within a 150 miles of the known crime scene locations: one in Nevada City, two in the Bay Area. The other four were in southern California, at least 350 miles from the closest crime scene associated with this case. The Bay Area vehicles were housed relatively close to Walnut Creek, the Nevada City vehicle was a similar distance from Ruck a Chucky.

Because JARS had generated no alerts when the seven names were added to the case, Jake knew that these names hadn't showed up in any part of the investigation. He took a look at the license plate entries in JARS and, sure enough, the system had automatically added notations about every time a particular license plate had been detected by one of the Automated License Plate Readers out in the field. Jake checked on the three northern California plates. There had been only one detection in the last week, and that was Friday morning. One of the Bay Area plates had been read on highway 101 near Palo Alto. That plate couldn't have been at Ruck a Chucky on Friday morning and Jake added a note to the effect onto the license plate reference.

Celia had been thinking about Mason Resto using an empty house to kill the victims. She made a call to a friend, then got Jake's attention. "It turns out that modern lock boxes transmit a record of who opens them and when. That information gets put in a database and the listing agent gets an email about the event. If we get that database we can do a couple of things. First, we find out if Resto visited houses on Friday morning as he claimed. Second, we can extract all the houses that Resto has visited, then match that up to MLS data on homes that went off the listing without a sale. That gives us a list of potentially empty houses he might have used for a kill."

"Great thinking C. If we can get the raw data from them, it won't take a lot of work to extract what you suggested. Why don't you go after the lock box data and I'll try the MLS people?"

"Sure Jake," said Celia as she picked up her phone.

An hour later, Celia turned back to Jake. "The lock box people agreed to give us just the data for Resto."

"The MLS people didn't want to give us their data, but said that if we'd give them MLS numbers, they'd give us the information for the associated property. It looks like we can find the potential houses. We can turn the project over to Suzie for now.

"I'll do that," responded Celia. "You know, Resto would have to have been planning way in advance to line up a place like this."

"True. Your friend Kaya says our guy is a real planner, so it's a possibility.

Jake decided to review the case documentation in JARS to refresh his memories of the details and see if it would trigger new insight or ideas.

Late in the afternoon, Jake was interrupted by the sonar ping from his phone indicating that a text message had arrived. The message had come from JARS, indicating that a plate reader had identified one of the license plate numbers that Suzie had just entered into JARS around lunchtime. The plate had been detected entering I80 from Raley Boulevard, heading west. Curious, Jake downloaded the actual photo that showed a white Chevy Suburban. Zooming in on the license plate, it did indeed match one in their list: 5XCS387.

"Hey C, this is cool," said Jake. "You remember that I'm working on the integration of JARS with the plate reader system?

"I do recall that, mister geek."

"Hey, I'm not a geek, just a tool user. You might remember that tool use is a primary distinction between humans and other animals."

"Your knowledge is like a hundred years old Jake. Even some birds use tools."

"Yeah, anyway, the car carrying one of the plates we came up with has been detected by one of the plate readers and the system texted me."

"OK, and I care about that why?"

"Well, we now know that the vehicle is white and a Suburban."

"The same model and color that was observed down at Ruck a Chucky. I think that particular plate and its owner are more interesting now."

"You're right, C. I'll note in the system that that plate is indeed a white Suburban. If I can find some time I'll check out the owner a bit. I see no reason at this point to care about the vehicle being in that location."

"How much of my tax money is being eaten by this project?"

"The JARS integration is maybe a couple of hundred thousand. The full blown statewide plate reader system will cost maybe twenty million."

"I hope it's good for more than telling what color a car is."

"Just raining on my parade eh? Forget I mentioned it."

"How about I soothe your damaged ego by buying you a drink?"

"That's the third good idea you've had today."

32. YUBA CITY

He walked at a normal pace down the Garden Highway in Yuba City, just another guy in a t-shirt and jeans. The straw cowboy hat kept the strong sun off his head as well as shadowing his face. A backpack was slung over one shoulder.

After a mile he reached an area with sidewalks. After two hundred yards on the sidewalk, he turned into a trailer park. Walking past the trailers emoting confidence, he entered a farm field and angled left. Five hundred feet further, screened by some trees, he entered the back yard of a midsized house. Watching the neighbor houses for activity, he walked up to the house's back door.

Now screened by landscaping, he kneeled down and opened his backpack. Out came a long sleeved shirt, hair cap, bicycle clips and surgical gloves. After donning the gear and clipping his pants tightly around his legs, he pulled out lock picking tools.

Noting that the cheap lock installed by the house's developer was still in use, he used a torsion wrench and raked the lock with a snake pick. In three minutes he'd bounced all the pins and used the torsion wrench to turn the plug and open the lock. He walked inside and closed the door behind him. He settled down to wait alongside the door between the kitchen and the garage.

After two hours he heard a car drive into the garage. He pulled the Taser out of his backpack and stood against the wall next to the door. A car door slammed. A key slid into the lock. The door opened and a mid-height woman stepped inside. From the back he could see a full head of brown hair with blonde highlights. He fired the Taser, she jerked into rigidity and fell, making a thumping sound as she hit the floor. Her keys skittered across the vinyl.

Stepping over, he picked up the keys, walked back and rolled her onto her back. She was dressed in brown with a crisp white blouse. In a beauty contest with his first two, she would have come in fortieth. Not ugly, just older, not attractive, and a fish belly white complexion. Her eyes were wide open, terror showing as she looked at him.

He applied duct tape to her mouth, wrists and hands. A zip tie went around her ankles. Pulling out a dark brown plastic tarp, he rolled her against the cabinets, spread out the tarp, and then rolled her into the middle of it.

He spoke for the first time, "You will lie still in your current position and make no sound. If you do not follow these directions, you will receive another charge from this Taser. Nod your head if you understand."

She nodded. There was a pleading look in her hazel eyes. Her mascara was smearing, tears trickling down her cheeks. Her heart was pounding, trying to escape her chest.

He picked up her purse, sat down, and rummaged through it. He pulled out her cell phone, removed the battery, and dropped them both back in the purse. He got up, found her vacuum cleaner and vacuumed the room to pick up the AFIDs from the Taser. He then sat, leaned back, and waited for dark.

An excruciating hour went by before she tried to plead. No intelligible words passed the duct tape, but the tone was clearly pleading. He looked at her as if she was a bug and lifted the Taser. The sound stopped.

Time passed. After what seemed like hours, her mind began to escape the grip of terror and organized thinking returned. She realized that he hadn't gone through the house and hadn't asked her anything. He also hadn't made any attempt to conceal his face from her. Since he hadn't killed her, she guessed that he was going to kidnap her. Either that or he was waiting for something to happen; she had no clue as to what it could be. Since he'd let her see his face, he probably planned to kill her. God, she didn't want to die. All tied up like she was and lying on the floor, she couldn't think of any way to fight him. Damn, she wished that she had kept going to the gym so she'd have some strength to fight with.

Just before nine, he pulled a vial and a large syringe out of his bag. He loaded the syringe and stood up.

She thought this might be her last chance. Bending her knees and lifting up her bound feet, she kicked out as hard as she could. He was in the middle of a step, with his weight on the leg she aimed for, so he was unable to avoid her. Both of her feet, shod in hard soled shoes, impacted. Her left foot caught his knee, her right his shin. He yelled in pain, shifted his weight to the other leg and reflexively bent to grab the painful leg. She used both arms to strike his head with her bound hands acting as a club. Her blow glanced off his head and had no visible effect. As he straightened up, she tried to get up off the floor, but it was the wrong move: Her bound ankles and hands made her slow and clumsy. She saw his leg draw back. Pain burst through her head as it recoiled from the kick. She couldn't think. Then he was on top of her, rendering her legs useless and holding her arms captive with one of his. She arched her back trying to throw him off, but he rode her like a bronco. His free arm plunged the syringe's needle into her chest and she felt another pain as he rammed the plunger home. Leaving the syringe in her chest, he slapped her face hard. "You fucking bitch, you're going to suffer for this!"

He rode her bucks and twists for the minute it took the drug to put her under. Getting up, he pulled out the syringe and sat down, breathing heavily. His face was angry and his eyes stared at her with hatred. Sitting down, he massaged a shin that still hurt like hell.

Capping the syringe, he returned it to his backpack. Folding the tarp around her, he strapped it up into a package. After using the windows to check for activity out front, he took his backpack and her purse out to her car. Returning to the kitchen, he picked her up, grunting with the exertion. Depositing her in the trunk, he went back to the kitchen, straightened the chairs and examined the room for signs of disruption. Seeing none, he locked the door, backed the car out and drove away at a moderate pace.

Once out on the Garden Highway, he drove a mile then turned right into a short street ending in a cull de sac. The street must have been built as a part of some building scheme that had never happened, because it was surrounded by weedy fields. Pulling into the dirt, he backed her car up to the rear of his SUV. He moved her limp body and strapped it to his backboard, then covered her with the furniture pad. Grabbing her purse and his backpack, he locked her car, entered his and drove away. Starting out heading north east, he turned onto Highway 70 south after three miles.

Jake was sipping tequila at home, contemplating emptiness, when his phone pinged. After a minute he picked up the phone and checked. It was another plate reader message from the same location, except that this time the vehicle was exiting the freeway. At the moment, he didn't care much, thinking that he should change the importance level of these licenses so that he didn't get text messages.

He drove the SUV and its cargo into the garage and closed the door at ten thirty. Following his normal routine, he got his latest acquisition into the bathroom and folded over the stool. She was recovering as he finished, the anesthetic impact of the drug coming to an end.

Ten minutes later he began applying the belt. He grabbed himself but shortly realized that he wasn't aroused. All he felt was hate. This bitch had fought back, it wasn't to be tolerated. He put both hands on the belt and lashed her harder, putting his whole body into the strikes. Blood began exploding into the air, reaching every surface in the room. Her muffled screams reached a peak and then stopped as she passed out. It took him three more strokes to realize that she could no longer feel the pain he was delivering. He stopped and let his pounding heart slow, his frenzy subside.

He dropped the belt into the tub and removed the ice pick from the medicine cabinet. After a step toward her, he stopped. Not now, he thought, she needed to see and feel this. He sat on the toilet and gazed at the patterns made by blood spatter on the walls and ceiling.

Twenty minutes later he heard low moans from her as she woke up. When she turned her head and opened her eyes, he got up. "Did you enjoy that, bitch? I told you that you were going to suffer. You have only yourself to blame for your pain."

He held the ice pick in front of her eyes and said, "Feast your eyes on this delightful instrument. It was the coup de grace for your predecessors, but your behavior warrants more pain. Think about this wonderful point; it will enter your ear shortly. I'm going to go slowly and do some early stirring with you as recompense for your vicious attack on me. I'll give you just a minute to contemplate your demise."

Her eyes had widened and her moaning stopped when he showed her the ice pick. How could she fight this bastard? She was trussed up and bent over a stool that pressed into her gut. Her feet weren't on the ground so she had no leverage. Damn it, what could she do?

"Time's up," he said. He extended the pick towards her ear. Just as he reached the beginning of her ear canal, she began violently twisting and shaking her head, causing the pick to tear through part of her outer ear. Annoyed, he said, "Hold still slut." Grabbing her hair, he yanked her head back hard, sending a shock of pain through her and reducing her ability to move her head. He got the pick into her ear canal and, reaching the eardrum, began to stir as he slowly advanced the point. She reacted with a muffled scream and suddenly shifted herself toward him, in the process driving the pick all the way into her brain. "You cheating bitch!" he exclaimed.

An hour later, as he was leaving the property in his Toyota, he wondered. Are they good enough to figure out that I have her before I give her back to them?

33. SACRAMENTO; THURSDAY

Jake got another text from JARS before leaving for work. When he reached his office he bitched to Celia, "That damn JARS system is pesky. It texted me last night and again this morning about license plate detection. Damn Technology's run amok."

Celia laughed, looked at Jake and laughed some more. "Your monster's after you, Frankenstein."

"I'm going to put a stake in its heart," said Jake as he logged on to JARS.

"Stakes are for vampires dummy, monsters need to be shot. Don't you know any important cultural facts?"

"Wow, you're smart. I guess that's why I keep you around," said Jake, clicking away at his computer.

"No, I keep you around to keep you from making big mistakes," Celia came back as she turned to her desk.

Jake got to the appropriate display window on his screen. With one selection and click he set things up so that the plate reader data from the Ruck a Chucky possible plates would be recorded but not texted or emailed. He looked at the recorded data, all from plate 5XCS387, the one that belonged to a Tom Ditkam in Nevada City. For a guy from Nevada City, he spends a lot of time near Sacramento, Jake thought. Maybe he works down here, but the times seem odd.

Jake pulled up a map of the area where the SUV was being spotting. Wherever it was coming from or going to, it was north of I80. He'd never thought of using plate readers to search for somebody's origin or destination. After looking at the map and thinking, Jake reached for the phone and called the Automatic License Plate Reader lab.

"Tommy, this is Jake. Can I get you to move a couple of portable reader units for maybe a week?"

After a bit of silence, "Yeah Jake, we can do that. What's up?"

"The unit on I80 and Raley has been spotting a plate that we put into the JARS system. Everything's been working as we wanted, though I can't see that the info is useful for the case. This car has been getting on and off the freeway, I'm just curious to find out if more units could help us find where he's going."

"I guess that wherever you put them they'll still be picking up plates for its regular functions, so it can't hurt," said Tommy. "Where do you want them?"

"Put one on Raley just south of Ascot and another on Rio Linda Boulevard south of Crystal."

"Sure. We can get that done this afternoon Jake. Anything else?"

"Nope, that's all I need. If you need those units back for something, let me know."

"Bye Jake."

"Turning more monsters loose, Jake?" said Celia.

"Yeah, you're right. Think I get into gadgets too much?"

"Sometimes. I think that you need to get back into the people and forensics of this case."

"I'm on it, ma'am."

At four o'clock the third task force meeting convened. The first member with some information was Torrey Bonner from Walnut Creek.

"I've been through Mills College about our victims Sophia and Gina. It looks like they were both on the rowing team in 1995. I've got the list of their teammates but the school doesn't want to give out alumni information."

"I can understand that," said Celia. "It'd be kind of a turnoff to hear about two murdered classmates. There's no way we could get a warrant for alumni info without more cause."

"You're right," said Bonner. "I'll look for them using Accurint and DMV records. At least I have a connection that we can pursue. That's all I've got for now."

"Thanks Torrey," said Sam Nakamura.

Randy Moore's face appeared on their computer screens. "Jake and Celia came up with a total of seven Chevrolet UT class vehicles with licenses close to the bad number on our permit envelope. We've contacted six of them with soft calls. One of them was hostile, they all claimed that they hadn't been at Ruck a Chucky. None of them tickled our radar except for the hostile guy."

"Who was he?" asked Jake.

"A guy named Tom Ditkam from Nevada City," replied Moore. "We'll be checking him out after this meeting. That's all I have."

Rich Luton, Roseville PD. "We've found a witness who saw a man sitting in an SUV in the parking structure near Niebaums on the day Gina disappeared. She described a white male with a dark bushy mustache and a white cowboy hat."

"We're looking hard at the victim's ex-husband, Mason Resto. Jake and Celia have come up with a clever way to check out part of his alibi as well as identify possible empty houses that he had access to. That's it."

"Anybody else?" asked Sam.

After a bit of silence, "Jake here. "I just wanted to show you our timeline." The timeline popped up on everybody's screen and Jake used a large mouse cursor to highlight items. "Eleven days elapsed between the two kidnappings. Eleven days from the second kidnapping would be Saturday, two days from now. Remember that serial killers often ratchet up their pace, so a third victim might already be gone. Don't let down, folks. This bastard is killing good people while we're looking around."

"Thanks Jake," said Sam. "We'll schedule the next meeting for next Tuesday. Keep after him, people."

That evening Jake was sipping tequila while the case kept spinning around in his head. Even though he knew better, he was feeling responsible for the second victim's death because he hadn't caught the son of a bitch. These two women were law abiding contributors to society who had every expectation of many more richly filled years of life. Instead of seeing their kids grow up and traveling the world with their husbands, they almost certainly experienced some unbelievable terror before their future was snuffed out. "Damn it," Jake said as he got up and headed for the bedroom.

34. SOUTH FORK, YUBA RIVER; FRIDAY

Shortly after dawn, the SUV finished the downhill gravel road trip to Purdon Crossing. He'd driven slow enough that only a minor plume of dust followed him and then spread out to add to the existing coating on millions of leaves lining the road. Backing into a small cleared area, he turned off the engine and sat looking around. As expected, no vehicles were in sight.

From the back of the vehicle he extracted waders, wading boots, a fishing vest, fishing pole and gloves. He removed Sally Tomwick's head from a cooler and placed it in a plastic bag inside a creel, whose strap then went over his shoulders.

He slowly walked about 450 feet up the hiking trail on the north side of the river, always scanning his surroundings. Seeing no sign of humans, he walked down the steep bank to the river, stepping past poison oak that grew near the oak trees. He paused on a shore covered with medium sized rocks. After looking around again, he picked up a couple of rocks, waded one step into the river and arranged them on a boulder whose top rose above the torrent. After fetching and arranging a third rock, he made a few casts with his fly rod to cover another survey of the area.

Satisfied that he was alone, he opened the creel. Removing Tomwick's head, he positioned it on the rock, facing downstream. Grabbing a hairbrush from the creel, he brushed her hair. Dropping the brush into the open plastic bag, he pulled out a small zip lock bag. Removing a medium length black hair from the bag with tweezers, he positioned it into the hair of his display. After one last gaze at his work, he headed back to the SUV.

As eleven o'clock arrived, Alyssa and Arin had already been sunbathing for almost an hour. They were both bleached blonde and two years out of Nevada Union High School. There the resemblance stopped. Arin was five foot three and retained about 10 pounds of baby fat. Her breasts were shapely but small and her hips were more than ample. An attractive face unfortunately featured a tiny mouth that produced high pitched sounds. Alyssa had been one of the school beauties; she was five ten and possessed a whole body of excellent parts, delightfully displayed in a bathing suit made from a small number of threads. Alyssa had successfully depended on her beauty for much of her short life.

They had been sharing a joint of Ed Rosenthal Super Bud, a favorite of Alyssa's connoisseur uncle who had a farm of mixed marijuana varieties up 'on the ridge' as the locals referred to the North San Juan area. Both girls were relaxed, laughing and chattering in the sun.

At the current high water flow rate, even the lit up girls knew better than to wade into the river. The people who drowned here were generally men from out of the area who didn't know better.

Most of the riverside beaches were submerged this time of year, but there was one tiny beach on the north shore about a hundred feet upstream from the bridge. Next to the beach were some massive flat topped boulders, ideal for sunning. They had chosen the boulders. Tired of sitting on a rock and having a full bladder, Alyssa worked her way upstream so she wouldn't be visible from the bridge. Finding a location screened from both the trail and the bridge, she relieved herself.

Walking to river's edge, she slowly turned in a circle, marveling at the wild beauty that was always there but only penetrated her awareness when she was high. She saw something strange upstream, but couldn't figure out what it was. As Alyssa walked through the rocks toward the strange object, her mind continued to fail its decoding task.

At a distance of 15 feet, her brain got it together. "Mother fucker!" Alyssa shrieked as she toppled backwards into the chilly shallows. She sat there in the water looking at a perfectly arranged woman's head sitting on top of a boulder that protruded 2 feet from the river. "Oh shit, oh shit," was all Alyssa could say as she wrapped her arms around herself and shivered.

After a minute it dawned on Alyssa that whoever had done this might still be around. In a panic, she jerked her head in all directions trying to spot danger. Seeing nothing didn't calm her much. She stood up, dripping river water, and began a hurried but uncoordinated trip back to the bridge.

When she got close to where Arin was laid out, Alyssa yelled "Get up, we've got to get the fuck out of here."

"Huh? What're you talking about?"

"There's a dead head up there," Alyssa said, pointing upstream. "Come on, get to the car, we gotta go."

"What?" said Arin as she stood and began climbing the bank.

Alyssa's head was on a swivel as she climbed to the trail. They ran to Alyssa's car, climbed in, locked the doors and headed south, up the hill.

"What'd you see up there?" asked Arin.

"There was this woman's head, like, sitting on top of a rock," responded Alyssa. "It was freaky."

"Damn. There was something like that on the news last week, my mom and dad were talking about it. We gotta call the cops."

"But we've got weed," complained Alyssa.

"Not that much. Your uncle can come up with more. Give it to me and I'll dump it out the window."

"No, I can't just toss it," said Alyssa.

"OK, stop here," said Arin. "We'll stash it behind that cluster of boulders over there. You can come back and get it."

After hiding the bag, they continued up the hill. "Cell doesn't work till we get almost to the ridge top," said Arin.

Alyssa didn't respond. She was shivering and concentrating on her driving on the narrow winding road.

Five minutes later, Arin said, "I've got good bars here, stop so I can call."

Arin placed the 911 call. After describing what Alyssa had seen and who they were, she was asked about her current location.

"We're three or four miles up the road from Purdon's Crossing on the way to Nevada City. We passed Lake Vera a couple of minutes ago."

"What make and model vehicle are you driving?"

"Alyssa, what's the make and model of this thing?" asked Arin.

"It's a blue 2002 Toyota 4Runner," replied Alyssa.

After receiving that information, the 911 technician said, "Stay in your vehicle in that location with your doors locked. sheriff's personnel will be there in minutes."

As they waited, Alyssa began sobbing. "It was so awful, that fucking head staring at me. How could somebody do that to me?"

Arin, down a bit from her high, replied, "Like, they did it to the woman whose head you found, not to you, stupid."

"Don't call me stupid. You didn't see it. It was unreal at first and then it was scary, really scary. Kind of like in Saw, you know? You got a dead person and the killer's around, ready to get you next."

"Didya see or hear anybody?"

"No, but there's all those trees and bushes around, you can't hear shit because of the river."

"I'm sure that was scary but you're OK now."

A sheriff's car drove up and stopped, two deputies stepping out.

"Are you, uh, Arin and Alyssa?" one of them asked.

"Yeah," said Alyssa.

"Please lock up your vehicle, come with us and show us what you found."

"We gotta ride in the back of that thing?" Alyssa asked, pointing to the sheriff's car.

"You'll be safe with us and I promise that we'll let you out," said the deputy. The girls felt safe but claustrophobic in the patrol unit, separated from the deputies by Plexiglas and imprisoned by doors with no handles.

Reaching the river, the deputy parked the car, radioed in their status, and let the girls out of the back. They walked out on the rickety bridge and asked the girls to point out what they'd seen.

"Like, I didn't see nothin'," said Arin.

"I'm the one who did," said Alyssa. "I walked up river and saw it on top of the rock out there." She pointed up river. "It was a woman's head and her eyes were looking right at me. The eyes were wrong though, they looked real flat."

"Without tears, they do that," said the deputy, holding up a pair of zoom binoculars. "Sure as hell looks like a head." He handed the binoculars to his partner.

"Yup," said his partner after looking. "We've got a crime scene. Let's call it in and block it off."

Twenty minutes later two more patrol cars and Sheriff's Detective Ned Purdy from the Major Crimes Unit had arrived. Purdy was 36, had been a detective for four years and worked two murder cases. His brown hair was cropped short, mostly covered by a tan felt rancher's hat. Purdy's green eyes and wide nose were centered in a round face. His blocky body was dressed in slacks and a blue sport shirt left untucked to conceal his weapon.

"My crime scene," said Purdy after getting a report from the first deputies. "Charlie, you start a log, John and Marty, you block the road at least 50 yards uphill on both sides. See if you can block it someplace where drivers can turn around. I'm going to walk in for a closer look at the head. I'll keep up a conversation on my handheld, you guys pay attention and be ready to back me up if needed."

Purdy started walking up the narrow trail, watching where he stepped, trying not to spoil any evidence and at the same time staying aware of his surroundings. He figured that the perp was probably long gone, but you never knew; the guy could be hanging around. The trail rose away from the river and oak trees obscured much of his view of the water. He walked about the distance he had estimated, then spotted a faint trail leading towards the water. He got 15 feet before he spotted a partial footprint. Stopping, he looked past the trunk of an oak and through a bush to the boulder and its topping. Raising binoculars, he could see the shape of a head with hair moving in the river breeze. From his angle, only part of a nose was visible. He took three pictures, then backed out to the main trail and returned to the road.

Using the radio in his car, Purdy connected with his Sergeant. "Phil, it looks like we have a human head out here; maybe the perp that's been in the papers has paid us a visit. I couldn't get closer than twenty five feet and be comfortable about possible evidence."

"Preserving the scene was the right move Ned," said Phil Dorsey. "Since this looks like the case that the DOJ has been working on, I'll call in their forensics crew and investigators. This is our turf however, so I'm going to send the rest of our team down and call the DA. Work with the DOJ people, but for now it's our case. You have trouble with them, call me."

"Got ya, Sarge. I'll start interviewing the girl that found the head. If you want to avoid a bunch of angry citizens, you could get the roads closed higher up so people won't drive all the way out here to find out they have to turn around."

"Good idea Ned. Anything else? I need to get to these calls."

"I'm good. Talk to you later."

Purdy was excited. Back in the 1850s, the county had at least twenty homicides a year, but these days it was around one a year and some of those were bones found by hikers. A case like this would get his juices flowing even if it ate all his spare time for a while.

By the time Willy Jackson arrived with his DOJ forensics crew, at least 15 Nevada County law enforcement personnel were on scene. Some were there because this is where the action was, a few were guarding the crime scene, and the others were waiting for Willy to clear the area for their access.

Willy and his crew met the locals and got a briefing from Ned Purdy. Two techs went up Purdon road, looking for evidence in the dirt and gravel. When they were done, they were to process the dirt trail. With two other technicians, Willy was going to boulder hop up the side of the river to the head. He said, "Alyssa and Arin, I'd like you to point out every place you went, but let us look at things before you step on them again."

"Sure," said Arin, staring at Willy. African-Americans were rare enough in Nevada County that locals paid attention. In the vast majority of cases, the attention was merely curiosity, but the objects of their attention were often uncomfortable with it. Willy ignored her rude behavior.

The girls pointed out their route to the beach, Willy and his crew worked it, finding nothing. At the beach, the girls identified the boulders they had used. The crew found nothing in the area other than a few cigarette butts that they bagged and tagged. Willy sent Arin back to the bridge and had Alyssa show him her route to the head. It soon became clear that she didn't remember much of the walk. The crew took thirty minutes to travel the couple of hundred feet to the head rock, finding nothing of interest on their route other than the faint smell of urine at one spot. Alyssa's admission about using the location saved them from having to collect a soil sample.

Observing the head from 15 feet away brought back memories of their Ruck a Chucky experience. It was a real head, the flies told them that much. Pictures were taken and Alyssa was sent back to the bridge using the route they had already checked. Using waders and safety ropes, they were able to take a full set of pictures on three sides. The current was so strong on the fourth side that even wading to knee depth would have been dangerous, so they did without pictures from that angle. The pictures done, they began a slow and careful search for the perp's ingress and egress routes.

Jake got the call at 2:21. Even though he had expected another victim, it drove a wave of frustration through him.

Despite knowing how hard serials were to solve, he had a feeling of inadequacy, like this woman's death was his fault.

"Celia, we've got another head."

"Crap." Celia had her own feelings. A mix of empathy for another lost life, frustration at their lack of progress and excitement at continuing the hunt with new information.

"Chocolate will be doing their crime scene, so we don't need to hurry up there," said Jake. "Let me put the event in JARS so everybody will get notified. We should take a department SUV and our travel bags. Changing into field clothing would be smart." Jake and Celia both kept a packed bag in their cars for the regular situations where a case took them out of town without warning.

Celia tried to contact Kaya Lane, but got voicemail for both her office and cell phones. She left a message about what was happening and where.

A half hour later they were heading for the hills in the ubiquitous government SUV; large, black, with tinted windows. Jake didn't like the cumbersome vehicle much, but didn't want to take his Boxter on dirt roads and didn't want to run home to get his truck.

As the SUV began the climb into the foothills, Jake said, "We should call this guy the Friday killer, he's blowing up a lot of Fridays for people.

"Even better would be the weekend killer," said Celia. "I haven't had a full weekend to myself since this case started."

"You're right about that."

Celia's phone began singing. "Moreno," she answered.

She listened for a minute, then said, "Great work. I assume you've put it in JARS connected to Resto?"

More listening. "Thanks Suzie."

"That was Suzie, Jake," said Celia. "She's gotten the results from Resto's lock box usage data combined with the associated MLS data. Over the last year we have eleven houses that Resto's been in that have been removed from the listings without selling. We don't know how many of those are unoccupied. Suzie put the data into the system connected to Resto, so Luton will get an email notification."

"Good," said Jake. "I hope that he checks those places out."

As they passed the monument on Highway 49 marking the beginning of Nevada County, Celia said with a faint smile, "So I guess that Nevada County isn't in Nevada either."

"Duh," said Jake. "I'll give you the quick summary. The county is about a thousand square miles, the size of the European country Luxembourg. It stretches all the way from here to the state of Nevada. The population is about a hundred thousand. There's a lot of socioeconomic diversity and not much racial diversity. Most of the people are in the western half of the county. The eastern half is mostly national forest. Only two towns are larger than ten thousand: Grass Valley in the west and Truckee in the east. Truckee gets over seventeen feet of snow a year and hits freezing or below sixty percent of the days in an average year."

"The encyclopedic Jake strikes again," cracked Celia.

"I just like the area enough that I want to be able to describe it to people. Being part engineer, I like to have some facts. For a touchy feely person like you I should talk about vast hills enveloped by lush greenery, rugged mountains with glaciated lakes, a land dotted with mining and railroad towns, many of them extinct."

"Consider me touched."

The highway turned to freeway as they passed through Grass Valley then Nevada City. Above Nevada City they followed 49 to the left then turned right onto North Bloomfield. After half a mile they jogged onto Lake Vera – Purdon road. Soon the road changed from narrow and paved to narrow and partly paved and they arrived at the crime scene roadblock. Jake grabbed his crime scene bag and they walked down to the river. Running across a deputy with a clipboard, they signed the crime scene log and asked for Ned Purdy.

"That's him at the other end of the bridge; the guy with the tan rancher's hat," was the answer.

Starting towards the bridge, Celia asked, "This thing looks like it could collapse any minute. You sure that it's safe?"

"Well, it looks like those cars made it over, so we should be fine," responded Jake as they stepped onto the one lane bridge with two rows of extra boards for vehicle tires. Seeing a group of people upriver, he stopped in the middle of the bridge. He pulled binoculars from his bag and looked. "Looks like the same MO," he said, handing the glasses to Celia.

After a minute, her response was "yup".

They introduced themselves to detective Ned Purdy, who then introduced Cliff Stover, the DA's lead investigator.

Having seen that Chocolate was still at work, Jake asked, "Why don't you tell us what's happening and then we'll give you a summary of the case we're working?"

"Sure," said Purdy, who proceeded with a summary of what they knew, ending with, "I interviewed the girls, but they don't know anything of value. Your forensics people haven't cleared the site for us yet."

Celia gave the two men a summary of the case, finishing with "The perp seems to be escalating. It was ten days between the first and second discoveries, only seven between the second head and this one. That's assuming that it's our guy and not some copycat."

"Your guy's a nastier bastard than we normally deal with up here," said Purdy. "We'd be real happy to make this his last killing, or at least his last killing in our county."

"So far, we don't know where any of them were killed," said Celia. "All we have is kidnap and head pose locations. We haven't found any other remains either."

Jake took another look at Purdy, wondering why the man looked strange to him. Then he had it. The man had no earlobes. The outer curve of his ear just swooped down and connected to his head. Different.

Chocolate walked up to the gathering and said, "Hello everybody. It's beautiful here isn't it?"

"I think I could appreciate it better if this case wasn't involved," responded Celia.

"It can be difficult to appreciate beauty in the presence of death," admitted Chocolate. "We've cleared you a route to the pose site, so you can take a look now. It appears that the perp got there by the same route I'm taking you. So far we haven't found much other than a partial boot print. I think that the print matches the wader boot prints we've seen before. The pose setup is the same as the previous two. Since that level of detail didn't get published, I expect that this is the guy we've been looking for."

"Let's go check it out," said Cliff Stover.

They walked upriver on the narrow dirt trail. "Here's the first of the poison oak," said Stover, pointing to a small shrub with shiny green leaves in groups of three. "You don't want your skin or clothes to touch it. My rule around here is to never touch a green thing unless I'm sure it's not poison oak." He was speaking to the DOJ people, not knowing whether they were clueless flatlanders or not.

"This is prime poison oak country all right, middle elevations where oak trees like to grow," said Jake, not wanting to be seen as a city boy.

After carefully working his way up the trail, Chocolate turned downhill towards the river. "Careful of these tall poison oak plants," he said, twisting around them.

They worked their way down thirty feet of steep bank to the rocks at river's edge. In front of them, just offshore, was a head, sitting on a boulder and facing downstream. The head had attracted at least a dozen blue bottle flies, disturbing its gruesome serenity.

Jake walked a few steps downstream to get a better look at the face. "She's not Italian at all," he exclaimed in a voice loud enough to overcome the roar of the river. "We should have brought your shrink, Celia."

Celia ignored him, taking in details of the scene. She decided that this had to be a new victim of the same guy. Because this woman was unlike the previous victims she'd show Kaya a picture as soon as she could.

Celia poised to jump onto a boulder protruding from the water just below the head rock. As she began to jump, Jake grabbed her arm and spun her back onto shore.

"What the hell?" growled Celia, annoyed.

"If you'd gone into the water beyond that boulder, the river would have taken you and there's a good chance that you wouldn't survive," said Jake.

"It can't be more than knee deep out there," protested Celia.

"At knee depth, I doubt that you could stand against the force of that current. You would have fallen and been taken downstream. The shock of immersion in snowmelt water and the force of the water would make you helpless. Hypothermia would rapidly reduce your ability to function even if you got past the shock. No rafts or kayaks are around to rescue you; you'd drown or break your head on a rock. You wanna know why there aren't even kayaks out here?"

"Why?"

"I checked the water flow rate before we came. The water flow today is way over the safe limit for kayaking this stretch, nobody but a suicidal idiot would run it. At this spot right here, we're seeing the water come through at almost 20 miles an hour."

"OK Jake, thanks for pulling me back. I owe you one," said Celia, blushing. She was embarrassed, but nothing could be done about it now.

The two Nevada County deputies had watched all this in silence, then gave each other a look. They knew that this river killed careless waders and foolish swimmers on a regular basis. Every once in a while it got a kayaker. Apparently Appleby knew his stuff about rivers.

Jake and Stover both took pictures of the scene, even though they knew Chocolate's team had taken many. This done, they climbed the bank and walked back to the road, leaving the head for Chocolate to retrieve and deliver to the morgue in Auburn.

Jake suggested that they retire to the detective's office; there was no benefit to hanging around the river. Purdy agreed and began dividing up the immediate work between the detectives. Jake asked Chocolate to stop by the sheriff's office on his way out and summarize what he'd found.

35. NEVADA COUNTY

It was crowded in the detective's office on Maidu Avenue. Five of the six desks in the small room were occupied by sheriff's detectives. Jake and Celia shared the sixth.

Cliff Stover, sharing Ned Purdy's desk, got on the phone to Assistant DA Marti Nelson. Marti handled prosecution of violent crimes for the county.

Purdy called the Chief Deputy Coroner, who was down in Sacramento for the day. Without mentioning that it was already happening, Ned convinced him that the DOJ forensics unit could properly transport the remains to the morgue. By emphasizing that this was part of a series of killings that they needed to stop, he convinced the deputy to make a Saturday autopsy happen.

Jake and Celia had been setting up their laptops and getting on the sheriff's local network. When Purdy finished his call, Jake suggested that he check the DOJs Missing Person's database and with local agencies who might have received information about a missing woman. Purdy agreed and got started.

Celia had uploaded their photos into the JARS system and was on the phone with Kaya Lane talking about the different appearance of the new victim.

Jake authorized access to the case in JARS for the Nevada County detectives and DA personnel. JARS automatically sent each person an email with notification of access. Jake remembered the plate reader notifications he had been receiving about the car registered to a Nevada City address. Asking Celia to find out what the Roseville person of interest Mason Resto had been doing this morning, he started looking into Tom Ditkam.

Jake knew that their connection to Ditkam was extremely thin – his license plate number was a transposition of the number written on the suspicious Ruck a Chucky fee envelope. Looking in JARS he saw that the Ditkam license plate had been spotted in Sacramento again this morning, but being in Sacramento had no obvious connection with this case. Jake started up Google Earth with the case's placemark file. A placemark for Ditkam's home address had automatically been added when Ditkam was added to the case. Looking at the satellite image, Jake realized that Ditkam lived over ten miles outside Nevada City, in the area called North San Juan. Jake was surprised and then he remembered how the city part of an address reflected the post office delivery area, not the city limits. Zooming to a higher altitude view, Jake realized that Ditkam's house was on an extension of the line between Nevada City and the Purdon Crossing pose site. Pulling up a tool that put the case's placemarks on a Google Map, Jake looked at roads in the area. Ditkam's residence was about four miles from Purdon Crossing. As his heart rate increased with excitement, he noted to himself that this was too big a coincidence to ignore. They had another person of interest.

When looking at the list of plate reader sightings of Ditkam's vehicle, he'd noticed a link to another report in the system. Clicking on it, he found Randy Moore's report on Ditkam as part of his work checking out the small group of possible plates from the Ruck a Chucky pose site. Jake got another boost looking at the report: Ditkam had a record. Going back twenty years, the guy had a burglary conviction, a skate on a murder charge and a robbery bust that got him a term in Folsom Prison. He'd been paroled two years ago and had no recorded offenses since then. Maybe he'd been saving up for a big murder spree.

Celia interrupted his thoughts, "Resto hasn't been seen since Tuesday night. Roseville just had loose surveillance on him; they look for his car at work, home and around town. When they didn't see the car Wednesday morning, Luton checked work and the house and came up empty."

"So Resto's in the wind just in time to pick up this woman, kill her and pose her," said Jake. "Did you give Luton some motivation to find Resto?"

"I did indeed. Gave him some grief about not being on top of it, not letting the team know he was missing. He knew the guy was missing when we had our task force meeting yesterday, didn't mention it."

"I thought Luton was better than this."

"So did I," replied Celia. "Let's hope that it was a onetime screw up."

"Let me see if a plate reader spotted Resto's vehicle," said Jake, turning to his computer. After a minute, "Yup, Resto's Expedition was spotted heading west on I80 at Raley Wednesday morning. That doesn't help much; he could go most anywhere from there. I'll set things up so Luton and I get texted if he's spotted again."

Ned Purdy walked over to Jake and Celia. "Nothing useful in the missing person database," he said. "I checked with our Missing Persons guy and Grass Valley Police and they don't have any reports for us. How'd you ID the other two vics? It sure wasn't through fingerprints."

"Both of them came up through our Missing Persons system," replied Celia. "We confirmed with teeth. It may be that she just hasn't made it into the system yet. I'll set it up so we'll get text messages whenever an adult female is added."

"That sounds cool. I didn't know you could do that."

"Jake's working with the people running all of these systems, trying to make them more active. He's our super geek, so I end up learning this stuff," she said with a smile.

Jake gave her an annoyed look. He didn't like the term geek, particularly when it was applied to him. Of course he egged her on when he got annoyed about it. "Why don't you tell Ned and Cliff Stover about Resto?"

Ned motioned Stover over, and then Celia gave them the rundown on Mason Resto. "He has motive for killing his ex-wife, but we have no significant evidence. He's more interesting because he's been missing for the last few days. The guy could be bookending the killing of his ex with a couple of random killings to throw us off."

"That gives us somebody to look at," said Purdy. "The details on this guy are in JARS?"

"They are," said Celia. "You may want to check to see if he's on any local radar."

"And while you're at it," added Jake, "I've got somebody else for you." He told them what they knew about Tom Ditkam and his slim connection to the Ruck a Chucky victim. "This guy's an ex-con who once got a not guilty in a murder trial. He got paroled up here."

"I'll check them out with the narcotics task force," said Stover. Noticing a questioning look from Celia, he said, "Narcotics has the best intelligence in the county. They have eyes, ears, and informants."

"I can see if there's any other action with one of the local police departments," said Purdy.

Chocolate walked in, spotted them and headed over. "Looky here, we've got a whole passel of dicks," he said with a grin.

"Excuse me?" said Celia, trying to look insulted.

"Sorry Celia, I meant to say dicks and a lovely lady detective."

"You're excused then."

"Good. I need to get down the hill, so I'll run through what we found, or what we didn't find. As before, we found nothing on or around the head. We've got that partial boot print I expect to match the wader boot we've seen before. In a cleared space on the north side of the river we found our favorite tire tread and a boot print that all look like what was found near the Tuolumne. For what it's worth, the vehicle left going north."

"Towards Ditkam's house," commented Jake.

"Whatever," said Chocolate. "I'm outa here, I need to drop a package at the Auburn morgue. I'll wait until Monday to confirm all this unless somebody tells me they need it earlier."

"Thanks Willy, I think Monday works," said Jake, figuring that the locals didn't know Chocolate well enough to hear his nickname.

When Chocolate had left, Celia spoke up, "I should tell you what Kaya's thinking now that we have a victim that looks different than the others."

"I suppose," said Jake without enthusiasm. To the others, he said, "Kaya's part of the DOJs profiling program and she's part of the task force for this case."

Feeling a need to defend her friend, Celia said, "Kaya's done good work on other cases. She's given us a profile of our perp; you can find it in JARS. Part of the profile is that the guy's killing women who resemble somebody important, but hated, in his life. Since the first two victims were similar in appearance, we were expecting subsequent victims to look Italian. Kaya suggests that our new victim may not be a victim of opportunity intended to represent an abusive mother. She thinks that this one was selected for some different reason. If this analysis is correct, there's a connection between this victim and our killer where there wasn't a connection with the first two vics."

"Connections we can find," spoke up Cliff. "Knowing that the guy has an Italian mother is not helpful at this point."

"Right on both points," responded Celia. "Though knowing about an Italian mother is helpful when you've got a person of interest. For example, Mason Resto doesn't, though the abusive hated figure could have been his Italian heritage wife."

"So not a lot of help there," said Jake.

Ignoring Jake, Celia continued, "Kaya talked about another possibility, though one that has a much lower probability than her primary theory. The perp could have done the first two just as a smoke screen to obfuscate this killing. The real target was this third victim, the other two were just a diversion."

"So again, for our purposes, we focus on this victim and expect a connection between her and her killer," said Cliff.

"Right," agreed Celia.

Jake frowned, but decided to keep his mouth

Stover got a call from the Chief Deputy Coroner. Some arm twisting and a lunch bribe had gotten the autopsy scheduled for the next day at eleven. After talking it over, the group decided to get started on reports and meet in the morning at nine.

Jake and Celia drove over to the Magic Inn and got keys for two rooms. Paul gave Celia the house tour and history lesson. Celia enjoyed the antiques and detailed period décor. She knew that Jake didn't care about these but he enjoyed the good beds and their hosts.

When she finished the tour they walked over to Fiona's house to say hello. Kaitlin was happy to see dad, but he couldn't get a word in edgewise as, in a relentless stream of words, Kaitlin described her plans for the weekend in excited detail. It became clear that she didn't have much time for him, but Jake set up a tentative late Sunday hike with her. He got a meager hug from Fiona, who gave Celia a somewhat chilly, "pleased to meet you." Leaving Fiona to finish cooking dinner, they headed downtown for their own meal.

"Your daughter isn't shy anymore," said Celia.

"You got that right. She's back in a motor mouth stage, kind of like when she was four. I've got to say it's fun to see her bubble like that."

"Soon she'll be a teenager and won't want to talk to you. She won't want you knowing details of her social activities."

"I guess that you're right C, but I'd be real happy to avoid that kind of behavior. I'd like to stay connected with her through her teenage years."

"Good luck. So what was with Fiona?"

"What do you mean?"

"That hug she gave you was pitiful and she definitely didn't want to meet me."

"Maybe she was just distracted because she was in the middle of cooking dinner."

"I don't think that's it, Jake."

"Maybe Fiona was jealous of you, that'd be a good thing," said Jake, always looking for a rekindling of their early relationship.

"Could be, but I doubt it. She would have given you an extra big hug if she was jealous."

"We're going to get back together, I know it."

"So how about those Giants?" said Celia, changing the subject. She didn't know or care much about baseball, but was uncomfortable with the current conversation. Jake kept hanging on to his hope, but she couldn't see that anything had changed to get Jake and Fiona back together. He seemed blind and stupid on the subject, but then he was a guy.

"Got it," said Jake, knowing that neither of them paid a lot of attention to baseball. "So why don't you learn how to kayak? It's a blast and you're in shape for it."

"Thanks for the compliment, I think. I've thought about kayaking, but taekwondo takes up a lot of my free time, such as it is."

They talked about kayaking through the dinner. Jake consumed a filet mignon with a glass of Nevada City Syrah, Celia a garlic chicken fettuccine with a glass of Sierra Starr's Reserve Chardonnay. The locally grown wines, meats and produce were a tasty change from their normal menu. Sticking with one drink since they had work to do, they finished by eight and walked back to the Inn.

After grabbing their gear from the SUV, they walked up the stairs to the rooms. Jake was up front, as usual ignoring chivalrous behavior when with a female workmate. He walked into the "gold miner's daughter" room and started to unload.

"Whoa cowboy," said Celia. "This is my room."

"Oops," responded Jake. "Sorry 'bout that." He headed for the door where Celia had stopped. Passing through sideways, belly to belly, left him short of breath.

"Uh, see you, uh, in the morning," he said.

"Yes Jake, I'll see you in the morning," was the soft reply.

Jake got to his room, unpacked, and sat silently for a minute. Then he pulled out his phone and called Chuck Browning for the evening report.

"You're late, Appleby. Eight o'clock is when I expect your call. What don't you understand about eight o'clock?"

"Sorry Sir," Jake said, suppressing his anger. Deliberately not responding to the insulting question, he began his report of the day's activities.

"So we have another posed head, cause of death unknown, identity unknown, in yet another jurisdiction," summarized Browning.

"Yes," said Jake, giving the minimum.

"So resolve those unknowns, and quickly. It's time that we solved this case and apprehended the perpetrator."

"Yes sir."

"Are the locals cooperating? I expect their full cooperation."

"We're doing just fine sir."

"Tomorrow, eight o'clock sharp, agent," emitted the phone before the connection dissolved.

Jake snarled, "*Grrrrr.*" He began a series of deep breaths, letting them out slowly.

Recovered, he opened his laptop and began the work of recording today's activity. There was no longer paper involved, but it was still "paperwork," the most unglamorous but necessary part of a detective's job.

36. NEVADA COUNTY; SATURDAY

Jake was up and dressed by seven. He walked downstairs for coffee and the paper. He sat down outside next to a green slate patio table in the shade of a massive oak tree. The morning was perfect: clear blue sky without a hint of clouds, temperature already in the mid sixties. When he unfolded the Sacramento Bee, his joy disappeared. The bold headline read *NCAL WOMEN IN DANGER!* The lead quote from Browning was *"Our northern California serial killer has struck again, this time at yet another innocent middle class woman in yet another jurisdiction. Fortunately, my office is running the perpetrator to ground using the combined forces of five local agencies. In the meantime, women need to be extremely cautions and avoid being alone in public lest they become a victim of this fiend."*

The self aggrandizing asshole, thought Jake. The women out there are more likely to die from poisoning than from any homicide, much less being killed by the monster we're after. Browning and the media are happy to use these deaths and generate fear, each for their own reasons. He put down the paper and went inside for more coffee, rolling his shoulders to relieve the tension he'd just built.

Celia joined him for an eight o'clock breakfast. Jake didn't mention the newspaper headline, just talked about a tentative plan for today. Breakfast under the oak was juice, roasted potatoes and a cheese and ham soufflé. Coffee was from the local coffee roasters, five blocks away. This was a great way to start Saturday, thought Jake. Too bad that the remainder of the day will be work.

Just as they got up from the table, Jake received a text message. There was a new adult female in the missing person's database. Celia had her laptop downstairs and pulled up the report.

"That could be her," said Jake, looking over Celia's shoulder. Pull up our victim's picture out of JARS.

Celia did that, looked for a few seconds, said "I think that we've identified our victim, Jake."

"I agree. Let's get over to the sheriff's office and check it out."

Fifteen minutes later they were meeting with Cliff Stover and Ned Purdy. Purdy had gotten the same text and checked it out, coming to his own conclusion that they knew who their victim was.

"According to the missing persons report, she's from Yuba City and hasn't been seen since leaving her shop on Wednesday," said Purdy. "We've got a good conference phone in our meeting room, let's connect with Yuba City."

They reached the Yuba City Police Department contact for the missing persons case and gave her the basics. Within minutes the Sergeant in charge of investigations was patched into the call from his home. They gave the Sergeant the short version of the story, mentioning that it was part of a multi-jurisdictional task force.

"We don't get many homicides," was the Sergeant's reaction. "Half the ones we do get are gang related. I'll chase down a detective for the case and have him call you."

While they waited, Cliff read the missing person's report out loud. "Sally Tomwick, five four, 150 pounds, brown hair, hazel eyes, white with light complexion. No distinguishing marks. Last seen 7:00 PM Wednesday leaving Tomwick's Fine Jewelry on Bridge Street in Yuba City. She didn't show up at the shop on Thursday and her employee couldn't reach her. The employee reported her missing at 4:50 PM Friday. Tomwick has no spouse or known significant other."

"Not only are her hair, eyes, and complexion different from our other vics, but she's noticeably heavier as well," said Celia. "You'd think if the other two were done as distractions, they'd have looked more like this one."

"Who knows what craziness lurks in the minds of men?" cracked Jake with a tiny smile.

"The Shadow knows!" responded Celia. "But wait, did he know about craziness or just evil?"

Jake came back with, "Whatever he knew, the Shadow probably can't remember anything. He'd have to be at least a hundred years old."

The phone rang, saving everybody from further banter. "This is Ned Purdy, you're on a speakerphone."

"This is Stan Voss, Yuba City Police Detective. I've been assigned a missing persons case and understand that you think you've found her."

"We think we've found a part of her," said Purdy. "I'm the Nevada County Sheriff's lead on this case. Yesterday we found a woman's head posed on a rock in the South Yuba River. Comparing what we found with the pictures in the missing persons report we think it's her."

"Just a head? Is this part of the serial case that's always in the papers?"

"Jake Appleby, California Department of Justice here. We believe that she's the third victim of our whitewater killer. We started up a task force a week ago when we found the second victim. Here's a brief summary. Victim one was kidnapped in Walnut Creek, her head was found posed at the Tuolumne River. Victim two was kidnapped in Roseville, her head was found posed at the Middle fork of the American River. You will now be the sixth jurisdiction involved in the case. For the other two we've used dental records for positive ID, we should try that for this one."

"Whoa, this is a big deal," said Voss. "All I know at this point is what's in the missing persons report. I need to start digging."

"Celia Moreno, DOJ. Do you guys use the JARS system?"

"Yeah," answered Voss.

"Good. We'll give you authorization to the case. You can see the reports and pictures on the head we found up here. When you have time, everything about the other two vics and the investigation is also there."

"That'll get me started," said Voss. "I'll need some time to get up to speed. How about I check with you guys about two?"

"That'll be good," said Purdy. "The autopsy on the head is at eleven in Auburn, we can give you the results when we talk."

"Talk to you at two," said Voss before he hung up.

Jake, Celia, and Ned Purdy met the pathologist at the second street morgue in Auburn. Already smelling death, Celia girded herself for the autopsy room sights, sounds, and smells. As a woman, she couldn't afford to show a reaction to the upcoming proceedings. If a guy complained or even got sick, he'd catch a lot of shit. If a woman did the same, she'd be looked on as weak, a chick, not a real cop.

Much of the external exam was eventful, not like the exams of the first two victims. The pathologist found a bruise on her left cheek, a bruise and torn skin behind her right ear, and tissue damage to the auricle of her right ear as well as an ear drum perforation. "The bruising and tissue damage are premortem," he said. "You can tell that the cheek bruise was caused by a hand – you have a solid bruise with four short stripes coming out one side." He took some measurements and said, "With a high probability this is an adult male's right hand."

"I thought the dark area on her cheek was just a shadow," said Celia. Of course we couldn't get a good angle on that side when she was on the rock."

"Maybe the guy got violent when he grabbed her," said Jake. "I'd bet that Kaya would make something of that. What would cause that ear damage, doc?"

"I understand that the previous victims were killed by a sharp instrument inserted into the brain via the ear?"

"Yeah, we think it was an ice pick."

"This damage to the outer ear is consistent with something like an ice pick being pulled sideways across the auricle. That could be caused either by the wielder of the weapon or movement by the victim."

"Maybe she fought back," said Celia. "I hope so."

"If you look closely at the bruise behind her ear," said the pathologist, "it suggests the toe of a boot. See the straight line of a sole, then an almost circular patch of a toe?"

"So he kicked her in the head, slapped her on the cheek, tore her ear, then punctured it," said Jake. "A lot more action than the first two."

Carefully combing out her hair, the pathologist reacted, "look what we have, a hair that doesn't belong." He held up a black hair with his tweezers, clearly not a match for her brown frosted hair. "We're in luck, it's got a root."

"That could be golden," remarked Celia. "Nothing that good was found on the first two victims."

With a root, they should be able to get a full DNA analysis and look for matches in the DNA databases. Tom Ditkam, for example, would be in the state database because he was a convicted felon.

The remainder of the autopsy went as expected, she had the same brain hemorrhage as the first two victims, and the neck had been severed by a sharp instrument. After arranging for the head to go to their forensic odontologist and the hair to go to Chocolate, they headed back up the hill to Nevada City.

They stopped for lunch at Mo Manje in downtown Nevada City. The Cajun restaurant's name meant "I'm Hungry". They took a seat outside, both Jake and Purdy managing to get their backs to a wall, Celia depending on them to keep an eye out. Celia didn't have an appetite after the autopsy, but started her red beans and rice dish anyway. Halfway through, she forgot that she wasn't hungry. Jake had a Po' Boy and Ned had blackened catfish.

Back at the office, Cliff Stover joined them and they talked through what they had on Ditkam. The potential for his vehicle to have been at the previous head pose site, his record, his home's proximity to this head pose site.

"This guy feels good to me," said Jake. "I'd like to go through his place, but there's no way to get a warrant given what we have."

"If Ditkam's still on parole, all we need is for the parole agent to decide to make a search," said Stover. "He can run a search whenever he wants. There's one guy who handles most parolees up here, Burt Greesom. Let's check to see that he's got the case."

A computer verified that Greesom was Ditkam's parole agent.

"I know the guy," said Stover. "He's easy to deal with. It'd be nice if we had more on this Ditkam before we talk to him."

"You can't do a drive-by of Ditkam's house," said Purdy. "He's at the end of a dirt road. People up there in North San Juan pay attention to who's driving around. If he sees you drive to his place he's liable to get spooked."

"So we keep plugging for now. It'd be nice if he didn't know we were looking at him until we do a search," said Jake.

"Time for Yuba City to call," said Purdy. "What was his name?"

"Stan Voss," answered Celia as they headed for the meeting room.

At two, the conference phone rang and Purdy answered. "Ned Purdy. Is this Voss?"

"It is," said the speakerphone. "I've picked up some more information, but it's mainly about what to look at next. The woman who called the station Friday worked in the jewelry store for four years and knew Tomwick's routine. Tomwick's the owner and manager of the store. As far as she knows, Tomwick didn't have any current boyfriend or partner. She didn't know about any family or who Tomwick's dentist was. I did get the names of some bars and restaurants that the victim liked. I checked out her house. It's locked and there's no evidence of a break in or disturbance and her car isn't there. I've got one of our ADAs working on warrants for her house, car, credit card and phone records."

"You've been busy," said Jake. "Is there a Niebaums in town?"

"Are you kidding? This town's never had an economy to support a store like that. We've got one small mall with a Penny's and a Sears."

"Does it have a parking structure?"

"No, it's surrounded by ground parking."

"The first two victims were picked up in the ground floor of a parking structure after shopping at Niebaums. You might look for her car in your shopping center lot."

"I can get that done. I'm planning to hit her known hangouts tonight, I expect we'll get the warrant and do her house this afternoon."

"Why don't I join you for that, Stan," said Celia.

"That's fine. Call me when you get to town."

"I will."

After Voss hung up, Celia asked Purdy, "Can I get a ride over to a car rental outfit?"

"Sure," said Purdy. "Let me get you somebody."

"Jake, I'll pick up my stuff from the B&B," said Celia as she walked out of the room. "I plan to work with Yuba City tomorrow, so I'll sleep at home tonight."

"Good plan. Find us something good," responded Jake.

Jake logged in to JARS and noted that Ditkam was a person of interest in the latest murder. The entry already included everything they knew about him: license number, phone, address, a link to his criminal record, and the license plate detections by plate readers. Stover led him to the county information on Ditkam's address. Owned by somebody with a Nevada City address, the place had twenty acres of land but only 1248 square feet of house. It had been purchased at the peak of the market for $178k.

Next Jake added Tomwick to JARS as a probable victim in the case. He was going to find out Ditkam's work situation when an alert window popped up on his screen. JARS had discovered a connection between Sally Tomwick and Ditkam. Clicking on a link, Jake got to the data containing the connection.

"Got him!" Jake exclaimed. "Ditkam was convicted of robbing Sally Tomwick's jewelry store. We've got a solid connection."

"All right," said Purdy with enthusiasm. "An actual clue."

"Yeah," said Jake. "Take a look at his 2001 robbery conviction."

The other two scrambled to get at the information on their laptops while Jake went back to reading. He had read it and was thinking when Stover said, "They never recovered most of the jewelry – Ditkam only had a few pieces when they picked him up."

Jake responded, "Look at his life style: He's living in a small, inexpensive rental and driving a Chevy. That's not the life style of a guy that has two and a half million dollars of jewelry."

"Unless he's waiting to move it," said Purdy.

"We haven't found any agency watching him, looking for the jewelry to surface," said Jake. "You'd think he'd be getting some income off of a stash like that, even if he was being careful."

"If anybody was watching him, it'd be the insurance company that paid off Tomwick," said Stover. "I'll check on that on Monday."

"Good point," said Jake.

"So what if Ditkam had a partner in the robbery who kept the jewelry and never gave Ditkam a share?" said Purdy. "That could be why he never sold any of the stuff."

"But why wouldn't Ditkam turn the guy in?" asked Stover. "He'd already done time for the robbery, so he wouldn't be on the hook. Putting the guy in jail would be good revenge."

"Maybe Ditkam's afraid of the guy," said Purdy. "Or he hates the system so much he wouldn't help it in any way."

"Maybe his choice would be to kill the guy," said Jake.

Six seconds passed in silence, then "Tomwick," came from Jake and Stover simultaneously.

"What better place to sell stolen jewelry than in a jewelry store?" said Jake.

"Ditkam might have no proof that she was involved," contributed Purdy. "He was an ex con, she was a successful businesswoman, who would have believed him?"

"If she moved the goods, there'll be financial tracks," said Jake. "If there are financial tracks, you can compare what her customers bought to the robbery inventory and to her purchase records around the time of sale. It'll take some serious digging, but we can find out."

"In the meantime, we've got enough on Ditkam that I'd bet we can get a parole search," said Stover. I've got a cell number for his parole agent, let me try him." He dialed and waited. "Burt, this is Cliff Stover with the Nevada County DA's office. Am I interrupting something? Good. You might have read in the paper that we had a murder up here on Friday. A guy who's one of your parolees is looking good for it and we'd like to talk to you about him."

Stover ended up giving Greesom all the information over the phone. After hanging up, he said, "We got it. Greesom's going to do a parole search on Ditkam early Monday morning. We are invited along as is DOJ forensics."

"Great news," said Jake.

Stover and Purdy began organizing the local forces for the Monday event. Jake arranged for Chocolate's crew to participate, catching some grief about the early start time.

On a whim, Jake called his contact at the California Highway Patrol's Valley Division office in Rancho Cordova. The CHP, the largest state police agency in the USA, had a lot of resources and some responsibility for helping local agencies. Jake arranged to have one of their choppers come to the sheriff's office Sunday morning.

Jake caught Purdy between calls and interrupted Stover's mad typing. "Since we can't drive around to scout out Ditkam's house, I've got a CHP copter coming tomorrow morning."

"But that'll be worse than …" exclaimed Purdy before he was stopped by Jake's raised palm.

"We'll make a single pass over the house, just like we're in transit from town out towards Bullard's Bar Reservoir," said

Jake. "We'll get eyes on the area and some HD video to review. A single pass isn't going to make anybody nervous."

"I guess you're right Jake," responded Purdy. "It'll be a real help to know the lay of the land before we go in."

Jake went back to Ditkam's file and started reviewing his criminal record. He had served six months in county jail for a 1993 burglary conviction because he'd had the bad luck to be stopped for speeding when he had contraband in his back seat. This certainly was an indication that he wasn't a master criminal, but maybe he'd learned. There was only basic information on his 1996 arrest and trial for murder because he was acquitted and records from that era were not all digitized.

After they finished for the day, Jake called Fiona and made plans for a family afternoon and dinner on Sunday. It made him feel good. He yearned for a family life but had great difficulty making time for it. Intellectually, he knew that he was bullshitting himself, that if it was important, you prioritized it and made it happen. The compulsion to take down killers, awakened by Diane's death, drove him to devoting much of his life to his job. Interest and excitement about a job were good things. Jake realized that being compulsive about the job was doing damage to his life, but he wasn't willing to attack it as a problem. All this thought, of course, was at a level that he generally avoided. When he did go there, he rarely came back happy.

Instead of getting into his own head, Jake sat back and tried to get into the head of his prey. Why was this guy posing heads in a river? Why didn't he do it in a more public place? Did he have some special connection to whitewater rivers?

37. YUBA CITY

It was late in the afternoon by the time Celia and Stan Voss drove up to Sally Tomwick's house on Desert Wind Drive in Yuba City. Celia had checked out the house on Zillow and found a twenty year old 1900 square foot house worth about $170,000 in today's down market. For someone owning a jewelry store it didn't seem like much of a house, but then she didn't know how successful the store was. Houses in the area looked well kept; most of them had small front lawns with a tree. Unlike some neighborhoods in this price range, the street wasn't cluttered with cars.

They parked in front of the house, a pale blue California ranch home with white trim. A squad car and the Yuba City crime scene detail pulled up behind them. They sent one of the uniforms around back and waited for the radio confirmation that he was in place. Voss rang the doorbell twice, and then waited just in case somebody was there. They each put on booties and gloves, announced their presence and tried the door. It was locked, so Voss broke the sidelight window, reached in and unlocked the door. The two of them cleared the house then began a close exam while the crime scene guys took pictures. It looked like a tidy person lived here, but wasn't home at the moment. Nothing looked disturbed or unusual. The answering machine was blinking, so they listened to it. "Hi, this is Jason. Where've you been? Let's do dinner." A computerized voice followed with "Saturday, 11:20 AM. End of messages."

While the crime scene crew searched the house and made a mess with their fingerprint powder, Celia moved into a bedroom being used as a home office. Scanning folders in file drawers, she found business records and personal records. From the personal records she extracted a dentist's bill, writing the name and number in her notebook. She dipped in again and found phone and mobile phone billing records, as well as credit card records.

Voss joined her and suggested that they take her credit card records and go through them over dinner.

Leaving the scene to the techs they headed for JJ's, one of Tomwick's favorite restaurants, to troll for information, check her records for more bars and restaurants, and have some dinner. After they were seated in a booth enclosed by dark wood paneling, they asked to speak with the manager. Shortly, she emerged from the kitchen and sat down with them. After introductions, Voss asked her for information about Sally Tomwick, showing the manager her picture.

"Yeah, I know Sally," she said. "She's, like, in here once or twice a week."

"Does she come in to eat, drink or both?" asked Voss.

"She does both. I don't think that she likes to cook, so she eats out a lot."

"Does she eat alone or with others?"

"Used to be she was alone a lot. The last couple of months there's been a guy with her. She introduced me, but I can't remember the guy's name."

"How about a description?"

"The guy's kind of a turn off. He's old, has grey hair, a black nose, a double chin and a pot belly. He always seems to wear a wrinkled grey suit. The good news for our profit margin is that he drinks a lot, Jack Daniels on ice."

"So what's old to you?" asked Celia.

"Oh, maybe fifty," replied the twenty something woman.

"When's the last time you saw either of them?" asked Voss.

"I'm thinking that I might have seen her in here on Monday. Could have been Tuesday. She was alone."

"Anything else you can remember?"

"Well she, like, kisses him on the mouth when she gets here after him. When he's here last there's nothing happening."

"How about your staff, might they know his name?"

"Possible. That's a good way to get better tips. Sheila's our regular during the week. Lucky for you, she's pulling a shift tonight, she's your waitress."

The manager got up, waved the waitress over, and left for the kitchen. The waitress, a tired and lean brunette in her forties, took their dinner order then came back for their questions.

"Do you know this woman?" asked Voss again, showing the picture.

"Yeah, that's Ms. Tomwick," responded Sheila.

"Do you know her well?"

"No. She's the kind who looks down on servers, if ya know what I mean."

"But you know her name?"

"From the credit card. I try to use customer's names when I can."

"We understand that she's been in with a man in recent months."

"Yeah, Mr. Sellers."

"Thanks for the name. Do you know his first name?"

"Naw, he's even less friendly than she is."

"So he pays with a credit card?"

"Sometimes he does."

They talked with Sheila for several more minutes without learning anything useful. Minutes after they finished interviewing her, she delivered their dinner.

After a few bites Celia spoke up, "I hope that you can find better food than this in town."

"Well, a couple of places are better," said Voss, "There isn't much demand for high end dining around here. How about I take you out to a nice restaurant in Sacramento tomorrow night?"

"Uh," responded Celia, surprised at the quick come on. "That's a nice offer but there's somebody in my life."

"Well, if you change your mind, I think I'd enjoy some time with you," said Voss, letting it go easily.

To get past a feeling of awkwardness, Celia suggested that they split up the credit card records and look for bars and restaurants. Through the meal they compiled a list of eight places they could check out.

"If we can find him, I'd suggest we go for this Sellers guy before we go out trolling," said Celia.

"I agree," responded Voss. He pulled out his smart phone and had it search for *Sellers, Yuba City*. From the seven results, there was only one private individual and the app provided a phone number and address. As a bonus, the first name on the entry was Jason. "Let's just head over to his house."

"Works for me," agreed Celia.

Yuba City was small; it took them all of ten minutes to reach Sellers' address. Sellers' place was a large two story brick home with a three car garage, looking like it sat on two lots. The landscaping looked like it had been designed and maintained professionally. The place stood out among the basic homes on the rest of the street.

"Upscale for Yuba City," said Voss. "Wonder where the money comes from."

Their guy responded to the doorbell. Though he was in shorts and a golf shirt instead of a grey suit, the restaurant manager's description fit perfectly, down to the black nose. The nose was probably caused by far too many tumblers of whiskey like the one he was holding.

"Yeah?" he said.

Voss held out his badge, "I'm detective Voss from Yuba City PD, this is agent Moreno from the California Department of Justice. We'd like to ask you some questions."

"Really," said Sellers, the word a bit slurred. "Ask away."

"Would you mind if we came in, Mr. Sellers?. It'd be more comfortable and private," Celia nodded toward the next door neighbor working on his car in the driveway.

"I guess," said Sellers as he turned his back and walked into the house.

They followed him in and found him in a big leather recliner, taking a large swallow. When he didn't speak, they sat on a matching leather couch across from him. Looking around, it was obvious that a competent decorator had spent significant money here. Several bronze sculptures were strategically placed around the large high ceilinged room. The walls had a tasteful number of what looked like original art pieces. Unlike the neighbor, this guy probably didn't work on cars.

"Do you know Sally Tomwick?" asked Voss.

"I do indeed," responded Sellers. "She owes me a phone call."

"You're not going to get that call, Mr. Sellers. We believe that she's been murdered," Voss said, watching Sellers for his reaction.

He was slow on the uptake. Blinking several times and thrusting his head forward, his response was "Huh?"

"We haven't scientifically confirmed it, but we're quite convinced that her remains were discovered on Friday."

"Remains? Holy shit. Remains?"

"What can you tell us about Sally Tomwick, Mr. Sellers?" asked Celia. "It would help us to understand her better, know about her friends and enemies."

"What am I, her social secretary? I don't know any of that crap, don't care about it. Maybe she said a few things like that but I didn't pay attention. That wasn't the deal."

"So you don't know anybody that might want to hurt her."

"No, I don't. She was a businesswoman, so she must have pissed some people off, but I don't know who they'd be."

"Yes sir. What was your relationship with Ms. Tomwick?"

Sellers drained his whiskey glass, got up and walked to his wet bar. As he filled his tumbler from a bottle of Wild Turkey Russell's Reserve Bourbon he said, "Relationship. Yeah, I guess we sort of had one. We ate and drank and fucked each other."

Not expecting such a raw description, Voss said, "So not exactly a romantic relationship?"

"Romance? I had romance. It cost me half a million fifteen years ago. Fuck romance. Sally and I just sort of got it on a couple of times a week, that's all. Too bad she's dead."

This guy's money hadn't bought him any class, thought Celia. His mind's as black as his nose. "When did you last see Sally, Mr. Sellers?"

"That'd be a week ago. Yeah, last Saturday. We ate at Angeline's then came back here to drink and do the nasty. She was good at it, even if she was kind of flabby."

"And where were you this week, Wednesday night through Friday morning?" asked Voss.

"Where was I? You think I was involved?" Sellers was getting a bit sharper on his feet.

"We just need to be able to rule you out," said Voss, trying to keep the discussion low key.

"You can do that. I was in LA Tuesday night until about eleven this morning. Played in a golf tournament with a buddy."

Voss took notes on the trip details so he could verify Seller's alibi.

"Have you lived in this area all of your life, Mr. Sellers?"

"Not yet."

"This is a nice house, Mr. Sellers," said Celia. "What business are you in?"

"I'm in the business of enjoying my money," was the reply. "I rode the mortgage business hard all the way to the top, ended up with three companies. I sold them in 2006 before the buyers figured out that the boom was done."

"So you were into subprime mortgages?"

"Was I ever. You know about the sucker born every minute? They were all in the housing market back then. They bought over their head, signed ridiculous mortgages and dropped money in my pocket. Back in the Gold Rush the shopkeepers mined the miners. I mined the house buyers."

Voss' cell phone rang. He answered, listened, and said, "Where." Listened some more, said, "Be there in ten."

He stood up and said, "We have to go. Thanks for your time, Mr. Sellers."

Celia was ready to leave even though she didn't know Voss' reason. This guy was a complete sleazeball. Nastier people were out on the street, but this guy had damaged more lives than any hundred of them and was proud of it. She wanted a shower.

Back in Voss' car, he spoke up, "A patrol unit found Tomwick's car."

"In a shopping center?"

"No, down near her house."

"So another break in the pattern."

"Seems like it."

They drove back south on the Garden Highway. Shortly after they saw the flashing red and blue lights they joined three official vehicles in a cull de sac, surrounded by a huge weedy field. The only civilian vehicle was a silver Lexus GS sedan. A patrol car had spotted it out here, an unlikely spot for anything but an abandoned junker. When the plate matched the Tomwick plate listed in a BOLO, crime scene and Voss were notified. The same crime scene crew that had done Tomwick's house was at work on the car. The quick exam of the interior and trunk had found nothing.

"I'm surprised to see this thing here," said Voss. "It disappeared at least a day and a half ago. I would have expected somebody to spot it out here and have it parted out or headed for Mexico by now."

"Dumping it out here is a different MO," said Celia. "You've got to wonder about the logistics. Where did it come from, who drove it here, how did he or they get Tomwick out of town."

"He or they? I thought you had it figured at one man."

"We did. Having this car here raises the possibility of one person driving her car, one person driving another."

"Or, he could have left his car here, walked out to the Garden Highway and taken a bus to most places, including the mall. Then he could jack her and the car, drive them back here, load her up and go."

"That's plausible. The chance of getting useful ID information from a bus ride at an undetermined time is zero."

While the detectives had been talking, the crime scene crew had set up a series of powerful lights, angling towards the field from the road. Lighting from an angle created shadows that highlighted tracks and footprints. "Stan, we've got something for you," called one of the techs.

Celia and Voss walked over to the edge of the pavement at the front of the Lexus. The car straddled the curb, its right two wheels were in the dirt.

"You can see by these tracks that the Lexus was backed into this spot," said the tech.

"Then we look behind the car," he said, leading them around the Lexus. "and we see a different set of tire tracks and a set of boot tracks. I'd say that the two vehicles were backed up to each other. The boot tracks show the driver getting out and walking around the front of his vehicle. There's another set of tracks where the driver walks from the back of his vehicle to the driver's door. There are no tracks next to the passenger side doors of the Lexus."

"The boot tracks and other vehicle tracks look like they match what we've found before," said Celia. "You'll record them like the DOJ crews do?"

"We will," said the tech. "We're going to wait until morning to process details."

"Stan, I suggest that you have the DOJ do the detail on the car. They're good at it. This time it appears that our perp may have been in the victim's car. There should be a good chance of some kind of transfer; at least a hair."

"I was planning on it," responded Voss.

"Thanks. We've collected history, friends and family data on the first two vics to do connection analysis. If you could gather history info on Tomwick we could look for connections to either of the other two."

"That stuff is in my to-do list. I'm about done in for today though, I'll start back in tomorrow."

"Yeah, it's been a long day for me too. Can I get a ride back to my car?"

38. NEVADA COUNTY; SUNDAY

Jake enjoyed another Magic Inn breakfast, this time thick slices of French toast with a custard topping, thick cut applewood smoked bacon, and fresh fruit. As much as he hated to, he passed on the coffee cake that beckoned to him from the center of the table. Ten years ago he could and would have gotten away with eating half of it, but now it would result in unwanted growth.

Two couples from the Bay Area were also at breakfast, tourists visiting the gold country. Jake had pleasant conversation with them but responded to their career questions with generalities, not wanting to talk about his business in the county. It turned out that three of the four worked for startups in Silicon Valley. This was the first weekend they'd taken off in two months. Jake remembered the excitement and enthusiasm that kept you going at a startup, not to mention the lure of getting rich if the company went public in a big way. It had worked for Jake – he'd had fun, learned a lot, created a lot, and made lots of money. On the other hand, these kids had about a one in five chance of real success.

Excusing himself, Jake took the Sunday paper outside. The article today was one column, below the fold. *Promising Forensics in Whitewater Killer Case.* Browning had done another interview, once again mentioning that he was running for State Attorney General. This time he said that Saturday's autopsy produced valuable but unspecified forensic evidence. He also disclosed that his team was now working with six jurisdictions because the latest woman was from Yuba City.

Jake kept himself at a slow boil, though his dentist wouldn't have been happy at the way he clenched his teeth. Deciding to distract himself, Jake called Celia to get an update on the Yuba City action. He got the facts as well as an earful about what an asshole Tomwick's fuck buddy was.

"I gather you don't care much for this Sellers character?" Jake said with a grin that Celia couldn't see.

"Jake, I have two good friends from college who have been financially destroyed by the housing crash. They had insane mortgages from a white collar thief like this Sellers. The guy convinced them that after a year they could refinance into a better mortgage, and then everything turned to shit. They lost everything but their 401K."

Losing the grin, Jake said, "Sorry C, I know that lots of people got hurt. Guys like your new friend made money off the top, and then sold the mortgages to other people who ended up holding useless paper. In the meantime, your buddy's laughing all the way to the bank."

"He's not my buddy, you jerk, he's a total asshole."

"Whoa C. You're right and I'm sorry if I got you worked up. Go kick something and get it out of your system."

"It's a good thing you're not here; I would have kicked you."

"It is a good thing," agreed Jake, thinking of her taekwondo prowess.

Jake told Celia about the connection between Ditkam and Tomwick as well as the search planned for Monday.

At the sheriff's office, Jake looked at the license plate reader data for Ditkam's plate again. He realized that Ditkam was down in Sacramento late in the day that Sally Tomwick disappeared, and then the following two days including early morning on the day Tomwick's head was found. All it really told him was that Ditkam didn't stay in the hills on those days and where he was on a few specific times. The plate reader unit had only been at the current location for a few days before its first detection of Ditkam. There was no way to tell if he had been in that area when the earlier abductions and murders had taken place.

Purdy hung up his phone and turned to the other two. "That was my Narcotics Task Force contact. He says that they've only observed Ditkam because he works with a known meth seller. The two of them were observed going to the Crazy Miner's bar together."

"What's the bar like?" asked Jake.

"Our local rednecks, young punks and lowlife drug users hang out there. You can sample the bunch by driving by; they hang around the sidewalk to smoke."

Twenty minutes later Jake, Stover, and Purdy were outside the building, watching the Eurocopter AS350 B3 copter land in the field next to the parking lot. Flying bits of dry grass filled the air, striking them hard enough that they turned away to protect their faces. The wild grass in the field had recently been mown to eliminate the fire danger posed by the tall ripened stalks. The unforeseen side effect was the creation of thousands of tiny missiles to be fired by the copter's downdraft. Hearing the turbine winding down and seeing the missile barrage stop, the three men turned and walked to the six person copter. Climbing inside and donning headsets so that they could communicate despite the turbine noise, Jake explained what he wanted to accomplish and why. He pulled out a map and worked out a route with the pilot, who created a waypoint for Ditkam's house in the GPS navigation unit.

After spooling up the turbine, the pilot lifted off and climbed to eight hundred feet above the ground while turning towards Ditkam's house.

Jake pulled an HD video camera out of his field bag and set up to record their overflight. Once they had the river in sight, the pilot backed the speed down to a hundred knots to give them a bit more time over target.

"I'll pass by the house about a hundred feet to the right so you can see it and get your video," said the pilot through the headset intercom system. "When we pass this vineyard up ahead we'll be one minute out. I'll be about five hundred feet above the house."

"Twenty seconds. Ten Seconds. The next house near the left side."

They passed by the house, seeing a small and simple structure with a detached garage sitting in a clearing. The dirt access road continued past the house for about three hundred yards and came to a dead end. No nearby structures were visible, but they had only a second to look as the copter continued on a straight line towards Bullards Bar Reservoir.

At the reservoir the pilot turned southwest and sped up to the machine's cruise speed 132 knots or 150 miles per hour. They followed the combined North and Middle forks of the Yuba for about 10 miles before a slow turn took them over the Bridgeport covered bridge on the South Yuba and headed them towards the sheriff's office. When they disembarked after thanking the pilot, Jake checked his watch and noted that the entire activity had taken twenty minutes. The copter was a great tool.

Back in the office, they reviewed the video and decided to send a pair of deputies through the woods to cover the back of the house. That way, if Ditkam tried to book out the back when the search crew arrived, the deputies could bag him. Since the operation briefing was set for five thirty the next morning, they decided to call it a day.

Jake drove over to Fiona's house, expecting to have some family activity hours. Without explanation, Fiona declined, so Jake and Kaitlin took off.

They drove up Highway 20 to Five Mile House and parked. They hiked part of the Pioneer Trail, loosely following the route of the 1850 cutoff of the emigrant trail. When they finished, Jake let Kaitlin choose their dinner restaurant and they ended up sharing a combination pizza.

When he got Kaitlin home, Jake found a serious Fiona. She listened to Kaitlin's account of the afternoon with only one comment, and then said, "Kaitlin, why don't you go to your room for a while. I need to talk to your father."

Kaitlin opened her mouth to object, but her mother's stern face halted the process. She looked at her dad, who shrugged and said nothing.

When Kaitlin was gone, Fiona said "Sit Jake."

When they were both sitting, she began. "Jake, as much as I've loved you, the two of us just don't work as a couple. What I want from a partner and what you are willing to provide are too far apart. Life is too short for me to keep hanging on, hoping that you'll change. I'm dating a man and we want to pursue a relationship. To make that work, you're going to need to fulfill our custody agreement and take Kaitlin every other weekend."

Jake sat, stunned. He felt like he had been hit in the chest with a sledgehammer, he couldn't take a breath. He had thought that they were doing well, that they had a good chance for getting better. "Why didn't we talk this through before you got involved with somebody?"

"Jake, we've talked it through. Many times. Your commitment to law enforcement not only causes me too much worry, but it eats so much of your time that there's none left for a relationship. You've known this, but haven't changed. I'm done waiting. You now need to spend significant time with your daughter; she needs you and I need the relief."

"But every other weekend just doesn't work, Fiona. When a case gets hot, it's a seven day job. I love Kaitlin and do want to spend more time with her, but a rigid schedule just doesn't work."

"That's your problem Jake, not mine. You figure out how to make it work. I expect you to take her every other weekend. Pick her up Fridays, return her Sunday evening."

"But," Jake started, then stopped. He didn't know what to say. In a daze, he got up and began the walk to his SUV.

Fiona called after him, "Next Friday Jake. You pick her up."

Jake drove down the street towards the Magic Inn. After two blocks, he turned off his route and drove to the biggest liquor store in town. Finding an acceptable bottle of reposado tequila, he bought it and headed for the inn.

Back in his room, he poured tequila into the wine glass in his room and sat down. It's right that I spend more time with Kaitlin, he thought. She needs a dad actively involved in her life and that should be me. This thing with Fiona though, I've got to turn that around. I love her and I know she loves me; we should be together. I've got to figure out a way.

Three glasses of tequila later he stumbled to the bed without a solution.

39. YUBA CITY

By the time Jake started at the Nevada County Sheriff's office, Celia was walking into the Yuba City Police Department building on Poole Boulevard. Stan Voss met her and walked her back to his desk in Investigations. As they walked, she told Voss about the Ditkam connection and the planned search.

Two computer monitors sat on Voss's desk. One was attached to a mini tower PC standing in the isle. "Our tech guys got past her logon password for us, so we can do some data mining," said Voss. I've been looking through her contacts, but it's a big list and you don't have a clue what the relationship is. Like you look up Jason Sellers and there's no note that he's an asshole or a good lay or anything. Just phone numbers and addresses.

"How about email?" asked Celia.

"Let's try. Here's an Outlook icon; if she uses Outlook at least I'll understand how to use it."

"Yup, Outlook is her mail program," said Celia as the program came up displaying a list of items in the inbox. We can use the search option to save a lot of work. Try searching on 'Ditkam'."

"Sure," said Voss, selecting the search option and keying in Ditkam. "No luck. I'll try 'Tom'."

Thirty messages with 'Tom' showed up, but ten minutes of wading through them produced nothing that appeared to be about Tom Ditkam.

After slogging through emails for an hour, they had identified a sister and a female friend. The PC's contacts list gave them phone and address information: The friend was in Yuba City, the sister in Sacramento. Another hour of digging produced nothing of real interest.

They switched to the Outlook calendar function, but it appeared that Tomwick didn't use it.

Celia's cell phone started up with the ring tone she had set up for calls from Jake. He asked her for an update on the Yuba City investigation.

"We've gone through Tomwick's email, but haven't found any references to Tom Ditkam or Mason Resto."

"Too bad, that could have helped a lot. Nothing about this case is easy. I'd like you to get a handle on Tomwick's financial situation. We're hypothesizing that she sold all the goods stolen from her store in 2001 after she collected the insurance."

"I'll take a shot at it Jake. Not today though. Hey, I'd like to bring Kaya to tomorrow's search of Ditkam's place."

"It'll be a bit crowded, but better you two than a bunch of suits. See you bright and early."

Celia hung up, then called Kaya's cell. The phone connected on the fourth ring.

"Hi Celia, what's up?"

"Are you enjoying a personal Sunday?"

"I am, and it's delightful," responded Kaya.

"Nice that somebody gets one. We're going to do a search on our Nevada County person of interest first thing tomorrow morning. I'd expect that we'll also interrogate him. Would you like to join us?"

"Yes indeed. Seeing his place and his behavior will give me significant information."

"I'll pick you up at the Park n Ride on Taylor in Roseville at four fifteen."

"Four fifteen in the morning? Really?"

"Yeah. The briefing for the event is in Nevada City at five thirty."

"That's going to be painful. I'll see you then."

Back at Tomwick's computer, Voss pulled up her income tax software and looked at her last tax return. The return indicated about $105,000 in net business income, not a lot for an established small business. Celia asked for and got a copy of her returns going back to 2001 so that she could look at them later.

Looking at Tomwick's browser history they figured out that she dealt with Vanguard, so they tried her logon password and got access to her portfolio. She had just over two million dollars spread across four accounts.

"That's a lot of assets for somebody with her income," said Voss.

"You got that right," responded Celia. "Though she could have inherited a lot of it or earned a lot in another job or business."

"That's true. You get one fact and then you need a bunch more. As best I can tell, she's only had these accounts for three years, so we have no meaningful history."

Voss had set up appointments to interview Tomwick's employees, so they shut down the computer and headed off for the first of the three. Two hours of work did the job since the small town made driving times short. All three employees did the same kind of work. They sold jewelry as well as keep the place neat and appealing. One of them also had basic skills for resizing rings and minor repairs. None of them dealt with the books or the purchasing side of the business, that was Tomwick's domain. None of them had a personal relationship with Tomwick. Two of the employees had been hired in October of 2007 at the same time as all of the existing employees were let go. One had passed them the rumor that Tomwick had also replaced all her employees after the 2001 robbery.

While they were driving back to the department to pick up Celia's car, she said, "I'm thinking that the idea that Tomwick sold the goods stolen from her has some merit. Her assets and the firing/hiring activity both support that notion."

"What about the hiring and firing?" asked Voss.

"Think about it. If she's going to start moving the stolen goods, the whole business is going to change. She'd have to keep buying some goods to avoid a big red flag, but she'd have to cut retail prices to get her volume up and sell the stolen stuff. Old employees might even recognize the stolen pieces when Tomwick came up with them. Same kind of thing when she finishes moving the goods – the business has to change. She didn't want employees figuring out that things were hinky."

"Good analysis, you could be right," responded Voss. "How do you think we should pursue that notion?"

"I'll look at her tax returns as soon as I find time. Unless she was also cheating on her taxes, the extra income will show up there. You could get a warrant and analyze her business books. You could also interview her employees in the 2001 to 2007 time frame, comparing their memories of the business with the descriptions from the current bunch."

"So we're chasing a crime here, but it's not finding her murderer."

"It's giving us solid motive for the guy who robbed her store to turn around and kill her."

They reached Celia's Mustang. "Nice car," said Voss.

"I enjoy it," replied Celia. "It makes my dad nostalgic; he owned a '65 stang. Young guys get off on the exhaust sound. So you know how to get to the sister's house?"

"Yeah, I've got a portable GPS for that."

"I'll follow you."

During the drive south to Sacramento, Celia ignored the soupy green rice fields bordering the highway while she made calls. First she left a message on Torrey Bonner's work phone, asking him to check on Mancuso's activity for victim three's snatch and dump days. She skipped his cell and called the office because she figured that Mancuso was a real long shot; let Bonner have a weekend. Next, she called Rich Luton's cell to ask him about Resto. His annoyed response was "Look, when I find the bastard I'll let you guys know. In the meantime, give it a rest."

"OK Rich, sorry to bother you on a Sunday," was Celia's mild response. She didn't like being snapped at, but she also knew that being pestered made her irritable, so she couldn't blame him. She had learned to roll with it when pestered by the suits, but from another detective, maybe not.

They rolled through most of Sacramento on I5, exiting on Sutterville road then turning south again on South Land Park Drive. After a few blocks they turned onto Kennedy Circle and pulled up in front of an aging, but well kept, ranch house. The homes in this area sold for twice as much as most of the homes in Yuba City even though this was not the high end part of Sacramento.

The woman who opened the door was about five six wearing a colorful summer blouse tucked into white capris. Limp black hair topped a long face with dark black eyebrows and lashes surrounding dark brown eyes. Her stand out feature was a long jaw descending from a pair of small crimson coated lips. She was a bit broad of beam and looked to be in her late thirties. Wafting past her was the smell of bacon.

Voss introduced the two of them to Donna Simpson, the sister of Sally Tomwick. As soon as Simpson knew that they were law enforcement, Simpson moved those small lips around in ways that Celia had never observed before. She realized that the woman must have more facial muscles on that long jaw than any ten ordinary people.

Celia let Voss take the lead because it was his case and because she could then concentrate on observing. Once they were sitting in a living room furnished in 1990s overstuffed that was heavily floral, Voss started. "I don't know if you're aware that a missing persons report was filed on your sister last Friday?"

"No I'm not. Nobody contacted me and I had no idea that she was missing," responded Simpson, her eyes widening and her lips roaming to the right.

"So you're not in frequent contact with your sister?"

"Not really. We email every couple of weeks and talk on the phone maybe once a month. You haven't found her?"

"We're not positive, but there's a high probability that we have."

"Oh my God." Lips moving impossibly high on the left, she said "What's happened to her?"

"We believe that she's a victim of murder, ma'am."

Her face dissolved into a portrait of misery, lips moving down towards her chin. "This can't be. Sally was my older sister, my only remaining family. She can't be gone."

"Does this look like her ma'am?" said Voss as he held out an eight by ten photograph, mercifully void of flies and cropped to show only the chin up.

"Oh God, that's her. That's my sister." The tears began draining from her eyes, destroying her eye makeup before running down her face. She brushed at the tears with the back of her hand, drawing a black line across her cheekbone.

"We're so sorry for your loss Mrs. Simpson," said Celia, with all the warmth she could muster. "Losing family is painful."

Voss gave Simpson a minute. He hated notifications, especially to women. Crying had always been a challenge for him to deal with.

"We'll be able to get confirmation that it's your sister in the next couple of days ma'am. In the meantime, we're trying to learn as much as we can about her. Are you up to helping us?"

Donna Simpson struggled to regain her composure. At her core she was a caring, helpful person so Voss' appeal struck a chord. She sniffed repeatedly, trying to get her running nose tamed, pushing her lips up to her nose in the process. Accepting tissues from Celia, she wiped and blew and got herself under control.

"I'll try, detective. Go ahead and ask."

"Are you aware of any enemies that your sister had. Is there anybody who might want to harm her?"

Simpson thought for a moment then replied, "I don't know of anybody, but I wouldn't be terribly surprised if there was somebody like that."

"Why do you think that?"

"Sally is … kind of hard. She's nice only to those people she thinks she can get something from. That's why we weren't close; she didn't see much value in me anymore." Her lips formed an upside down "U". Another tear began its way down her cheek and she brushed it away.

"Anymore?"

"John, my husband and I helped her start her jewelry business in 1999. She asked for more money in 2001 but John said we couldn't risk it and we said no. She hasn't visited us since and only communicates when I initiate it."

"Have you observed other examples of this behavior?"

"Yes, detective. Our mother and I both observed Sally as a child repeatedly being an exploiter. Even though mom knew what was happening, she let Sally exploit her until she died. I always hoped that Sally would grow out of it, but I didn't see it happen. She could be cruel."

"Do you know of anything criminal that your sister has done?"

"Oh no, detective, nothing like that. Except for speeding, of course. That's not really criminal though, is it?"

Ignoring the rhetorical question, Celia asked, "What do you know about your sister's financial situation?"

"That's not something she talks, uh talked, to me about. I guess I get hints over time though. She seemed to be living well a couple of years after she asked us for more money. In fact, she gave us back our loan money, surprising us. In the last couple of years she seemed to tighten up though. I wasn't hearing about fancy travel, things like that."

"How about her friends," asked Voss.

"Sally never had friends that I knew about. People who she was using thought that she was their friend, but they generally found out that they were wrong. It was sad."

"Can you think about anything else that might help our investigation?"

She thought a minute, her lips moving around in a large circle, then said, "I guess that I didn't know much about my sister's life, detective. I'm sorry, but I can't think of anything right now." The tears started again.

The two of them got up, thanked her, gave her cards, and left her with her grief.

When they reached their cars, Voss spoke up, "She paints a picture that fits what we've found."

"Yeah, Tomwick seems like a piece of work. Well, it's still a crime to kill a bitch. Did you see the way the sister's face moved around?

"Yeah, weird."

"I've never seen anything quite like it. Maybe she should be a mime," said Celia.

I'll call you tomorrow after we finish up in Nevada County."

"See ya," said Voss, getting in his car.

40. NEVADA COUNTY; MONDAY

The large group involved with the Ditkam search gathered just before the 5:37 sunrise. Burt Greesom was running the show and made it clear that only he and sheriff's personnel were to be involved before the scene and Ditkam were secured. Since the house might be the scene of multiple murders, the order was out that any law enforcement entry was to be with booties and gloves to prevent contaminating the scene. Two deputies were sent off early in an unmarked car so they could work their way through the woods and be on station behind Ditkam's place. The biggest initial concern was that somebody in the area would see the operation unfolding and alert Ditkam. Many people on the ridge had no enthusiasm for the law. When Greesom decided that the scene was secure, he would call in the DOJ contingent to check the place out in detail.

The remainder of the group headed out from the sheriff's office on schedule for a six thirty knock on the door. The goal was to have Ditkam awake, but not ready to leave for work. They drove northwest on 49, down into the river canyon followed by a steep climb out. Turning right on Tyler Foote Road, they drove five minutes to the staging area at Dad's Market.

As soon as they received radio confirmation that the deputies had the back of Ditkam's house in sight, Greesom and Purdy pulled their car onto the dirt road that led to Ditkam's and stopped two hundred yards short of the house. A patrol unit pulled up behind them to prevent civilians from driving down the road. Greesom, Purdy and a deputy walked carefully up to the corner of the house. Leaving the deputy, Greesom and Purdy walked to the front door. While ninety percent of a wall on a frame house provides no protection from a serious weapon, there is a five inch vertical strip of real protection provided by the framing at the edges of a typical door. At about four inches of wood thickness, the frame would stop a forty caliber pistol slug, though not a serious rifle. Using this cover as much as possible by turning sideways in front of it, Greesom knocked on the door.

They heard a noise from inside that sounded like a chair scraping back on a wood floor. Silence followed. This was not an area where people came up and knocked on your door, so it was understandable that Ditkam might be concerned. On the other hand, you didn't know what he was doing with all the time. Greesom waited fifteen seconds that felt like sixty, then knocked again.

The door opened and a stocky, muscular man a bit shorter than average looked at them. His angry brown eyes bounced back and forth between the two men. "What the fuck are you doing here?"

The two men had checked Ditkam's hands as the door was opening. Seeing them empty took away some of the tension, seeing no weapons on his person took away more. "You're the subject of a parole search," said Greesom, pulling out the paper.

"Damn. Why are you hassling me? I ain't done nothin'"

Ignoring the man's statements, the same bullshit words he heard all the time, Greesom asked, "Are you alone in the house?"

"Yeah."

Greesom signaled the deputy to come to the door.

Leaving Ditkam at the door with a deputy, Greesom and Purdy put on booties and gloves, then cleared the house. When done, they cleared the garage. Purdy then got on the radio and invited the remainder of the sheriff's contingent to the house. Greesom explained to Ditkam that he'd have to stay with the deputies while the search was in progress.

Greesom and Purdy began a careful walk through the house. Not touching anything, they tried to take it all in while looking for anything that might be evidence of a crime. There was no obvious evidence and no indication that more than one person lived there. Disappointed, Greesom radioed clearance for the DOJ contingent.

As Jake drove the DOJ SUV to Ditkam's place, he was thinking about Fiona and what he was going to do about her announced plan. Realizing that he needed to focus on the task at hand, he mentally slapped himself and worked to compartmentalize his thoughts of her.

When he arrived, Jake let Chocolate and his crime scene crew get to the house first. He, Celia and Kaya took their first in-person look at Ditkam. Topped with long, coarse black hair tied in a ponytail, his stocky body looked to be in good shape except for a bit of a belly, His tanned face was ordinary other than a few pockmarks on his full cheeks and a thick black mustache. He was dressed in auto shop blue pants and a plain white t-shirt, white socks but no shoes. His eyes and demeanor gave Jake the simultaneous impression of anger and resignation. Ditkam's right arm had a tattoo that they couldn't decipher from twenty feet away.

The house and its immediate surroundings were underwhelming. About the size of a doublewide, the house was stick built and shabby. The area around the house was a combination of packed dirt, ripened native grasses and outright weeds that had been cut with a weed whacker. Jake always thought of the grass as brown, but California's public relations people called it golden. Further away from the house was oak forest dotted with ponderosas and some manzanita thickets.

Entering the house they were assailed by the look and smell of a bachelor's pad. The small living room looked barren. A midsized flat screen television was sitting on a beat up blond wood table next to a satellite receiver. A dark brown, heavily distressed table sat next to a recliner covered in a fabric that had once been pale green. Fishing magazines were neatly stacked in a magazine rack on the other side of the chair. The walls were a dirty white, a theme that would be continued throughout the house. No pictures were on the wall, no decorations of any kind. Barren.

The kitchen fit the same theme. Cheap white cabinets, Formica counter tops and a basic set of white appliances covered two walls. A small, well used wooden table sat against a third wall, accompanied by a single chair. Apparently Ditkam didn't host dinner parties. The place was neat, but looked grimy.

Opening the refrigerator, they found a large supply of Budweiser to go with the large bottle of Ancient Age bourbon sitting on top. Two packages of cheese, four packages of lunch meat and condiments were in the refrigerator, not a single fruit or vegetable. The freezer was packed with frozen dinners and trout. Clearly Ditkam wasn't a member of the area's organic and natural food faction.

They glanced in the other rooms and found more of the same. The crime scene techs filled the master bedroom and bathroom. The small spare bedroom had two tables set up in an "L" shape, covered with materials and tools for fly-tying. It was neat and organized with materials all stored in small plastic boxes.

Leaving the house to Chocolate, they headed for the garage. Outside was a twelve foot aluminum fishing boat with a five horse Honda outboard sitting on a trailer. The garage had more fishing gear neatly hung from peg boards attached to the walls. A set of waders was hung in a cabinet, the boots were beneath them. Most of the space was taken up by the vehicle, a white 2007 Chevy Suburban half ton four wheel drive K1500 LS. It had the license plate they already knew about and the Bridgestone tires that they were looking for. The rear seat was sitting on the floor of the garage.

A fully suited crime scene tech got in the Suburban, backed it out of the garage and into position to be winched aboard a tilt bed truck. Ditkam was yelling. "God damn it, that's my only ride. How the hell am I supposed to get to work? You bastards." Nobody bothered to answer him.

Greesom, Purdy and Stover joined them by the garage. "What do you think?" asked Stover.

"The guy's not much of a decorator and likes fishing," said Jake. "I hope Chocolate finds something, because I sure didn't see anything useful."

"We didn't see anything either," said Purdy. "We're going to take him in for interrogation, you folks are welcome to watch and listen."

Kaya spoke for the first time, "Unless he gives it up, I'd like to see how he reacts to a woman. Can you give Celia a few minutes with him?"

"We'll see how it goes," was Purdy's noncommittal response. He turned and walked over to Ditkam, introducing himself and Stover. Purdy asked, "Where's your cell phone?"

"I don't have one."

"Bullshit, everybody has one."

"Not me, I don't need to talk to nobody."

"We'll see." Purdy would have loved for Ditkam to have a smartphone that logged GPS coordinates about where it went. He'd check with the two cellular companies that provided service in the area to see if Ditkam had an account. Given that there wasn't a landline in the house, you'd expect Ditkam to have a cell.

"Since you don't have any transportation, why don't we give you a ride to town?" said Greesom.

"That'd be good," responded Ditkam.

"How about we talk for a while, Tom?" asked Purdy.

"I guess so."

"We can't do it inside until these guys are done, so let's go to town and get comfortable."

They drove back to the sheriff's office and a deputy took Ditkam to an interrogation room. The room, plain on the inside, was soundproof and contained hidden mikes and cameras. This particular room didn't have one way glass, but it did have a room nearby with screens and speakers for observers. Stover, Jake, Celia and Kaya settled in the observation room. Jake sat next to a speaker and pulled out his smartpen. He wanted a recording for JARS that had indexed access.

Greesom entered the interrogation room with a cup of coffee, Purdy followed him. Greesom offered the coffee to Ditkam, who took it and began to drink.

"So far, it appears that you've been clean in Nevada County Tom," said Greesom.

"Damned right. I am clean, so why are you hassling me?"

"We'll get to that. Tell detective Purdy about your job. Who do you work for, what do you do, when do you work?"

"I'm a car mechanic. I work at Kirby's on Gold Flat. I do everything but trannys though I haven't trained on the high end Kraut cars yet. What else did you want?"

"Work schedule."

"Yeah. I work Monday, Wednesday, Thursday and Saturday, eight to four thirty.

"Kind of a screwy schedule."

"Yeah, it sucks. I wanted five days and two days in a row off, but I'm low man on the totem pole. At least I've got a steady income."

"So what do you do with your spare time? It sure isn't cleaning house."

"Fuck cleaning. I got no bitch to do it and don't want one."

"You don't care much for women?"

"Hell no. They ain't good for nothin' but dipping my wick and gob jobs."

"Back to your spare time."

"Oh yeah. I fish and I watch TV."

"What kind of TV do you watch?"

"I sure don't watch cop shows. I do reality shows and good movies like Steven Seagal makes."

"Where have you been fishing?"

"The water's been too cold up high so I've been doing the Yuba below Bullards Bar and Collins lake."

"What about the American and the Tuolumne?"

"I've fished em both, but not in a while. Tuolumne's too far for a one day trip."

"What about the South Yuba?"

"Not now, man, it's running way too high."

"Where were you last Wednesday?"

"I work on Wednesdays."

"What about after work?"

"Sometimes I go to the Crazy Miner's on Wednesdays. I think I went last week."

"What do you mean, think? It was just last week for Christ's sake," broke in Greesom in an annoyed voice.

"It all runs together man. Doesn't matter anyway."

"It does matter, stump. You're going to want an alibi."

"What're you talkin' about?"

"Later," said Purdy. Tell me about the take from your robbery in Yuba City. The jewelry never turned up but you're not looking too wealthy."

"That fucking bitch was supposed to give me my cut when I finished my time," said Ditkam, getting red in the face. "She blew me off so I told the cops down there, but they fuckin' ignored me."

"Which cops did you tell?"

"I dunno. Some detective in Yuba City."

"If she ripped you off I can understand why you killed her."

"Whadya mean, killed her. I didn't kill nobody."

"You did it Tom. You killed her last week and cut her head off."

"That one last week that was in the Saturday paper? That was Tomwick?"

"You knew before the papers, stump. You put her head on the river just down the road from your house," was Stover's comeback.

"You know what, it couldn't have happened to a better bitch. I'd buy the guy who did it drinks for a whole night."

"You'd be buying yourself drinks, stump."

"I ain't no stump. I didn't kill that bitch. I did seven long fucked up years for that robbery. There's no way I'm doing anything that would send me back. That's why I'm clean."

"You're going down, stump."

"You might take me down, but I didn't do it."

Purdy got up, gave Greesom a nod and they walked out, locking the door behind them.

Back in the observation room, Purdy said, "Jake, why don't you and Celia take a crack at him on the other murders. You two know the details better than we do. Since he hates women, having a woman in there might produce something."

"We'll give it a shot Ned," responded Jake.

Kaya spoke up, "He's going to hate having a female in control of him. Be aggressive and pushy. Jake can be his buddy, understanding how hard it can be to tolerate women. I expect him to get hostile and foul mouthed; ignore it, don't let it goad either of you. Find out if he's got a woman in his life."

"Sounds right to me," said Celia.

They entered the interrogation room and introduced themselves. They could read the tattoo on Ditkam's arm now: *Life's a Bitch and then you Die.*

"So you're familiar with the Tuolumne River?" asked Celia.

"Yeah," responded Ditkam, his angry eyes starting at her breasts.

"Which spots on the river do you fish?"

"It's kinda tough to get to the river but I go down around Lumsden campground and the Lumsden bridge. A couple of times I've hiked down to the river from that forest road."

"So where were you on Tuesday, May 24th?"

"How the fuck would I know? If it was Tuesday, I wasn't working. I was probably fishing somewhere but I don't remember. Where the hell were you on Tuesday the whatever?"

Ignoring the question, Celia said, "You don't have much of a memory do you? Does the rest of your brain perform as poorly?"

"The hell with you, bitch," yelled Ditkam, starting to get up.

"SIT DOWN!" was Celia's forceful comeback. "We're not done. Where were you on Friday June third?"

Ditkam had sat back down on command. His face was red and he was radiating anger. Looking at the wall, he was quiet for a minute, then said, "After Memorial Day? I was fishing the Yuba, down where the middle fork joins the water out of Bullards."

"Do you have any witnesses?"

"A couple of guys were there, but I don't know 'em."

"You were on the middle fork all right, but the middle fork of the American where you left the remains of another woman. We have evidence that puts you there."

"Quit yellin' at me, I ain't done nothin'. I was on the Yuba."

Jake spoke up, quietly in Ditkam's ear, "You'd better give her something man, she'll just tear you up. These women have all the power now."

Showing relief at talking to a male who wasn't hostile, Ditkam said, "I've got nothin' to give up, I didn't do nothin'. For the first time in my life I've been clean and now you people are all over me. I don't keep track of when and where I go but that don't mean I'm a killer."

"So what do you do for fun besides fishing?" asked Jake. "You have a woman?"

"I get laid when I need to, but I sure don't want a woman around all the time, messing with my life."

They continued working on him for forty minutes, Celia playing the aggressive woman and Jake the friendly guy. Ditkam wouldn't budge off his story and ended up looking wrung out. Finally, he said the magic words, "I want a lawyer."

"You can have one if you can find one," replied Celia. "We've not detained you or arrested you so we have no obligation to provide you with a lawyer."

"You're shitting me. I don't have to be here?" asked Ditkam, looking at Jake.

"You did have to be here. Condition of parole."

"I'm gone." Ditkam got up and walked out the door.

Jake and Celia followed him out and watched him head for the exit. "That wasn't worth much." said Jake.

"We learned that he hates women," answered Celia. "He didn't give us much that's useful, so if he's our perp he's not a complete melon."

Back in the observation room, Greesom said, "We didn't find anything to violate him on. If you do, let me know. I've got too big a caseload to spend much time on any one of these people."

"Thanks for running the search Burt," said Purdy. "I'll let you know what forensics comes up with."

"That's good Ned. See you later."

After Greesom left, Purdy said, "Ditkam's got motive for our killing. This guy not only hates women, but he really hated Tomwick."

"She gave him good reason, if what he said was true," added Jake. "He seems to have opportunity for all the killings, but we need some solid evidence to nail him."

"Let's hope your crime scene guys find some," said Stover.

Kaya spoke up, "This guy's kind of a mixed bag relative to our profile. Everything he has at home is organized and in place, almost to a level of compulsion. He seems to be smart enough and he's got the anger. On the other hand, the standard profile includes middle class status and a relationship with a woman."

"So another profile down the drain," retorted Jake.

"Maybe the guy's had enough bad experiences with women that he's given up on relationships," said Celia, annoyed at Jake's firm, mindless opposition.

"I think that Ditkam's our guy for now," said Purdy. "We'll go where the evidence goes."

They were taking a break when Chocolate walked in, paying them a courtesy visit on his way back to the lab. Once they gathered together, he started. "I've got some preliminary results for you. We have some reasons to be optimistic, but nothing is dead bang yet. He's got boots that match what we're looking for and a ragged blue sweatshirt that might match the Tuolumne thread. We found some blood between the vinyl floor and the bathtub and we pulled a hairball from the tub's trap that looks to have hair other than the occupant's.

Ditkam had a lot of fishing gear, including wader boots matching what we're looking for. He had a sharp filleting knife, but he also had fish fillets in the freezer. We did not find weapons or drugs or an ice pick. With the priority that Browning's providing, we should get DNA from the extra hair on the victims head by this Friday. The rest of the DNA we won't get until Tuesday of next week."

"That's good stuff Willy," said Jake. "We need one solid piece and we've got this guy."

"Thanks for the briefing," said Purdy. "We'll be looking forward to the results."

When Chocolate had left, Purdy asked Stover, "We need to chase down his credit card and phone records. How about I get with the cellular companies, you do the credit cards?"

"Works for me."

Jake spoke up, "You guys have lots of empty forest around here, but if Ditkam got lazy he might have buried remains somewhere near his house. You might want to get out there with some cadaver dogs. Until you get to that you might want to keep an eye on the area since Ditkam's out and around."

"Good idea, Jake," agreed Purdy.

"Ned, are you OK with Celia and I interviewing Ditkam's boss?" asked Jake. "I think it would be a good idea to get to him quickly."

"Sure. That'll save me from one report at least."

Jake and Celia drove the mile to a deli in downtown Nevada City for lunch. Jake got pastrami, Celia vegetarian. Both sandwiches were far larger than they needed. Eating on the patio, Jake pointed out the old gold mining equipment that decorated that part of town.

"That thing over there that looks like a big pipe is called a monitor. It's a water cannon that shot high pressure water at hillsides and eroded them away so that imbedded gold could be extracted. These things could shoot a stream of water four hundred feet. This was such an effective form of mining that the companies running these operations created a massive water infrastructure. A mine out near Ditkam's house used something like fifteen billion gallons of water in a year. The first long distance telephone line was built in the mountains to manage water flow. Hydraulic mining is incredibly destructive. These monitors blasted away well over a billion cubic yards of hills and much of the debris was flushed downstream, choking the rivers and killing the fish. In the Sacramento valley, mining sediment caused serious floods and buried a lot of farmland. Hydraulic mining started up in these mountains around 1855 and was outlawed in California around 1884 after a major court case."

"It sounds like an environmental disaster, Jake."

"You're right, it was unbelievable. You can still find immense gravel fields down towards the valley. The court decision is viewed by some as one of the early environmental laws."

"Thanks for the history lesson. How do you remember all this stuff?"

"It just interests me, C. I got into it when I was exploring this area with Kaitlin. I'll give you the story on this other equipment some other time."

A three minute drive took them to the auto shop where Ditkam worked. The concrete block building had four work bays and an office. It was surrounded by hundred foot ponderosa pines.

Introducing themselves to the shop's owner Dale Kirby, they left the tiny and messy office, moving out back for a private discussion.

"So you guys are why Tom was late today?" asked Kirby. "Is he going to be arrested or what?"

"At this point, we'd call him a person of interest, Mr. Kirby," responded Celia, trying to play down the situation. "We'd like to know his work schedule and any other information about him that you can give us."

"I gave him a schedule he doesn't like, but it's what I need," responded Kirby. "Business is tough these days. I've got him working Monday, Wednesday, Thursday and Saturday."

"And what time does he start and finish?"

"I've got him working eight to four thirty."

"Is he always here between those hours?"

"Yeah, I watch the hours on my guys. He doesn't leave early and you can bet that he doesn't stay late."

"What kind of a worker is he, Mr Kirby?"

"He knows what he's doing and doesn't make many mistakes. That's a good thing because he doesn't take criticism well. I don't think of him as a hard worker, but he gets his job done. Are you planning to arrest him? Do I need to find a replacement?"

"We have no current plans to arrest him," said Jake. "I can't speculate about the future. Do you keep accurate records of the days and hours that he works?"

"I do. Do you need to see them?"

"Not right now, thanks. Maybe in the future. I do need a close look at his work area."

"Sorry, but my insurance only allows employees in the work areas."

"You don't want to make me get a warrant do you?" responded Jake with a tone and a look intended to make Kirby nervous. "That wouldn't be pleasant for either of us."

"Uh, well, OK. Just for a minute though, alright?"

"That's all it should take."

They walked around the building, stopping in front of the bay where Ditkam was bent over under the hood of an older Honda. Kirby had Ditkam step out front. Ditkam, clothing now grease stained, looked at them but he didn't say a word.

Walking to the front of the Honda, Jake said quietly to Celia, "I wanted to pick up a grease sample to compare against the grease found on victim two."

Celia responded, "You know Jake, we can get some grease from the shop, but what if the grease came from some customer's car? There's no way to track that down."

"Good point C. We'll just do what we can, pick up some grease from the shop." Opening an evidence bag, Jake used a tool resembling a popsicle stick to scrape up some grease from the lift and insert it into the bag. Sealing and labeling the bag, they took a quick look around but saw nothing of interest.

As Jake drove them back to the sheriff's office, Celia commented, "That shop was sitting in the middle of a ponderosa pine forest Jake. Any other shop around here is also in the forest. There's got to be ponderosa pollen everywhere so I don't see what good this evidence is going to be."

"I'm not sure that it has any value. The lab would have to be able to find something unique about the grease or something in it, otherwise the grease won't be helpful in court. To us, it'll be just another indicator that Ditkam fits the known evidence."

Back at the office, they found out from Purdy that Ditkam was a rare American adult, he didn't have a phone or a cell phone.

"He could have a prepaid cell phone," said Celia.

"But where is it?" was Purdy's comeback. "It wasn't on him, in the house or his car."

"What if he's got it at work?" asked Jake. "We didn't search his work area thoroughly enough to find one. Let me call his boss."

Kirby had never seen Ditkam on a phone or with a phone. They agreed to leave the question open and move on. Purdy headed out to manage the canvass of Ditkam's neighbors.

Jake talked Celia into writing the report on the auto shop visit and interview. While she worked on it he logged into JARS and pulled up the case calendar. As he thought, every abduction and head discovery had been on a weekday that Ditkam had off: Tuesdays and Fridays. There was one exception, the abduction of Sally Tomwick, who they believed had been taken on a Wednesday evening though it could have been on Thursday.

Pulling up Google Maps, Jake got directions from Kirby's auto shop to where Tomwick's car had been abandoned in Yuba City. The drive would take an hour. Unless Ditkam had an alibi for the previous Wednesday evening, he could have easily been down in Yuba City before Tomwick even left work.

Jake couldn't remember what Ditkam had said about last Wednesday so he pulled out his smartpen and notebook. Scanning down his notes to where he'd noted *Wed*, he tapped the pen and the pen played back the associated audio, quickly getting to the important part: *"Sometimes I go to the Crazy Miner's on Wednesdays. I think I went last week."*. The bar might be Ditkam's alibi.

Jake was getting hungry. Looking over at Celia, he saw that she was on the phone so dinner would wait a while. Plugging his smartpen into his laptop, he started the process to upload the recording and notes into JARS. The recording would be transcribed into text in the process so you could retrieve either the audio or the transcript and be indexed into either format. Once the uploading was done, he initiated the same process for the interview with Kirby, linking it to Celia's report.

Celia ended her phone call and spun her chair around to face Jake. "I just got an update on what's happening in Yuba City."

"Anything earthshaking?"

"No."

"Give me the highlights. Purdy and Stover can get it from JARS if they want."

"Voss got Tomwick's dental records. He scanned them and sent them to our forensic odontologist. We should have results tomorrow morning."

"We need to dot that 'I', but we know that we've got Tomwick," commented Jake in a bored voice.

"I said, 'not earthshaking', didn't I?" was Celia's response.

"Sorry, I'm just getting tired. Go on."

"Voss and crew are interviewing the sister again looking for connection information that might tie Tomwick to the other two vics. They've found a couple of friends and will be doing the same interviews with them."

"That's good. They just might stumble on something to connect Ditkam with the first two."

"Voss is also trying to find the people who worked at the jewelry store when it was robbed. He figures they might remember Tomwick's behavior. That's about it."

"OK, thanks for the update, C. How about some dinner?"

They drove down the hill on Broad Street into Nevada City and found a parking place on the really narrow Commercial Street. A short walk got them to the town's only fondue restaurant that also had a good menu of other fine meals. Inside, they were greeted by delicious odors and dark cozy booths.

Jake ordered a Cabernet Franc from the Nevada City Winery, one of more than a dozen local wineries. Celia decided to start with an appletini. After delivering some warm, crusty bread, the waiter took their orders. Celia was having macadamia nut crusted halibut, Jake a prime rib. Sitting back with their drinks, they enjoyed the guitar music leaking around the corner from the bar.

Jake began to lighten his burden. "Last night my life kind of turned sideways. Fiona didn't go out with Kaitlin and me like she usually does. When I brought Kaitlin home, Fiona told me that we're done. She's seeing some guy and wants a relationship. She needs some time alone with him, so I am supposed to take Kaitlin every other weekend."

Celia felt hope blossom in her chest. Suppressing the desire to take advantage, she chose to be a friend. "Has Fiona done this kind of thing before?"

"I think that she's had some dates, but as far as I know, nothing serious. Even though she initiated the divorce, we've stayed real close. I always had hope we'd get back together. Now she's saying that we're done, there's no chance. This sucks."

"What do you want to do about it Jake?"

"I don't know. I think I have to respect her wishes and go along, but I can't stand the idea of losing her. I want her to talk through things with me, we were always good at that."

"Is she open to talks?"

"I don't think so; she seems to have made up her mind."

"Jake, maybe you have to go along, but this relationship might not work out for her. It's hard to find a good partner once you're a full adult. She could well find this guy's a loser and change her mind about talking."

"Maybe you're right, but damn it, I hate this. Something hugely important to me is out of my hands."

"I'm sorry that you're going through this Jake." Celia had conflicting feelings running like a Ferris Wheel inside her. On top was empathy for a friend in pain. Going down, anger at Fiona for hurting him. On the bottom, hope for his freedom. Climbing to the top was annoyance at herself for giving him a reason to hang on.

Jake sat with his face in his hands, his elbows on the table. After a minute, their food arrived and quiet eating began. Jake picked at his food but drank a second glass of wine. Celia found the moist fish with the nut flavor delicious and ate the whole serving.

"Let's go check out this Crazy Miner place," said Jake. "See if they give Ditkam an alibi."

"Not a good idea Jake," responded Celia. "Purdy should be involved. You're in a bad place over Fiona. The Wednesday customers might not be there on Monday."

"I'm going. Your option to come along or not."

"That's democratic."

"It is what it is."

They finished their meals in silence, then paid the bill and walked out into the cooling evening air. The sign above the Crazy Miner's door was visible down the street. Jake started in that direction.

"You're just going to leave me here?" asked Celia.

"Here," said Jake as he tossed her the car keys.

This isn't good, thought Celia. He's not thinking this through, he's upset and angry. Combine that with being a cop in a redneck bar and it's like lighting a match in a fireworks stand. She called out, "Hold up Jake, I'm coming with you."

Partway down the block they spotted three scruffy looking men standing at the curb in front of the bar, having their smokes.

"I bet in the winter they stand out in the rain and snow to get their nicotine hit," said Celia.

"Yeah," grunted Jake.

Going through the door they were engulfed by thick air that smelled like unwashed men. Details weren't visible in the darkness, but it looked like there were about six empty seats in the place, two at the far end of the bar. On the route to the empty stools, none of the clientele they passed looked like they enjoyed theater or orchestra music. Mixed grooming patterns were evident; shaggy hair and beards or shaven heads and tattoos. As they sat down, their nostrils wrinkled from an odor of stale beer combined with urine smells wafting from the nearby bathroom. No more unwashed smell, just a stench.

As their eyes adjusted to the dim light, they noticed that they'd attracted a fair amount of attention. The bartender finished loading the tired looking waitress' platter with bottles of beer, then headed their way.

"I thought I knew all the cops around here," was their greeting by the bartender. A big man, his forehead glistening with sweat, he wasn't smiling.

Only a bit surprised at being made, Jake said, "DOJ. We're working with the sheriff on his piece of a larger case."

"Big time pigs eh? Why don't you leave before you get my customers worked up?"

"We'll be going after you answer a couple of questions. You know Tom Ditkam?"

Heads turned toward them. Jake ignored the action, focusing on the bartender.

"Yeah I know him. Regular customer. Why are you after him?"

"Was he in here last Wednesday?" asked Jake.

"Hell yes, he's in here every Wednesday, wasn't he boys?"

Grunts of "yeah,"" yup," and "fuckin' A" came from the patrons around them.

A mountain of flesh moved up to Jake's stool. The man stood at least six foot six and had to weigh well over three hundred. A massive belly made you think of him as a fat boy until you noticed his large, well defined arms. Prison tats circled the thick neck that held up a large shiny head. He held his left forearm in front of Jake's face. Jake read the blue and red artwork: Fuck You.

"That's not friendly," said Jake in a mild voice.

"You get outa here now or they'll have to scrape you off the floor," rumbled the mountain.

"Excuse me," said Jake as he began standing up off the stool.

Celia was already on her feet, but a man was standing behind her, inches away, flexing his hands. Others were packing around them, sensing action.

Jake used his legs, shoulder and right arm to drive his fist into the mountain's groin. The big man drew back his right arm before the pain hit him, then grabbed for his damaged testicles. Jake put all he had into a left handed uppercut to his assailant's jaw. The blow snapped the mountain's head back, his eyes rolled up in his head and his body fell backwards into the two men behind him.

The man behind Celia reached around her with both arms, grabbed her breasts and lifted her off the floor. She bent her right knee then kicked downward at an angle, raking the man's shin with the heel of her shoe. Before he felt the screaming pain from his shin, she tilted her head forward and snapped it back, crushing his nose. She was free, but another man was swinging at her head.

Jake took a fist to the cheek from a new assailant, snapping his head towards the bar. He blocked the next blow with his right forearm, spun and drove his left fist into the man's gut. From behind him, a beer bottle descended, hitting his head and disgorging a full load of beer as it shattered. Jake went to the floor.

Celia ducked under the blow and drove her fist, middle knuckle extended, into the man's solar plexus. Without pause, she spun around, using that force, her shoulder and arm to drive her elbow into the next man's throat. Stepping inside the third man's blow, she slapped both his ears with flat palms, instantly disorienting him and breaking his right eardrum. Stepping back, a kick to his knee put him down.

Seeing Celia destroy four men in seconds motivated the rest of them to back off. Hearing thumps behind her, she glanced and saw two men kicking Jake's inert body. Spinning and leaping she kicked the nearest man in the temple and he collapsed in place like one of the twin towers. The other kicker saw what she'd done and backed off, holding his hands in front of him as if to ward her off.

Pulling her weapon with her right hand and her cell phone with her left, she dialed 911. "Two police officers attacked in the Crazy Miner Bar, Nevada City," she announced. "We have at least three injured." She listened, said "yes," listened again, said "yes" then snapped the phone closed. "Cops are coming boys," she announced in a loud voice.

Men began leaving. First a couple, then a few more, then a rush. By the time the Nevada City Police arrived, only Celia and the bartender were standing. Jake and two other men were still on the floor. Celia had checked Jake. She knew that he was breathing and there were no major crush injuries to his skull so she left him on the floor, knowing that moving someone with unknown injuries was dangerous.

Jake had awakened while they were waiting for help. He was groggy and didn't quite know what was going on. He did know that he hurt, so he stayed down. The paramedics arrived soon, checked him out, put on c-spine protection and loaded him up. Next was the five minute ambulance ride to the Sierra Nevada Memorial Hospital. As they wheeled him into emergency, Celia joined them. She'd put off the Nevada City Police and driven the SUV to the hospital. After two hours of x-rays, prodding, poking, questions and waiting, Jake was in a hospital bed.

"So what happened C?" asked Jake when they were alone. "The last I remember was punching somebody."

"Given that the back of your head was wet, stunk of beer and bottle shards were in your hair, the detective in me theorizes that you took a beer bottle to the head."

"It feels like it. Damn, do I have a headache."

"You're lucky that's all you have, though I suspect you'll be sore all over tomorrow from the kicking you took. You were stupid tonight Jake, you could have gotten killed."

"God, I could have gotten you killed. You look fine, did they leave you alone?"

"They had to be convinced. I'm fine other than my complete exhaustion. I've been up since three this morning. Coming down from the adrenaline rush is leaving me with nothing."

"Don't drive home. That's too nasty a drive in your condition."

"Agreed, no way I'd try that."

"I've got an unused room at the Magic Inn. Take my key."

Fiona walked into the room. Ignoring Celia, she hurried to Jake's bed. Sitting on the edge of the bed, she cooed, "Jake honey, are you all right? What happened to you baby?"

Knowing that this woman was the root cause of all the damage, Celia's depleted adrenaline gland gave her a weak squirt. She held back the anger, gave Fiona a withering look, and walked out.

41. NEVADA COUNTY; TUESDAY

Jake woke at six thirty. Despite the hospital he had managed to sleep. He felt OK – no headache and his face only hurt when he moved his jaw. Deciding that there was no reason to stay in the hospital, he rolled over to get up and was hammered by pain. His ribs didn't want him to move and were voicing loud complaints. Carefully rolling onto his back again, Jake decided to wait for breakfast and to talk to a doc.

By ten, Jake had consumed a breakfast not worthy of the Magic Inn and had talked to the hospitalist assigned to him. She reviewed his x-rays and checked out his torso, giving Jake a chance to see the massive bruises. She asked him a number of questions looking for concussion symptoms. Finally, he got the news that despite the pain, nothing was broken. He had a concussion and she'd like him to stay under observation for another day. Jake said that he appreciated the hospitality, but not enough to stay another day. The doc gave him a list of concussion symptoms and told him that consequences of a repeat injury in the near future were likely to be severe. "Look Jake, a grade two or three concussion like you had is a mild form of traumatic brain injury. A repeat, particularly before you are free of symptoms from this injury, is something we worry about a lot. You really don't want to end up with these symptoms being long-term."

"I'll be good, doc, I just need to get out of here."

Jake drove to the sheriff's office to check in with Ned Purdy. He described the Crazy Miner experience and got a cool reception.

"Jake, I gotta tell you that I'm not happy with what you two did there last night. This is our killing and our investigation; you need to coordinate stuff like that with me. After last night,

Ditkam will have twenty witnesses who'll swear on their mother's life that Ditkam was at the bar last Wednesday. Not to mention that you pissed off the Nevada City Police and I'm getting blowback from them."

"You're right Ned, I'm sorry. I was in a bad mood and made a couple of bad decisions. For what it's worth, I think the people in that bar would have testified for him whether we showed up or not."

"I guess that's true. Some of the people that hang out there are real lowlifes."

"They do like to fight, though."

"From what I heard, most of that bunch won't be picking fights with Celia though."

"Yeah, taekwondo's been her hobby for a long time. Messing with her is a bad idea."

"On another subject, Jake, we've got cadaver dogs lined up to search Ditkam's place tomorrow. The property owner's been cooperative. He's given us permission to search and, if necessary, dig. "

"Great. I hope Ditkam was stupid and we get lucky. I'm going to head back to Sacramento to get some work done and do the afternoon's task force meeting."

"Sergeant Tom Max at the Nevada City PD needs a statement from you about last night. Why don't you stop by on the way."

"Sure. I owe them for creating a mess in their town," said Jake as he stood up with a groan.

42. SACRAMENTO

Celia arrived at work about ten after a Magic Inn breakfast and driving down the hill. She had decided to take a hard look at Tomwick's finances with the hope of finding proof that Tomwick had sold the jewelry that Ditkam had stolen from her store. On the way down she called Jake's hospital room and found him awake, sore and grumpy. "You're like most guys, a crappy patient," she said. "If you insist on checking out, come on down the hill and get some rest."

Worried about him, but knowing that she couldn't help, she got down to work. First she looked into the jewelry business. In half an hour she had some generalities about the finances of small jewelry shops. You charge double the cost of goods, so your gross income gets split into three major buckets: 50% for goods, 40% for operating costs, 10% for profit. Sell a million dollars worth of goods and take $100,000 profit.

If Tomwick started selling stolen goods she'd have no cost of goods and reduce her operating costs since she wasn't paying to cover an inventory. She could get maybe 70% profit from their retail price. Unless she's also trying to cheat the IRS by not putting the extra income on her tax returns, the returns should show part of what's going on.

Setting up a spreadsheet, Celia started extracting tax numbers and plugging them into the sheet. Luckily for her, Tomwick had tax data going back to 2001. It became quite clear that something major had happened. The business income doubled in 2002 to $250k, then up in the $330k range for the years through 2007, falling until she was down to $105k in 2010. Of course the great recession of 2008 probably hit her volume hard, even if she was still trying to sell stolen goods. Let's see, if she was selling only stolen goods through 2007, she would have sold ballpark $3.2 million worth. What was the value of the stolen goods?

Looking up the reports on the 2001 robbery, Tomwick claimed to have lost $1.25 million worth of goods. That would be wholesale value, so they would have had a retail value about $2.5 million. Tomwick must have sold some legitimate goods during the 2002-2007 time frame to make her business look legal.

So maybe Tomwick had just had great business success before the recession hit? Celia pulled out the cost of goods sold from the tax returns and put them in the spreadsheet. That made it all crystal clear: During the years when her profit went up, her cost of goods sold went down. Thank God she was apparently afraid of the IRS, who might audit cost of goods sold, but didn't argue about high profit.

This whole thing needed business records and a forensic accountant but the lawyers could deal with that, she had more than probable cause. Sally Tomwick was dirty, Ditkam's claim that she kept the goods was almost certainly correct and he had a great motive for killing her. Tomwick pulled almost two million from the robbery Ditkam had done, he'd pulled seven years in prison.

When Celia got back from lunch with Kaya she found Jake at his desk. Looking him over, she said, "You've got a bruise on your cheek, what's the rest of you look like?"

"You'd like to know, eh?" he said with his wry smile. "It's not a pretty sight right now. According to the doc, the big thing is not banging my head for a while."

"I guess I'll have to take a holiday from slapping you upside your head. Too bad." Shifting gears, she said, "I've got probable cause that Tomwick sold the stolen goods in her store over the seven years after the robbery, making a ton of money selling them at retail. Her insurance company might want to run with this and get their money back, but it sure creates great motive for Ditkam to kill her. Take a look at these numbers."

Jake looked for a minute, and then said, "Great work C, you've got her. Why don't you put together one chart graphing these numbers that you can show at the task force meeting?"

"Sure."

"I did my interview with the Nevada City PD. They want one from you soon. Here's the guy's card," said Jake.

"Yeah, I know. I'll deal with it tomorrow."

Sam Nakamura started the task force meeting at four on the dot. There were now six jurisdictions plus the DOJ. He started with Ned Purdy.

"I'm Nevada County Sheriff's Detective Ned Purdy. A local young woman discovered the severed head of a woman in the South Yuba River last Friday. We believe that the head belonged to a Yuba City woman by the name of Sally Tomwick. Saturday's autopsy of the head indicated fatal brain damage caused by a sharp instrument inserted through the right ear. That's the same method used on your previous two victims. A single strand of black hair was found mixed into the hair of the victim. Based on information from Jake Appleby, we began looking at a local named Tom Ditkam. On Sunday, the JARS system found a connection between Ditkam and Tomwick. It turns out that Ditkam had robbed Sally Tomwick's store in 2001. He did time in Folsom Prison for it. We searched Ditkam's house yesterday. We found no smoking gun, but we're pending on several lab analysis. We interviewed Ditkam and didn't get much other than that he hated Tomwick. Tomorrow we'll have his credit card information and we'll be doing a search of the area around his house with a cadaver dog."

"Next is detective Stan Voss, detective with the Yuba City PD.

"Hi. We got a missing persons report on Sally Tomwick late last Friday. The woman owned and ran a jewelry store in town and lived alone. We got the call suggesting that she was a murder victim on Saturday morning. She has just been confirmed as the victim by the DOJs forensic odontologist. We found her vehicle abandoned about a mile from her house, it's at the DOJ lab. We have no idea where the actual abduction happened. We've been interviewing family, friends, and employees. Nothing that seems useful, though we do have some connection data on her life. We've got a team canvassing near her home, though the home itself looks clean."

"Next let's have Willy Jackson, DOJ Forensics," said Sam.

Willy's smiling image popped up on the upper left of the participant's monitors. "We're getting more action on this killing than the other two, having some fun and keeping busy. The hair mixed with the victim's is in DNA analysis. We're expecting results Friday thanks to priorities given this case by Chuck Browning. We're working on Ditkam's SUV, nothing has turned up yet. We're also working on Tomwick's car and have found no blood, no hair other than hers. The tire tracks and boot tracks found next to her abandoned car match what we found near the Tuolumne scene.

The grease sample from Ditkam's job is consistent with that found on the head of victim two. Ponderosa pine pollen was in both at similar proportions. We have no science regarding matching grease samples so I'd suggest treating this as circumstantial evidence of low value.

Now to Ditkam's house search. We have a sweatshirt consistent with the fiber found near the Tuolumne scene, but again that's only circumstantial evidence since it's a common fiber. We have two different blood samples found in the seam between the bathtub and the vinyl floor. The blood types match victims one and three and the samples are in for DNA analysis. We're working through the hairball from the tub's trap, excluding Ditkam's hair based on other samples from the house. There was a sharp fillet knife in his fishing gear that could have been used to sever a head. There was some blood residue between the blade and handle but it turned out to be fish blood. The house video, still shots, and inventory are already in JARS. That's it for now."

"Torrey Bonner."

Torrey's image replaced Willy's and "Torrey Bonner, detective, Walnut Creek PD" appeared below the image. "Pauli Mancuso claims to have been in New Orleans at a convention last week. If it confirms, we can eliminate him as a person of interest. I've talked to four of Sophia Mancuso's college rowing teammates. They don't recall that Sophia and Gina Roberts had any relationship other than teammates. What I've seen so far on this new victim shows no connection to Sophia."

Rich Luton was next. "Mason Resto is still missing, but we found out that he'd arranged for another realtor to cover some things for him, an indication that he intends to return. We've checked out the houses Resto had access to that have gone off MLS. Five of them appear unoccupied, we're chasing down the owners to get access. Like Torrey, so far I don't see a connection between our victim and this new one."

"Celia Moreno," said Sam, keeping the meeting running.

"I've been working on the idea that Sally Tomwick had possession of the goods stolen from her store in 2001 by Tom Ditkam. The notion is that she sold them through her store." Celia's face and description was replaced on everybody's displays by a graph that plotted two sets of data. "This graph has the years 2001 to 2010 on the X axis, dollars on the Y axis. The blue line shows that her profits rose dramatically for the six years after the robbery, and then dropped like a stone. The red line shows that her cost of goods sold dropped during the period of high profits. I have no doubt that Tomwick was selling the goods stolen from her store and that Ditkam's claim of her being a partner and cheating him is correct. We're arranging for a forensic accountant to do a professional analysis."

"So Ditkam was telling the truth and we have proof that he has one hell of a motive," said Purdy as his image popped up on the right of everybody's displays. "Good work."

"Thanks," said Celia. "That's all I've got for now."

"Kaya Lane, DOJ profiling."

"I'd like to point out that these killings have occurred in a small period of time. From the first abduction to the discovery of the third victim was only three weeks. Given that these are well planned killings by an organized offender I find it hard to believe that the killings were planned serially. Our perpetrator had to be planning multiple killings in parallel. This is unusual if not unique."

"Tom Ditkam fits the profile of our killer in some ways, doesn't fit in others. Profiling isn't perfect, but it tends to be accurate for this type of crime."

"Are you saying that Ditkam isn't our perp?" Jake's image popped up on the right side of the participant's screens.

"Strictly from a profile perspective, I'd rank the probability of Ditkam's being our perp as about sixty percent. You've got hard evidence though, that certainly trumps a profile. That's all I have today."

"Jake?"

"I've got a couple of things to talk about. First a timeline." A calendar popped up on their displays, showing part of May and part of June. "This is the JARS timeline/calendar tool set to show only abduction dates and head discovery dates. You'll notice that five of the six events occurred on Ditkam's days off: Tuesdays and Fridays. The sixth event appears to have occurred the evening of a Wednesday, but Ditkam could easily have done it after work because Yuba City is about an hour from where he works."

"Secondly, I'd like to compare what we know about the first two crimes with this latest crime. First the similarities: woman's head found posed on a rock in a whitewater river. Apparently killed by something like an ice pick through the right ear. The location of the remainder of the body remains a mystery."

"Now some differences. The first two women were in their thirties, attractive and Italian with olive skin, black hair and brown eyes. Our third victim is ten years older, heavier, brown/hazel and not very attractive. The first two were abducted in the covered parking lots outside upscale stores, the third was not done that way."

"The third abduction could have changed because the perp knew we were on top of his pattern," injected Celia.

"True. Also, if there was some reason to abduct from the Yuba City area, the covered structure and upscale store combination doesn't exist there. Worth considering though. The thing is, we've got a live one with Ditkam, but we need to keep looking and thinking on all fronts. If any of you come up with ideas or info, I'd like to hear it."

Nobody responded. A strange artifact of online meetings is that people didn't tend to make casual remarks or simple acknowledgements, thus the occasional awkward moment like this.

"OK people, does anybody have anything else?" asked Sam. After a few seconds of silence he said, "We'll do our next meeting Friday at two. Good hunting."

Jake owed Chuck Browning an update so he took a couple of calming breaths and made the call. "This is Jake. You wanted an update after our task force meetings?"

"Indeed I do," was Browning's response. "Be succinct, I'm busy."

Taking another deep breath, Jake went through the information brought up during the meeting. Browning interrupted with snide questions twice, Jake managed calm answers and completed the briefing.

"Appleby, it's time for you to get decisive and arrest this Ditkam. You have motive, means and opportunity. Put this man away so that we can tell the public they are safe."

"Ditkam's probably the guy," responded Jake, "but he'd have to be nuts to kill another woman now. The public is safe and we have time to get some hard evidence before an arrest."

"The man is 'nuts' as you so crudely put it. Killing and beheading three women qualifies him as insane. Appleby, I'm not making a request, I'm directing you to perform. You will have this man arrested."

"Yes sir," answered Jake through gritted teeth. "I'll pursue this with the Nevada County people who will have to do the arrest. You might want to talk to their DA about it."

"When I require suggestions from you, I'll request them. Stick to performing your duties as directed."

The connection dropped.

Jake spun his chair and exploded, "God damn, what a complete asshole! I can't stand working for that son of a bitch."

"Another good chat with Browning?" asked Celia.

"The asshole just 'directed' me to go arrest Ditkam. He knows that if there's a case, Nevada County is going to try it and they'll arrest him when they think it's appropriate. I think they're doing things right, but he doesn't give a damn."

"I agree that they're doing fine. So tomorrow talk to Purdy, Stover and Marti Nelson about arresting Ditkam, letting them know where the order is coming from. They'll ignore the request and Browning will have to push the DA if he wants an early arrest."

"That's about what I had in mind. I've got to stop letting the arrogant bastard get to me."

"Good idea, you'll be happier. I think that passive-aggressive behavior often works well for somebody like Browning. Changing the subject, I'm bringing Indian food and a bottle of wine to your house about six thirty. We're going to have a good dinner and do some talking."

"Yeah?" said Jake, giving her a quizzical look.

"Yes. See you then."

By a quarter to seven they had waded into a meal consisting of chicken tikka masala and vegetable curry on saffron rice accompanied by peshwari naan and mango chutney. Their first glasses of chardonnay were nearing empty. Pausing to suck some cooling air over a tongue assaulted by curry, Jake poured more wine.

"This was a good idea C. I haven't had Indian in quite a while, but I wasn't up for going to a restaurant."

"I suspected as much. How're you feeling?"

"Honestly? I'm beat up. It feels about twice as bad as a rough football game in high school."

"And you're not seventeen anymore."

"Not even close; I don't heal as fast as I did. I think I'm going to have to use the Jacuzzi tub tonight and when I get up."

"Do you use that thing much? I know that they've been the thing to have for a while. I've never used one."

"This'll be the first time I've used it. I'd prefer the serious unit over by the pool, but I'm not going to display this body for a while – too many colors. I've got your basic black, several shades of blue and purple, some yellow and a bit of red."

"You're a regular United Nations."

"Temporarily. Hey, I need to thank you again for saving my ass. I'd guess if you hadn't stopped those boys I'd be in a lot worse shape. When I've healed up we'll figure out a good reward for you."

"You do owe me. First you drag me into that place, then you abandon me to those Neanderthals while you play at fighting."

"From what I hear, you left some repentant Neanderthals behind."

"Maybe so, they deserved it. So look, for part of my compensation I want you to talk to me tonight. You were so worked up over Fiona the other night that you made bad decisions and put us both in danger. I know that this thing with her is tough on you, but let's talk through it so you can get back to functioning something like normal."

"I hear what you're saying C, but I don't know how to talk about it. It's even worse now. At the hospital she was all loving, then the next day it was back to 'you're just the father of our child'."

Celia had observed the loving part and was pleased to hear about Fiona's emotional retreat. "I'm going to lead you through it, maybe digging a bit. You just do your best to think, feel and talk."

"OK, I'll try. I'm going to switch to tequila," he said as he drained his wine glass. "Can I get you something?"

"More wine if you have it."

Settling down with more alcohol, Celia started. "So you two have been divorced for how long?"

Jake thought for a few seconds. "It'll be seven years this September. That's longer than I thought."

"You two must have dated other people since then."

"I did some. I just never dated anybody that clicked. I learned that for me, sex without real emotional attachment is like dry toast. In the last three years the only dates I've had are when I needed somebody for a particular event. They were more like companions than anything else. Look, this conversation is private right? Just between you and me, forever?"

"You're safe Jake. I won't ever talk about it to somebody else. So has Fiona dated?"

"Yeah, she has. She never talked about it but Kaitlin told me about a couple of guys. I wasn't happy about it, but what could I do. We've stayed close though."

"Sexually close?"

"Well, yeah, at least until recently. We were always good together."

"You've told me that she left you because you were so committed to police work after Diane was murdered that you had no time for her."

"That's what she said and she's stuck to it."

"Are you just as committed and just as unavailable now as you were when she divorced you?"

Taking a sip and a bite of lime, Jake responded, "I guess you're right. I still have that drive to get these bastards before they ruin more lives. The problem is that there's a never ending supply of bastards. It's been hard for me to even spend much time with Kaitlin."

"So despite your continued and almost exclusive love for Fiona, since you've become a cop you've never given her the kind of time and attention she wants?"

"Yeah," said Jake, looking at the floor.

"So here's what this all looks like to me," said Celia. "Fiona figured out seven years ago that love was necessary but not sufficient. She couldn't see you changing to give her enough time for her definition of partnership so despite the love that both of you had, she sent you packing. Either she hasn't met any worthwhile men since then or she hung on hoping for you to change. You haven't changed and she's moving on. Most people are done after a divorce, Jake. She's telling that she's done now."

"Oh man. But I …"

"But you still love her?"

"Yeah."

"Jake, you're lucky to have loved her like you did, luckier still to have love returned for a few years. Continuing to feel that kind of love for somebody who's moved on is like having an engine without oil – things are going to work poorly."

Jake was silent, contemplating the wreck of his love affair and marriage, that his passion for police work had doomed them. Looking up at Celia finishing a sip of wine he thought, maybe a cop relationship could work better. Her lips glistened in a face he knew so well and stopped to admire so rarely. I can't go there now, he thought.

Tossing down the rest of his tequila shot, Jake said, "C, you've done a lot for me. Tonight was kind of painful but I think it was a good thing. Your friendship is truly a wonderful thing; just don't go telling anybody that I said that. I think that you need to head home and I need that Jacuzzi. How about I send you home in a cab then pick you up in the morning?"

"I guess a cab's a smart move Jake. They seem to be getting fussy about cops driving drunk."

Jake pulled out his phone and called a cab. "They said five minutes. Can I get you anything?"

"No thanks Jake, let's just sit."

43. NEVADA COUNTY; WEDNESDAY

Jake got to Celia's place at seven fifteen. She was on the porch waiting. What kind of woman is this, he thought; they all make men wait. Driving back to his house, Jake avoided serious talk by posing the question: What was he going to do with Kaitlin for a full weekend?

"Consider making that room she sleeps into her own personal bedroom," suggested Celia. "Most women like to nest and, like it or not, Kaitlin's a young woman."

"Great idea, C. That might make her feel like it's one of her two homes since she's going to be here a lot. The work will keep us busy. Thanks. I bet you have some ideas on what we should do."

Jake's eyes glazed over as Celia, with enthusiasm, gave her decorating ideas with him muttering the occasional affirmation.

After dropping Celia at her car, Jake turned his Boxter around and headed for Nevada County.

At eight o'clock, after Ditkam was at work, two detectives, an evidence tech, two patrol deputies, a dog handler and his cadaver dog started working the property surrounding Ditkam's house. At Ditkam's house, the handler addressed the group. "This is Simon. He's a chocolate lab and cadaver certified with California Office of Emergency Services. Simon is trained to detect airborne scents from human remains, follow the scent to the source, then let me know he's found a source and lead me there. He ranges on his own and it works better if we all stay in one place."

The handler took the leash off of Simon and gave him the "go find" command to begin his work.

When Jake walked into the detective's work area he found Purdy and Stover going over Ditkam's credit card records. They weren't enthused because Ditkam hardly charged anything. He had only been carrying one credit card, so the assumption was that he used cash for most everything.

Jake asked them to get Marti Nelson on a speaker phone so they could talk. When they got it done, Jake started with, "I think that the three of you know about Chuck Browning. He's the head of our Bureau of Investigation and Intelligence, is running for Attorney General, and is the source of most of the newspaper pieces on this case. He has been closely following this case from the beginning. I work with cops and DAs all over the state and a good working relationship is important to me. I know that this latest murder is your case, you'll prosecute it and you'll make an arrest when you choose. Browning has 'directed' that I get Ditkam arrested. If an arrest doesn't happen I'd expect him to pressure your DA."

Jake could see Stover getting red in the face, but Nelson spoke up first. "The way our office works is to only arrest on circumstantial evidence if we have no expectation of direct evidence. So far in this case, we have good circumstantial evidence. We also have hopes for direct evidence on several fronts. One solid piece and he'll be arrested. For now, he stays free. If this Browning wants to talk to my boss, let him. I'm sorry that you can't follow your directive, but you'll have to deal with that."

"I'll deal with it and I understand your position perfectly," said Jake. "Thanks for listening."

Nelson disconnected the call and Purdy said, "So this is the asshole who gives the press all the case details and tries to churn up fear in the public?"

"That's the guy; a real joy to work for," was Jake's sarcastic response. "Luckily he's a couple of layers up in our structure so I don't have to deal with him much. I'll have to call him with the good news this morning."

"It seems like there are people like that in a lot of jobs," said Stover. "The DA job's political, so we sometimes get directions we don't care for, but our guy's good."

"That's good, but sometimes it's not the cream that rises to the top," said Jake.

"Shit floats," responded Purdy.

"Well said," agreed Jake. "You mind if I go over and have a casual chat with Ditkam? I'd like to get a feel for how he is one on one outside of a threatening environment."

"That's fine, just put a report in the system," said Stover.

"I will. Call me if the cadaver dog finds something?"

"No problem."

Back in his car, Jake called Browning's work number and reached Browning's secretary. A touch relieved at not having to talk to him, Jake left the message, "Nevada County won't arrest until they have direct evidence." Five minutes later, Jake pulled up at Kirby's and walked into the office. "You mind if I talk to Ditkam for another five minutes?"

Kirby looked annoyed. "I'd rather you talked to him on his own time, but if you have to do it now, OK."

"Thanks," said Jake, walking out to the service bays. "Tom, I need to talk to you for a couple of minutes."

Ditkam looked back towards the office, then slumped his shoulders and wiped his hands on a red shop rag. He walked out front of the bay and followed Jake around back.

"Why can't you guys just leave me be?" was Ditkam's whiny opening.

"You know why Tom. You're a person of interest for several murders."

"I didn't do nothin', I'm clean." The familiar mantra.

"The people you hang out with don't make you look clean. Your buddies at the Crazy Miner gave me a concussion."

Trying to hide a smile, Ditkam responded, "Yeah, I heard. I also heard that you and your girlfriend put four on the floor."

"Agent Moreno is a black belt. Your buddies made a mistake messing with her."

"Look, those guys aren't my buddies. I don't even know most of their names. I just go to that place with Konrad once in a while."

"Konrad works here?"

"Yeah, he's in the bay next to me. He likes the Miner, goes there a lot. I just go when I've had a rough day."

"This Konrad the same one that sells meth?"

"I don't know nothin' about him and meth. I don't do drugs and want nothin' to do with em. Look, I've done some bad things in the past and done time for a couple of them, but I'm done with that. Prison was my worst nightmare and I never want to go back. I keep to myself most of the time, just work and fish. I'm clean."

"With your record, it takes us a long time to believe that you're clean."

Ditkam didn't respond.

Jake asked, "When's the last time you went down to the flatlands?"

"Dunno. Maybe a month or six weeks? I don't have much cause to go down there anymore."

Jake knew that he had Ditkam in a lie. A plate reader had spotted his vehicle in the valley."

"You loan out your ride, Tom?"

"Last time I did that, the fucker wrecked it. No more."

"Good policy. You planning any fishing?"

"Yeah," Ditkam brightened, "I'm goin' up to the Yuba North Fork Friday. Supposed to be workin' good now."

"Good luck. I'll see you," Jake turned and walked to his car.

Jake drove to Bob's Café for lunch. He got a booth and used his laptop to write his report over coffee after he ate a Joe's special.

At Ditkam's house, Simon the chocolate lab ran back to his handler, barked once and placed a paw on his handler's leg. "Show me," ordered the handler and the dog headed out. Following, the handler gave a "come on" wave to the other men.

Simon led the men on a winding route through the manzanita. A couple of hundred yards from the house, the dog began to walk around in a circle. His handler released and rewarded him, then turned to the men. "I'd expect you to find human remains in this area that Simon was circling. I have no way to tell how old they are, but you'll find something."

The two patrol deputies and the evidence tech went back for their vehicles while one of the detectives called Purdy. "The dog's found a spot and his handler is sure that we'll find remains here."

"Good," said Purdy. Just be careful until you find something and then stop. I'll alert the DOJ people but they won't come until a find is made."

The evidence tech set up a large framed screen on legs ten feet from the search area. "We'll want to run all material that you remove through this screen so we don't miss small items," he said.

They began raking leaves off of their search area and the tech looked through the debris. Once the leaves were gone it was clear that they had a recently dug area. There was an oval shaped area with loose pieces of soil. The surroundings were undisturbed smooth red clay. Small shovelfuls at a time, they transferred dirt to buckets and then screened it. A little more than an hour later, one of the deputies hit something with his shovel that didn't feel like dirt or a rock. Using his gloved hands, he removed dirt until he had exposed about four inches of flesh.

They stopped and made another call to Purdy. "We're about two feet down and have exposed what we believe to be human flesh," the detective said.

"Good work. Can you tell what it is? What body part?"

The detective looked around and got shrugs. "Not without excavating more dirt."

"Better not do that," said Purdy. "Leave a deputy and the evidence tech there to protect the site and come on in. It'll take a couple of hours to get DOJ out there."

Hanging up, Purdy called Willy Jackson. "We've got flesh in a hole about two feet down. We'd like you here as soon as you can make it."

"I've had good results with cadaver dogs, so I got us loaded up after you called," Jackson responded. "We should get up there in less than two hours unless we hit a traffic problem."

"We don't have traffic problems up here," teased Purdy. "You might hit one down in your metropolis though."

"We'll be up in your boonies soon," was Jackson's comeback before he hung up.

Turning to Jake and Stover, Purdy said, "Less than two hours till he's shovel ready, he says."

They finished their discussion with the two detectives that had canvassed Ditkam's neighborhood. "So nobody knew him?" asked Purdy.

"Nobody I talked to," answered one of the detectives. "A couple of people knew about his car coming and going and one person saw him running a weed trimmer. That's all I got. A couple of people refused to talk, but that's normal up there."

Purdy looked at the other detective.

"Same deal for me. None of my people saw weed trimming though."

Purdy said, "Thanks guys, we had to give it a shot."

"We know, Ned."

Purdy had a departmental meeting to attend, so Jake called Celia for an update. "Hey C, it looks like we have a buried body near Ditkam's house."

"Only one?"

"You're never satisfied. Only one body so far."

"Jake, you're wrong again. I'm frequently satisfied. For example, I was satisfied with our dinner last night."

"Uh, yeah," grunted Jake, caught off guard. "So what's happening in Yuba City?" trying to change the subject.

"They canvassed Tomwick's neighborhood. The only thing they came up with that might be interesting is a sighting of a guy walking through a trailer park to a farm that backs up to Tomwick's house. Here's the description: White man, t shirt and jeans, white straw cowboy hat, black pony tail, and backpack. Something sounded familiar so I checked in JARS. Roseville PD interviewed a elderly woman who was helped by a man in the parking structure where victim two was picked up. The man had a white straw cowboy hat and a pony tail."

"That's good stuff C. Ditkam has the black pony tail and I remember seeing a white straw cowboy hat hanging up in his house. It's got to be in the pictures the forensics people put in the system. Of course thousands of those hats are around the West but the circumstantial stuff on Ditkam is piling up."

"I'm thinking that if the trailer park guy was Ditkam, he was headed for the back of Tomwick's house. I'm going to ask Chocolate if he can look at her house with that thought in mind."

"Didn't Yuba City already go through the house?"

"They did, but they didn't have this additional information and it was Yuba City people, not DOJ. Even if we don't find direct evidence, knowing that she was picked up at home makes her not a random victim, points at Ditkam."

"Give it a shot. I'll talk to you tomorrow."

"Bye Jake."

Chocolate's team was well under way by the time Ditkam arrived home. Seeing the mass of vehicles just down his dirt road was a bit of a shock. After stopping and thinking for a minute, Ditkam drove up to the vehicles and started walking towards a cluster of men. Purdy moved out of the group to greet him.

"What the hell's going on here? What're ya doin' on my land?" said Ditkam, anger in his eyes again.

"The land belongs to your landlord, not to you," responded Purdy. "He gave us permission to search the property. You'll have to stay clear of the crime scene tape."

Ditkam couldn't see what was going on, the manzanita was too thick. He said, "How can there be a crime scene? There's nothing out here."

"I have no information for you," said Purdy, watching how Ditkam responded to the activity. "I think you know what's out here without us telling you."

"I don't know shit. I ain't never been out here, it's just a bunch of damn manzanita. You guys are tryin' to screw me." Ditkam turned away and took his vehicle back to the house.

When Purdy saw Ditkam pull into his driveway, he called one of the patrol deputies over. Purdy told the deputy to park his vehicle on the departure side of the property and to follow Ditkam if he left. Ditkam might rabbit now that he knew they had found the body. Pulling out his cell phone, he called his Sergeant and requested approval for twenty four hour surveillance on Ditkam.

Jake left the scene for the ride home at seven. By then they had unearthed a Taser and knew that they had a female with no head. It was clear that they weren't going to finish before dark. They'd have to guard the site overnight and finish the next day.

On the way home, Jake stopped at a supermarket that had a salad bar. After building a twelve ingredient salad he finished the drive home.

Back at the house he greeted Tank and then called Browning, wanting to get that chore behind him.

"I understand that you failed, Appleby. This Ditkam character is not in custody."

Jake took a deep breath, thinking of how he'd like to respond. Instead, he said, "I laid out why you wanted him arrested, but the Nevada City team is waiting for serious direct evidence. Maybe they'll change their mind now that we have a body."

"You have a body?"

"Yes, we've found a headless female buried a couple hundred yards from Ditkam's house. The excavation will be finished tomorrow."

"You have a mountain of evidence. It's unfathomable to me that the man is free. If he runs, the recalcitrance of these Nevada County people could be the cause of further butchery."

"They have him under twenty four hour surveillance," said Jake. Sensing Jake's anger, Tank ran away.

"This is not at all foolproof. He must be incarcerated. Since you seem ineffective in this arena, I'll look for another solution." Browning hung up.

Jake took a deep breath, then poured a glass of wine to go with his salad and sat down to eat. When the salad was gone, Jake grabbed his sipping tequila and settled into his Stressless chair. He started up an Alan Jackson song, *Gone Crazy. Here I am all alone tonight … But ever since you left I've been gone, Gone crazy, goin' out of my mind.*

44. NEVADA COUNTY; THURSDAY

At eight in the morning the DOJ team restarted the excavation near Ditkam's house. By ten thirty they had finished. Besides the Taser, the only content of the hole was the nude body of a headless woman. Below the body they had run into a solid soil layer indicating that they'd reached the bottom of the hole. The body was transported to the Auburn morgue. They'd managed to schedule the autopsy for early the next morning.

"You think we can get a discount on the autopsy?" said Purdy to Stover with a straight face. "They already charged us for the head. Paying for two autopsies on one person seems like a rip-off."

"You've got to be ..." Stover stopped as Purdy cracked a wide smile.

"I hope that Auburn prints the body and IDs her quickly," said Stover. "If we had our own print specialist we'd already know. The body shape seems to match with Tomwick, not the two earlier vics. It'd be good to know for sure who we dug up."

Purdy pulled up the Taser report from JARS and found that the Taser in the grave was the device that had been stolen.

Purdy's phone rang.

"Hi Ned, this is Marti. A guy named Don Foreman, the Deputy Attorney General assigned to this serial case, is meeting with me in an hour. I'd like you and Cliff to be here for the meeting."

"I can make it," said Purdy. "Cliff, can you make a meeting with Marti in an hour?"

"Sure."

"We'll both be there Marti."

"Thanks."

Purdy and Stover drove to the DA's offices in downtown Nevada City, a short walking distance from the courthouse. Marti, a good-looking woman of about forty with close cropped brown hair, hazel eyes and a serious expression, was wearing a black pinstriped business suit this morning. Standing up from a visitor chair was a tall skinny redheaded man dressed in a blue pinstriped suit with a white shirt and striped tie. "I'm Don Foreman," he said.

Introductions completed, they talked through the prosecution plans for Tom Ditkam, Foreman making a couple of useful suggestions.

"We'd like to see Ditkam prosecuted for the other two murders as well," said Foreman. "Given the identical mode of killing and posing, it's quite clear that he committed those crimes as well."

"At this point, I don't see enough evidence to try him on the first two murders," said Marti. "There's also no evidence yet that those murders were committed in this county. With budgets being what they are, we're not interested in trying crimes for other jurisdictions."

"This blood that's in for DNA could well give you solid evidence as well as jurisdiction," responded Foreman.

"We'll cross that bridge if and when the DNA comes out that way."

"On another topic," said Foreman, "we'd like to see you arrest Ditkam today."

Nelson's eyes turned cold. "What is it with you guys about pushing the arrest?"

"Well, we just feel that there is ample evidence and that he's a flight risk as well as a risk to public safety," answered Foreman.

With annoyance in her voice, Nelson said, "By my definition, we'll have ample evidence when YOUR lab gets us DNA results from the extra hair found mixed with our victim's hair. I believe results were promised for tomorrow."

"Yes, Friday was my understanding as well. We still have the flight and safety issues though."

"We have this guy under twenty four hour surveillance. He's not going anywhere, he's not hurting anybody."

"But we ..."

"No buts," interrupted Nelson, now showing anger. "You can tell *We* that our office is comfortable with its decisions and needs no more suggestions about arrests. It's time for you to find your way back to Sacramento. Good day."

After Foreman had left, Nelson said, "Annoying twit."

"You sent him home with a limp," said Stover.

"Yeah, I suppose that I should hold my tongue. The DOJ has lots of resources that they share; I don't want a problem impacting our access to them."

"That might be an issue," said Purdy. "According to Jake Appleby, the source of this pressure is Chuck Browning. He's high enough to be able to hurt us now, but if he gets elected attorney general he could hurt us a lot."

"Guys, be ready to go on Ditkam as soon as you get positive DNA results from that hair. I want him in the bag within a couple of hours."

Jake had slept in, knowing that he had a nine o'clock meeting and nothing else pressing. He read the paper while having breakfast at Pauline's, happy to find no mention of the Whitewater Killer. The meeting this morning was the JARS steering committee; Jake and eight people representing areas of the state who had users of JARS. Jake didn't enjoy meetings much, but this group was important to the continuing evolution of JARS as a high quality law enforcement tool. All of the members took feedback and suggestions from users and boiled the most interesting of them down in the meetings. The lead developer of JARS was a member and their primary conduit to accomplish change.

Jake was able to give the participants a real example where the active component of JARS provided critical help to an investigation. The detectives would probably have found the

Ditkam-Tomwick connection themselves, but the system had saved them time.

Jake went to lunch with the two members of the JARS team who had been physically present at the meeting. While at lunch he received a text message. It notified him that Mason Resto's SUV had been spotted by a plate reader. Jake didn't care much about Resto at this point.

Touching bases with Purdy late in the afternoon, Jake got the full story on the body excavation. He also heard about Don Foreman's effort to pressure Nevada County into arresting Ditkam. "This bullshit is a turnoff," said Purdy.

"Sorry about that," responded Jake. "Overall I think we've helped you guys. Foreman is Browning's boy; he'll do what he's told and relate everything he knows to Browning."

"Yeah, we figured as much," said Purdy. "If the hair DNA comes in as Ditkam tomorrow we'll bag him, so we won't be hearing about the issue any more."

"Browning is actually providing some help, you're getting DNA results faster because of his intervention. Talk to you tomorrow," said Jake as he disconnected.

45. DREAMLAND

The killer was daydreaming about his conquests.

He relished the precision of his operations that placed him in complete control, the delicious helplessness of the women. The progression of expressions in their eyes was fascinating. It started with the shock and fear after he Tased them. When they woke up in the tub they were bewildered. As he started to whip them they descended into pain. He cherished the terror in their eyes as he moved the ice pick through their field of vision. Best of all, he consumed the empty stare of death.

There were also the great physical sensations that made him feel godlike. He gloried in his dominance when he unleashed the Taser, dropping his prey to the ground. The violence of wielding the belt as he repaid long-ago debts. The sense of ecstasy he experienced when the ice pick slid smoothly into the brain, turning their light out forever. His feeling of power as he hung them up like the dead meat they were. He was a vengeful god.

As icing on the cake he took much pleasure from his art. Selecting the rivers and rocks had provided a pleasing environment for his spectacle. Displaying only the head guaranteed shock waves through the discoverers and the public. He had been surprised at the pleasant sensations he felt while he gently arranged the heads and lovingly brushed their hair for a final time. He felt such pride in his marvelous creations.

It's unfortunate that I have to stop now, he thought. I'll always have the memories though.

46. SACRAMENTO; FRIDAY

Purdy and Stover spent much of the morning observing the autopsy of the excavated body in Auburn. By the time the autopsy was finished, Auburn's print tech had identified the body's fingerprints as those of Sally Tomwick.

Celia used up her morning walking through her work on Sally Tomwick's taxes and finances with a forensic accountant.

Jake was reviewing everything JARS had on the case when he was interrupted by a text message: JARS, Whitewater Killer case, high priority entry. Body excavated near Ditkam house identified Sally Tomwick via fingerprints.

So we've located all of Tomwick and have great evidence on Ditkam, thought Jake. Unless they find some proof from the grave that Ditkam put her there, the evidence is still circumstantial though. So where are the bodies of the other two women? Maybe he put Tomwick nearby because she was the only victim that meant anything to him? He could have planned regular walks so he could piss on her grave.

The fifth meeting of the Whitewater Killer task force began at two PM. The first person with status was Torrey Bonner from Walnut Creek.

"We've gone through all the information from Yuba City on victim three. We found zero connections with our victim. We also looked for a connection between our victim and your guy Ditkam, but came up dry as dust. We've confirmed that Pauli Mancuso was in New Orleans when Tomwick was abducted and killed. He's not our guy."

"Next is Roseville, Rich Luton," said Sam.

"We caught up to Mason Resto late yesterday. One of Appleby's gadgets spotted his SUV on I80. He claims that he went to Grant's Pass Oregon to visit his brother. We're checking on that. If true, it'd be his alibi for victim three. On the other hand, it turns out that he was selling real estate in Yuba City back in 2001 when Tomwick's store was robbed. He, of course, claims to know nothing about her, her store, or the robbery. We've been through three of the five potential houses he might have used for killing the women, no results so far."

"Yuba City, Stan Voss."

"Our canvass has turned up a sighting of a guy that may have been heading for the back of Tomwick's house. The report's in JARS, but the general description matches Ditkam, though it's not good enough for an ID in court. Your DOJ crime scene people reprocessed Tomwick's house yesterday. They found tool marks on the back door lock. They also found Taser AFIDs in the vacuum cleaner bag. The numbers matched those in the JARS case file. Tomwick must have been abducted from her home."

Jake spoke up, "This tells us that Tomwick was specifically targeted; more evidence against Ditkam. The description that came up in your canvas mentions that he was wearing one of those hard shell straw cowboy hats. A hat like that turns up in two other places in the case. The potential sighting of our kidnapper in the Roseville mall parking lot includes the hat. The search evidence of Ditkam's house includes a photograph of such a hat."

"Ned Purdy, Nevada County."

"We've found and excavated a grave two hundred yards from Ditkam's rental house. The grave contained a single headless body that was determined via fingerprints to belong to Sally Tomwick. The grave also contained a Taser. During the autopsy, injuries consistent with application of a Taser were found. The device found in the grave was stolen at the same time as the Taser cartridge used on our second victim and the cartridge used on Tomwick. Our working assumption is that burial of the weapon indicates intention to end the murders."

"The autopsy gave us some other relevant results. Premortem bruising and severe lacerations were on the buttocks suggesting many strong strikes with something like a one inch belt. There would have been significant blood spatter from these wounds. There was duct tape residue on hands and ankles plus ligature marks on the ankles. There was no evidence of sexual activity. It appeared that the body had been washed with a bleach solution."

"Kaya Lane, DOJ profiling."

"Again I have to point out an incongruity. Burying a body and a weapon near one's home is stupid, particularly when one has immense empty forest country nearby. These abductions and head placements were not done by a stupid person. A second concern I have is that there's only one body. Where are the other two?"

Jake jumped in. "I had the same thought about only one grave. It's possible that Ditkam's hatred for Tomwick made him want her nearby so he could defile her grave. It's also possible that the cadaver dog stopped looking when it found the grave. There could well be other graves still out there. I'd recommend another cadaver dog search of the area to look for the other two bodies."

"Good idea, we'll do that next week," answered Purdy.

"Willy Jackson."

"We've got some excellent news. I reported to Ned Purdy late this morning that the foreign hair found in Sally Tomwick's hair has been DNA matched with Tom Ditkam's DNA record in our California's database. We'll want to match it again to a current sample from Ditkam when we can get it."

"We've worked through the hairball found in Ditkam's tub drain. Apart from his hair, we have long fine black hairs that could match either or both of the first two victims. We also have brown pubic hair consistent with those found at Tomwick's house. We expect DNA results on these by next Wednesday. The blood samples from Ditkam's bathroom are on track for a Tuesday DNA results."

"Tomwick's car was a bust. The tires on Ditkam's SUV match the Tuolumne tread marks except that the right front tire has a chunk missing next to a tire repair made with a plug. The damage could have been done before or after the Tuolumne event, we have no way of telling. At the other scenes we don't have tracks of the full circumference of the right front tire so the damage has no relevance. The remainder of the SUV contained no relevant evidence."

"Next is Marti Nelson with the Nevada County DA."

"I think that you'll be happy to know that the arrest warrant on Tom Ditkam for the murder of Sally Tomwick is being processed as we speak. We expect to arrest Ditkam before he leaves work today. As a courtesy we've notified Chuck Browning with the DOJ." On the displays, Nelson appeared to wink with her left eye.

"We've got a great case, thanks to many of you in this task force. I'd like to summarize it for you. We've got Ditkam's DNA on Tomwick's head. Tomwick's body and a Taser were buried near Ditkam's house. We have blood from Ditkam's bathroom matching blood typed for Tomwick; pending DNA. We have pending DNA on Tomwick's pubic hair from Ditkam's tub. We have a Ditkam connection to Tomwick and excellent motive. Tomwick's head was dumped close to Ditkam's home. SUV tires and boot treads match though they're weak evidence. Ditkam has a weak alibi for the time of Tomwick's abduction, none for the dump day."

"At this time, we have no evidence that the other two murders were committed in Nevada County, though that may change with DNA results next week. For now, those two cases belong to Tuolumne and Placer counties. That's all I have for now."

"Great summary Marti," said Sam. "It looks like we have the third killing nailed, with evidence for the first two in the pipeline. Our people will continue to work with everybody on getting the whole case resolved. Jake?"

"I'd like to thank everybody for all their participation and efforts. You've all shown great professionalism and teamwork. Celia, I, and Don Foreman will stay involved until everything is nailed down, but for now, we won't schedule any more task force meetings."

Jake and Celia walked together back to their office. Celia said, "This arrest feels great. I'd been concerned that these killings were so free of evidence that we weren't going to solve them."

"You know," said Jake, "that same concept is making me just a bit uncomfortable with the arrest."

"How so?" asked Celia.

"We went through three abductions and two head placements without any hard evidence and very little circumstantial evidence. Now all of a sudden we're inundated with hard evidence, particularly if next week's DNA analyses match our victims. Kaya is skeptical. As much as I hate to agree with a profiler, what's gone on indicates that Ditkam was crafty and careful for weeks then dumb and sloppy. It all just makes me uncomfortable."

"That's pretty funny Jake. Those are the kind of things I'd normally say. In this case I think that we've got good evidence on Ditkam. He just got lucky until he filled out that permit envelope at Ruck a Chucky. We might have found him through his connection to Tomwick even if we didn't know of him from before. I'd say we finish cleanup on this case and move on."

"You're probably right C."

Jake's phone played a tune and he answered. "Appleby."

"Uh, well I don't know…"

"I do have to be up there anyway."

"OK, I'll do it. Where do I meet you?"

As he disconnected, Jake said, "That was Marti Nelson, wanting me to come up for the arrest and press conference."

"But you hate press conferences."

"I do, but she'll just use me as a shill to point out that the DOJ task force contributed. It's good for the DOJ to get some kudos. I have to pick up Kaitlin for our weekend anyway, so I'll be up there."

"You know that'll piss off Browning."

"Fuck him."

At four PM, Jake joined the party at the Nevada County sheriff's parking lot. Two carloads plus a patrol vehicle drove to Kirby's auto shop. While Marti Nelson and the others watched, Purdy and Stover entered Ditkam's work bay from both sides of the vehicle he was servicing, blocking any escape. Purdy performed the actual arrest.

"Thomas Ditkam, you're under arrest for the murder of Sally Tomwick. You have a right to remain silent …"

Ditkam said only, "This sucks, man. You're fuckin' up my life."

Back at the sheriff's office, Ditkam was booked before the press conference began outside. The place was a zoo, with satellite vans from three of the four networks with stations in the valley as well as several print reporters. The press outnumbered the law enforcement attendees, but only by a small number.

Chuck Browning was present, his wavy black hair topping his big boned, average height body. His brown, almost black eyes were a distinctive feature on an attractive face tipped by a cleft chin. He was wearing a charcoal suit by Armani with a red tie. When Browning saw Jake he looked surprised and then angry, but the conference was starting and nothing could be done.

The sheriff, whom Jake had only met once, described the crime and investigation. He gave solid credit to the DOJ task force and pointed out Jake as the lead agent, making Jake uncomfortable. The sheriff then said, "And over here, we have Chuck Browning from the DOJ management team."

Browning reddened at the underwhelming mention. Jake had to fight to keep the grin off his face. The sheriff has some stones, he thought.

The District Attorney said a few words about prosecuting Ditkam and ended the press conference.

As Jake walked over to Purdy, he saw one of the TV news crew moving to Browning. Kiss their ass and they will come, he thought. To Purdy, he said, "The sheriff doesn't seem impressed with Browning."

"He knew about the pressure for an early arrest," said Purdy. "He mentioned to me that he didn't care for Browning's press statements."

"I guess he's a stand up guy."

"Yeah, he's good, particularly for a guy who needs to be elected."

"I'll talk to you next week Ned. I'm looking forward to a weekend where I'm not working."

"Me too. See you Jake."

47. SACRAMENTO; MONDAY

Jake walked into the office with their morning drinks. "How was it having a weekend to yourself?" he asked Celia.

"It was great, Jake. After weeks without real free time I truly appreciated the freedom. I got in a great workout on Saturday and went wine tasting with Kaya on Sunday. How did you do with Kaitlin?"

"She signed up for the bedroom decorating you suggested, so we spent the weekend on it. It was fun doing a project with her, though she was surprised by how much work it was."

"But that's such a great learning experience Jake. Kids should learn that things aren't free and projects take work. If they grow up without that knowledge, moving to adulthood gets more difficult. You could teach her more by introducing a budget."

"That's a good idea, C. How do you know this stuff?"

"I've observed my family and other people's families for a long time. I've also read a few books on the subject."

"OK, you're my child rearing consultant. To tell you the truth, I had some trouble concentrating on things this weekend. Being with Kaitlin kept Fiona in my head."

A flash of exasperation crossed Celia's face. Before talking, she took a slow breath and let it out. "It's time you recognized reality and move past Fiona, Jake. If you don't, your life is going to be miserable. Just realize that you chased Fiona for seven years after the divorce and you never caught her. She's moved on; you need to."

"You're making sense Celia. Unfortunately, the part of me that's doing this doesn't seem amenable to sense."

"If you can't work that out, maybe you need some therapy. A good therapist made a world of difference to me after the rape."

"You did therapy for that?"

"I was messed up Jake. I couldn't get past it so I tried therapy. The first woman I went to was useless, but I spent some time checking out local therapists and got a good one."

"I'm glad you got help C. I've always thought you had your head on straight. I appreciate your suggestions; I'll just have to see how things go."

Responding to Jake's hint, Celia changed the subject. "Did you see the Saturday paper?"

"Nope, I threw the papers directly into my recycle can this weekend."

"There was what seemed like a reasonable article on the news conference, it even mentioned your name. There was a separate article about an interview with Browning. He was crowing about what a great job he did and the writer seemed to eat it up."

"What do you expect, it's the press. Chucky the hound feeds them so he's their baby. I'm glad I missed the article. Let me tell you what the sheriff did to him." Jake repeated the sheriff's statement about Browning.

"Wow. Are they enemies?"

"I don't know, but for sure the sheriff is on Browning's shit list now," said Jake.

"Let's hope Browning doesn't find a chance to carry out vengeance."

Jake's phone played a tune. "Appleby."

"This is Chuck Browning. What were you doing at the press conference last Friday Appleby? You know that department policy required authorization for media contact."

"Yessir. I had a last minute request from the Assistant DA to be involved in the arrest. I tried to beg off, but she pushed hard. I didn't want to sour a relationship. Besides, I didn't talk to the media."

"Talking or not, you were involved in violation of policy. See that you do not repeat that error."

"Yessir." Jake raised his eyebrows and rolled his head.

Celia mouthed 'Browning'?

Jake nodded 'yes'.

"Moving on, I want to congratulate you on running a good investigation that reflects well on the DOJ. Without your work, Nevada County might never have found the perpetrator."

"Thank you sir. You know that Celia Moreno played a critical role as did Willy Jackson's organization."

"Yes, I suppose so. Pass on my congratulations to Moreno."

"I will sir."

The connection dropped.

By the way, Browning congratulated you."

"Yeah, after you brought up my name. I'm quite happy that he doesn't talk to me," said Celia.

Hours later, Jake scooted back from his desk and said, "I'm going to meet Terry and Steve at the Blue Ball, you want to join us?"

"Sure Jake, it beats cooking for one."

"Plus it's an opportunity to be around wonderful people."

"Well, people at least."

At the Blue Ball, Terry and Steve wanted to hear about the arrest. By the time they were into their second round of drinks, Jake and Celia had covered the highlights of the investigation and the evidence.

"We've got this guy dead bang, but Jake still has his doubts," said Celia.

Terry said, "Hey, this guy's a dirt bag and you've got all kinds of evidence. Move on man, there's other dirt bags that need nailing."

"Yeah, I could do that," said Jake. "I certainly don't want this woman on my back." He nodded towards Celia.

An image flashed in Celia's mind. She took a long sip of her drink to hide the rosy color that appeared on her cheeks..

48. SACRAMENTO; TUESDAY

The early morning was gorgeous, perfect for Jake's top-down drive to work. It wouldn't stay that way though, Sacramento was headed for one of its triple digit days. Dry heat, sure, but that doesn't make hundred plus degrees comfortable.

Jake had decided on tan Dockers, sandals and a red golf shirt today in support of his comfort and in violation of the dress code. Walking into the office Jake was assaulted by cold air. The classic overly chilled air was done with the thought that since people were hot outside they'd like to be cold inside. Or maybe the concept was that people worked harder when they were fighting off the cold. In any case it made hot coffee a reasonable drink in summer.

Celia was looking delicious in a loosely flowing sundress in swirling blue on white. She had made her own decision for comfort instead of rules.

Jake settled in at his desk thinking about the plate reader detections of Ditkam's SUV. Ditkam had claimed not to have been in the valley, but the same reader had detected his license plate several times. Could this lead to more evidence against Ditkam? Would this be another demonstrable value of the plate reader system?

Jake pulled up a map of Rio Linda using Delorme's Street Atlas USA product. While Google Maps was valuable, it didn't yet have features allowing him to mark up a map the way he wanted to. Next he located the plate reader detection reports in the JARS system. He selected a map data file where he had marked the locations of the plate readers. The next step was to put the detection times and dates next to the associated reader location:

READER1: From Raley southbound, I80 entry westbound; Wednesday 6/8 16:11.

READER1: I80 eastbound exit to Raley northbound; Wednesday 6/8 22:23.

READER1: From Raley southbound, I80 entry westbound; Thursday 6/9 06:31.

READER1: I80 eastbound exit to Raley northbound; Thursday 6/9 10:36.

READER1: From Raley southbound, I80 entry westbound; Friday 6/10 05:34.

READER1: I80 eastbound exit to Raley northbound; Friday 6/10 09:42.

Thinking about the data, Jake concluded that: Ditkam had visited the area three days in a row, starting with the day of Tomwick's abduction and ending with the day her head had been exhibited. He's visiting some place convenient to and north of the Raley/I80 interchange. He comes from some unknown location, probably Nevada County, enters the local area by an unknown route, leaves the area by I80 westbound and later returns I80 eastbound. Then he must make his way back to Nevada County by some unknown route. He didn't pass by reader units two or three, so those routes in and out of the area were not used.

So what was Ditkam's route into the area? If he could figure that out, he'd have a much better handle on the location that Ditkam must be visiting. We know he's not entering the area after passing by the Raley interchange on I80 because we have no plate reader record. There were two main routes down the hill from Nevada City. One route would have him approaching Raley from the west, the other from the east. From the west doesn't make sense because you'd think he'd use the Raley interchange. Jake decided that arriving and departing from the east made the most sense; Ditkam probably got off of I80 at Winters Street. It's too bad that they hadn't had a plate reader unit there. Given that logic, Ditkam was visiting someplace north of I80 in between Winters St. and Raley Blvd. Houses, warehouses and some farm plots were in that area, but not very many because the old McClellan Air Force Base was just to the north.

Jake picked up his laptop and walked downstairs to the ALPR project lab. Setting his laptop on Tommy's desk, he said, "I'm trying to make use of some plate reader detections and I need somebody with a good analytic mind to critique my thinking." Celia had such a mind, but he figured that she wanted to be done with Ditkam.

"Thanks for the compliment," said Tommy. "What're you thinking?"

Jake went through the records and explained his thinking using the map.

"I can follow your logic and think that your theory is the most likely. Reader 2 and 3 plus McClellan rule out an approach from the north. It doesn't make sense to approach from the west using other than the Raley Interchange. Approaching from the east on I80 would only be possible on Winters St."

"Another solution would be to have him enter the area from the south on Raley. That's not a direct route from Nevada County, so I'd assign a lower priority to that theory. This is an interesting use of plate reader data Jake. In most cases I think this would take a dense network of devices to do this kind of work."

"Thanks Tommy. I agree with you about the dense network."

They talked about the project for a few minutes and Jake headed back upstairs. On the way up his phone pinged that a text message had arrived, but he ignored it.

As he reached his desk, Celia said, "Did you read the JARS text?"

"Not if it's the one that just arrived."

"Chocolate's people just finished the DNA work on the blood found in Ditkam's bathroom. There's a positive match to Sophia Mancuso and Sally Tomwick. The bastard butchered those women in his house. Nevada County's now got two murders to prosecute and solid evidence for both. Ditkam's dead meat."

"That's some good news," said Jake. It's nice to get closure on the cases and for the Mancuso family. As for Ditkam being dead meat, only figuratively. The way the death penalty works in this state, he'll end up dying of old age."

"I know Jake, I just meant that his days on the outside should be over."

"You're right about that."

Jake got back to the plate reader data. Wasn't Ditkam supposed to be working during some of these times? From JARS, Jake pulled up the smartpen record of the initial interview with Ditkam's boss. Yup, Ditkam's supposed to work Wednesday and Thursday. There was no way for him to work and be down in the valley during the time that his vehicle was spotted on those days.

Jake called Dale Kirby, Ditkam's boss, and asked if he had time cards for those days.

"Sure I do. Hang on a minute and I'll dig them up."

Two minutes passed and Kirby came back on the line. "I've got them. Ditkam worked eight to four thirty on Wednesday the eighth and eight to four thirty on the Thursday. He didn't work Friday. What's this about?"

I'm just checking some logistics for those days. Is there any chance that your records don't match what he actually worked?

"Not by more than a couple of minutes. I learned a long time ago to have guys check in and check out with me. That prevents a lot of screwing around."

"That's great, Mr. Kirby. It's good to know that you have reliable records. Do you know if he drove his Suburban to work those days?"

"I don't recall those specific days, but I've never seen him drive anything else. I think that I'd notice if he did, I keep track of what's in our lot."

"Thanks for your help." Jake disconnected.

Celia spoke up, "So what's that about?"

"You know about my work with license plate readers, right?" asked Jake.

"I'm afraid that I do, mister geek."

"I'm only part geek. Much of the time I'm a superstar agent."

"With a fat head."

"You got me. Anyway, I'm just working through the plate reader detections of Ditkam's license plate, trying to see if they're of any value. Every good use I can find for the data will help support the project."

"Quit wasting time on Ditkam."

"I'm not. This is about the technology project," said Jake.

Back with his own thoughts, Jake had thought about what he'd learned. Ditkam's SUV was in Sacramento at the same time he was working. It didn't make sense. He had already checked that the plate reader database had an image of the Suburban with Ditkam's plate. Sitting back, he thought for a minute, letting his mind bounce around possibilities. Kirby must be wrong. Somebody else was driving Ditkam's vehicle. Did he have an accomplice?

Enough of this, Jake thought. I'm going to hit the gym, get some takeout and go home.

49. REFLECTIONS

The killer was comfortable in his mahogany brown leather recliner, sipping Macallan single malt scotch from a crystal glass. This project has worked to perfection, he thought. These law enforcement clowns are so easy to manipulate. Making them hungry for any leads had been joyful, akin to teasing a dog with a snack. I finally gave them a snack with the third unit. Before they even knew how good it was, I gave them a feast. How delicious. Manipulation was a high art and he was a master at it.

The project had created quite a windfall. The pleasure and release he achieved dispatching the first two units was beyond anything he'd expected. Such joy. It made him want more, but he must restrain himself for the moment.

It was time to clean up loose ends. Rising from his chair, he opened the gun safe in his paneled library and retrieved a bag containing a mustache, wig, cheek pads and a hard shell straw cowboy hat. He piled a lot of kindling in his fireplace and ignited it with the gas log lighter. He waited for the fire to build. He thought that it was a bit warm outside to be having a fire, but what was air conditioning for, anyway. Into the fire went his tools of disguise. A few minutes of flame assisted by some poker manipulation did the trick.

Back in the chair with the scotch, he thought about how gratifying it had been to see Ditkam arrested with a mountain of evidence proving he was a murderer. And he had murdered, just not these women. When he got a not guilty verdict at his murder trial back in the nineties, Ditkam had sneered at the law and thought he'd gotten off. No, he'd just had a temporary reprieve.

He decided to once again relish last week's visit that established an iron-clad case for the helpless law enforcement minions. He'd started by using his surveillance system to ensure that Ditkam was gone by the time he reached the loser's home. Burying unit three was more work than he preferred, but was useful. It had been nice when the locals had decided to look for a body without his encouragement. Next he'd picked the cheap lock on Ditkam's rental and deposited the treasure. A nice hairball and drops of the appropriate blood lubricated Ditkam's slide towards death row. Retrieving a nice hair from Ditkam's pillow provided a snack for the autopsy of Tomwick's head. All that was left was the retrieval of the surveillance system from the woods across the road and he was done. How sweet it was.

I have to get out to my rental and dispose of everything there. I can take the hiking boots and waders along. A fire would be a pleasant way to deal with the house, but I'll have to dispose of units one and two as well as the vehicle. No problem, I just need to find some time.

50. SACRAMENTO; WEDNESDAY

Jake walked into the office to find Celia dressed in a short black skirt and a white silk blouse that highlighted her narrow waist and small but shapely breasts. A concave top met a convex bottom at a pert nipple. Whoa, man.

"You have a date?" asked Jake as he handed over the latte.

"No, I just figured that this was going to be an easy day and decided to cut loose. Maybe I'll go out at lunch and tease some men. It's so easy."

"Only for a woman as good looking as you," said Jake. "You're revealing a cruel streak."

"Lots of men out there deserve teasing, but it's not my thing, I was just jerking your chain."

"Happy to hear it. Save your cruelty for criminals."

Celia's phone rang. "Moreno."

Chocolate spoke, "I've got some good news and decided to provide personal delivery to you two since you've given me so much business lately. I called you 'cause you're prettier."

"Well thank you," said Celia in a sweet voice. "He is ugly."

"What's that?" exclaimed Jake. "Who are you referring to?"

"You of course. Is your ego sensitive today? It's Chocolate, I'll put him on speaker."

"Hi Jake. You taking grief again?"

"It appears so. What's up?"

"We've got DNA results on the hairball from Ditkam's tub. We have Ditkam, of course, but we also have victim two's head hair and victim three's head and pubic hair.

"So," said Celia, "combined with the blood evidence, we show all three victims in that bathroom."

"Indeed we do," responded a pleased Chocolate. "We're happy to make your case for you."

"And we're happy too," said Jake. "Why don't we have hair from victim one?"

"I don't know, Jake," answered Chocolate. "Maybe Ditkam cleaned out the trap after victim one."

"Who does that? If Ditkam was smart enough to clean it out, why didn't he clean it out after the last two victims?"

"I don't know Jake. It feels like you're looking a gift horse in the mouth."

"Sorry Choc. You did good stuff and I'm glad you called."

Celia said, "I think that this is the final nail in Ditkam's coffin. This should mean that Nevada County will try him for all three murders. It'll be a lot cheaper this way and it wraps up the entire case. Thanks for calling, Chocolate."

"Talk to you later. I need to get this stuff into JARS."

Jake and Celia turned back to their desks. Ten minutes later the texts came, notifying the team of high importance data being added to the case. Jake settled into a pattern of thinking, writing a note, thinking, …

At eleven thirty, Sam Nakamura walked into their space and said, "Let's go to lunch."

Knowing that a lunch invitation from Sam was for food and business, they both agreed. Walking out the front door was like jumping into a giant toaster. The difference between the chilly indoors and the high and rising outdoor temperatures was a shock. Jake didn't mind much. By the time they'd walked the three blocks to Ruby Anthony's Restaurant his chill had worn off. During the walk, Jake noticed that Celia was getting a lot of attention from people on the street.

After they'd been seated in a booth and ordered, Sam started.

"Browning called me a while ago and made it clear that he wants us out of the Whitewater case. He said that the latest DNA results wrap it up so well that Nevada County can handle it and we can move on. What do you two think?"

"I agree," said Celia. "I think that we're done and can move on to something else."

"I'm not ready to stop, Sam," said Jake. "I'm uncomfortable with the results at this point."

Celia rolled her head in exasperation.

"What is bothering you?" asked Sam.

"A lot of things combine to give me a gut feeling that we may not be right."

"But nobody else feels that way?"

"As far as I know," Jake admitted.

"Look," said Sam, "Browning made it clear as a shot of vodka, we are done with the case. If you insist on working it some more, I'll have to go back to him. You know how well that will go over."

"I hear you, Sam," responded Jake. "You tell Browning whatever you need to tell him, but I'm not done yet."

"You like your job, Jake?" asked Sam.

"You know I do Sam, but if I don't tie down some things on this case the job won't seem so great."

"No job's perfect all the time Jake, you know that."

"I do. This time I'm pushing back."

"OK, but I don't have much control over what Browning chooses to do to you Jake."

"Whatever."

"I've got another case for you two. Celia, I guess that you'll have to start on your own. We've got a gang based crime operation going on in the valley that is threatening highly placed police personnel. We need to stamp this out right now. We don't want Mexico style craziness to get a start up here."

"That sounds like a worthwhile cause," said Celia. "Is there an open case?"

"I opened it yesterday and authorized you two this morning."

Jake said, "It sounds challenging, Sam. Before I can start though, I need a few days off. The Whitewater case has been exhausting and I need to work out some personal issues."

Sam just stared at him. After a bit he said, "OK Jake, but just a few. I don't want Celia getting too deep into this case on her own."

"Me either, Sam. I'll finish out today and should be back at work next Monday. I'm hoping to wrap up my concerns on Whitewater soon."

Back at their work area, Jake said, "C, I know you think the Whitewater case is done, but I value your mind so I'd like you to hear my list of issues with Ditkam being our guy."

With a sigh, Celia replied, "You're a real bulldog Jake. OK, just this once."

"Here we go. First, bodies for the first two victims are missing. Purdy ran another cadaver dog search at Ditkam's yesterday and came up empty. Why would he bury the third victim's body in such an obvious place after doing a better job hiding the other two?"

Celia responded, "The other two are probably sleeping in dirt up in the forest. Ditkam probably got tired of hauling bodies into the mountains. I remember you suggesting that Ditkam wanted Tomwick nearby so he could desecrate her grave."

"I don't like any of those reasons. Next, the clothes from victim three are missing. Why wouldn't he just bury them with the body?

"He probably forgot to bury the clothes and then dumped them somewhere."

"I guess that's possible. That'd be a touch risky for him, but possible. On to the next incongruity; where's the ice pick?"

"Good question Jake. He'd keep a filet knife since he uses it in fishing. An ice pick isn't too necessary these days – you get cubed ice most places."

"Next, why is the SUV so clean of evidence when the house is full of it? The nooks and crevices in a vehicle make it impossible to clean completely."

"Maybe he kept the victims in something like a body bag when he transported them so they couldn't transfer any evidence to the vehicle."

"I suppose, but we didn't find anything like a body bag. He could have used a tarp and gotten lucky. So next, I have the chunk out of Ditkam's tire that doesn't show up on the Tuolumne. Yeah, the damage could have been done later, but that hole in the evidence should be plugged."

"Is that a pun, Jake? Hole in the evidence, hole in the tire?"

"Not on purpose, I'm sorry to say. I'm also not comfortable about the plate reader detections of Ditkam's SUV in the valley at the same time he was working. The only solution I can come up with is that somebody else was driving his vehicle, despite what his boss says."

"So what's the relevance?"

"I don't know, it's just another thing annoying me. The last thing on my list is that maybe the assholes in the Crazy Miner were telling the truth, Ditkam was there on the abduction night."

"You can't be giving them credibility Jake. Those guys would screw with any cop every time they could."

"You're right, I don't believe them. But the truth could have matched what they'd normally lie about. So that's all that I have on my list."

"Jake, you forgot to include in your list that Ditkam doesn't fit the profile of the killer all that well. I know that you don't care for profiling, but we're not talking voodoo here, Kaya's profile utilizes well known serial killer behavior and traits."

"Sure," said Jake, not wanting to argue the point right now.

"Also don't forget that Ditkam may have gotten away with murder back in the nineties."

"Yeah, it'd be nice to know more about that. Only a summary of that case got digitized so it would take some digging."

"You've come up with some interesting questions Jake, but some of the things on your list are weak. The evidence we have on Ditkam is just too conclusive to make it worthwhile pursuing your questions. Is this worth fighting Browning?"

"The hell with Browning. I'll be off the case when I'm done. In the meantime, you can get up to speed on the new case. Just be real cautious with the gangs, C. To those people, humans are no more important than a bug."

"I know as much about gangs as you do, Jake Appleby. Given what happened at the bar in Nevada City, I can take care of myself better than you, so don't pretend you're my daddy or something. As for Browning, he's the guy in charge, remember? You know what happens to people who cross Browning."

"I do know that. That's why you won't be crossing him."

"Damn it Jake, we're partners. Don't go off half cocked and screw things up. If you have to do this, you know I'm with you, I just think that it's a bad idea."

I don't know about half cocked, C, but I am going off. I'll see you on Monday."

As he stood up, Jake's phone played the Beatles *Nowhere Man*. His reaction was "shit". Stroking the answer icon, he said "Appleby."

"Appleby, I understand that you insist on continuing to work the Whitewater case," said Chuck Browning.

"Yessir."

"You should know that I'm quite displeased with your behavior and expect you to wrap up your concerns today. We have other important work for you."

"Yessir."

"Next Wednesday I plan to kayak the Tuolumne River. I expect you to come along as my guide."

Jake had hoped that this request would never come. A day on the river with Browning would be worse than cleaning out a septic tank. "A permit is required to run the Tuolumne, I doubt that you can get one on short notice."

"Don't worry about a permit, I'll take care of it."

"The Tuolumne is a challenging run sir. I'd have to be comfortable with your skills before I could guide you."

"Don't you worry about my skills Appleby. I just did a refresher run down the South Fork of the American and I'm ready."

"Which stretch did you run?"

"Riverton to Peavine Ridge Road. Some class IV's are in there, I handled it with aplomb. I'll expect you to drive your truck. I'll discuss details with you next Monday." The connection dropped.

Jake sat back down. "Browning?" asked Celia.

"Yeah. If he's elected AG I may have to find another job. I can deal with normal assholes, but he's got one the size of Meteor Crater."

"He wanted you to kayak with him?" asked Celia.

"He *directed* me to guide him. He hung up before I could tell him no."

"Just think about how much you like this job before you say no, Jake. How bad could taking him down the river be?"

"About as bad as having a bunch of teeth pulled without pain killer. There's an off chance that the bastard could get me killed. I don't trust him to help if I got into trouble."

"Then you should tell him no. Just remember how vengeful he is."

"I remember. This job loses a lot of appeal when Browning gets involved in it."

"With luck, he'll lose the election and will have to leave."

"That'd be a cause for serious celebration. I'll think about blowing him off. I've got a few days to decide. See you on Monday C."

"Enjoy your vacation."

51. NEVADA CITY; THURSDAY

Jake loaded his backpack with clothes and gear for a four day trip to the mountains. Getting on his Fireblade, he rode over to Pauline's for breakfast. After chatting with Patty about her kids, he settled in with his newspaper. *DOJ Lab Nails Killer.* In yet another Browning news conference, Chucky the hound discussed the DNA analysis that would result in Ditkam's being charged for the first two murders. *The women of northern California are safe again; the serial killer who has terrorized them is in jail and will be convicted.*

I've got to admit it, Jake thought, that jerk has gotten a tremendous amount of free publicity out of this case. I've hardly seen anything from his opponent. Damn, I hope Browning loses this election.

Back on the bike, Jake took I80 up to Auburn, and then jumped over to 49 using Bell Road. The traffic was heavy coming downhill, but not bad in his direction.

Half an hour later Jake pulled up to Kirby's auto shop. Kirby saw Jake and said "Again? I want to support law enforcement but I'm trying to run a business here."

"This should be short and sweet. You have one guy who does tire work, right?"

"I do. Young kid named Jesse."

"I just need to ask Jesse a couple of questions about Ditkam. Jesse's not in trouble, I'm just gathering information."

"Jesse's a good kid, try not to spook him. He's in the first bay on the left." Kirby walked away.

Jesse was a skinny kid, looked to be about twenty. He had the remnants of teenage acne showing red in contrast to his blue coveralls. He greeted Jake with a shy smile.

After he introduced himself, Jake asked, "Have you done a repair job on any of Tom Ditkam's tires in the last couple of months?"

"Yeah," answered Jesse. "Something cut a chunk of tread off and just barely punctured the tire. A plug patched it up fine."

"When did you do the work?"

"Oh boy, I'm not sure. Let me think … You know what, it was the day after my girlfriend dumped me. I remember being hung over and annoyed that I had to do a freebee for Tom. Lemme look that up on my iPhone. Yeah, it was May 18."

"Can you remember which wheel the tire was mounted on?" asked Jake.

"Yeah. Tom pushed me to rotate his tires when I fixed the flat. It, uh, came off the right rear and I put it on the right front."

"Thanks Jesse, I appreciate your help," said Jake, thinking how nice it was to be young, to have room in your head to store such trivia as on which wheel a tire was mounted.

Sitting on the Blade, Jake thought about this new fact. Ditkam's tire was missing a chunk before the Tuolumne head display. The tire tracks found there were not Ditkam's.

52. SIERRA NEVADA

Jake had planned a trip designed to relax his conscious mind, unwind, and hope that his subconscious mind would do some good work. He started his Fireblade and headed in the direction of the sheriff's office. Passing the office at speed, he followed 49 deeper into the mountains. After an exciting ride of forty minutes he stopped for a break in Downieville, once a Gold Rush town of 5,000. Downieville has the dubious distinction of hosting the 1851 lynching of a female, the only such event in California's history. These days Downieville's population is under 300 and its major attraction is mountain biking. As he washed his hands in the restroom, he noticed that they were shaking just a bit in reaction to the adrenaline generated on his ride. He bought a cup of decaf coffee and sat on the river bank watching the Downie River join the North Yuba. Watching the dancing waters and absorbing the river sounds brought him down from the riding high to a state of relaxation.

Getting back on the Blade, Jake idled through town in first gear, crossing the one lane bridge where they had hung Juanita for stabbing Jock Cannon in the heart. Picking up to a leisurely 50, he had time to glance at the tumbling river, a challenging kayak run that he'd done three years earlier.

In Sierra City Jake was able to get a riverfront room at O'Doul's Resort. The room was basic but it had a balcony twenty feet from the river. Leaving his pack in the room, he got back on the Blade and headed uphill to the Gold Lakes Basin.

Parking at the Gold Lake Lodge trailhead, Jake hiked up to Long Lake. After hiking about a mile and a half, he settled on a rock perched a hundred feet above the lake. Enjoying the bright and hot sun on his t-shirt, Jake took in the views. A cobalt blue lake surrounded with trees and glaciated rock, topped by a cloudless deep blue sky. Relaxing, he absorbed his surroundings: young pines anticipating greatness, a fallen giant whose punky insides had been torn and scattered by a bear looking for grubs, a chipmunk scurrying back and forth in search of food. He gazed at the lake and the mountains behind it, letting his mind lose focus.

An hour later his subconscious mind brought him back. The SUV spotted by the plate reader wasn't entering and exiting the Rio Linda area through some unknown route, it lived there and the reader was recording its comings and goings. If this theory was true, it wasn't Ditkam's vehicle, it was a copy. That would explain how the plate reader photographed the vehicle while Ditkam was at work with his vehicle. Somebody other than Ditkam was involved.

Jake got up and headed back towards the trailhead. He knew that there was no cell coverage in the area so he had to find a landline. By the time he got to a phone at O'Doul's it was six thirty. He called the mobile number of his tech assistant Suzie Eckerling.

"Suzie, this is Jake Appleby. I'm sorry to call you in the evening like this but I need your help."

"No problem Jake. What's going on?"

"I've been working on a problem and a new way of looking at it just occurred to me. I'd pursue it myself, but I'm on a road trip up in the Sierra. What I need you to do is find a rental house with a garage in about a two square mile area near Rio Linda. Most likely this place would have rented out in April or May. You could start by looking at new utility customers in that time frame."

"An interesting task Jake," said Suzie. What case is this for?"

"Right now it's just for me, Suzie. I'd appreciate it if you could keep it just between you and me and out of JARS."

"Really. Even more interesting. This is legal, isn't it Jake?"

"It's legal," said Jake, not mentioning Browning's dictum but figuring that Suzie was safe because she didn't know about it.

"OK, I can work on it tomorrow. What're the boundaries of this area?"

"I80 on the south side, Rio Linda Blvd on the east, Ascot on the north, Winters on the east. It could be done under any name, but if you come across the name Ditkam, it'll be significant."

"Ditkam eh," said Suzie, knowing that a Ditkam had been arrested in Jake's Whitewater case. Deciding not to raise the point, she said, "I'll get on it first thing tomorrow Jake. Anything else?"

"Not now Suzie. If you come up with anything, call my cell phone. I may have no coverage where I am, just leave a voicemail. Thanks for your help."

"No problem Jake, but I think you'll owe me one."

"I think you're right. Bye."

53. SIERRA NEVADA; FRIDAY

Jake slept late and woke to the rushing, bubbling sounds of the river. There was dim light coming through the windows; sunrise had happened on the mountain tops, but not yet in the canyon. Over breakfast of corned beef hash and eggs he decided to cut his trip short and head back home. By the time he got back Suzie might have results for him.

It was afternoon when he rode up to his condo. He turned on his smartphone and checked for messages. "Jake, this is Suzie. I've found six new utility accounts in the area you described. One of them is in the name of Ditkam. I used Google Earth to check the place and I think it has a garage. Call me."

Jake's heart started beating faster. This felt like big news. He deleted the message and called Suzie.

"This is Jake. It sounds like you've got great results."

"I think so Jake. Some trees were in front of the house so I'm not positive about the garage. Do you want me to drive out there?"

"Absolutely not. Don't go anywhere near there."

"OK Jake. I thought you might say that. I did check out the other five accounts using Google. Three don't have garages, one does and the other I can't tell."

"Give me the Ditkam address and then the other two possibilities."

"Sure Jake. The Ditkam place is at 1154 Martz Avenue. The others are 5022 Bobby Way and 310 Chester Street."

"Thanks. That's great work. Can you dig up the contact information for the owner of the Ditkam place and put it on my voicemail?"

"I'll try. Sometimes that's hard to find."

"Do your best Suzie. Thanks again."

"Bye."

Jake pulled up a map and searched for 1154 Martz, then the other two houses. He figured out a route that he could follow to ride by each of the properties.

A half hour later he was in the Rio Linda neighborhood. Population wasn't dense here; there were scattered farm plots and large lots. He made a single pass past the Ditkam rental at the speed limit without turning his head. What he saw was a rundown house with a garage and a gravel driveway on a large lot. There were no close neighbors and there was no traffic. The Bobby address was the same type of neighborhood but as far as he could tell with one drive by it didn't have a garage. If the house he was looking for was connected to the abductions, the killer would want a garage so that he could deal with his SUV's contents in privacy. The final house on Chester was in a dense residential neighborhood with a garage and a front yard littered with children's toys.

Hungry by now, Jake headed to Pauline's for a quick meal. After ordering he checked his phone and listened to his voicemail. Suzie had gotten him the contact information for the owner of the house on Martz. This could be the kill house. If so, nobody would live there. If he could put up surveillance he might catch the killer visiting. That tack had issues though. It was difficult to do surveillance on country property; you just couldn't blend in. He couldn't use DOJ personnel because of Browning's position on the case. Since the Taser was found in Sally Tomwick's grave the killer might be done with killing. He'd certainly be done if the objective was framing Ditkam. If he was done, why would he visit the house? In fact, he might have already cleaned up the place.

Given that surveillance wasn't a good option, they needed to search the house. It should happen sooner rather than later to minimize evidence destruction or deterioration. How was he going to get that done? He couldn't use DOJ resources to get a warrant, couldn't use DOJ crime scene or forensics resources either. A minute's thought gave him a solution. He pulled out his phone.

When Steve Devlin's cell phone answered, all that came out was jumbled noise. Jake said, "Steve, this is Jake. I need some help."

More jumbled noise and the word "outside".

Jake hung on and soon the noise subsided and he could hear Steve speak. "What's up Jake? Party at the Blue Ball, I had to get outside to talk."

Jake explained the Browning edict and how he'd discovered the house. "I need to search the place Steve, but I need you to do it. It's in your jurisdiction anyway."

"Do you have probable cause?" asked Steve.

"Sure. We have good evidence on Ditkam, his name's on the utilities and his vehicle has been in the area. We're looking for evidence that murder and/or dismemberment occurred in the house."

"Sounds workable Jake. When?"

"I'd like to see if we can reach the property owner in the morning, then do the warrant and the search. How about I call you between now and eight in the morning with a time for the owner?"

"Sure Jake. I may not be answering tonight, I plan to get lucky. I'll make sure to check voicemail before eight."

"Have a ball."

"That's the plan. Talk to you tomorrow."

The chance that Ditkam had a partner or had been framed created other angles to work on. Who would he partner with? Who would go to such elaborate lengths to frame Ditkam? Celia could work on these questions, but he didn't want to expose her to Browning's wrath. He'd get to it when he could.

54. SACRAMENTO; SATURDAY

Jake called Steve at 7:45 and said, "did you get lucky?"

"I'm sorry to report that I struck out, Jake. She couldn't appreciate what a manly man I am. She ran off with some patrol stud. What's happening?"

"We're meeting the owner of the house at eight thirty. I'll meet you at 2350 Keith Way then?"

"Keith is over near Arden and Howe?"

"Yeah."

"I can make it, see you at eight thirty."

Steve was already there when Jake pulled up. The yellow ranch house looked to be in good condition and the landscaping was lush and green; a far cry from the rental house. John Clark answered the doorbell. He was built like a Santa Claus: no extra padding required. For a Santa gig he would have needed a wig and beard though. The man seemed friendly but worried, not an unusual reaction for people after the police request an interview.

After introductions, Jake started. "We're investigating a crime and have reason to believe that your house on Martz may contain evidence. We expect to get a search warrant today and we'd like your cooperation."

"A crime? What kind of crime?"

"I'm sorry, but at this point all of that information is confidential," said Jake.

"Jesus, I wish I had unloaded that place. My father bought it in the fifties and I inherited the dump. You think he's growing pot inside? I hear that's happening all over."

Ignoring the question, Steve spoke up, "What can you tell us about your renter?"

"I've got the paperwork right here," said Clark, brandishing a file folder. "His name is Tom Ditkam and he started renting on May first, paid first and last month as well as a cleaning deposit. He's paid his June rent."

"How did he pay?" asked Steve.

"He gave me cash the first time, then mailed a money order for June. I would have taken a check, but I've had other renters who used money orders. It's not a big deal."

"Do you still have anything that he may have handled?" asked Jake. "The cash, an envelope, an application?"

"Uh, I've got the application, but the cash and old envelope are gone."

"We'll need the application as evidence, but you can make a copy to keep," said Steve.

"Can you give us a description of the man?" asked Jake.

"Oh boy. I'm not real good at that kind of thing. I guess around average height. He had a black ponytail, but he sure wasn't a hippy. Yeah, he had a bushy black mustache too."

"Any distinguishing marks like a scar or tattoo? Was he thin or fat?"

"I don't remember any marks. I guess he had an average build, I really don't remember."

"Did he give you contact information or any references?" asked Steve.

"He gave me a phone number. I've got it here on the application."

"Let's get a copy for you. Do you have a copier?"

"I do," said Clark, getting up and walking into a bedroom set up as an office.

Steve took a set of Clark's fingerprints so his could be ruled out when they examined the application. He pulled out gloves and gave them to Clark for handling the original.

As the multifunction printer was making a copy, Jake asked, "Do you have an extra key to the rental that we can use? That will avoid a need to break in if your renter isn't present when we serve the warrant."

"Why don't I just accompany you?" asked Clark.

"You can, but it would be a large waste of your time. You can't be inside the building when we search. If we find evidence the house will be marked off as a crime scene, so you couldn't enter after the search either."

"I guess it would be a waste. I can give you a key. Can you call me and let me know what happens?"

"We appreciate your cooperation, Mr. Clark," said Steve. "When the search is complete, we can let you know whether the house has been designated a crime scene or not."

"Thanks."

"One more thing, Mr. Clark," said Jake. "This is an active investigation. If you contact your renter or discuss our planned search before it occurs, you'll be impeding an investigation. That's a chargeable offense."

"Oh. I promise that I won't make any attempt to contact him."

"Thank you for your help," said Steve as he and Jake got up to leave.

Outside, Jake said, "Clark gave a description of Tom Ditkam, that should make the warrant easy to get. When do you think you'll have it?"

"The description he gave would match a few thousand men in Sacramento, but it'll work," replied Steve. "I've got an ADA set up to do the warrant. I'm guessing we'll have it by lunchtime."

"Can you use DOJ forensics? Your call, of course, but they've been doing the work on the case and do superb work."

"Can't do it Jake. I'll piss off the DA's office if I don't use their people, and my boss would have my ass."

"Yeah, you're right. You want me to check out the phone number the landlord gave you?"

"Nope, Terry needs some work to do."

"OK," said Jake. "Give me a call when you get the warrant."

At 11:50, Jake got the call from Steve. "We've got the warrant; we're set up to serve at 1:30. Meet me at the department at one."

Steve put four patrol officers around the perimeter of the house, just in case somebody was inside. With Terry and Jake, he went to the front door and knocked. After a second knock produced no results, he announced that they had a search warrant and tried the key. The key slid into the lock, but wouldn't turn; the lock had been re-keyed.

"I think it's your turn Terry," said Steve.

"With pleasure," replied Terry, already walking to their car. Returning with a door ram and a big smile, Terry put on heavy gloves and stroked the ram into the lock side of the door. Lots of sound and a few splinters, but the door held.

"Real cops do it with one," said Steve with a straight face.

Terry raised the ram again, putting his whole body into the stroke and with a large bang the doorjamb splintered away and the door flew open, slamming into the wall behind it. Weapon drawn, Steve took one step into the room and yelled, "Police. We have a search warrant." At the same time he was scanning the portion of the house visible from the door.

Steve waited five seconds for a response from within and then said to Jake and Terry, "This room is clear. I'll watch while you two get booties and gloves on."

After a minute, the three of them entered with weapons drawn and methodically cleared every space in the house. Once it was known to be safe, they brought the DA's forensics team in.

Their first impression of the house was *empty*. Next was the smell of bleach. The single piece of furniture in the entire place was a short, wide stool found in the hall outside the one bathroom. The garage proved interesting. More bleach smell but lots of items. The centerpiece was a white Chevy Suburban. Jake checked the plates and they matched Ditkam's plates. How in the hell did he do that? The forensics people should be able to tell him. The interior of the SUV appeared empty when they looked through the heavily tinted windows using flashlights.

Terry had walked over to a chest freezer and opened it. Inside was a large black plastic bag, the shape of the contents resembled a human in a fetal position. There was no head shape. After Jake and Steve took a look, he closed the freezer's lid and left it for forensics.

Cabinets lined one side of the garage. Before anybody looked in them, Jake noticed a tiny blinking red light on the wall and walked over. "Shit," he exclaimed, "the bastard had an alarm. Here's the keypad. There's a conduit running up to the attic; the controller's probably up there."

A strange ring tone emerged from the killer's leather bag. He reached inside and pulled out what they call a 'disposable cell'. Looking at the caller id produced a jolt of adrenaline as anger washed over him. Pulling the battery out of the phone he thought *they've found the place before I burned it.* Putting the phone and battery in a pocket, he walked out of the building and down the street. He walked into a Starbucks and ordered the largest cup of coffee they sold. Walking down the street, he stopped by a refuse container, dropped the battery inside and followed it with a third of the coffee. He dropped the phone in the cup, replaced the cap and walked another block. After he rounded a corner, the coffee cup went into the next refuse container.

Jake got one of the evidence techs, already bundled in a Tyvek suit, to climb into the attic, photograph and retrieve the alarm controller. The device had been connected to a telephone line and when they used the controller's setup function to find the phone number called when the alarm tripped, it turned out to be the same number that 'Ditkam' had put on the rental application. Our perp is damn sharp, thought Jake.

"I checked that number this morning," said Terry. "It's a throwaway. I'll get with the wireless company to get a call list and service locations."

"Good," said Jake. "Ditkam's in jail. If that phone is moving around, either Ditkam has a partner or it's the guy trying to frame him. After seeing this place, my bet's on the frame."

Leaving the house to the crime scene people for now, the detectives walked outside and started making calls. Jake reached Celia who had just finished cleaning up after a taekwondo morning. "Why don't you meet Steve, Terry and I at the pizza joint on Raley south of 80?"

"What's up Jake?"

"Come and find out. Bring Kaya if you can find her."

Seeing that the other two were still on the phone, Jake called his boss but got voicemail. "Sam, this is Jake. I wanted to give you a heads up that the Sacramento PD has just searched a house that appears to be the kill house for the Whitewater case. I think that this case is wide open again."

They staked out a large corner table in the pizza place, ordering a couple of Coke pitchers and a pizza to snack on. As the pizza arrived, Celia and Kaya walked in. It was the first time Jake had seen Kaya without a business suit. Not only did she have an attractive face and great hair, she had a great body. Something stirred, but it disappeared as Celia got in his face.

"What's going on Jake? You were supposed to be on vacation."

"Steve, brilliant detective that he is, found a house in his jurisdiction that Ditkam had apparently rented. With his talented, but not too muscular partner, they got a warrant and Sacramento forensics is going through the house as we eat pizza. There appears to be a wealth of new evidence."

Celia gave Jake a hard look. "You're going to make Browning look like a fool and he's going to know that you're behind it." She then turned to Steve. "I've never seen the Einstein side of you Steve, where's it been?"

"I'm crushed," responded Steve "that you haven't detected my immense intellect. I try to keep it shielded so that my friends won't feel inadequate."

Terry, who'd been trying to hold it in, burst out laughing. Jake joined in while Steve managed to look offended.

"All right, enough bullshit," said Celia. "Kaya's going to think your department's full of clowns."

After Kaya was introduced, Steve and Terry took them through the day, sticking with Jake's version of what started things.

"Terry," said Celia after hearing about the incident with the ram, "I've got a new name for you. From now on, you're Terry Two Strokes."

Jake chuckled, Steve said, "One interpretation of that name might require some intimate personal knowledge, Celia."

Her face reddening, Celia said, "Personal knowledge I don't have, but I have it on good authority."

Terry said, "I take a beating like a man. Just bury me when you're all done."

"Back to work guys," said Jake. "Kaya, I think that you were right with your organized offender thing. Whoever set up this house did some excellent planning and execution. Ditkam's not dumb enough to put his own name on the rental and utilities. I'm thinking that Ditkam is not the killer."

"I agree with your assessment Jake," said Kaya. "While organized offenders make mistakes, gross blunders like using your name and duplicating your license plate are inconsistent with the type."

"So we need to find ourselves a new suspect," said Steve. "I'm going to get the department to ask for DOJ investigative help. In the meantime, how about we go see what forensics has come up with?"

Back at the house on Martz, George Ely came out front to talk to them. "This looks like the house where your serial killer dispatched at least two women. It's clear that the house was just for storage and killing, there's no way that anybody lived here. There is no furniture, there's lots of dust without footprints, and there is no food in the cabinets or refrigerator."

"The garage is a windfall. We have two headless female bodies in the chest freezer. They had been folded into a fetal position, put in plastic bags and placed in the freezer. I'm guessing that the coroner will find evidence of a thaw/refreeze on part of the bottom body, caused when the second, warm, body was stacked on top. The coroner wants to thaw the fingers before he prints them. That should happen by this evening."

"In one garage cabinet we found surgical gloves, blue nitrile gloves and two full Tyvek crime scene outfits. These were all new. We found no garbage of any kind but there were plenty of plastic garbage bags. That cabinet also contained a roll of duct tape, a bag of zip ties, two new chemical cartridge respirators and a package of vacuum cleaner bags for the shop vac."

"A rescue style backboard with straps was propped up in a corner. It may have been used to restrain victims during transport. Next to it was a Black and Decker battery powered blower and a two gallon garden sprayer that smelled like it contained a bleach solution. In another cabinet is a fly fishing setup: wader boots, rod, vest and a large wicker creel."

"No waders?" asked Celia.

"No. Too bad, because we'd have a chance of recovering DNA from inside them. Next to the washing machine there's a box of laundry detergent and two big containers of bleach. "Nearby is a shop vac without a filter and an open bag of commercially sold rags.

Before we towed the SUV I took a quick look. It's empty and clean. The only thing inside was a thin moving pad, neatly folded. The plates are interesting. They're made of some sort of casting material and have the proper raised letters and numbers for a plate. If you look closely you can see that the colors are painted on but it was done with skill. The stickers belong to the plates that should have been on the vehicle. Here's the VIN number."

Terry took the slip of paper from Ely. "I'll check it out."

"The kitchen has some items of interest," continued Ely. "A large stainless steel bowl was upside down on the counter as if it was draining. The refrigerator contained a vial of ketamine and a box of syringes."

"What can ketamine be used for?" asked Steve.

"Historically it was used as a general anesthetic, though it's no longer used on humans in the states. It's still used here on animals. It's also used as a recreational drug. I'll have to research dosage and effects."

"Back to the refrigerator. Two sets of items were labeled 1, 2, and 3. One set was stainless steel water bottles that appear to contain blood. The other set is zip lock bags that contain hair. There was one additional, unlabeled, zip lock bag with hair. In one of the cabinets were boxes of plastic garbage bags in three sizes and a roll of duct tape. Finally, we found a mop and bucket, cleaning supplies, a coil of rope and a box cutter."

"You thinking that our perp is drinking blood?" asked Terry.

"I don't know, but it would be nice," replied Ely. Seeing a disgusted look on the women's faces, he said, "I don't mean that drinking blood would be a nice thing in itself, but that he could well have left saliva and DNA on the lip of the bottle. We'll be checking."

"The bathroom looks to be the killing location. It contains no towels, rugs or shower curtain; it's easy to clean. The only sundry is a pump bottle of hand soap. Taped to the medicine cabinet mirror is an eight by ten photograph of an attractive adult woman who looks Italian or Hispanic. Inside the cabinet is a scalpel, an ice pick, and a heavy serrated knife. A large hook is screwed into a ceiling joist over the center of the tub. The room looks clean but I have a guy doing a Leucocrystal Violet blood identifier test as we speak."

The detectives had been paying close attention, taking notes even though Ely would produce a detailed report. Jake said, "This place is a mother lode of evidence. I know you've just started, but what about prints and DNA?"

"We haven't finished looking Jake. Prints are in the house, but remember that it's a rental. We didn't find a single print in the bathroom, where we assume that our perp spent most of his time. So far we haven't found any blood or hair in there that we could test for DNA. Even if we did, it's likely that it would be degraded by bleach. I've never seen a crime scene as organized against evidence that might ID a perp. I think that there's a good chance we'll get something, but it's not going to be easy. We'll be working here through tomorrow, then in the lab. They'll go through the SUV on Monday."

"What about the bodies?" asked Celia.

"The coroner has them. He should be able to print them by this evening after the fingers have thawed a bit. If they're your victims, we'll know then."

Nobody spoke for a moment. "Thanks for the briefing," said Steve.

"Welcome," replied Ely. "Let's go see whether the LCV showed us anything."

As they crowded into the bathroom, it was obvious. The wall opposite the shower head and half the wall behind the tub were covered with violet spots and streaks.

"The spots are the original splatter," said Ely. "The streaks are mostly from his cleanup work. There's a reasonable amount of blood here, but it's not like arterial spatter. I'd guess that this was some sort of beating, not a knife attack."

Ely went back to supervising his crew, the detectives and Kaya moved to the driveway.

"This house was used by the real killer in this case," said Kaya. "The planning and organization here is impressive. The killer is highly organized and quite intelligent. I'd also suggest that the picture on the mirror is likely to be your perp's mother. She was there to witness what he was doing to his victims. This was payback for her physical and/or sexual abuse of your perp."

"He did it because he had a mean mother?" asked Terry.

"No, he did it because he's a psychopath," responded Kaya. "One of the many items in the standard profile for an organized killer is the abusive mother. Another is that the perp tends to choose victims that resemble a significant female in his life. You're looking for this guy, you should review the information that's been collected on organized offenders."

"We should and we will," said Steve. "You can work with us?"

"I can. I haven't been told to stay clear of the investigation."

"It's Sacramento's case at this point," said Jake. "The evidence points to at least two and probably three murders being done at this house so you have jurisdiction. Finding this house has saved Nevada County a lot of work."

"And generated a lot of work for us," said Terry.

"You love it, two strokes," responded Celia. "If that blood and hair belongs to our three victims, it seems hard to believe that Ditkam did the killings. Somebody has been framing him. How else would blood and hair turn up in his Nevada County bathroom when the victims were killed here?"

Steve said, "If our old suspect is clear, we need a new one. How about Terry checking out the SUV ownership and the rest of us canvassing the neighborhood?"

Before Jake started, he called Nevada County's Ned Purdy. "Did I catch you at a bad time?"

"I'm at my kid's soccer game. I love her, but watching little kids run around a soccer field can get old. What's up?"

"I've got some bad news Ned. The Sacramento PD just searched a house down here that looks like the kill house for these three murders. It's looking to us that Ditkam was set up, that somebody else actually did the killing." Jake recounted what had been found at the house and why they thought Ditkam didn't do it.

"That sucks Jake. We've been played."

"You're right, it's looking that way. I think we'll know for sure when the lab gets their work done. I got played first with the Ruck a Chucky license plate thing. Sorry I brought you Ditkam but whoever set him up was very talented."

"You're right about that, Jake. I'll tell everybody up here. Will all of this show up in JARS?"

"It will, Ned. I'll talk to you later."

On his walk over to the first house he was to canvass, Jake got a call from Sam Nakamura. Jake explained what had happened and, without telling a lie, left Sam with the impression it had all been Sacramento PD's doing. When Sam disconnected, Jake thought about how tiring it was to repeatedly update people on a case. Suits were the worst; many of them wanted to hear it from the officer in charge. For a lot of people, JARS could distribute the information, saving him from repeating it. Too bad that the suits were too self-important to read.

"Browning."

"This is Sam Nakamura. There's been a significant development in the Whitewater case and I think we need to revisit our stance on it."

"What's the development?"

Sam went through what he knew about the kill house.

"How did Sacramento become involved and find this house?" asked Browning. "As I recall, they hadn't been involved in this case at all."

"I don't know the specifics, sir. I believe it had something to do with the license plate reader system spotting Tom Ditkam's license plate near Rio Linda."

"This plate reader thing is Appleby's pet project isn't it?"

"He's one of its advocates, yes. It looks like it's going to be a valuable tool for us."

Silence.

"Nakamura, my Bureau will no longer play an active role in this case. Is that clear?"

"You're the boss, sir."

"Indeed I am, and you people would be well served by remembering that. See to it that the people associated with this case are off and stay off it. No pushback will be tolerated. Appleby and Moreno are assigned to a case that is important to us; ensure that they get to it."

"Yes sir."

Celia, Steve and Jake got back together to discuss the results of the canvas. They had to cover only nine homes because of the sparsely built neighborhood. They had found residents at seven of them. The general observation was that there were almost never signs of life at the kill house. One person remembered that a green Toyota had pulled into the driveway a couple of times. Several people mentioned the SUV. They got Terry on speakerphone to see what he had found out about the vehicle.

"The registered owner is a short bald guy. We should put him in JARS and check his record but I can't see him as our perp. He claims that he sold his SUV in April. I asked him why he hadn't submitted a notice of transfer to the DMV and his response was 'huh?'. The guy remembers that the buyer paid cash and no, he doesn't have any of the bills left. He remembers the buyer having a cowboy hat and a pony tail. Other than that this dude was as empty as a stadium after a big loss. Ownership of the SUV looks like a dead end."

"OK Terry," said Steve. "You want to meet us at the Blue Ball?"

"Just for a couple. My wife'll be on the warpath anyway."

"Save me a seat," said Jake. "I need to put a summary of all this in JARS and give you guys full access for this case."

Before Jake finished, he received a text message from Sam Nakamura. He was to attend a meeting in Sam's office at nine Sunday.

Several drinks and appetizers later, Steve got a call. "That's good. OK. Thanks for getting right on it and calling." After hanging up he said, "We've got confirmation that the house is about the Whitewater case. The two bodies printed out to be victims one and two. They'll do the autopsies Monday but he told me that both bodies had premortem bruising and lacerations on the buttocks."

Jake had a hard time getting to sleep. For once he wasn't thinking about Fiona, he was churning about the case. He hadn't been comfortable about Ditkam, now there was a lot more information and areas to look into. He'd always been highly motivated, but the challenge of catching this smart bastard had him cranked up.

55. SACRAMENTO; SUNDAY

Jake walked into Sam's office at nine. Celia and Kaya were already seated. Jake was drawn to the long slender legs emerging from Celia's filmy pastel sundress. Realizing what he was doing, he turned his attention to Sam.

"Sorry to call you in on Sunday," said Sam, "but you need to hear this and hear it well. Chuck Browning climbed a long way up my ass about you continuing to work the Whitewater case. He has directed me to ensure that nobody in his bureau works on it. We are done with the case; it's up to local agencies now. There is no doubt that his wrath will descend on anybody who touches it. Since his wrath would also descend on me, you'll have me to deal with as well. Kaya, I've talked to your boss and she understands the directive."

Jake was quiet but Celia spoke up. "But the case is wide open again, the guy we had didn't do those women. We can make a difference and get this monster off the street."

"Sure we could make a difference," responded Sam, "but we're not going to. From what you tell me, the whole case looks like it belongs to Sacramento and they're capable of handling it on their own. I'm sure that the Bureau of Forensic Services will continue to support the case."

"But," Celia began.

"No buts," Sam broke in. "We're off the case, period. You know that messing with Browning is a losing proposition. You didn't hear this from me, but Browning is heavily exposed in the press. He made a big deal with the them on how 'his' agency did all the work and apprehended the vicious fiend that was preying on women. Now he's set to have egg on his face. He wants to be as far away from the case as possible."

Jake was thinking that at a minimum Browning deserved egg on his face. For once he kept his mouth shut.

"Anything else?" said Sam.

Silence.

"Kaya, I appreciate your help on this case, I'm sure that you have other work to do. You two take the rest of the day off. Tomorrow you need to get into the threat case."

While walking down the hallway, Celia said, "I'll put something in JARS tomorrow indicating that the bureau is off the case."

"I suggest you couch it in terms of Sacramento taking over and the case no longer being split among jurisdictions," said Jake.

Jake thought about the meeting with Sam and Browning's forceful interference with what normally was Sam's decision. Browning had some reasons for his decision, but most of them were bullshit. Law enforcement had been deceived by the real killer and the press was going to make them look stupid when they found out. Browning would be the prime idiot because he'd been out there claiming credit. Too damn bad, he had been stupid. If it gets him defeated on election day, it would be a good thing. The hell with Browning, Jake thought, I'm going to keep looking.

Jake began thinking about "why Ditkam?" The guy was kind of obscure, living quietly up in the hills. Why was he set up for these killings? He either had a serious enemy or happened to be convenient to divert suspicion. So maybe the real killer wanted to do Tomwick and Ditkam was perfect to take the fall. It could have been a third person involved in the jewelry heist, wanting to take care of his partners. Or maybe Ditkam did somebody wrong in the past and this was all a payback. You'd think it would be easier just to kill Ditkam, but twisted people think in twisted ways.

Back at home, Jake booted up his laptop and logged onto JARS. With "why Ditkam" in his mind, he began reviewing the entire case. He'd been through the records so many times that it took serious concentration to do it again. Without the concentration he'd just glaze out and get nothing done.

An hour later it was something that was not in the record that aroused his interest. The record showed that Ditkam had been charged with murder and acquitted, but none of the details were there. The event had happened in a time when most law enforcement records were on paper and only the highlights recorded electronically. Computer storage was more expensive back then and software to support online record keeping had been a bit rigid and primitive.

Shutting down the laptop, he climbed into his Boxter and headed across town to the Sacramento Police Department headquarters on Freeport. Since it was Sunday, it took him over an hour to get the Ditkam murder case file.

Ditkam's live-in girlfriend had been beaten to death behind a bar and thrown into a dumpster. The coroner had determined that the perpetrator had been right handed and used a pair of sap gloves. One good punch with such gloves would put many men down, let alone a five foot two one hundred pound woman. The woman's head had been pounded to a pulp: jaw fractured, nose crushed, and three bones of the left orbit broken. Her left temporal bone had been fractured and driven into the brain; this was the blow that killed her. Investigation showed that she and Ditkam had argued a lot, most recently about her being unfaithful to him. Ditkam had an alibi: He had been fishing up north on the Klamath River with a buddy. The buddy had done time twice for assault and no corroboration of their story was found. Ditkam was arrested and charged with murder.

The remainder of the report was just a summary of the case disposition. Ten seconds into reading it, Jake exclaimed, "Son of a bitch!" Charles Browning was listed as the prosecuting attorney. Jake knew that Browning had worked in the Sacramento DA's office but had left about the time Jake joined the police department. Browning had never said a word about prosecuting Ditkam, had given no indication that he'd ever heard of Ditkam. This was hinky. Reading on, Jake found that the jury verdict had been *not guilty* and Ditkam had been released.

Packing up and returning the file, Jake's head was spinning. Why would Browning cover up his connection to Ditkam? He had pushed hard to get him arrested. Given Jake's observations of Browning, he would have been full of anger about losing a case.

Driving back home, Jake called Steve. "How ya doing buddy?"

"I'm working my ass off on a Sunday, thanks to you and your case, that's how."

"It's your case now, my friend. Look at all the preliminary work we've done for you and be grateful."

"Yeah, right. What's up?"

"My place for salmon tonight?"

"Uh … good. Girls or not?"

"Sure girls. Let's relax a bit. If Terry's around, ask him."

"Yeah, hold on."

"Terry's a go Jake. I think I've got a girl to bring, I'll call you if she can't make it."

"Good. Do you have a good connection that worked in the DA's office in 1996?"

"Ah … yeah. Why?"

"I just want to talk to somebody about what was going on in the office back then. Can you give me contact information and then prime him for my call?"

"It's a her, Jake. She got married and I haven't talked to her for a couple of years. She likes to talk though, so it might work for you. I'll call her and get back to you."

"Thanks," said Jake as he disconnected.

Jake called Celia and invited her for the dinner. Minutes after that call was complete his phone played the William Tell Overture, his ring tone for most working cops in his contact list. His dad had been a Lone Ranger fan and they had watched the show together when he'd been a kid.

"Appleby."

"Jake, this is Steve. You may have done me a favor here, she's single again. She'll talk to you if you call. Her name is Camille Emory."

"Hold on Steve, let me pull off the road."

Jake took down the woman's name and number and thanked Steve. He drove to his favorite market to pick up some wild salmon fillets and corn on the cob. He assembled an extra large custom salad and checked out. With the price of wild salmon today, it was nice to have money.

At home, he put the dinner fixings away and then called Camille Emory.

"Hello."

"Hi, this is Jake Appleby, I'm a friend of Steve Devlin's."

"Oh hi. Steve said you'd call. What can I do for you?"

"I'm trying to get some background information on the DA's office as it was back in the mid nineties. Anything you tell me is off the record."

"Interesting. I left the DA's office on good terms with the office and most of the people. Why don't you start asking and I'll see if I can help?"

"I'm looking for background on Chuck Browning. Can you tell me about how he fit into the office and what his work was like?"

"Our potential Attorney General? Is this connected to the media in any way?"

"Absolutely not, Camille. None of what you tell me will go to the media in any manner."

"Well, Steve says you can be trusted, so here goes. Browning was an ass kisser that would climb over anybody for advancement. Most of the people in the trenches had him figured out and disliked him. Chuck was also one of the few men around that didn't put some sort of move on me so maybe he's a closet gay. He had an excellent conviction record and he used that to ride up the ladder. The thing that the record didn't show was how he managed to slough off the risky cases to keep his record great. Did I say that he was an asshole?"

"I've heard that last description before. Do you remember the Tom Ditkam murder case?"

"The guy that beat his girlfriend to death?"

"That's the one. Browning prosecuted it and lost."

"I do remember that. Browning steamed for days and everybody was laughing behind his back. He'd gotten so egotistical that he thought he couldn't lose, and then he lost on a guy with a flaky alibi. If I remember right, this spoiled his perfect record on violent crime convictions."

"I'm not too surprised at what you just told me, but your information is helpful. Thanks Camille."

"Are you going after Browning in some way?"

"Not at this point, I'm just collecting information."

"OK Jake, call again if you like."

"I will. Thanks for the help."

While Jake was grilling the salmon and corn, he talked about the case with Terry and Steve. He didn't mention Browning to them. They had dotted some I's and crossed some T's, but not come up with anything of significant value. The autopsies were scheduled for first thing in the morning and Terry had drawn the assignment. They decided to forget about the case for the evening and began talking about the upcoming football season.

Celia had been with the women and, as usual, found herself conflicted. She enjoyed female company and conversation; the two women were intelligent and interesting people. On the other hand, she wanted to be part of the detective crew that she knew was talking about the case.

An hour after the food had disappeared, Terry and Steve left with their companions. Celia was still helping Jake clean up, so she ended up alone with him again. She brought up the Whitewater case and Jake just said, "That's Steve and Terry's case, they haven't gotten much yet."

Relieved that Jake was staying out of the case, Celia changed the conversation to Kaitlin. Jake brightened up and talked about his plans for her the following weekend. He walked Celia to Kaitlin's room and showed her the progress on their redecorating project. Celia praised the work while thinking that a young teenager has some strange tastes. Their conversation tailed off as Jake ran out of things to say about Kaitlin. They found themselves just gazing at each other. Celia was thinking what a good man he was; caring, but also competent and tough when he needed to be. She felt herself softening up and pulled back on the reins. Wait girl, she thought, don't screw this up. She told Jake that she had to get home and headed out.

Jake sat in his chair for a while, sipping his tequila as thoughts of Fiona were interrupted by flashes of Celia standing there looking at him with soft eyes. Confused, he headed off to bed.

56. SACRAMENTO; MONDAY

Terry Rocker was going through the second autopsy of his morning. He figured that he might be able to eat by dinnertime, but lunch wasn't happening. Earlier in his career Terry had thought of bodies during autopsy as objects labeled as "victims". He had since decided that it divorced him from reality too much, so he thought of them as people with names. That made autopsies emotionally wrenching, but it heightened the fire inside that drove him through the boredom and bullshit of investigations.

So far the exam of Gina Robert's body was turning out the same as Sophia Mancuso's exam. Her ankles had zip ties on them. Her wrists and hands had been duct taped. The perp had been smart. Taping just the wrists left the fingers and nails free as tools and weapons. The tape on her hands had been removed the night before in order to get fingerprints. This morning the zip ties had been removed. The skin at the neck where her head had been removed was a clean cut, just like that found on her head.

Both women had additional ligature marks on their ankles. The remainder of the external exam found no damage except on the buttocks. She had taken a beating there – seven straight line lacerations were on Sophia Mancuso and now five similar wounds on Gina Roberts. The pathologist had stated for the recording that the wounds were from ¼ to ½ inch deep, enough to generate only moderate blood spatter since no arteries were near the surface of the buttocks. The nature of the wounds indicated that they had occurred premortem, so the women had suffered. Terry recalled reading that the damage to the third victim had been much worse.

Examination of both women's genatalia showed negative for sexual activity. There was no tearing, bruising or semen. Rape wasn't part of the killer's agenda.

The only item of note found during the internal examination was that both Sophia and Gina had been drained of blood. That explained the ankle injuries; they had been hung up like a beef carcass. The draining didn't impede the autopsy process because the pathologist was able to extract blood samples from the women's hearts.

Terry was wrung out like a mop by the time the second autopsy was completed. They had more information, but none of it seemed to lead toward a perpetrator.

Jake was up early, sifting through their new case on JARS. Satisfied that he had a good overview of the case, he called Celia. They discussed the case briefly and then Jake told her that he would work from home today.

Jake called Rich Luton in Roseville. "Morning Rich, how's it going?"

"Doin' OK, though my new case isn't as interesting as the murder. What's up?"

"Did you ever confirm Mason Resto's alibi for victim three? He was supposed to be up in Oregon."

"We did, Jake. The department up there checked with the brother and managed an independent confirmation. Why?"

"Oh, just trying to tie up loose ends in my head. How about checking out the last two vacant houses that Resto had access to?"

"We looked at them, but came up empty again."

Thanks Rich, I'll talk to you later."

As Jake climbed into his Boxter and headed downtown, he thought about Resto's alibi. Resto couldn't just sneak out and kidnap somebody, it was a ten hour round trip to come down here from Grant's Pass and go back. The alibi looked good.

Jake parked, then walked to the DA's office on G Street There was a line at the records department counter even though two clerks seemed to be hustling. After five minutes in line and another five minutes waiting, Jake got the files for the Ditkam case. Sitting down at a table, he read through the material looking for insight. The files exuded a sense of Browning's efficiency and arrogance. Jake could see that the average man might not have been convinced by Browning's intellectual arguments and circumstantial evidence when Ditkam had an alibi, albeit from somebody with assault convictions. Jake would have voted for conviction, but the jury had taken two days and then voted for acquittal.

Jake started up his laptop and checked the Department of Motor Vehicles registration database. Browning had a four door Mercedes that Jake had seen him drive, but he also owned a four door Toyota. The database didn't contain vehicle color, so he couldn't check whether the car was green. Jake had never seen Browning driving a Toyota. Somehow it didn't fit the man's ego.

Walking back to his car, Jake thought: What the hell am I going to do with this. If I do anything within the DOJ, Browning will get wind of it. This is too hot to take to an Internal Affairs unit. I guess I could go to the Feds or the Sacramento DA, though Browning has history with the DA and the Feds are a bitch to work with. Maybe I just give it to Steve. For sure if Browning's not the perp and he finds out I've investigated him, I'm done at the DOJ. Maybe I'll keep looking at Browning by myself.

A tall woman with black hair down past her shoulder blades walked in front of him, making him think of Kaya. She had called it that Ditkam wasn't their guy. The profile she gave fit much of what he knew about Browning, too bad he couldn't get her involved at this point. Browning was indeed a white male, above average intelligence, at least middle class. At 47 he was just beyond the age range Kaya had listed. He's a self-centered person who manipulates people, feels no guilt or remorse for his actions. He pays lots of attention to the media. He loved power. Jake didn't know about any abuse by Browning's mother or whether the victims resembled his mother. Wait. Kaya said that the picture taped to the kill house mirror was probably the perp's mother.

How to establish the identity of the woman in the photograph? I think that Browning's parents are dead, so I can't check there. Maybe there's other family around. Maybe Browning has other pictures, but a search warrant would tip him off.

Jake drove ten minutes to the Police Department. Walking into homicide, he found Steve and Terry at their desks. Terry volunteered an autopsy summary. Steve had checked on trophies: All the jewelry that had been described on the victims had been found in the bags with their bodies. Other than heads, nothing had been found missing from the bodies. There was no evidence that trophies had been taken so they weren't going to find that kind of evidence.

Steve then asked, "What's up? It's good to see you Jake, but you're not working the case."

"You're right," responded Jake, "I'm not working the case. I'd like to see a piece of evidence from the kill house."

Steve said, "You forgot the wink wink. I'm sure that you need to see evidence to further your development as a DOJ Agent."

"You're always right, Steve, what a mind."

They pulled the box containing the photograph from evidence storage. Jake looked at the photograph and decided that his memory was correct, it looked like a studio portrait. Jake turned the photo over and at first glance saw nothing. Holding it up to the light and turning it, Jake thought he saw a faint "S". "Steve, I want to take this over to Chocolate and see if he can pull a photographers name off the back."

"You can sign it out," said Steve, "but you'll be leaving a record of being involved."

"Screw it," said Jake as he signed the evidence form.

"You going to tell us what you find out?" asked Terry.

"Would I hold out on you?" answered Jake.

"Yeah."

"I'll make sure that you get what I have."

"Maybe we should tell you about the cell phone when you get back to us," said Steve.

"The phone called by the kill house's alarm?" asked Jake.

"Yup,"

"So where was the phone?"

"I don't know if I have the time for this," said Steve. "I'm busy."

"Hey," said Jake, "I just fed you a great salmon dinner."

"That's true, you earned some consideration. Tell him Terry."

"The phone was powered off after the alarm call went to it and hasn't been powered back on," said Terry. "The only call made on the phone was to John Clark, the owner of the rental house, in late April. When the alarm call was received, it was somewhere in a six block area, roughly bounded by 13th and 15th, I and K streets. That includes the Convention Center, so it's not too useful."

"It also includes the DOJ building," said Jake.

"OK, a few hundred more suspects," said Terry.

"Thanks guys," said Jake as he stood up to go. "Keep on truckin'".

At the DOJ forensic lab, Jake found Chocolate in his office, clicking away at a keyboard. "Hey Chocolate, I need some of your magic."

"I have lots of magic, what particular form do you need?"

"I think that there's a photographer's stamp on the back of this photograph. I think I can see an "S," but can't pick out anything else."

"Let's go look." Chocolate got up and started walking down the hall, Jake following.

In a lab full of equipment, Chocolate walked up to a collection of gear arranged around a device that looked like it was the flat bed from a giant copier. Powering up a computer, he put the photograph into the flat bed and clicked on a "START" button. "This gear looks with many different wavelengths of light, from the low infrared through the ultraviolet. The computer looks for contrasts in the image and combines what it finds. Give it a minute."

Chocolate started talking about golf, to which he'd recently become addicted. Since Jake was collecting a favor, he listened with interest even though he had a hard time thinking that it would be fun to hit a small ball that just sat there, defenseless.

A bugle sounded the call to post tune that you heard at horse tracks. "What the hell?" said Jake.

"The guy who set up this system is a fan of the horses. That's the signal that it's done." Chocolate looked at the screen, clicked the mouse a few times, then moved to let Jake see the large high resolution display.

He could read *Stephan's Fi e Ph ography, 762 Je sie St, San Francis.* "That's great magic, Choc. Can you get me a printed copy and a good copy of the photograph?"

"I can. Give me a minute and I'll get this test into your JARS case."

"Uh, Choc, how about you forget to do that?"

"Really."

"Yeah. There may come a time when I'll want it in the file, but right now it's a bad idea."

"OK, we never had this conversation."

"Thanks, Choc."

Back at home, Jake searched the internet for the photo studio. He found one, but it was back East, not in San Francisco. There was no date on the photograph, but the woman looked like she was about thirty. If she was Browning's mother and had him at twenty five that would make her 72 now and would make the photograph in the vicinity of 42 years old. No wonder he couldn't find the studio.

Jake checked JARS for his new case, reading the meager amount of new material so he'd be current. As he finished reading it, the sound of *Nowhere Man* emerged from his pocket. It was Browning.

"Appleby, it's time to get the details set for our Tuolumne trip. I've arranged for the permit as well as a shuttle from the bottom so we can just drive your truck to the shuttle location."

"There's not much to plan," said Jake. "You pack your gear, including some food, and I'll pack mine. I'll pick you up about six on Wednesday morning. Eat before I get there."

"That all sounds reasonable. I'll be ready." As usual, Browning disconnected without a goodbye.

Jake idly scratched Tank behind the ears as he contemplated Wednesday and what to do with the photograph.

57. SAN FRANCISCO; TUESDAY

The morning traffic made Jake's drive to San Francisco last two hours. As he reached Vallejo he transitioned from cloudless bright sunshine to the chilly gloom caused by a layer of coastal stratus. The tourists in San Francisco wearing shorts would be freezing their butts off. Stopping to pay the Bay Bridge toll generated a moment of future shock: The toll was now six bucks during rush hour. The toll had been a buck the first time he'd paid it as a sixteen year old driver.

The photo studio had been a couple of blocks from Civic Center, a crowded area during workdays. As he drove by the address, he spotted a "Photography" sign in the window. Maybe this was going to be a lucky trip.

After ten minutes of driving around the area, Jake nabbed a parking space then walked the three blocks to the studio. Wedding pictures and portraits filled the window, brightening up what was otherwise a dingy brick building. Inside he introduced himself to a forty-something Hispanic man who turned out to be the owner.

"How long have you owned the studio?" asked Jake.

"Let's see," said the owner, "it must be eighteen years now.

"I'm trying to determine the identity of the person in an old photograph. Here's a copy of the back, indicating *Stephan's Fine Photography* at this address."

"Yes, I bought the business from an old couple; Stephan was the man's name."

A couple that was old eighteen years ago, Jake thought. There's some chance they may be alive. "Do you have contact information for them?"

"I guess I could dig up their names, but I haven't seen them since we closed the deal. You can search my files for that picture if you want."

"Your files include their work?"

"Sure. I bought the business and that included the customer files. All my recent stuff is on my computer but I've never gotten around to cleaning up the old files. It's all filed by customer last name though. It'll be a big job looking through all of them."

"I've got ideas about the last name," said Jake. "Where are the "R's?"

There was no file with a name that resembled Resto. Jake scanned the file cabinets until he found the drawer for "B". Two Browning files sat in the drawer. The negatives in the first file didn't match his photograph. The second file was a treasure trove. He found the negative for his photo as well as family photos of the woman, a grim faced man and a ten year old kid who resembled Chuck Browning. The receipt in the file listed Ava Browning and an address of 2514 Pacific Avenue. Using his smartphone, Jake found the house in the Pacific Heights district known for expensive housing. Using a real estate web site, he found the house to be about six thousand square feet with an estimated value of over seven million. Some shack to grow up in.

Jake put the file in an evidence bag, gave the owner a receipt and thanked him. He started walking to the Office of Vital Records across the street from City Hall. On the way, he thought damn, it really is Chuck Browning. I know that the guy's an asshole, but murdering women? This is going to be the scandal of the year in Sacramento. No wonder we thought it was Ditkam, Browning knew just how to set him up and knew every step we took by talking to Foreman.

The four story grey concrete block that housed the Public Health Department was rescued from boring by bits of blue railing. Inside, Jake managed to get a copy of Charles Able Browning's birth certificate in fifty minutes. Ava Browning and Edward Browning were listed on the certificate as the parents. Confirmation; Chuck's mommy had been watching what he had done to those women in the kill house bathroom.

Heading back towards the warm Sacramento sunshine, Jake's mind spun like a top. He was sure that the experienced law enforcement professional running for attorney general was a serial killer. The problem was that the evidence he had was too weak to even get a search warrant on a man with such a high profile. Even if they could get a warrant, Browning had been so careful that there was a good chance that his residence was clean. Having that photograph at the kill house was a mistake though, so Jake hoped that Browning had made or would make other mistakes. I'll be with the bastard for the whole day tomorrow; maybe I can work his ego and get something.

58. SACRAMENTO

Jake stopped at a coffee and pastry shop in Dixon. With an apple fritter for fuel, he documented what he knew and suspected about Whitewater/Browning on his laptop. After reviewing the document, he got back in the car and back onto I80.

Exiting the freeway in downtown Sacramento, Jake made his way to his office and was happy to find that Celia was out. He felt badly about not carrying his share of the new investigation and didn't want to lie to his partner. It was best to not see her.

After printing out his report he put it, the photograph copies, the birth certificate copy and the photographer's file in a giant sized manila envelope. Sealing it, he wrote on the front and locked it in his desk.

Jake stopped at Pauline's for an early dinner, and then went home to prepare for tomorrow's kayak trip. By seven he had his gear bags filled and his kayak strapped to the truck. Anticipation of the trip began filling his gut. Every downriver trip was a new experience because the water was never quite the same. The big new experience tomorrow would be kayaking with a serial killer. Hopefully, he doesn't know that I'm on to him.

At seven thirty he called Kaya Lane's office and, as expected, got voicemail. After the tone, he said, "Kaya, this is Jake. I wanted to thank you for the great profile work you did on the Whitewater case. It looks like my skepticism was unfounded. I now believe that you were right on. Thanks again."

Jake had just sat down with his tequila and was having a one-way conversation with Tank when his phone played its Celia music. He let it play while he considered not answering. Caving, he connected and said, "Hi C, how ya doin'?"

"I'm doing a little slow, Jake Appleby, because I don't seem to have a functional partner."

Jake thought: I was afraid of this. Temper time. He said, "Sorry C, I had some personal things come up and now I've got this kayak trip. I should be back on it Thursday."

"What do you mean, *back on it?* You haven't done a damn thing on this case and you've been bullshitting me about working it. I'm covering for you with Sam, but he's going to catch on soon."

"C, you're a smart woman. I've always liked that about you. I've got to get ready for tomorrow's trip now, we're heading off early." He hated keeping her out of the loop, but his need to protect her was stronger.

"OK, but come Thursday you're either working the case with me or telling me what's going on."

"You're sure playing the strong but not silent type."

"I mean it Jake. You be smart on the river tomorrow, I know you haven't been paddling much recently."

"I'll be good. It's a bit like riding a bike. Not to worry."

"Thursday." She disconnected.

Raising his glass, Jake said, "Tank, there's something to be said for being a loner like you."

Tank lifted his head for an instant, then went back to sleep.

Chuck Browning was pressing the flesh at a cocktail party in the Sacramento suburb of Carmichael. The party was in a large stucco McMansion owned by an area developer. The crowd was full of real estate and development types, down a long ways from the bubble times, but ever hopeful. While Browning didn't care much for these people, compared to ordinary drones they were more comfortable and a better source of votes. They, of course, were interested in an attorney general who would overlook their behavior.

Browning was looking for a way out of a discussion with an egotistical broker. She was a blonde who he guessed had been a knockout in her twenties, but didn't seem to realize that her goods should be displayed more subtly at her current age. Spotting somebody he knew, he said, "I appreciate your viewpoint and you have a great argument. I'm looking forward to discussing it further after I'm elected. I see somebody I need to speak to, please excuse me."

Walking over to a short, overweight red faced man in his fifties, Browning said "I haven't seen you in years William, what are you up to?"

"I'm up to more of this scotch," said William, holding up a crystal tumbler brimming with amber nectar. "I'm still at the DA's office. My wife dragged me to the party, she's now a broker and she socializes with these types. I see you're making a run at attorney general."

"I am, William. I hope to be graced with your vote."

"Sure, Chuck. I was thinking about you yesterday."

"Oh?"

"I was down in records and heard a guy request the files for the Tom Ditkam case. Wasn't that one you handled?" said William with a tiny smirk.

"It was my case, yes," was Browning's stiff response. "Who was looking at it?"

"I don't know, Chuck, some thirty-something stud. I did catch that he was from the DOJ though."

Feigning boredom, Browning said, "Well, I hope that he's making good use of his time. Good to see you, William."

"Good to see you too, Chuck."

Turning away, Browning was seething inside. It had to be Appleby. Putting him on the case had been a mistake.

After twenty more minutes of schmoozing, Browning thanked the host and hostess and left.

Arriving at his office, Browning logged into JARS using Foreman's ID and password and reviewed the case. There was nothing new from Appleby and so far, forensics hadn't come up with anything from the house. Grabbing the set of master keys that he had insisted on possessing, he headed for Appleby's office space. He verified that nobody was working late before sitting down, gloving up and opening the desk. Nothing in the file drawer seemed interesting. The drawer above contained only a jumble of office supplies. He opened the center drawer and found a large manila envelope with *for Steve Devlin* written on it. Looking at it, Browning thought: I can copy the handwriting on a new envelope if I need to. Tearing it open, he scanned the contents. He locked the desk, looked around, and walked away with the envelope.

59. TUOLUMNE; WEDNESDAY

Jake arrived at Chuck Browning's house at six AM. Calling the place a house was like calling a Smart Fortwo a car. This property was more on the level of an AMG Mercedes. It had manicured grounds, walls of glass and a huge deck looking down on the pool and American River. Jake had attended one party at the house, enjoying the beautiful great room with eighty other people. In today's market, this place was only worth a few million. Browning had family money; he didn't buy this place using a government salary.

Today, Jake's exposure to the house was limited to the six car garage. The bay whose door was open held Browning's kayak, river gear and two sets of golf clubs. As he helped Browning load the truck, Jake spotted a black Mercedes S550 sedan blocking most of the view of a green car. *That must be the green Toyota* thought Jake.

It took only minutes to load the truck and then they were off on the drive to the Tuolumne. Browning had arranged for a morning shuttle from the takeout area so they needed only one vehicle and the truck would be waiting for them when the run was over. The drive south on US 99 and east on Highway 120 was going to take two and a half hours. Jake and Browning talked kayaking until they reached the town of Stockton. It was clear by then that Browning knew how to talk the talk. What he could do on the river would be known in a few hours. Conversation stopped as Browning fell asleep.

At Wards Ferry Bridge they switched their gear to the shuttle van. The trip to the put-in at Meral's Pool took almost an hour. The last five miles of the drive were in low gear on the steep, rutted, dusty Lumsden Road. The shuttle driver talked for a while about the rafting business. It had taken a big hit last year when Lumsden Road was closed by a slide.

When they arrived at Meral's Pool, two rafting companies and their customers were already there and getting set up. Jake and Browning donned their dry suits, spray skirts, flotation vests and helmets, transforming themselves into aquatic creatures. They were in the river at ten o'clock, ahead of the rafts.

The river flow yesterday had been 6800 cubic feet per second due to the wet winter and generally mild spring. At this rate, the river was a major challenge for rafting and a thrill ride in a kayak. Jake still had concerns about how Browning would do. He figured that he'd know soon.

"Appleby, I'd like you to describe the route and maneuvers while we're above each rapid, then lead me through it," said Browning.

Jake responded, "I can give you what I think is the route, but I've not been down the "T" at this flow, so we'll be winging it to some extent. Rock Garden is coming up. We'll scout what we can from the right. Plan to stay 50 feet behind me in rapids."

In the clear water above the rapid, Jake maneuvered to the right side of the river, trying to spot changes that would affect his normal route. Seeing nothing, he yelled out over the roar of the frothing water, "Enter just left of center and stay there all the way down." Jake paddled upriver a bit and began his move to the center, glancing at Browning to ensure he was hanging back. At this water flow, the rapid wasn't difficult. Jake felt his boat accelerate and all thoughts of Browning were pushed aside as he entered the whitewater. At Jake's skill level, this rapid just took a few strokes here and there to keep the boat on a good route and avoid the boulders emerging from the flow. Near the bottom he found a hydraulic below a short drop, spun his boat around and sat in it so that he could watch Browning.

Browning was 150 feet up river, maneuvering. He looked a bit clumsy but he was getting it done. When he reached a rock 50 feet above Jake, Browning miscalculated and was pushed to the right into the rock. Contact was violent, but he didn't get pinned and he just managed not to roll, so it worked out.

Turning around, Jake paddled back into the current, finished the rapid, and waited in an eddy for Browning.

Browning pulled in next to him and said, "Whew, the first one always gets me going."

"Yep, you're in another world now. About 17 more of these between us and the take-out. Nemesis is just below us and there's no way to scout it. Start left, then work right before the big rock, Nemesis, sitting in the center. Avoid the far right until you pass a drop of several feet, then look for some slaloms."

Jake paddled into the current then floated on the short stretch of calm water above the rapid. He worked with the river, maneuvering so it would take him where he wanted to go, until he reached a recirculating eddy below the drop and watched for Browning.

Again, Browning looked clumsy but he was getting it done until he got sideways above the drop and rolled over as he went over the edge, hitting the bottom head first. When Browning didn't immediately roll back upright, Jake watched the bottom of Browning's boat and began counting. Browning started a roll, but raised his head too soon and rolled back under. One more try and Browning was upright on a count of seven. Way too slow. The river doesn't stop when you're under, but your maneuvering does.

Jake headed down, having some fun slaloming through boulders, then eddying out left at the bottom. Browning joined him, panting and not saying a word. Jake liked him that way. "We've got Sunderland Chute next. It's tougher than what we've done. It's big and powerful and there's not going to be much of a break before we're into the next rapid, Hackamack's Hole. Let's enter Sunderland left of center and stay there, avoiding the big holes on the right. Below Sunderland, get right and stay there through Hackamack."

Seeing Browning nod, Jake paddled into the current and let it take him around the bend and into the rapid. Big standing waves were at the top and he got slapped in the face by one. Following his own instructions, he crashed through the rapid and found an eddy at the bottom so once again he could watch Browning. Being a babysitter for an asshole wasn't his notion of fun. He watched Browning start fine, but misjudge the power of the river and get swept right over a rock and into the big hole. He spun, thrashed and rolled in the hole where the racing water was forced down and then back upstream, entraining so much air that the kayak lost flotation and sank deeper. This could get bad.

With three powerful strokes, Jake beached himself in the rocks on the right. Popping his spray skirt and climbing out, he grabbed his rope bag and scrambled upstream. Reaching a spot across from Browning, he looked to see what was going on. Browning was still in the hole, with the bow of his boat sticking almost straight up. The boat was being pushed left and then right, Browning was working too hard with his paddle but going nowhere. Jake opened the neck of the bag, grabbed the end of the rope, and threw the bag out over the river upstream of Browning, hoping that Browning saw it and had enough sense to grab the rope. The dirty orange bag flew out beyond Browning and the rope was carried downriver to his body. He did manage to grab it and not drop his paddle.

Watching his footing, Jake pulled the rope tight as he moved downriver. Finding stable footing he began to pull. Browning stayed in the hole. Getting into a tug of war position, Jake started walking the rope backward. The resistance was huge and his muscles bunched with the strain. Suddenly, Browning popped out of the hole as if a toaster had ejected him. Falling on his butt, Jake watched Browning drop the rope and paddle for shore.

Jake stayed seated, panting from his exertion. After a moment, he began coiling the throw rope. Browning got to shore, climbed out of his kayak and collapsed in the rocks. Jake walked over to him and said, "That wasn't a lot of fun. You OK?"

"I'll be all right in a few minutes. Why in hell did you tell me to go right? That hole could have killed me, damn you!"

"I told you to stay left of center to avoid the holes," said Jake, keeping his anger under control.

"I do not recall it that way," complained Browning.

"Whatever," said Jake. "Are you sure that you want to run the "T" today? There are lots of holes and other places that are dangerous, maybe you should bail." Jake was hoping that Browning would quit. As much of a hassle as that would be, it would be better than having the jerk drown or get broken up.

"We will continue," commanded Browning. "I expect you to pick the easiest routes and give me clear directions."

"We can continue, just know that after a couple of miles we head away from Lumsden Road and there's no decent way to walk out."

Browning, climbing to his feet, said, "What's the route from here through this next rapid?"

Jake thought about how he was going to get this asshole down the river in one piece. He needed to take every sneak route he could and let Browning stay close even though that added some risk. He should have a competent paddler behind Browning, but that wasn't happening. He'd make Browning portage around Clavey Falls. This was not going to be fun. "We'll stay right on this rapid, you'll need to follow me carefully. Try to stay close, maybe 20 feet."

At the bottom of the second rapid, Jake paddled over to the left side of the river. Watching Browning , he said, "This is where we found Sophia Mancuso's head."

Browning didn't blink. "That's quite a display stand," he said, referring to the boulder. "Finding the woman's head there must have been quite a surprise."

"It blew our minds," said Jake. Now he saw emotion in Browning's eyes: pride. Jake had used Sophia's name on purpose, but Browning's response had been about an object. The man had no empathy at all, people were objects to him. Jake was on the river with a psychopath.

It took them well over an hour to navigate five rapids and almost four miles. The good news was that they'd had no serious incidents and Browning's skill level seemed to be improving a bit. Taking the easiest routes and babysitting Browning was a drag for Jake, but Browning seemed to be enjoying himself.

Jake pulled out on the right to a beach covered with baseball to volleyball sized rocks called cobbles in the construction trade. Browning pulled in beside him, looking tired.

"We're just above Clavey Falls," said Jake. "We'll rest up and eat lunch here, then portage."

"Why portage? I understand that Clavey is the highlight of the run."

"It is the highlight, but it's also the most dangerous rapid on the river," said Jake. "It's caused lots of dislocated shoulders, broken bones and two deaths. It's just too risky for your current skill set."

Browning was quiet for once, not liking the reminder that he wasn't top dog here.

Jake had popped his kayak skirt, climbed out and removed his helmet. Next off was the flotation vest and spray skirt, leaving just the dry suit. Jake headed for a bush.

They ate lunch while sitting on a log, soaking up the sun that beamed on them from a clear blue sky. It was warm enough so that they unzipped their dry suits a bit to let cool air in. Loud music was provided by the river as it fell ten feet over Clavey Falls.

Finished with his meal and feeling rested, Jake got up and walked toward the kayaks.

"Stop right there, Appleby!"

Jake stopped and turned around. Browning was standing, pointing what looked like a .380 automatic at him. Shit.

"Down on your belly."

"This isn't very attorney general like," said Jake.

"Always a smart mouth. Don't think I won't shoot you Appleby," said Browning. "Down on your belly."

Seeing no good alternatives, Jake got down on his knees and then laid down on the cobbles. "So it was you."

"Of course it was me, you idiot. Too bad that you're the smartest of the idiots, that's going to cost you. You were clever in deducing my involvement, but stupid to think that I wouldn't catch on to you." Browning had an arrogant smile on his face.

"Killing me won't get you out of this," said Jake. "I left some tracks behind me."

"You mean that folder that used to be in your desk?" gloated Browning.

Damn, thought Jake. I shouldn't have left that stuff at the office. I need to buy some time here, let him gloat. "So was this all about getting back at Ditkam?"

"Of course not. Ditkam needed to pay for spoiling my perfect record, but he was just a component of my masterpiece."

"It was an amazingly clean set of crimes until you brought Ditkam in."

"Of course it was. I know how to do it; how you'd operate. Then, of course, I knew every step you took. That was why I had you find the first head, to have you involved in the investigation while I watched."

"We were sure that us finding the head wasn't a coincidence, but just couldn't find the connection."

"Of course not, I didn't want you to find it."

"You nailed Ditkam."

"With the blood and hair I collected from those bitches, I could have nailed the governor. I loved leading you in with the license plate – you lived up to my expectations when you deduced that it could have been Ditkam's."

"I don't understand why you had to kill Sophia and Gina. You could have gotten Ditkam with just one killing."

"Of course you don't understand, you're a drone. A smart one, but a drone nevertheless. Those extra units gave me priceless public relations. I was constantly in the papers and on television, showing the stupid voters that I'm in charge and will protect them from the crazy violent world out there. Then, the climax. My leadership brings the evil villain to justice. You should see what that did for my name recognition and approval numbers. The AG job is mine."

"You're right, I didn't see that angle," Jake said, thinking that this had to be as despicable as a politician could be. Most politicians had other people do the killing for them. "And then, of course, there's the joy of killing your mother a couple of times."

"What are you talking about?"

"Sophia and Gina looked like your mother. Did it feel like abusing and killing your mother?"

"I suppose it did. You're right, I did enjoy them more because of that. Not as much as when I actually killed mom though."

"You killed your mother?" asked Jake, knowing nothing about the death of Browning's mother.

"I did, she was my first," said Browning with pride. "I performed a masterful piece of work for a beginner. Vehicular manslaughter. I borrowed a car and got the pleasure of crushing her. The owner of the car was convicted before he knew what hit him."

"Mama must have whipped you, given what you did to the victims," said Jake. "You get off on that?"

"You're quite sassy for a dead man, Appleby. It's now time for your kayaking accident." Browning shifted the automatic to his left hand and picked up a rock the size of a pineapple in his right. As he reached Jake, he lifted the rock high and started it down toward Jake's head.

Jake pivoted on his hip, kicking Browning in the shin while moving his head away from the rock as it crashed into the ground. He grabbed a handful of pebbles as Browning pulled the trigger. Jake felt a tug at his right ear as he threw the rocks at Browning's face and leapt to his feet. The weapon fired again, the round missing as Browning reached for his damaged cheek.

Jake grabbed Browning's left forearm with both hands and spun around. Browning's response to the pain was to drop the gun. Jake dropped the arm and drove a punch toward Browning's solar plexus, realizing his mistake as the semi-rigid zipper of the dry suit absorbed the blow. Browning clasped his two hands into a big fist and crashed them into the back of Jake's head. Stunned, Jake went to a knee while Browning took two steps and bent over to pick up the automatic. Jake launched himself at Browning, putting his shoulder into the man's chest, just like he'd been taught in football practice. The impact and momentum drove them both into the water.

Struggling to stand on the sloping river bottom covered with slippery cobbles, they exchanged weak blows, then Browning landed a roundhouse right on Jake's ear. Jake was shaken, but managed to duck under Browning's next big swing.

Jake then put his whole body into an uppercut that snapped Browning's jaw shut and launched him back, spread-eagled, onto the water.

Browning's dry suit provided just enough flotation that he stayed on top of the water on his back. A weak current took him away from shore, towards the downriver current. He began thrashing, but before he got himself under control, he was being carried downriver. He got turned over and began swimming upriver as hard as he could. Jake, knowing better than to go after Browning, yelled, "swim to the shore, swim to the shore." Browning either didn't hear him or thought he could beat the current. Jake knew better, you can't fight the river, you have to work with it. Despite the swimming, Browning was moving downstream, his dry suit filling with water through the open zipper, making swimming more difficult. As his muscles tired, he moved faster and into stronger current. Another blink and he was over the falls.

Jake slipped and stumbled to the shore, then began running downstream, looking for Browning. Past the falls, he stopped and surveyed the river, seeing nothing. In a moment, Browning appeared, headed for dinosaur rock. It didn't look as if he were swimming. The current carried him up over the rock and he disappeared from sight. Jake stood there for ten minutes and didn't see Browning reappear. Two guys in kayaks had died on that rock; it may have taken a third today.

The adrenaline was wearing off and Jake hurt. Skin was missing from three knuckles on his right hand. He reached up to touch his right ear and his hand came away bloody. His left ear hurt. Man up guy, he thought. You've got work to do. He walked back to his kayak and pulled out a waterproof bag. Extracting his satellite phone, he powered it up and found that he had enough satellites to made a call. "Celia, this is Jake. We need to get a search going."

60. SACRAMENTO; TUESDAY

Jake was sitting at his desk, sipping his morning coffee. He had a yellow and purple bruise next to his left ear and the lower portion of his right ear was bandaged. His ears were no longer symmetrical; a bullet had taken off most of his right earlobe. He didn't mind much. A missing earlobe was a much better outcome than if the bullet trajectory had been an inch or two further to the right. For now, the injury was getting him a touch of sympathy from Celia, at least when she forgot to be angry about his working the case alone. The bruises were starting to fade, it had been almost two weeks.

Turning his attention back to the computer screen, he clicked the box titled *Case Closed.* One of those annoying message windows came up, asking *Are you sure?* He clicked on *Yes* and mumbled, "Damn right I'm sure." He had written his final report on the Whitewater Killer case.

Browning's body had not been recovered, despite an intensive two day search. He was presumed drowned and trapped under a rock or log somewhere in the river. The chance of him surviving without floatation gear and with a dry suit full of water was slim. Neither the helicopters nor the rescue crews nor the sheriff's men nor the rafters had seen any sign of Browning on the river or hiking out of the canyon. The rescue team had tried to use their underwater camera to look for Browning under dinosaur rock but the force of the water prevented a complete check. The rapids and high water flow also prevented effective use of a cadaver dog trained for water searches. The general opinion was that the body might turn up when the water level dropped in July.

Jake was happy that Browning was fish food; the guy was finally doing something useful. A couple of times Jake had thought that he might have rescued Browning if he'd gone right for his throw bag when Browning got into the current. He dismissed such thoughts, telling himself that Browning would have been too far downriver by the time Jake would have been able to throw the bag. Besides, this outcome saved taxpayers money and cut down on the embarrassment to the DOJ.

Initially, the Attorney General tried to keep Browning's guilt out of the media, but he soon realized that it wasn't possible. Skilled politician that he was, he turned around and crowed about what a great organization he had: The DOJ had rooted out its own highly skilled criminal who had foiled seven law enforcement jurisdictions. The revised PR strategy required Jake to do several news conferences and interviews. He only had one more interview scheduled and hoped that was the last of them.

The media still trashed the DOJ, but at a different level than they would have if the department had tried a cover up or hadn't found their own guy. The State Assembly had scheduled hearings on the case to get some PR of their own.

Even if Browning had killed Jake, he might have been caught. Since Browning had disposed of Jake's folder documenting his suspicions of Browning, Steve or Terry would have needed to come up with Browning as a suspect on their own. Then there was Jake's summary of his suspicions on Browning. Browning got the paper, but the file was still in Jake's computer if anybody had looked.

Browning had disposed of the kill house shop vac filter bags, but the lab found a hair imbedded in debris inside the vacuum's hose. DNA analysis of the hair failed to match it to anything in the California or CODIS database, but it matched a hair retrieved from Browning's house. Waders and hiking boots found at the house had little evidence value because they couldn't be tied to the crime.

Tom Ditkam had been released from jail. His job had been filled while he'd been incarcerated and there was so much press about his arrest that everybody thought of him as a murderer. The suits in the DOJ were worried about a lawsuit. Jake didn't have any sympathy for the man. Ditkam had gotten away with a brutal murder of his own fifteen years ago.

Jake had shared Browning's confession about killing his mother with the San Francisco DA's office. The man convicted of the killing would be cleared.

Jake rotated his chair around and looked at Celia. Her shiny black hair matched the knee length black skirt that had risen up, revealing a hint of shapely thighs. A blousy satin top created contrast while leaving her shape to imagination. "Celia, how about lunch?" asked Jake.

Turning around and looking at him, Celia said, "I'm with you, Jake."

Made in the USA
San Bernardino, CA
19 April 2013